Edward S. Holden

Elementary Astronomy

a beginner's text-book

Edward S. Holden

Elementary Astronomy
a beginner's text-book

ISBN/EAN: 9783337275631

Printed in Europe, USA, Canada, Australia, Japan

Cover: Foto ©Andreas Hilbeck / pixelio.de

More available books at **www.hansebooks.com**

ELEMENTARY ASTRONOMY

A BEGINNER'S TEXT-BOOK

BY

EDWARD S. HOLDEN, M.A., Sc.D., LL.D.

Sometime Director of the Lick Observatory

NEW YORK

HENRY HOLT AND COMPANY

1899

INTRODUCTION.

THE first notions of Astronomy are acquired in the study of Geography. Geography lays special stress on the fact that the surface of the Earth is in a state of constant change. Its oceans and its atmosphere are subject to tides ; its surface is leveled for the sites of cities and towns ; its mines and quarries are explored for substances useful to mankind. Men navigate its seas and use its soils to produce the food that supports them. Its ceaseless changes, natural and artificial, give to it a kind of life— for the sign of life is change.

Geography teaches, also, that the Earth is one of the planets, but in this larger relation says little or nothing of changes taking place in the solar system. The young student is very apt to conclude that the other planets of whose existence he knows— *Venus* and *Jupiter* for example—are changeless, immutable; that they are bright points of light without a history. This was the view of the ancients.

The special business of Astronomy is to develop the ideas of the student so that he may understand that all the bodies of the Solar system—the Sun and all the planets— are themselves subject to ceaseless changes and are thus endowed with a kind of life. Not only this; the bodies throughout the whole universe—Sun and stars alike—are perpetually altering both their places and the arrangement of their separate parts. Our life on the Earth, for instance, would quickly cease were it not for changes in the Sun. There are many stellar systems in which such changes have

already ceased and which are themselves now dead as the
Moon is dead.   Others again are in their prime of youth,
and still others are in their ripe maturity.   The Cosmos is,
as it were, alive; and it is still in a state of uncompleted
development.

The study of Astronomy should lead the student to com-
prehensive ideas of the universe at large.   He will gradually
become possessed of at least a part of the vast body of results that has been slowly amassed, and, what is even more
important, of the methods that have been invented by the
great men of past times for the discovery of results.   A
part of the lesson of the science will have been missed if it
does not teach a sympathetic admiration for great names
like those of Galileo, Kepler, and Newton.   Its history is
intimately connected with the history of the intellectual
development of mankind.

As Astronomy is one of the oldest of the sciences its
methods have been perfected to a very high degree, and
have served as models for the methods of the other sciences.
It is chiefly for this reason that it is so well fitted to be the
science first studied by the young student.

In teaching Astronomy every endeavor should be made
to have the student realize what he learns.   What is already known about the Earth will serve as a stepping-stone
to a knowledge of the planets.   When something is learned
of the planets, the knowledge will throw light upon the
past (or the future) condition of the earth.   Jupiter represents, in many respects, the past condition of the Earth,
just as the Moon, in all likelihood, represents its state in a
very remote future.   The Sun is like the bright stars
strewn by thousands over the celestial vault—not unlike
them.   Everything that can be learned regarding the Sun
helps us to comprehend physical conditions in the stars,
therefore; and the converse is true.

The nebulæ are not exceptional bodies of unique nature,

but they are examples of what our own solar system was in ages long past. Though we cannot see any individual nebula pass through all the stages of its life from its birth to its maturity, we can select from the vast numbers of such bodies particular nebulæ in each especial stage. As Sir William Herschel wrote in 1789, "This method of viewing the heavens seems to throw them into a new kind of light. They are now seen to resemble a luxuriant garden which contains the greatest variety of productions in different flourishing beds; and we can, as it were, extend the range of our experience to an immense duration. For is it not the same thing whether we live to witness successively the germination, blooming, foliage, fecundity, fading, withering, and corruption of a plant, or whether a vast number of specimens selected from every stage through which the plant passes in the course of its existence be brought at once to our view?"

It should be the aim of the text-book and of the teacher to so marshal the most significant of the results of observation that the student may acquire such wide and general views. If he at the same time gains a luminous idea of the most important of the methods by which such results are reached, his teaching has been successful. It is necessary to recollect, on the other hand, that it is not the province of an elementary text-book to present all the latest interpretations of observation, or to give more than the principles of the methods employed. Details of the sort cannot be thoroughly understood by the beginner. Questions that are still in debate, like the nature of the planet *Mars* or the constitution of comets, cannot be presented with fulness because the student is not yet sufficiently equipped to judge the points at issue. At the same time the materials for such a judgment should be, so far as possible, laid before him in such a way as to stimulate his thought and his imagination.

In all the natural sciences one of the very first matters is to make an orderly inventory of the visible universe. Things must then be grouped into classes, in order that the relations of the various classes may afterwards be studied. In Astronomy the classes are few; there are the Sun and the stars, the planets, the comets, the nebulæ. The next step is to study typical members of each class with the telescope. All that the text-book can do is to give descriptions of the appearances presented by telescopes. These must, in most cases, be taken on faith.

The Moon can be studied to advantage by opera-glasses or by such small telescopes as are available for use in schools. Something can be learned, by like means, of the spots on the Sun, etc. The existence of the brighter satellites of *Jupiter* and of *Saturn* can be verified. But for all the more significant facts the pupil must accept the verbal descriptions of the book. The apparent motions of the stars and planets can perfectly well be observed, out of doors, by the student who has time and opportunity. But here again there are difficulties. Dwellers in city streets, seldom have an uninterrupted view of the sky; and even those who live in the country rarely have time enough to give to actual observation. It is entirely impossible in a few weeks to even verify what it has taken centuries to disclose.

All the actual observing of the heavens that can be arranged for should be done. Its chief use will be to illustrate by actual examples the methods laid down in the text-book. Conviction will come to the pupil because he has learned *how* to prove or to disprove its theorems; not because he has actually made the proofs for himself. He knows that if he has sufficient time they can be proved or disproved by following a certain method. He thoroughly understands the method and he has applied it in a few cases. He is satisfied that the method itself is adequate and he accepts the conclusions—even those that he has not himself tested. If the student will take the time and the pains to actually make the observations suggested, he will learn much. Enough is here given to start him on his way and to make it easy for him to go on by himself.

The present book endeavors to place the pupil in this independent position by suggesting tests that he can himself apply. Quite as much stress is laid on the spirit of the methods of the science as on the results to which those methods have led. And the separate results of observation are prized mainly because each one bears on an explanation of the whole universe.

This book is condensed from two volumes previously written by Professor SIMON NEWCOMB and myself for the *American Science Series*. I have to express my sincere thanks to him for permission to print the condensation in its present form, and to the Astronomical Society of the Pacific, to Professor CHARLES A. YOUNG, and to Dr. J. E. KEELER, Director of the Lick Observatory, for permission to use some of the cuts here printed.

The book is addressed especially to pupils who are studying Astronomy for the first time. The chief difficulties of such students are not due to the intrinsic complexity of the separate problems that they meet, but rather to their apparent want of connection one with another, and above all to the unfamiliarity of the student with the methods of reasoning employed. It is therefore necessary to treat each new topic with great clearness, and not to dismiss it until its relation to other topics has been at least partially apprehended. The important point is to present the subject in a way to convince and to enlighten the pupil, and this object can only be attained in a text-book by some repetitions and by avoiding undue brevity. This volume contains more pages than one of its predecessors in the *American Science Series*. The increased space is given to very full explanations of difficult points, to lists of test-questions, and to pictures and diagrams. Where the mathematical equipment of the pupil is not yet adequate—as in the case of NEWTON's discoveries in Celestial Mechanics, for example—an historical treatment must be adopted.

It is probable that most of the students who will read this book will not pursue the subject further in the way of formal studies. Their ideas of the measurement of time, of the apparent and real motions of the planets, of the cause of the seasons, and of other fundamental and practical matters of the sort, will be derived from this one course of study. Especial stress is therefore laid on such topics, and many interesting subjects of less importance are passed by with a mere mention, or are omitted altogether. The prescribed limits of space do not permit a treatment of all the parts of a vast science like Astronomy.

It may sometimes be useful to the teacher, and it will always be so to the student, to refer to the questions printed in Part I, which will suggest new ways of testing the knowledge gained by the reading of each lesson. It is not here attempted to set down all, or any great part, of the questions which each topic may suggest, but only to give such as are most essential and important.

If the student finds that he has an answer in clear and definite English for each of the questions given here, he may be sure that he has comprehended the explanations of the text. And he should not finally leave any topic until he does so.

The second part of the book is mainly devoted to a description of the bodies of the solar system, one by one, and to some account of nebulæ, stars, and comets. It is to be expected that the formal studies of the pupil will have created a living interest in such information, and that he will, for his own pleasure, read some of the many admirable popular works on Astronomy that we owe to Mr. PROC-

TOR, Sir ROBERT BALL, and others. The text-book will have performed its part if such an interest has been awakened, and if at the same time a solid foundation for the student's future reading has been laid. For this reason Parts II and III of this book have been somewhat abbreviated.

If the class has sufficient time it is desirable that the teacher should supplement his instruction by reading, with the students, certain chapters from the books of the school library named in Chapter XXIX. Chapters bearing on a certain subject can be selected by the teacher from the books referred to, after the students have studied the corresponding chapter in the present volume. If such books cannot be had articles from encyclopædias will serve in their stead.

It will not be out of place to give a few practical hints based on experience. Excellent training in observation can be had from tracing the areas and the boundaries of the constellations. The positions of the brighter stars of each constellation should first be fixed in the memory. There are ten stars of the first magnitude and about thirty of the second magnitude in the northern sky. After these, or most of them, have been identified, the constellation figures may be taken up one by one and their boundaries traced. The six small star-maps of this book can be used for this purpose in connection with the Map of the Equatorial Stars. A celestial globe is even more convenient and satisfactory, and every school should own one if it is practicable. It should be constantly used to illustrate or to prove the theorems of the text-book.

The globe will be a material aid in planning any series of observations, and it should be always at hand to explain the results of observations already made.

The course of one of the bright planets among the stars

should be mapped from night to night. The path of the
Moon, also, should be followed whenever it is practicable.
The place of a planet can be fixed with considerable precision by noting its allineations with two or more stars. In
these observations it will be found useful to employ a
straight ruler three or four feet long. The phases of the
Moon can be studied with the eye, or better, with a common opera-glass. A watch regulated to sidereal time
should form a part of the equipment of the school.

If a small telescope on a firm stand is available much
may be done by its aid. Many of the surface-features of
the bright planets (*Mars, Jupiter*) can be made out. The
existence of the larger satellites of *Jupiter* and *Saturn* can
be proved. The ring of *Saturn* can be seen. Some of the
double stars can be separated. The brighter nebulæ can
be shown. Some of the principal star groups or clusters
can be studied. The changes in brightness of a short-
period variable star can be observed. The spots on the
Sun can be shown by projecting the Sun's image on a
screen.

In these observations it is important to do the work
thoroughly and systematically. If the satellites of *Jupiter*
are in the field every student in the class should see all of
the bright satellites that are then visible. If a double star
is viewed it should be looked at until both its components
are plainly seen, and so with other cases. No one should
leave the telescope unconvinced. The object of such
observations is to make an ocular demonstration of facts
that have heretofore been received on faith, not to make
additions to science. For this reason the instructor should
select the objects to be examined, with care. They should
be typical, but not difficult to make out. Each student
should be required to keep neat, accurate, and concise
notes of his own observations, and whenever a drawing or
a diagram will explain the observation he should be

required to make it. All observations should be dated and authenticated with the pupil's signature. He should be taught to feel a responsibility for the records that he makes.

The student should be practised in pointing out in the sky the principal lines and points of the celestial sphere— the meridian, the equator, the ecliptic, the vernal equinox, the poles of the two last-named circles, and so forth. There is no mystery in these plain geometric figures. A little practice will serve to make them quite familiar.

The school should own a small collection of works on popular and descriptive astronomy, which can be loaned to the students for reading at home. These can be selected by the teacher and added to the equipment of the school from time to time, as fast as circumstances permit. Simple models to illustrate the motions of the different instruments of astronomy are easy to make, and they are of great practical utility in the class-room. Most of them can be made by the pupils. If practicable, models of the sextant, the transit instrument, the meridian circle and the equatorial should be provided. Directions for making such models are given in the text.

Finally it is of the first importance that difficulties should not be shirked. To be useful, the student's work should be thorough so far as it goes. An instructor (or a writer of text-books) is often tempted to smooth away obstacles, forgetting that one great use of the study of science is to train the mind to resolutely meet and to conquer difficulties. The advantage of scientific problems is that they are capable of a definite solution, and that the student himself cannot fail to know whether he has or has not accomplished that which he set out to do. If our nation is to take and hold a foremost place in the world, it will do so through the predominance of certain qualities in its citizens that scientific education can foster to a very important degree. We cannot afford to neglect any means of developing thoroughness and faithfulness in the performance of duty in those who will soon be the responsible governors of our country. E. S. H.

New York, June 17, 1899.

TABLE OF CONTENTS.

(Consult the index at the end of the book also.)

PART I.—INTRODUCTION.

PART II.—THE SOLAR SYSTEM.

xiii

SYMBOLS AND ABBREVIATIONS.

SIGNS OF THE PLANETS, ETC.

☉	The Sun.	♂	Mars.
☾	The Moon.	♃	Jupiter.
☿	Mercury.	♄	Saturn.
♀	Venus.	♅	Uranus.
⊕ or ♁	The Earth.	♆	Neptune.

The asteroids are distinguished by a circle enclosing a number, which number indicates the order of discovery, or by their names, or by both, as ⓘ⓪⓪ ; *Hecate*.

The Greek alphabet is here inserted to aid those who are not already familiar with it in reading the parts of the text in which its letters occur :

Letters.	Names.	Letters.	Names.
A α	Alpha	N ν	Nu
B β	Beta	Ξ ξ	Xi
Γ γ	Gamma	O o	Omicron
Δ δ	Delta	Π π ϖ	Pi
E ϵ	Epsilon	P ρ	Rho
Z ζ	Zeta	Σ σ ς	Sigma
Π η	Eta	T τ	Tau
Θ ϑ θ	Theta	Υ υ	Upsilon
I i	Iota	Φ ϕ	Phi
K κ	Kappa	X χ	Chi
Λ λ	Lambda	Ψ ψ	Psi
M μ	Mu	Ω ω	Omega

THE METRIC SYSTEM.

MEASURES OF LENGTH.

1 kilometre = 1000 metres   = 0.62137 mile.
1 metre   = the unit   = 39.370 inches.
1 millimetre = $\frac{1}{1000}$ of a metre = 0 03937 inch.

MEASURES OF WEIGHT.

1 kilogramme = 1000 grammes = 2.2046 pounds.
1 gramme   = the unit   = 15.432 grains.

The following rough approximations may be memorized :
The kilometre is a little more than $\frac{6}{10}$ of a mile, but less than $\frac{2}{3}$ of a mile.   The mile is $1\frac{6}{10}$ kilometres.
The kilogramme is $2\frac{1}{4}$ pounds.   The pound is less than half a kilogramme.
One metre is 3.3 feet.   One metre is 39.4 inches.

ASTRONOMY.

CHAPTER I.

INTRODUCTORY—HISTORICAL.

1. Astronomy defined.—Astronomy (from the Greek ἀστήρ, a star, and νομος, a law) is the science that is concerned about the laws that the heavenly bodies obey, and with a description of the bodies themselves both as they appear to be and as they really are. For instance the Sun appears to us very different from a bright star; but astronomy shows that the Sun is itself a star like thousands of others that we see in the sky at night. The Sun appears to move across the sky from east to west, from rising to setting, every day. Astronomy explains that this motion is only apparent and that, in fact, it is caused by the Earth's turning on its axis, daily.

The Sun appears to move among the stars so as to go completely around the sky from one star back to the same star again every year. Astronomy proves that, in fact, the Sun does not move, but that its apparent course is nothing but the result of the Earth's real motion around an orbit—a path—with the Sun near its centre. The planets, like the stars, appear to shine by their own light.

1

Astronomy shows that the planets shine by reflected sunlight, while the light of the stars is native to them. Astronomy is the science that seeks the true explanation of the appearances presented by the stars. Astronomy is the science of the stars; or more particularly, it is the science that explains what the stars really are, how they really move, and why they appear to move as they do. The word star is used so as to include planets, comets, the Sun, the Moon, etc. It is used as the Greeks used it, to mean any heavenly body.

2. How we get our notions of the Universe of Stars.—We know things on the Earth through our senses, by touching them, tasting, smelling, hearing, or seeing them. A piece of iron can be felt and weighed as well as seen. If one of our senses makes a mistake, another sense often comes in to correct the error. A piece of cork might be painted so as to look precisely like a piece of iron of the same size. The sight alone could not distinguish between them. But if we take the two things in our hands, the sense of touch or of weight detects a difference at once.

Stars in the sky are known to us only through the sense of sight. If that sense is deceived, there is no other one to correct it. A blind person can know much about things on the Earth, but he can know very little indeed about the stars that he cannot see. All our first-hand notions of the universe of stars come to us through our sense of sight.

Our eyes tell us how things appear to be, and we do not know how they really are until we have reasoned about the appearances and sifted out the truth. A bright rainbow looks almost like a solid arch in the sky, while it is, in fact, not in the sky at all. It is in our own eyes. When we travel in a railway train, parts of the landscape seem to be moving about other parts ; yet nothing is more certain than that the landscape is really unchanged. It requires reasoning to interpret such appearances.

— What senses can you use to learn about things on the Earth ? Give an example of a thing that you can touch ? of a thing that you can taste ? of a thing that you can hear ? From all these separate senses you gain notions of things on the Earth. How do you get your ideas about a star ? It is by the sense of sight alone, is it not ? If you have only one sense to help you, you have to be extremely careful not to be deceived by it. Give some examples of how the sense of sight deceives in appearances on the Earth.

3. **The Heavens were carefully observed by the Ancients.**—The very first man could not fail to notice the rising and setting of the Sun. The coming of Night—often a time of terror and danger to him—was a mystery ; and the advent of successive days was a perpetual miracle. The Sun brought cheerfulness, safety, warmth, comfort. His rays made plants grow and provided food. He was worshipped as a God by the men of early times. When the Sun was darkened by an eclipse and the day itself grew black the people were filled with dread. Special men—priests—were appointed to observe such occurrences and to foretell them. It was by the diligent watching of these priests that the different appearances in the sky were first carefully noted, and the first lists of the stars made.

By and by, as men in general had more leisure, the science of the stars, like other sciences, was studied for its own sake. Men were curious to understand *why* the Sun rose and set; *why* it was sometimes eclipsed, and so forth. Moreover, their knowledge of astronomy was put to practical uses. In the earliest times navigators did not dare to venture out of sight of land, or to make voyages at night. They sailed from headland to headland during the day, and tied their little vessels to the shore at night. They steered their course by landmarks. But wise men had noticed that while the stars in general rose and set, there were some stars that were always visible—the North Star, for example. They could use the North Star for a steering-mark by night, then; and so they did.

Nearly three thousand years ago (1012 B.C.) Solomon built the Temple at Jerusalem and ornamented it with gold brought by ships from South Africa. The Phœnicians (who lived on the north shores of Africa) brought tin from England about the same time. These long voyages must have been made by using the stars as guides by night.

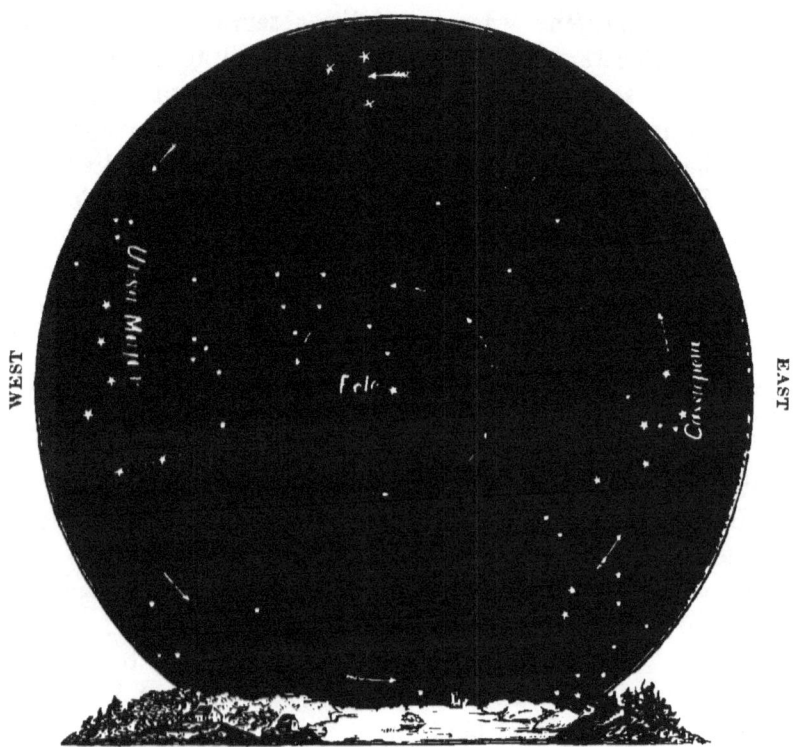

FIG. 1.—THE STARS OF THE NORTHERN SKY.

The Pole-star is at the centre of the cut. The Great Bear (the Dipper) is at the left-hand side. The arrows show the direction in which the stars move round the pole.

The mariner's compass, which is our guide nowadays, was not known in Europe before A.D. 1300, though the Chinese sailors used it long before that time.

— What was the earliest observation of astronomy ? Who were the first astronomers ? After the priests, who studied the stars? How did astronomy make itself useful to navigation ? What star is always visible on clear nights in our part of the world ? Does the North Star rise and set ? Mention some long voyages made by the ancients.

4. Some of the great astronomers of ancient times.

We do not know the names of the ancient priests and wise men of Assyria, Babylon, China, and Egypt who first studied the stars. A few of their records that have come down to us date back to 2200 B.C. in Chaldæa and to 2900 B.C. in China. Our history of astronomy begins long after their time, with the Greeks, about six centuries before Christ, about 2500 years ago. The Greeks of that time were a very intelligent, clever, hardy, adventurous people, eager to learn and to practice what they learned. They were good sailors and good soldiers.

THALES (pronounced thā'lēz), one of the seven wise men of Greece, was born about 640 B.C. He showed his countrymen how to divide the year into seasons. At midsummer the Sun at noon was higher in the heavens than at any other time of the year (about June 21). At midwinter the Sun, at noon, was lowest (about December 22). These were the two *solstices* (pronounced sŏl'stĭ-cĕs). About March 20 and September 22 the days and nights were of equal length (at the two equinoxes). March 20 was the vernal, or spring, equinox; September 22 was the autumnal equinox. Each and every year could be divided into seasons in this way because the Sun was always highest in the heavens (nearest to the point overhead) in June, always lowest in December ; because the days and nights were always of equal length in March and in September. THALES did not know why this was so. But he knew the facts. And he first showed the Greeks how to divide their year into parts. Before his time the Greek sailors had steered their ships by the stars of the Great Bear (see Fig. 1). He showed them, it is said, that the stars of the Little Bear, which were nearer the pole, would serve the purpose better.

ANAX'IMANDER, a friend of THALES (610 B.C.) invented the sun-dial. The shadow of an upright column made by the Sun moved during the day, and the motion of the shadow marked the passing of the hours. Sun-dials were the first clocks. He explained why it is that the Moon changes every month from a crescent (new Moon) to a full Moon; and other matters.

PYTHAG'ORAS (born 582 B.C.) travelled in Egypt and learned much of the science of the Egyptian priests. Several of the Egyptian pyramids were built at least a thousand years before Christ, and many of them were built by astronomical rules, so as to face the North Star and so forth. PYTHAGORAS brought much foreign science home to the Greeks. It was he who first taught his countrymen that the morning and the evening star (*Venus*) was the same body. It had formerly been thought that *Phosphorus* (the name for the morning star) and *Hesperus* (the evening star) were two different planets. It was a great discovery to learn that there was only one planet, sometimes seen in the west at sunset, sometimes in the east about sunrise. You know the fact, just as PYTHAGORAS did twenty-four centuries ago. He did not thoroughly understand why it was so, but the reason will be plain to you before you have finished this little book.

ANAXAG'ORAS (born 500 B.C.) knew all the bright planets—*Mercury*, *Venus*, *Mars*, *Jupiter*, and *Saturn*—and understood how they moved in the heavens, among the stars. He knew that the stars did not move among each other. A group of stars like the Great Dipper (see Fig. 1) keeps the same shape during centuries. Planets (wandering stars) move among the fixed stars. ANAXAGORAS explained eclipses too. He said that the dark body of the Moon came in between the Sun and the Earth and shut off the Sun's light, just as your hand held in front of a candle shuts off *its* light.

AR'ISTOTLE (born 384 B.C.) was the first Greek to prove that the Earth is a globe. He was the friend of ALEXANDER the Great and the pupil of PLATO, who was the pupil of SOCRATES. He studied every kind of science and wrote many books. (Books in his day were manuscripts of course ; printing was not invented in Europe till about A.D. 1450, though the Chinese had practiced the art long before.) ALEXANDER the Great founded a splendid city —Alexandria, in Egypt—and endowed it with schools, colleges, libraries, museums, observatories. It was full of learned men of all sorts : physicians, geographers, grammarians, mathematicians, and among them were many famous astronomers. EUCLID, the geometer, was born there about 300 B.C. ; ARCHIME'DES, the famous mathematician (born 287 B.C.), studied there ; ERATOS'THENES (born 276 B.C.) was the keeper of the Royal Library, and there he made a great map of the world and tried to measure the circumference of the earth.

HIPPARCHUS (born 160 B.C.) was an Alexandrian, too, and he is the Father of Astronomy. He collected all the observations of the men who had gone before him and made great discoveries of his own, of which we shall hear more. Most of his writings are lost, but his discoveries are described by PTOLEMY of Alexandria (who lived in the first century after Christ) in his great work the *Almagest.* This book, which sums up all the astronomical knowledge of the ancients, was the greatest scientific work of the Old World. Its doctrines were believed and taught in all the schools and universities of Europe from PTOLEMY's time up to the time of GALILEO (died 1642)—that is, for fifteen centuries.

PTOLEMY's book declared that the Earth was the centre of the Universe, and that the Sun and all the planets moved round it. Another great book was written by COPERNICUS (died 1543) to prove that the Sun and not the Earth was the centre of the system; and that the Earth was only one of the planets, all of which moved round the Sun. This was and is the truth; but it was not established until the discoveries made by GALILEO (1610) with the telescope that he constructed.

Still another great book, the *Principia*, was written by Sir ISAAC NEWTON in 1687, to prove that all the motions of all the planets and all the stars are the results of one single force—the force of gravitation or attraction exerted by every heavy body on every other such body. NEWTON is the Father of Modern Astronomy, just as HIPPARCHUS was the Father of the Astronomy of the Ancients. The books of PTOLEMY, of COPERNICUS, and of NEWTON are landmarks in the history of Astronomy. Their dates should be remembered: A.D. 140, A.D. 1543, A.D. 1687.

—When does the history of astronomy begin? To what nation did the first learned astronomers belong? What sort of a people were the Greeks? Who showed the Greeks how to divide the year into seasons? When did THALES live? Who invented the sundial? Who first explained the changes in the Moon's shape? When did ANAXIMANDER live? What Greek brought home the learning of the Egyptians? When did PYTHAGORAS live? Who first taught how the planets moved among the stars? and that the stars were fixed? and explained eclipses? About what time did ANAXAGORAS live? When did ARISTOTLE live? He was the friend of what great King? Who founded Alexandria in Egypt? What sorts of learning were encouraged there? Name some of the famous men who studied and taught there. Who is called the Father of Astronomy? What is the name of PTOLEMY's great book? How long was the *Almagest* the greatest authority on astronomy? Where was the centre of the Universe acording to PTOLEMY? Where did COPERNICUS (1543) place it? Whose discoveries proved COPERNICUS to be right? Who constructed the first telescope? When did

GALILEO live? Who is the Father of Modern Astronomy? When was the *Principia* of Sir ISAAC NEWTON written?

5. How Astronomy might be studied.

In the paragraphs just preceding, a few of the names of the great men of past times have been mentioned and something has been said of their discoveries. If there were time enough there could be no better way to study Astronomy than to follow its history step by step from the most ancient times until now. Six centuries before Christ, 2500 years ago, the earliest Greek philosophers began to study science for its own sake. They were curious about the world around them and about all the appearances they saw in the sky. They wished to understand the motions of the planets, their distances, the shape and size of the Earth, the cause of eclipses, and so on. One after another of their great men accurately described or fully explained motions or appearances in the sky.

Each philosopher taught what he had learned to his favorite pupils by word of mouth. They in their turn taught others in the same way. Finally in the time of Alexander the Great (332 B.C.) the city of Alexandria in Egypt was founded, and splendidly endowed with colleges, schools, museums, observatories, and so forth. Learned men were invited thither from every other city. For several centuries it was the centre of learning for the whole world. Its libraries contained 700,000 manuscripts. Here a succession of great astronomers and mathematicians laid the foundations of the science. The work of HIPPARCHUS was gathered together in a systematic treatise (the *Almagest*) by PTOLEMY, and this book held its place of authority for fifteen centuries.

Alexandria was conquered by Rome in 30 B.C. When the Roman Empire was ruined in the IV century the fortunes of the city declined, and it was itself captured and sacked by the Saracens in 641 A.D. Learning, especially scientific learning, was at a very low ebb in Europe during the Dark Ages (A.D. 400 to 1400). It was not until the time of COLUMBUS (1492) and COPERNICUS (1543) that advances were made, except by the Moors in Spain (709 A.D. to 1492). The universities and schools established in these centuries still taught the astronomy of ARISTOTLE and of PTOLEMY.

The great book of COPERNICUS (*De Orbium cælestium revolutionibus*—on the revolutions of the celestial bodies) was printed in 1543. It announced and proved the great discovery that the Sun and not the Earth was the centre of the celestial motions. The doctrine of PTOLEMY declared that the Sun and planets moved around the Earth. GALILEO constructed the first astronomical telescope in 1609, and in 1610 he made such discoveries by its aid that the Copernican doctrine was fully established in the minds of all competent judges. But there were few such judges in his day.

KEPLER discovered the laws according to which the planets move in their orbits in the years 1609–1618. But it was not until the appearance of Sir ISAAC NEWTON's *Principia* in 1687—a little more than two centuries ago—that modern astronomy was born. He announced and proved that all the motions and all the appearances in the Universe were mere consequences of a single law of gravitation, of attraction. Since his time immense advances have been made, but most of them are but consequences of his law, and are explained by it. Astronomical instruments have been wonderfully improved also, and great discoveries have been made. The system of COPERNICUS, as explained by NEWTON, has been firmly established by all these advances.

If there were leisure to follow out in detail all these discoveries and advances, the pupil could be taken through the experience of the race and could successfully master each great problem just as it was mastered by THALES, HIPPARCHUS, COPERNICUS, and NEWTON. There is no more satisfactory and thorough method of study than this. Unfortunately it requires far more time than is available. It is impossible, here, to explain the system of the world according to PTOLEMY and to take the time to prove it to be wrong. All that can be done is to explain the system of COPERNICUS and to prove it to be right. It is necessary, therefore, to study Astronomy in our High Schools in a different order. Each subject must be so treated as to prepare the way for other topics, and everything must be presented in the briefest manner. The science of Astronomy is so vast, and so many brilliant discoveries have been made by so many able men, that the limits of this little book do not permit an historical treatment.

— How long ago were the beginnings of the Astronomy of the Greeks? How did the ancient Greek philosophers teach their pupils? When was the city of Alexandria founded? How many manuscripts were contained in its libraries? (The National Library at Washington has not even now so many books.) Ask your teacher to tell you about the Dark Ages in Europe, or else read about them in an encyclopædia. What system of Astronomy was taught in European universities in those times? Where did PTOLEMY say the centre of the universe was? COPERNICUS (1543) taught that the centre of the world was—where? Which is right? It will be abundantly shown in this book that COPERNICUS was right.

6. General notions of Astronomy.

Even before beginning the study of Astronomy every
one of us has a certain knowledge of it. All of us have
studied Geography and know what is there said of the Sun
and planets; all of us have heard certain facts of Astronomy talked about; and every one of us has observed a few
things for himself. Let us set down something like an inventory of this general knowledge here. It is well to find
out just what we know now before going on to new things.

The **Earth** is a huge globe, so large that any small part of it, where
we live, looks flat and not round. Its diameter is nearly 8000 miles.
We know that the Earth is a globe because it was circumnavigated
by MAGELLAN'S ships in the years 1519–1522, and by hundreds of
vessels since that time ; and because nearly every part of it has been
visited by travellers ; and finally because surveys have been made of
most civilized countries. The Earth is certainly a globe ; and its size
is enormous compared to our houses, cities, etc. It is not large compared to the Sun and to some of the other planets. It is isolated in
space. It does not touch any other planet or star. Even the Moon
is very distant from it, and the Sun is much further away. The stars
are further off still.

The Earth turns round on its axis once in every day, and its turning makes the Sun and the Moon and the stars appear to rise and set.
Moreover the Earth, like the other planets, moves round the sun in
an orbit—a path—once in a year, and this revolution of the Earth
has something to do with the seasons—Spring, Summer, Autumn,
Winter—which recur regularly every year.

The **Sun** looks to us like a large flat disc, but it is, in fact, a huge
globe, much larger than the Earth. It is the source from which
comes all our light and all our heat. Our seasons—Spring, Summer,
Autumn, and Winter—depend upon the amount of heat received from
the Sun at different times. Just what makes the light and heat we
do not learn from Geography, and that is one of the important things
taught in our text-books of Physics. All the planets—the Earth,
Venus, Jupiter, etc., move round the Sun in orbits—paths—and together make up the Solar System—the Family of the Sun.

The **Moon** also looks to us like a flat disc, but it is, in fact, a globe,
smaller than the Earth. It revolves about the Earth, not about the

Sun, in an orbit—path, and it is very far away from us. Sometimes
its shape is that of a crescent; sometimes it is circular. It regularly
goes through all its shapes and comes back to the same shape again
once in every month, and so on forever. The Moon sometimes comes
between the Earth and the Sun and shuts off some or all of the Sun's
light in the daytime and makes an eclipse, just as a book held in
front of a candle will cut off the candlelight and eclipse it. The
Moon is usually bright, but it is itself sometimes eclipsed. The face
of the Moon seen by the naked eye at night (or seen through an
opera-glass or a telescope) is not everywhere the same. Parts of it
are much brighter than other parts; and there are mountains on the
Moon.

 The Planets look to us like bright stars. *Venus* is often seen towards the west at sunset, and is called the Evening Star; and sometimes we may have seen it towards the east about sunrise, when it is
called the Morning Star. It is brighter than most of the stars.
Jupiter, Mars, and *Saturn* are planets that look like stars, too.

 The Comets are sometimes very bright, we have heard. They
move about in space, and people say that if one should hit the Earth
there would be a great disaster.*

 The Stars lie all around us, and they are visible by hundreds at
night. Most of them rise and set, but there are some near the North
Pole that are always visible whenever it is night. They are
divided into constellations, or groups; and one of the groups is called
the *Great Bear* or the *Dipper*. Some of the stars are quite bright,
others much fainter. If a telescope is used, many thousands of stars
can be seen that are invisible to the naked eye. The stars are exceedingly far away from us.

If some one who had not yet studied Astronomy were
asked to give his notions about the heavenly bodies he
would probably say something like what has been printed
in the preceding paragraphs. The information is generally
correct so far as it goes, but there are many things lacking
to make it complete. We ought to know *why* it is that
the seasons come back to us year after year in order; why

---

 * It may as well be said here that in the first place such a collision
is very unlikely to happen; and that if it did happen it is probable
that the Earth would not suffer.

the Sun gives us light and heat ; why the Sun is eclipsed by the Moon sometimes, and why it is not eclipsed every month; why the Moon itself is sometimes eclipsed, and so forth. Perhaps the most important thing that is left out of this account is the fact that the Sun shines by its own light (just as an electric light does), while the Moon and all the planets do *not* shine by their own light, but by reflected sunlight. They appear bright just as a mirror that is shined upon appears bright. If you shut off the light, the mirror is no longer bright. If the Sun were to be annihilated, all the planets and the Moon would instantly be dark. They are only bright because the sunlight shines upon them and because they reflect the sunlight back to the Earth much as a mirror might do. All the stars are suns, and each and every star shines by its own light, just as the Sun does.

With these additional facts about the Sun, which shines by its own light; about the planets, which shine by reflected light; and about the stars, which shine, like the Sun, by native light, we can go on to study Astronomy in detail. We have a general idea of it to begin with, and we know some, at least, of the lacks in our present knowledge. This book does not take such general knowledge to be proved. On the other hand the facts above set down will be explained and proved. But as every one has some knowledge of astronomical facts, the book is not written as if no one had any information of the kind.

— How do we know that the Earth is a globe ? Who first circum-navigated it? How long ago? How do we know that the Earth is isolated in space? Two of the Earth's motions make the day and the year—which two? What heavenly body that you know of goes through a series of changes every month? Does the Sun shine by his own light? Does the Moon shine by her own light? Do the planets so shine? If you could stand a long way off from the Earth, would the Earth be dark or would it shine like the other planets? Do the stars shine by the light of the Sun? Suppose the Sun suddenly became dark so that it gave out no more light, what changes would this make in the appearance of the sky at night? What bodies would no longer be visible? What others would continue to shine unchanged?

CHAPTER II.

7. **Space.**—The Sun, the planets, and all the stars are moving in Space. It is often called "empty" Space because it contains no large masses except the Sun and planets, the stars, the comets, and so forth. It is necessary to have some idea of its vastness, for it contains all these bodies and every other thing that exists. It is infinite—without any limits or boundaries. For suppose it had a boundary, what would lie beyond that? Only more and further extensions of space. We cannot realize exactly or even imagine what Space is; but we can obtain a few correct ideas about it.

Suppose that on a clear night you look up at the full Moon in the heavens. It seems to be, and it is, extremely distant. It is 240,000 miles away. It is 240 times as distant from us as New York is from Chicago. Now think of the Sun, which is 870,000 miles in diameter. The diameter of the globe of the Sun is about $3\frac{1}{2}$ times the distance of the Moon from the Earth. The Sun is one of the stars, and there are hundreds and hundreds of bright stars visible to the naked eye. There are millions and millions of stars visible in a great telescope. All these stars are scattered about in space somewhat as pictured on page 16.

Space contains millions of stars, and each star (as a, b, c, etc.) is at least as far from every other star (as f, g, h, i, k, l, m, etc.) as the nearest stars (b, c, g, h, l, m) are from the Sun.

15

Try to conceive this arrangement of stars clearly. They are scattered everywhere in Space. There are millions upon millions of them. Each one of them is as distant from its nearest neighbor as the stars nearest to the Sun are distant from the Sun. Now how far is the nearest star from the Sun? We shall see by and by that it is at least 20,000,000,000,000 miles; that is, twenty millions of millions of miles. Every other star in the sky is as distant from *its* nearest neighbor as this. And there are millions of such stars in succession one to another as we go out-

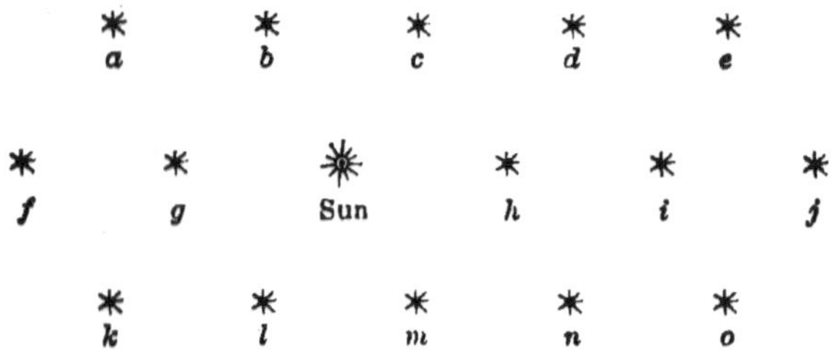

```
  *       *       *       *       *
  a       b       c       d       e


*       *       *        *       *       *
f       g      Sun       h       i       j


  *       *       *       *       *
  k       l       m       n       o
```

Fig. 2.

The stars are arranged in Space somewhat as in the picture, only not in a plane, but throughout a solid.

wards through Space. Space contains them all, and there is room for countless millions more. The spaces between them are empty.

Let us try to realize this in another way. Think first of the Sun—it is 870,000 miles in diameter. Then think of the *nearest* star. It is 20,000,000,000,000 miles from the Sun. Then imagine a whole universe of countless millions of stars no one nearer to another than twenty billion miles. All these stars may be thought of as a great cluster in the shape of a globe. Imagine this cluster to shrink and shrink, to get smaller and smaller. The stars will come nearer and nearer to each other, and the globe of the Sun (870,000 miles in diameter, remember) will also grow smaller at the same time and in the same proportion. Let the shrinking go on till the universe is 2,300,000,000 times smaller than at first—till the Sun's globe is only two feet in diameter,* and then stop the shrinking.

We shall have a model of the universe with everything in its true proportions, only the Sun will be two feet in diameter instead of 870,000 miles. Now how far off will the *nearest* star to the Sun be, in this shrunken model of the universe? It will be as far from the Sun as the city of Peking is from the city of New York! The *nearest* star will be so far off. The other stars will be arranged in order out beyond this one, and none of them will be any nearer, in this model, to its neighbors than the distance from China to New York. And the model must contain millions of stars. Even this model will be inconceivably large. The real universe—Space—is inconceivably larger than the model. An illustration like this entirely fails to give a *measure* of the size of Space, but it certainly does give some conception of its immense extension. In thinking of the universe of stars you must try to realize it in this way. The Sun and all the stars lie in space, none of them near together, with immense empty regions between the different bodies. Each star is inconceivably far from its nearest neighbors, and there are millions upon millions of stars. It is not at all easy to have clear ideas of an infinite extension; but it is absolutely necessary in beginning the study of Astronomy to have *some* idea of the space in which the Sun, all the planets, and all the stars exist.

— Why do we call Space "empty"? How far away is the Moon from the Earth? The *diameter* of the globe of the Sun is how much larger than this distance? Is the Sun a star? Space contains mil-

---

* Two feet is $\frac{1}{1500000000}$th part of 870,000 miles.

lions upon millions of stars. Each star is at least twenty millions of millions of miles from its nearest neighbors. Are the spaces between them empty of large bodies? Suppose you could make an exact model of Space with each star in its right place, and suppose you could make this model shrink until the 870,000 miles of the Sun's diameter had shrunk to two feet—how far off would the star *nearest* to the Sun be from the Sun itself? Would these words do for a definition of Space—Space is indefinite extension? If you have a dictionary, look up the word and see how it is defined there.

8. The Celestial Sphere.—In what has just been said about Space we have spoken of the universe as it really is. The stars are scattered all about through Space at enormous distances one from another. That is the way the universe really is. Now we have to ask how does it appear to be to us? If you look at the heavens on a clear night what do you see? In the first place you see hundreds of stars, some very bright, some less bright. They all seem to be at the same distance from you. They look as if they were bright points fastened to the inside surface of a great hollow globe —the celestial sphere—hung over the Earth. You see the bright points. The surface on which you imagine them to lie is called the celestial sphere. There is, in fact, no such surface, but there seems to be one. Let us make a formal definition of it which is to be learned by heart. *The Celestial Sphere is that surface to which the stars* seem *to be fastened.* No one ever thinks of the stars as if they were outside of the celestial sphere and shining through it.

In Fig. 3 the black square is a part of Space.* There are a few stars in it, namely p, q, r, s, t, t, t, u, v. In respect to the immense distances of the stars, the Earth, O, may be considered as a mere point. The configurations of the stars are the same whether you are at Lisbon or at

---

* The student must remember here and throughout the book that the drawings have to be on a small scale. All the Universe has to be drawn on a few square inches.

New York. No change of place on the Earth alters the grouping of the stars. You are on the Earth looking out at the sky at night and you see all these stars. If you look at the star which is really at q you are looking along the line Oq and see it as if it were on the surface of the celestial sphere at Q. If you look at r and s, you see them at

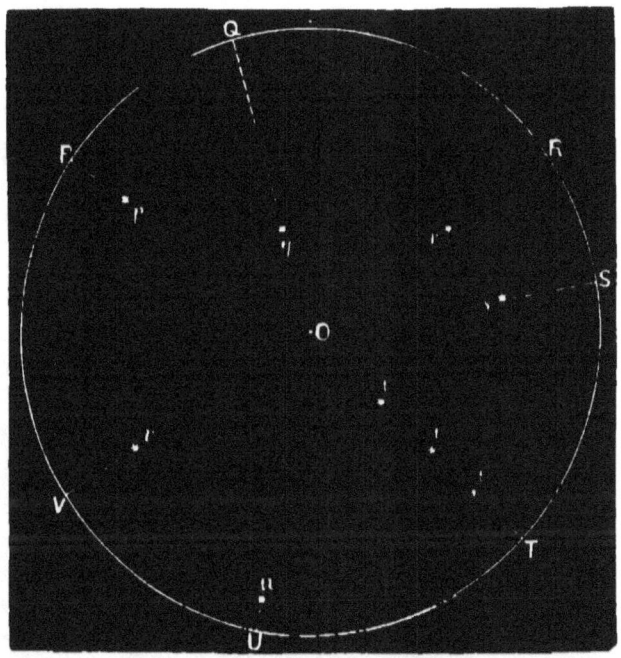

FIG. 3.—THE CELESTIAL SPHERE.

The Earth is supposed to be at O, a few of the stars at $p, q, r, s, t, t, t, u, v$. These stars are seen by us as if they were all on the surface of the celestial sphere at P, Q, R, S, T, U, V.

R and S. If you look at u and v you see them at U and V. All of them *appear* to be at one and the same distance from you, though they really are at very different distances. The point Q is in the line Oq prolonged; the points R, S, U, V are in the lines Or, Os, Ou, Ov prolonged. Now suppose there happened to be three stars, t, *t, t,* in a line. They would all three *appear* on the celestial sphere at *T*. You would never know there were three separate stars, because you could only see one bright point —at *T*. You do not see the other stars *r, s, v,* etc., where they really are, but at places on the celestial sphere at *R, S, V.*

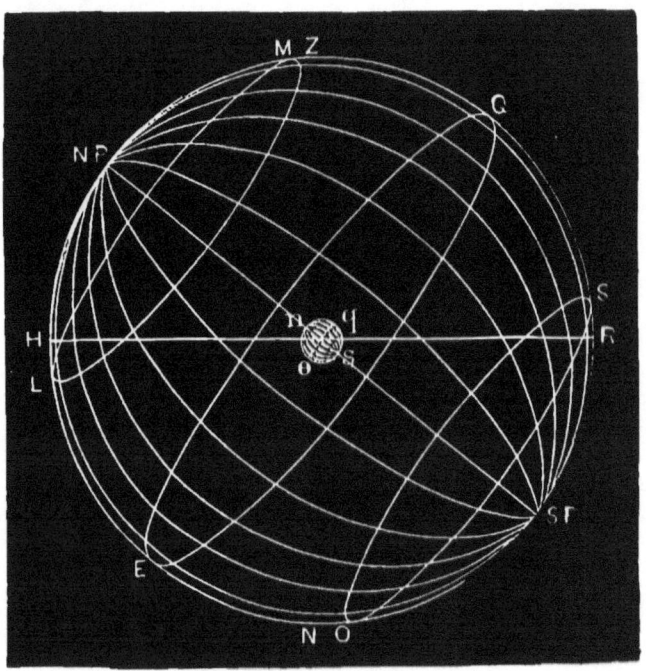

Fig. 4.—The Earth (*n, q, s*) in the Centre of the Celestial Sphere.

On the surface of the celestial sphere meridians and parallels are supposed to be drawn corresponding to meridians and parallels on the Earth.

What you *see* in a dark night is stars apparently studded over the inner surface of the celestial sphere. It is only by reasoning about it that you know they are not on this surface but scattered about inside of the sphere. The ancient astronomers thought that the sphere actually existed and that the stars were really fastened to it. Although it does not exist, the idea can be made to serve a useful purpose. For instance, if we want to know the angle between the two lines *Or* and *Os* (the angle between the two lines joining the Earth and two distant stars) all we have to do is to measure the arc *RS* on the celestial sphere. The arc *RS* is the measure of the angle *rOs* in space.

The sphere has other uses, too. Just as there is a terrestrial equator on the globe of the Earth (and terrestrial meridians, etc.), so there is a celestial equator (and celestial meridians, etc.) on the celestial sphere. The simplest part of astronomy deals with the apparent places of stars as they seem to be on the celestial sphere—it is called Spherical Astronomy for that reason. It is only after we have learned about the apparent places and motions of stars and planets that we can go on to study their real motions. So that the idea of a celestial sphere will be useful. Whenever you go out at night you will see it—it is the dark sphere on which the bright stars seem to rest. Imagine that the stars are not there ; yet the sphere will remain. Every one imagines the blue vault of the sky in the daytime as if it were a hollow sphere hanging over us. The Sun seems to be on its inner surface. When you see the Moon in the daytime it, too, seems to lie on the celestial sphere.

—The stars really are at very different distances from us; all are very far away, but some are much further away than others—do they *seem* to be at different distances when you look at them at night? Do they seem to lie on the inner surface of a sphere? What is the celestial sphere? Is it a sphere that really exists, or only one that appears to exist? Does the celestial sphere seem to exist in the daytime as well as at night?

9. Some Mathematical Terms used in Astronomy.—It

is convenient to use a few mathematical terms in speaking about the geometrical parts of Astronomy. All of the mathematical ideas here introduced are simple, but it may be well to set them down in order. If they are understood by the student he will have no difficulty in comprehending the astronomical matters that are to be spoken of. If they are not thoroughly understood some points will not be as clear as they should be.

ANGLES: THEIR MEASUREMENT. — An angle is the amount of divergence of two lines. For example, the

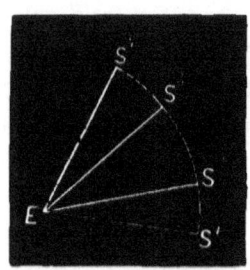

angle between the two lines S^1E and S^2E is the amount of divergence of these lines. The angle S^2ES^4 is the amount of divergence of the two lines S^2E and S^4E. The eye sees at once that the angle S^2ES^4 in the figure is greater than the angle S^1ES^2, and that the angle S^2ES^4 is greater than either of them.

FIG. 5.—ANGLES : THEIR MEASUREMENT.

In order to compare them and to obtain their numerical ratio, we must have a unit-angle.

The unit-angle is obtained in this way : The circumference of any circle is divided into 360 equal parts. The points of division are joined with the centre. The angles between any two adjacent radii are called *degrees*. In the figure, SES^2 is about 12°, S^3ES^4 is about 22°, S^2ES^4 is about 30°, and S^1ES^4 is about 64°. The vertex of the *angle* is at the centre E: the *measure of the angle* is on the circumference $S^1S^2S^3S^4$, or on any circumference drawn from E as a centre.

In this way we have come to speak of the length of one three-hundred-and-sixtieth part of any circumference as a degree, because radii drawn from the ends of this part make an angle of 1°.

For convenience in expressing the ratios of different angles the degree has been subdivided into minutes and seconds.

$$\text{One circumference} = 360° = 21600' = 1296000''$$
$$1° = 60' = 360''$$
$$1' = 60''$$

Smaller angles than seconds are expressed by decimals of a second. Thus one-quarter of a second is $0''.25$; one-quarter of a minute is $15''$.

The Radius of the Circle in Angular Measure.

—If R is the radius of a circle, we know from geometry that one circumference $= 2\pi R$, where $\pi = 3.1416$. That is,

$$2\pi R = 360° = 21600' = 1296000''$$
$$\text{or} \qquad R = 57°.3 = 3437'.7 = 206264''.8.$$

By this we mean that if a flexible cord equal in length to the radius of any circle were laid round the circumference of that circle, and if two radii were then drawn to the ends of this cord, the angle of these radii would be $57°.3$, $3437'.7$, or $206264''.8$.

It is important that this should be perfectly clear to the student.

For instance, how far off must you place a foot-rule in order that it may subtend an angle of $1°$ at your eye? Why, 57.3 feet away. How far must it be in order to subtend an angle of a minute? 3437.7 feet. How far for a second? 206264.8 feet, or over 39 miles.

Again, if an object subtends an angle of $1°$ at the eye, we know that its diameter must be $\frac{1}{57.3}$ as great as its distance from us. If it subtends an angle of $1''$, its distance from us is over 200,000 times as great as its diameter.

The instruments employed in astronomy may be used to measure the angles subtended at the eye by the diameters of the heavenly bodies. In other ways we can determine their distance from us in miles. A combination of these data will give us the actual dimensions of these bodies in miles. For example, the sun is about 93,000,000 miles from the Earth. The angle subtended by the sun's diam-

eter at this distance is 1922″. What is the diameter of the
sun in miles? (1″ is about 451 miles.)

An idea of angular dimensions in the sky may be had
by remembering that the angular diameters of the Moon
and of the Sun are about 30′. It is 180° from the west
point to the east point counting through the point immediately overhead. How many moons placed edge to edge
would it take to reach from horizon to horizon? The
student may guess at the answer first and then compute it.

It is convenient to remember that the angular distance
between the two "Pointers" in the Great Bear (see Fig. 1)
is about 5°.

PLANE TRIANGLES.—The angles of which we have spoken are
angles in a plane. In any plane triangle there are three angles A, B, C
and three sides a, b, c—six parts. If any three of the parts are given
(except the three angles) we can construct the triangle. For in-

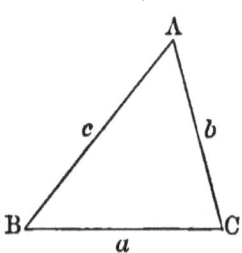

FIG. 6.—A PLANE
TRIANGLE.

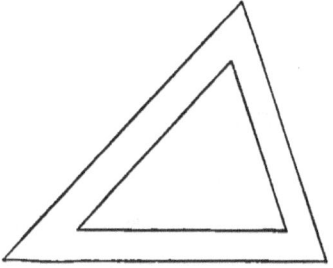

FIG. 7.—TWO SIMILAR PLANE
TRIANGLES.

stance, if you know the three sides a, b, c, you can make one triangle,
and only one, with these sides. If you only know the three angles
you can make any number of triangles with three such angles. All
of them will have the same shape, but they will have different sizes.
(See Fig. 7.)

THE SPHERE: ITS PLANES AND CIRCLES.—In Fig.
8, O is the centre of the sphere. Suppose any plane

as *AB* to pass through the centre of the sphere. It will cut the sphere into two *hemispheres*. It will intersect the surface of the sphere in a circle *AFBF* which is called a *great circle* of the sphere. *A great circle of the sphere is one cut from the surface by a plane passing through the centre of the sphere.* Suppose a right line *POP'* perpendicular to this plane. The points *P* and *P'* in which it intersects the surface of the sphere are everywhere 90° from the circle *AEBF*. They are the *poles* of that circle. The poles of the great circle *CEDF* are *Q* and *Q'*. It is proved in geometry that the following relations exist between the angles made in the figure :

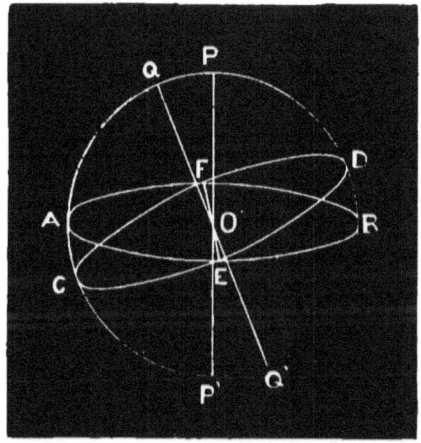

FIG. 8.—THE SPHERE ; ITS GREAT CIRCLES ; THEIR POLES.

I. The angle *POQ* between the poles is equal to the inclination of the planes to each other.

II. The arc *BD* which measures the greatest distance between the two circles is equal to the arc *PQ* which measures the angle *POQ*.

III. The points *E* and *F*, in which the two great circles intersect each other, are the poles of the great circle

PQACP'Q'BD which passes through the poles of the first two circles.

The Spherical Triangle.—In the last figure there are several spherical triangles, as *EDB*, *FAC*, *ECP'Q'B*, etc. In astronomy we need consider only those whose sides are formed by arcs of great circles. The angles of the triangle are angles between two arcs of great circles; or what is the same thing, they are angles between the two planes which cut the two arcs from the surface of the sphere.

In spherical triangles, as in plane, there are six parts, three angles and three sides. Having *any* three parts the other three can be constructed.

The sides as well as the angles of spherical triangles are expressed in degrees, minutes, and seconds.

If the student has a school globe, let him mark on it the triangle whose sides are—

$$a = 10°, \; b = 7°, \; c = 4°.$$

Its angles will be (*A* is opposite to *a*, *B* to *b*, *C* to *c*):

$$A = 128° \; 44' \; 45''.1$$
$$B = 33° \; 11' \; 12' \; 0$$
$$C = 18° \; 15' \; 31''.1$$

Latitude and Longitude of a Place on the Earth's Surface.—According to geography, *the latitude of a place on the Earth's surface is its angular distance north or south of the Earth's equator.*

The longitude of a place on the Earth's surface is its angular distance east or west of a given first meridian (the meridian of Greenwich, for example).

If *P* in Fig. 9 is the north pole of the earth, the latitude of the point *B* is 60° north; of *Z* it is 30° north; of *I* it is 27½° south. All places having the same latitude are situated on the same *parallel of latitude*. In the figure the parallels of latitude are represented by straight lines.

All places having the same longitude are situated on the same *meridian*. We shall give the astronomical definitions of these terms further on.

It is found convenient in astronomy to modify the geographical definition of longitude. In geography we say that Washington is 77° *west* of Greenwich, and that Sydney (Australia) is 151° *east* of Greenwich. For astronom-

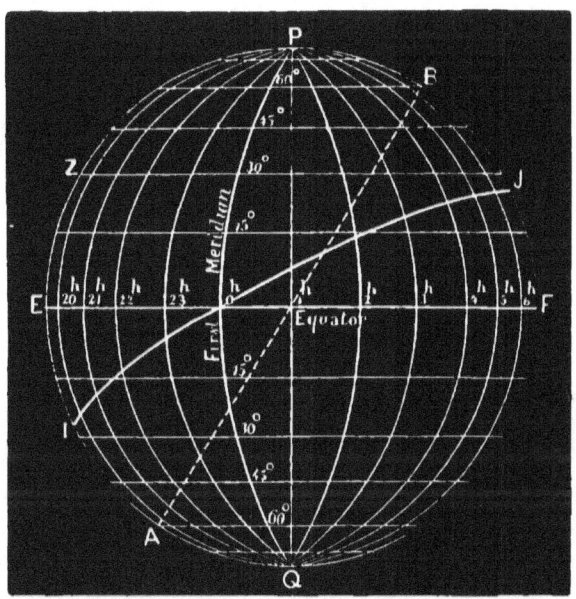

Fig. 9.—Latitude and Longitude of Places on the Earth's Surface.

ical purposes it is found more convenient to count the longitude of a place from the first meridian *always towards the west*. Thus Sydney is 209° west of Greenwich (360° − 151° = 209°).

The Earth turns on its axis once in 24 hours. In a day of 24 hours every point on the Earth's surface moves once round a circle (its parallel of latitude). Every point moves 360° in 24 hours, or *at the rate* of 15° every hour (360° divided by 24 is 15°).

Hence we can measure the longitude of a place in degrees or in hours, just as we choose. Washington is 5ʰ 8ᵐ west of Greenwich (77°) and Sydney is 13ʰ 56ᵐ west of Greenwich (209°). In the figure suppose F to be west of the first meridian. All the places on the meridian PQ have a longitude of 15° or 1 hour ; all those on the meridian $P5^hQ$ have a longitude of 75° or 5 hours ; and so on.

— What is an angle? What is a degree? What is a minute of arc? a second? The radius of a circle, if wrapped around the circumference of a circle, would cover an arc of how many degrees? What is the angular diameter of the Moon? of the Sun? How far apart in arc are the two "pointers" of the Great Bear? What is the difference between a plane triangle and a spherical triangle? Give an example of a plane triangle; of a spherical triangle. Define the latitude of a place on the Earth's surface. Define the longitude of a place on the Earth's surface.

10. The Points and Circles of the Celestial Sphere.—

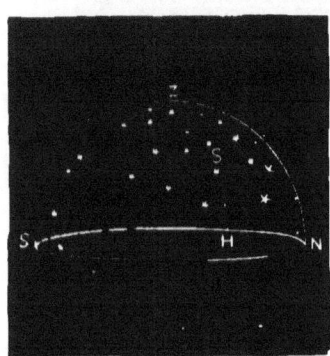

FIG. 10.—HALF OF THE CELESTIAL SPHERE, STUDDED WITH STARS.

The sphere seems to rest on the plane of the horizon. The horizon seems to be bounded by the circle *NHS*. *N* is the north point. *S* is the south point of the horizon. *Z* is the zenith-point or the point directly overhead.

THE HORIZON.—We only see one half of the celestial sphere; namely, the half above our heads. If we are at sea, or in a large open country on land, the concave vault of the daytime sky seems to rest on a flat plain, and this plain seems to be bounded by a circle. The flat plain is called the plane of the *horizon* (pronounced hor-ī'-zon). Its bounding circle is the circle of the horizon. A point on the celestial sphere directly overhead is called the zenith-point, or more briefly the *zenith.* A line joining the observer and the zenith-point is perpendicular to the plane of the horizon. If you wish to describe the situation of a star you can say that its *zenith-distance* is so many degrees—50° for example. The star *S* in the figure is distant from the zenith *Z* by an arc *ZS*. Its zenith-distance is 50°. The arc from the zenith to the horizon is 90°. That is, the zenith-distance of the horizon is everywhere 90°. The *altitude* of a star is its angular distance above the horizon. The altitude of the star *S* in the figure is *HS* = 40°.

The zenith-distance and the altitude of a star are measured on a vertical circle, *i.e.*, on a circle passing through the star and perpendicular to the horizon.

The zenith-distance of any star + the altitude of the star = 90°.

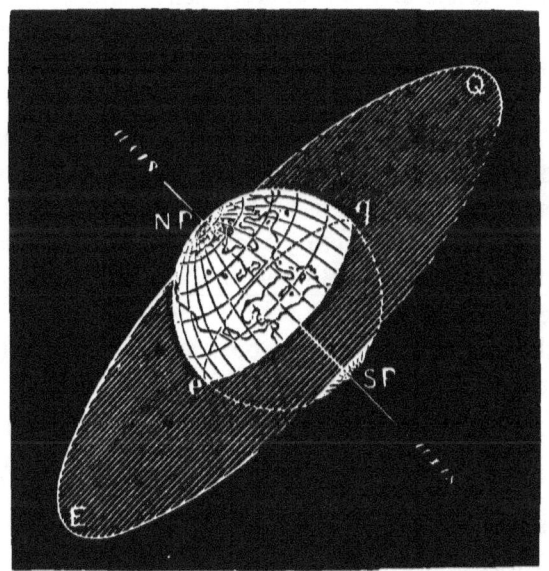

FIG. 11.—THE EARTH'S AXIS AND THE PLANE OF ITS
EQUATOR *EQ.*

NP is the earth's north pole; *SP* is the south pole; *eq* is the earth's
equator; *EQ* is the plane of the celestial equator.

THE CELESTIAL EQUATOR.—In the figure there is a picture of the Earth. *NP* is its north pole, *SP* is its south pole, and the line joining them is the Earth's axis. *eq* is the Earth's equator. It is a circle round the Earth. If we imagine the plane of that circle to continue out beyond the Earth on all sides till it reaches the celestial sphere the shaded surface *EQ* (a circle) will represent it. This surface is the plane of the equator of the celestial sphere—or more briefly, it is the plane of the *celestial equator.* If we imagine the axis of the earth prolonged both ways till it meets the celestial sphere the prolonged line is the *axis of the celestial sphere.*

If we imagine the planes of the meridians and parallels on the Earth to be prolonged outwards to meet the celestial sphere, they will meet it in circles that are the meridians and parallels of that sphere. They are not drawn in the last figure, so as to avoid confusing it ; but some of them are drawn in the next figure. In this *n* is the north pole of the Earth, *NP* the north pole of the celestial sphere; *eq* is the equator of the Earth, *EQ* the equator of the celestial sphere—the celestial equator; the planes of the meridians of the Earth are prolonged and make the meridians of the celestial sphere ; the planes of the parallels on the Earth make the parallels *ML, EQ* (for the equator is a parallel of latitude), and *SO.*

Z is the zenith-point of the observer—it is the point of the celestial sphere directly over his head. *N* is the *nadir*-point of the observer—it is the point of the celestial sphere directly beneath his feet. *HR* is a plane through the *centre* of the Earth and perpendicular to the line *ZN*. We shall now define *the plane of the horizon* to be *that plane passing through the centre of the Earth which is perpendicular to the line joining the observer's zenith- and nadir-points.* On page 28 the horizon was described as the flat plain on which the observer stands and on which the up-

per half of the celestial sphere rests. Such a plane is
called the plane of the *sensible horizon* (*i.e.*, of the horizon
evident to the senses). *HR* through the centre of the
Earth divides the celestial sphere into two equal parts. It
is called the *rational horizon*. The sensible and the rational horizons are parallel to each other.

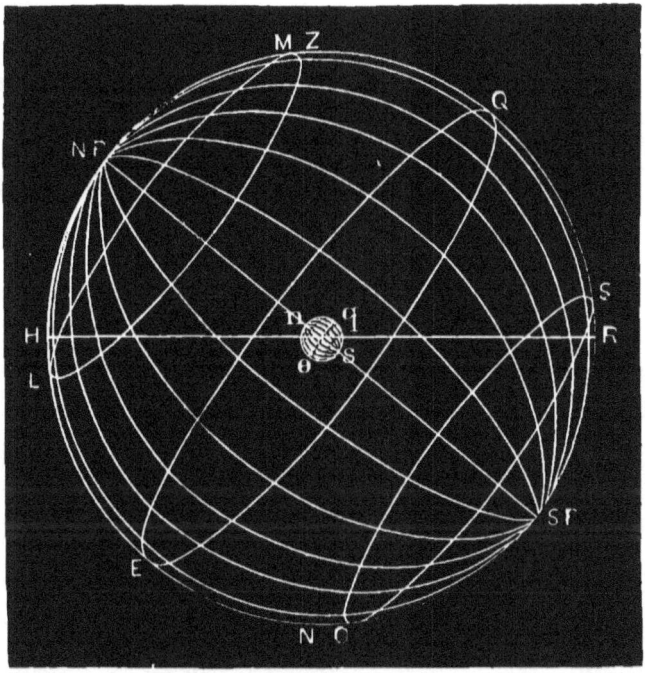

FIG. 12.—THE EARTH (*n, q, s, e*) SURROUNDED BY THE CELESTIAL
SPHERE (*N, Q, S, E*).

The meridians and parallels on the celestial sphere serve
the same purpose as the meridians and parallels on the
Earth. The latitude of a place on the Earth is its angular
distance north or south of the terrestrial equator. The
longitude of a place on the Earth is the angular distance
of that place *west* of the first meridian. If we know the

latitude and longitude of a place on the surface of the
Earth we know all that can be known of its situation.

Just in the same way we describe the situations of stars
on the surface of the celestial sphere. The *declination* (like
latitude) of a star is its angular distance north or south of
the celestial equator. The *right-ascension* (like longitude) of a star is its angular distance *east* of the first meridian. Declinations in the sky are like latitudes on the
Earth. Right-ascensions in the sky are like longitudes on
the Earth. The names are different, but the principle of
measurement is the same.

DECLINATION OF A STAR.—The declination of a star is
its angular distance north or south of the celestial equator.

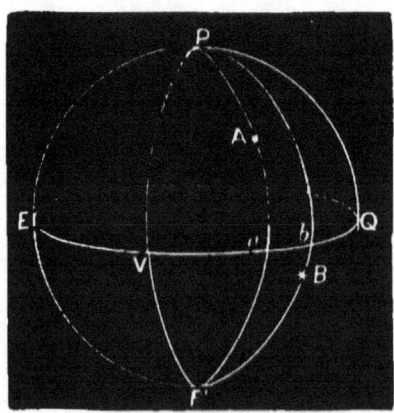

FIG. 13.—DECLINATION AND RIGHT-ASCENSION OF A STAR.

In the figure *EVQ* is the equator of the celestial sphere—the celestial equator. The Earth is not shown in the picture. If it were
shown it would be a dot at the centre of the sphere. *PAa* is a meridian of the celestial sphere passing through the star *A*. The angular
distance of the star *A* north of the celestial equator is *Aa*. *Aa* is
the north declination of that star. *PbB* is a meridian of the celestial
sphere passing through the star *B*. This star is south of the celestial equator by an angular distance measured by *bB*. *bB* is the south
declination of the star *B*.

If for a moment we should take the sphere *PEQ* to represent the
Earth and *EQ* the equator of the Earth, then the terrestrial north
latitude of *A* would be measured by *aA* and the south latitude of *B*
by *bB*. The declination of a point on the surface of the celestial
sphere corresponds to the latitude of a point on the surface of the
Earth. *PA* is the north polar-distance of *A ; P'B* is the south polar-
distance of *B*

The polar-distance of a star + the star's declination=90°.

RIGHT-ASCENSION OF A STAR.—The right-ascension of a
star is its angular distance east of a first meridian.

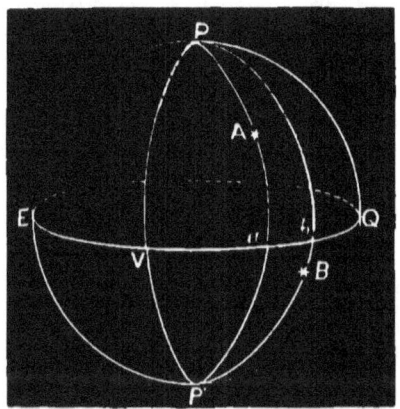

FIG. 13 *bis.*

In the figure *PV* is the first meridian. *PAa* is the meridian
through the star *A*. This meridian is east of the first meridian by
the angle *VPa*, which is measured by the arc *Va*. *Va* is the right-
ascension of the star *A*. *PbB* is the meridian through the star *B*.
This meridian is east of the first meridian by the angle *VPb*, which
is measured by the arc *Vb*. *Vb* is the right-ascension of the star *B*.

If for a moment we should take the sphere *PEQ* to represent the
Earth, and *EQ* the equator of the Earth, and *PV* the meridian of
Greenwich, (east) terrestrial longitude of a place *A* would be *Va;*
the longitude of a place *B* would be *bB*. The right-ascension of a
point on the surface of the celestial sphere corresponds to the longitude of a point on the surface of the Earth.

It is very important to understand these matters at the beginning, and it is necessary for the student to memorize the following definitions:—

The plane of the *horizon* is a plane through the centre of the Earth perpendicular to the line joining the zenith and the nadir of the observer. The *zenith* of an observer is the point of the celestial sphere directly over his head. Therefore each person has a different zenith-point. The *nadir* of an observer is the point of the celestial sphere directly beneath his feet. The zenith and nadir are points on the surface of the celestial sphere—not points on the Earth. The *zenith-distance* of a star is its angular distance from the zenith. The *altitude* of a star is its angular distance above the horizon. A *vertical circle* is a great circle of the sphere whose plane is perpendicular to the plane of the horizon. The *axis of the celestial sphere* is the line of the Earth's axis prolonged. The equator of the celestial sphere—the *celestial equator*—is that great circle cut from the celestial sphere by the plane or the Earth's equator extended. The *declination* of a star is its angular distance north or south of the celestial equator. The *right-ascension* of a star is its angular distance east (not west) of the first meridian of the celestial sphere. (This first meridian has nothing to do with the meridian of Greenwich on the Earth, as we shall soon see.)

The *terrestrial meridian* of an observer is that great circle of the Earth that passes through the observer and through the Earth's axis. All terrestrial meridians pass through the north and south poles of the Earth.

The *celestial meridian* of an observer is that great circle of the celestial sphere that passes through the zenith of the observer and through the axis of the celestial sphere. All celestial meridians pass through the north and south poles of the celestial sphere.

In figure 14 *n, e, q, s* is the earth, and some terrestrial meridians are drawn upon it. Some celestial meridians are drawn on the celestial sphere *NP, E, Q, SP. Z* is the zenith of the observer. Where must he be in the figure? He *must* be on the surface of *n, e, q, s*, where a line *ZN* (zenith to nadir) intersects it. Make a pin-prick at this point. His terrestrial meridian is the little circle *n, e, q, s* (because it passes through the observer's place and through *n* and *s*). His celestial meridian is *NP, Z, SP* (because it contains his zenith and the two celestial poles).

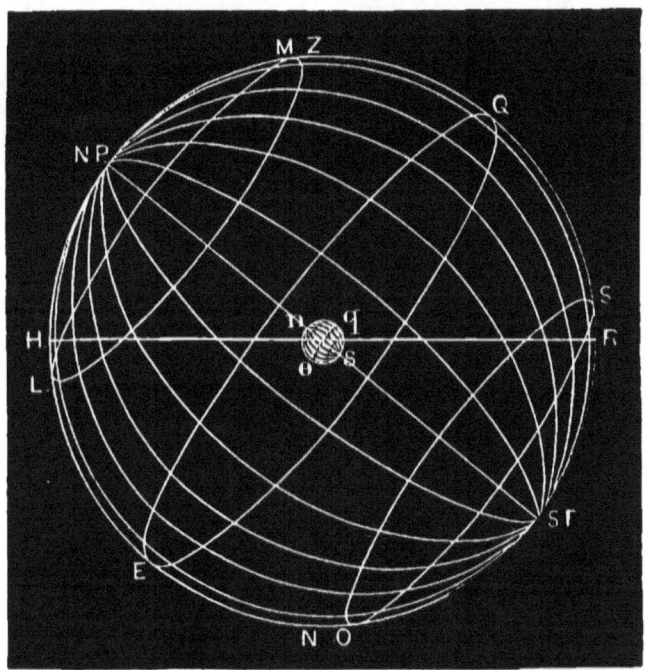

FIG. 14.—CORRESPONDENCE OF THE TERRESTRIAL AND CELESTIAL
MERIDIANS OF AN OBSERVER.

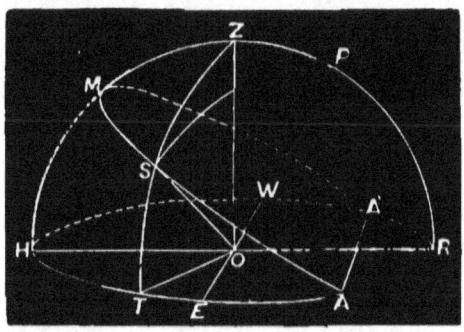

FIG. 15.—THE CELESTIAL SPHERE.

— It is so important for the student to understand the foregoing definitions clearly that the following exercises are added. The figures have been purposely drawn unlike each other.

In figure 15 P is the north pole of the celestial sphere; Z is the observer's zenith; HR his horizon; O is the position of the Earth.

What is the zenith-distance of S? What is the altitude of S? What is the altitude of Z? What is the altitude of P? What is the altitude of M? (Answers: ZS, TS, 90°, RP, HM.) Notice that an observer at O looks along a horizontal line OT; he sees the star S along the line OS; the angle TOS is the altitude of S, and it is measured by the arc TS. RH is the observer's north and south line, EW is his east and west line. His points of the compass are $R =$ north, $E =$ east, $H =$ south, $W =$ west.

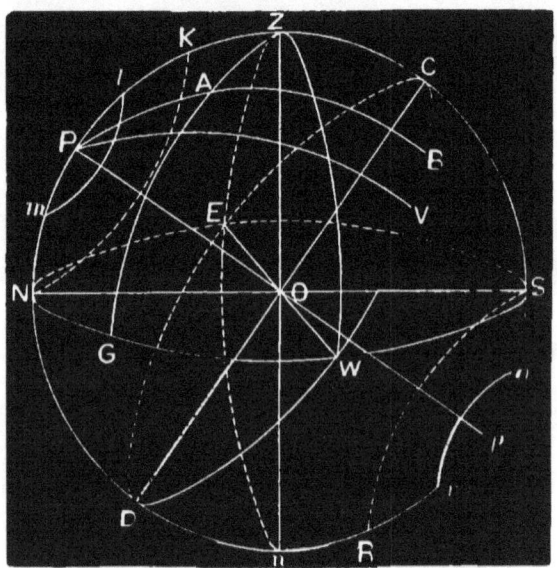

Fig. 16.—The Celestial Sphere.

In figure 16 P is the north pole of the celestial sphere, $ECWD$ is the celestial equator; PV is the first meridian of the celestial sphere. What is the right-ascension of the point V? of B? of C? of E? of D? of W? (Answers: 0°, VB, VC, VCE, $VCED$, $VCEDW$.) What are the right ascension and declination of the point A? (Answer: VB and north BA). What is the altitude of A? (Answer: GA.)

— What is the horizon of an observer ? Can you conceive a horizon without specifying an observer's place? What is a vertical line? If you had a string and a bunch of keys, how could you use them to show the vertical direction at your station ? Is this *direction* the same with respect to each observer, no matter where he is situated? Do you suppose this direction is absolutely the same *in space* for two observers 1000 miles apart ?

What is the zenith of an observer ? His nadir ? Have the words *zenith* and *nadir* any meaning if no observer or station is supposed ? When you assume a point on the celestial sphere as the zenith of an observer, is his place on the earth fixed? When you assume the

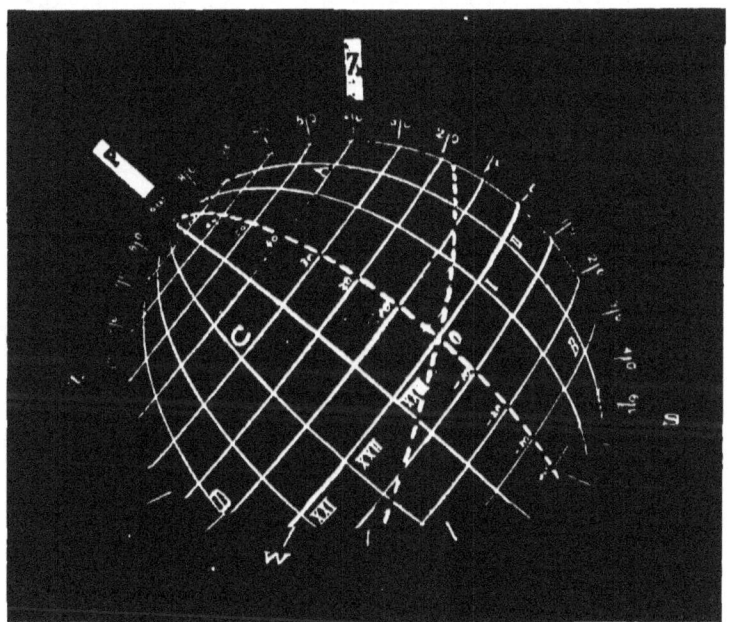

FIG. 17.—PART OF A CELESTIAL GLOBE:
Showing the principal circles of the celestial sphere.

place of an observer on the earth, is his zenith a determinate point on the celestial sphere ? Or may it be two points ? What is a star's altitude? its zenith distance? In answering these two questions, did you say its *angular* distance from, etc. ?

In figure 17 *Z* is the zenith of the observer and *NWS* his horizon. *P* is the north celestial pole. *PZS* is the observer's celestial meridian. *XXI, XXII* . . . *O, I, II* . . . is the celestial equator, and *O* is the vernal equinox—the origin of right-ascensions. *Parallels of declination* are shown (circles parallel to the celestial equator) every 10° both north and south of the equator. Meridians of the celestial sphere (*hour-circles*) are drawn every 15°; every hour. They pass from pole to pole across the celestial sphere and cross the equator at the points marked *XXI, XXII,* . . . *I, II* . . . Every star on the hour-circle *I* has a right ascension of 15°, or 1 hour; on *II* of 30°, or 2^h; on *XXII* of 330°, or 22 hours ; and so on.

All stars on the parallel of declination marked *A* have a north declination of 40° (+ 40°); on the parallel *C*, of + 30° ; on the equator, of 0° ; on the parallel *B* of − 30°. The student should mark the following places on the figure :

R. A. = 22^h and Decl. = + 80° ;   R. A. = 0^h and Decl. = − 40° ;
   = 23^h "   = − 30° ;   = 1^h "   = + 60° ;
   = 24^h "   =   0° ;   = 2^h "   = + 40° ;
   = 0^h "   = + 40° ;   = 2^h "   = − 30°.

CHAPTER III

DIURNAL MOTION OF THE SUN, MOON, AND STARS.

11. The Diurnal Motion of the Sun, Moon, and Stars.— It is a familiar fact to all of us that the Sun rises and sets every day. The Moon rises and sets. Stars also rise above the eastern horizon; they appear to move across the sky and to come to their greatest altitude on the meridian;

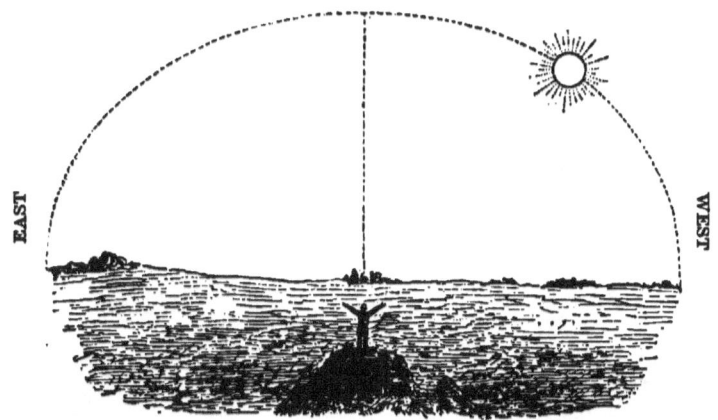

FIG. 18.—THE APPARENT MOTION OF THE SUN FROM RISING TO SETTING.

and then they appear to decline to the west and set below the western horizon. Every one is familiar with the Sun's rising and setting. It is too splendid a spectacle to be overlooked. We are all more or less familiar with the motion of the Moon from rising to setting. We may know

39

the fact that groups of stars also rise and set. But to thoroughly understand their motions we must actually observe some particular stars carefully. The student should himself make the observations that are described here so far as his time and opportunities will allow.

DIURNAL MOTIONS OF SOUTHERN STARS.—Let the student go out into a field or park at night where he can see the sky from his zenith towards the southern horizon,

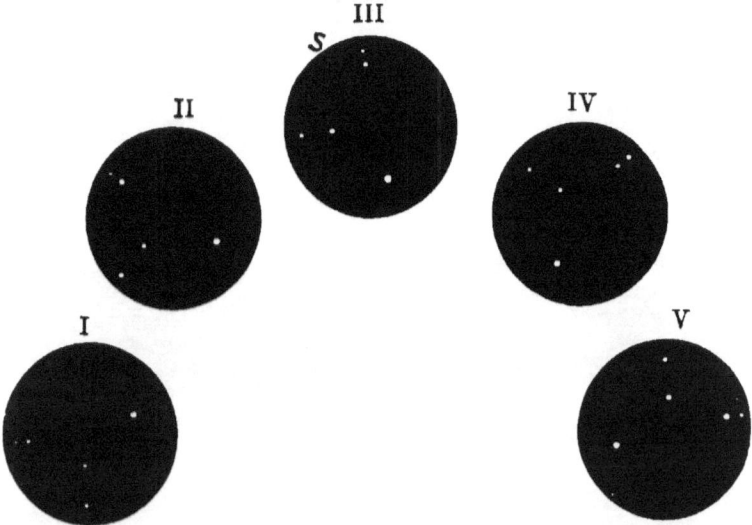

FIG. 19.—DIURNAL MOTION OF A GROUP OF SOUTHERN STARS.

The right hand of this picture is west: the left hand is east.

and where he can command an unobstructed view of the eastern and western horizon. Let him select a group of bright stars that are not very far apart, and that are not very far above the eastern horizon. He must learn the group so well that he can always recognize it in the sky no matter where it may be. Let him stand with his back toward the north. The group is *rising*, let us say (the lower left-hand circle in Fig. 19) when he begins to observe it. If he watches the group—looking at it every half hour or so—he will see that it is continually rising above the eastern horizon and getting higher in the heavens.

About three hours after the rising of this group it will be towards the southeast (the second circle counting from the left of Fig. 19). About six hours after rising, the group will be just south of him and at its highest —at its greatest altitude. The point in the sky where a star (or a group of stars) has its greatest altitude is called its point of culmination. It is due south of the observer at culmination (the uppermost circle, *S*, in the last figure). It requires about six hours for a group of southern stars to move from the eastern horizon, where it rises, to the point due south, where it culminates. Six hours of watching is quite as long as can be given by the student. But if he should watch longer than this, he would see the group of stars decline to the west and finally set (as in the two right-hand circles of the last figure).

Hunters, sailors, shepherds, as well as astronomers, have observed facts like these thousands and thousands of times. Any one who wishes *can* observe them whenever he likes on any clear night. So that the student can prove them for himself if he chooses; and we may take them as proved facts. The picture shows what actually does happen for a group of southern stars. When it is due south it looks like the upper circle, marked *S*. It is at its culmination. It is at its greatest altitude. Three hours *before* the time of culmination the group was as in the circle next *S*, to the left. Six hours *before* this time it was as in the lower left-hand circle. Three hours *after* the time of culmination the group has declined towards the west (see the figure), and six hours *after* this time it is setting in the west, as in number V.

It is not to be expected that a schoolboy will have the

leisure to watch throughout a whole night. If he were to do so he would see the group move as in the figure if he used a long winter's night for his observation and began his watch as soon as the sky grew dark. There is a simple experiment that he can try, however, which will make the diurnal motion of the southern stars quite easy to understand. Let him provide himself with a hammer and with a bundle of common laths, and let him sharpen one end of each lath so that it can be easily driven into the ground. Let him choose a spot of ground to stand on that is soft, so that the laths can be set in place without too much trouble. Let him select some one bright star that is near the eastern horizon, and remember it well so as not to mistake it for any other star.

Now he should kneel down, set the sharp end of a lath on the ground, and sight along the lath until it points exactly to the star. The lath is to be sighted at the star just as a rifle is pointed at a deer. The lath is now to be driven into the ground firmly; and *after* this is done it is well to take another sight along the lath at the star to be sure that it still points correctly. When all is right the observer should look at his watch and note the time and write it down, like this:

First lath set at 8^h 0^m P.M.

Things will look as in Fig. 20. The lath *OI* will point to the star at 8^h 0^m.

The observer need pay no more attention to the star for a couple of hours. A little before ten o'clock he should take another lath and make the same observation *on the same star.* He will find that the star has moved towards the west and upwards. Leaving the first lath in place, he must now fix a second one so as to point at the star at 10 o'clock. Its point will have to be set a few inches away

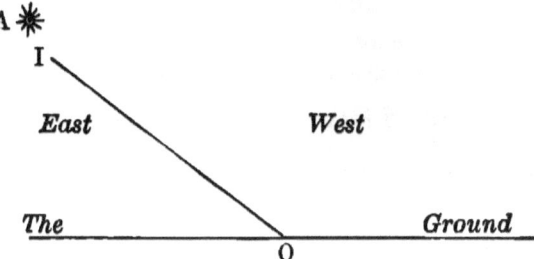

Fig. 20.—A Pointer Directed at a Star.

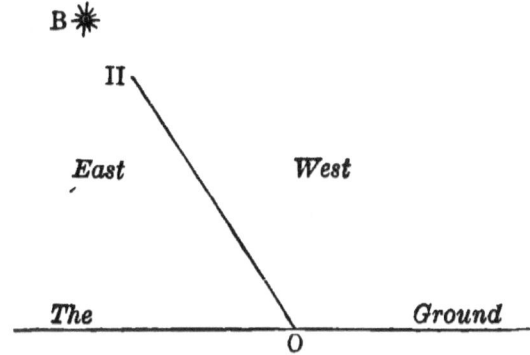

Fig. 21.—A Pointer Directed at a Star.

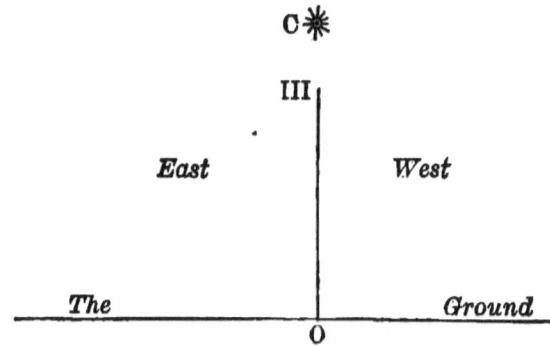

Fig. 22.—A Pointer Directed at a Star.

from the point of the first one, so as not to interfere with it. It will appear as in Fig. 21.

He should make a second record, thus:

Second lath set at 10ʰ 0ᵐ P.M.

Now the observer can go to sleep if he likes, setting his alarm-clock to wake him about quarter before twelve. At 12ʰ he should set a third lath to point *at the same star.* It will be like Fig. 22.

His note-book will read:

Third lath set at 12ʰ 0ᵐ P.M.

He should do the same thing at 2 o'clock in the morning, and the fourth lath will point as in the next figure.

Fourth lath set at 2 A.M.

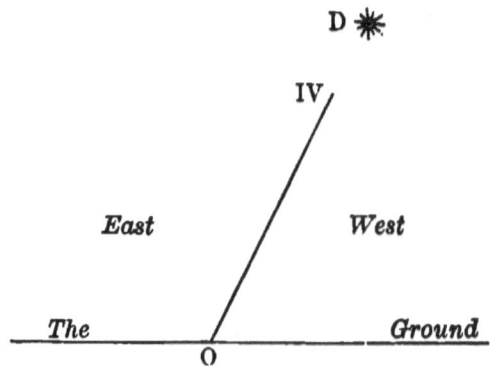

FIG. 23.—A POINTER DIRECTED AT A STAR.

These four observations will be enough, though the more that are made the clearer the motion of the star will be. The chief practical trouble will be that the points of the laths cannot be set very close together without interfering with each other. If they could be set just right and if a great number of them were so set, things would look like the group of laths, *B*, in the next figure, where the flat table represents the ground, and the lines in the circle *B* represent a number of laths accurately set at the point *O*.

This figure makes everything clear. The laths have been set at *equal intervals* of time and they are at *equal angles* apart. This proves that the apparent motion of the star *B* is such that it moves through equal angles in equal times. Its motion is uniform.

If the observer had chosen to select a star very far south (*A*, for example) and had set laths for it, also, the group

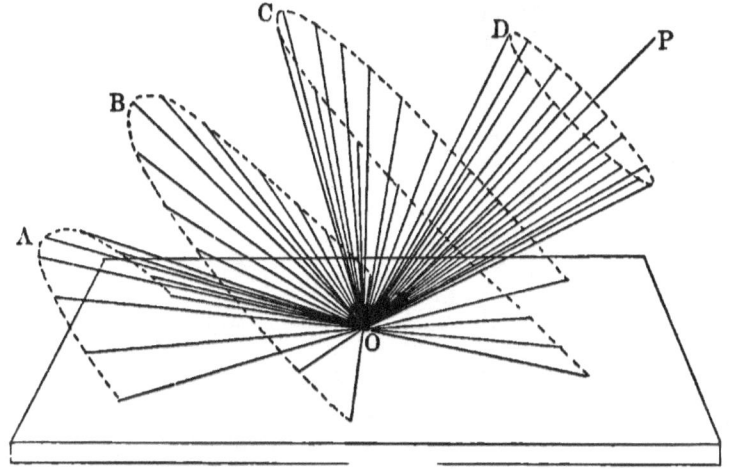

FIG. 24 —A MODEL TO SHOW HOW STARS SEEM TO MOVE FROM RISING TO SETTING IN THEIR DIURNAL PATHS.

of pointers for this star would look like the cone of rays marked *A* in the figure. All the laths would lie in the surface of a cone, and the vertex of this cone would be at *O*. If he had chosen a star nearer to his zenith (*C*, for example) and had set the laths for it, just as before, they would also lie in the surface of a cone *C*, as in the figure. Finally, if he had chosen a star much further north (*D*, for example) the pointers to that star would all lie in the cone *D*. The line *OP* is the axis of all these cones, and it points to the north pole of the heavens.

The north pole of the heavens is that point where the axis of the Earth, prolonged, meets the celestial sphere.

DIURNAL MOTIONS OF NORTHERN STARS.—After the motions of southern stars, from their rising to their setting, have been carefully observed and are thoroughly under-

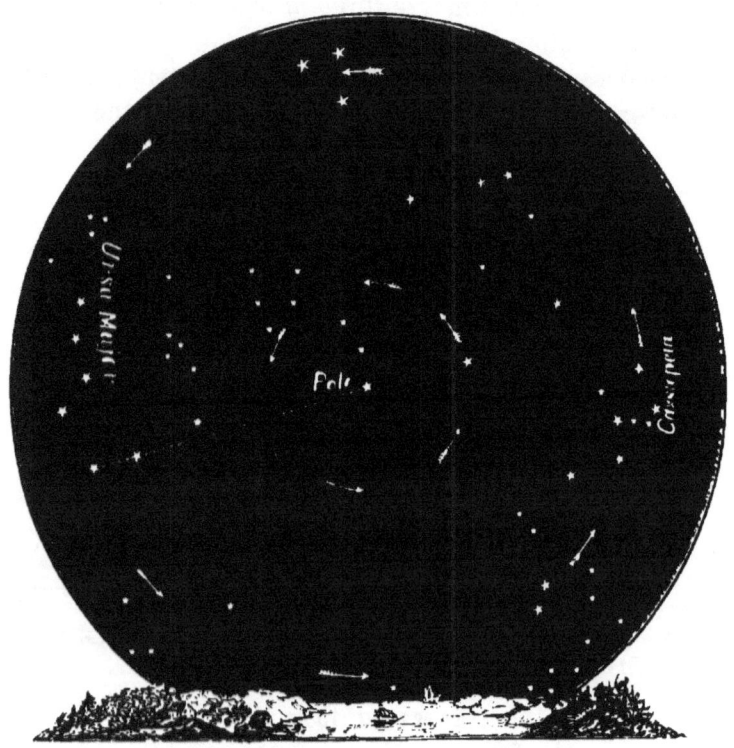

FIG. 25.—THE NORTHERN HEAVENS;

as they appear to an observer in the United States in the early evening during August. The right-hand side of the picture is east.

stood, the motions of northern stars must be observed. They can be studied in the same way as before. The drawings of the cones *C* and *D* in the last figure show exactly what would be observed. In every one of these cones, for any and every star in the sky, experiments will prove that the star moves through equal angles in equal times. The diurnal motions of all the stars are uniform.

The time required for the star D to go completely round its cone once and to come back to the starting-point again is 24 hours, one day; and the same is true for any and every star.

In Fig. 25 the stars of the northern sky are shown as they appear to an observer in the middle regions of the United States in the early evening in August. The same stars are visible all the year round, but they will not always be at the same altitudes above the horizon at the same hour of the night. No matter what hour of the night, or what time of the year you read this paragraph, you can see the stars of this picture (if the night is clear) by going—*now* —out-of-doors and looking towards the north. In order to make the picture look right you may have to turn the page of the book round somewhat (in the direction of the arrows) so as to put a different part of the page uppermost. But by taking a little pains you can hold the picture in such a position that it will agree with the configuration of the stars in the sky.

The first set of stars to find in the sky is the Great Bear —*Ursa Major*—the Great Dipper, as it is often called. It is made up of seven stars arranged somewhat as in the next figure:

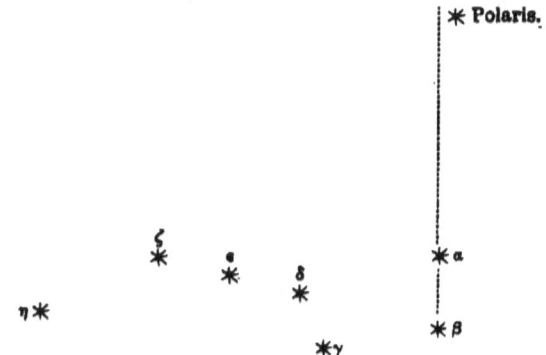

FIG. 26.—URSA MAJOR AND POLARIS.

They are called by these names : α (*Alpha*) Ursæ majoris; β (*Beta*) Ursæ majoris; γ (*Gamma*) Ursæ majoris;
δ (*Delta*) Ursæ majoris; ε (*Epsilon*) Ursæ majoris ; η
(*Eta*) Ursæ majoris; ζ (*Zeta*) Ursæ majoris.   The letters
α, β, γ, δ, ε, η, ζ are the first seven letters of the Greek
alphabet.   The stars themselves are a part of the *constellation* or group of stars named Ursa Major—the Great Bear
—by the ancients (see Fig. 25).   After you have found
them you must notice that two of them α and β (they are
called " the pointers ") point to another star, not so
bright, which is itself called *Polaris*—the pole-star—the
star near the north pole of the celestial sphere.

It is well to form the habit of glancing up at the north-

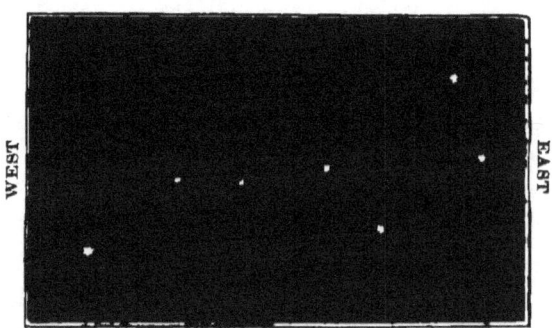

FIG. 27.—THE STARS OF THE DIPPER;
as they appear in the early hours of the evening in the month of May.

ern heavens every time you go out of doors on a clear
night, so as to be able to find *Ursa Major, Polaris,* and
Cassiopea quickly and easily.

If you study the motions of the northern stars you will
find that *Polaris*—the polar star—seems to be almost stationary.   If it were exactly at the north pole of the heavens (which it is not) it would be absolutely stationary; but
it is very nearly so.   All the other northern stars seem to

move round *Polaris* in circles. They move from the east, then upwards, then to the west, then downwards, then to the east again (in the direction of the arrows in Fig. 25), and so on forever. It takes 24 hours for each and every star to move once completely round the pole. Its motion has a period of one day—hence the name *diurnal motion.*

The diurnal motions of all the stars can be described in three theorems (following), and you should learn these theorems by heart, because that is the quickest way to get a perfectly definite and correct statement of the appearances in the sky. Recollect that the *north-polar-distance* (N.P.D.) of a star is its *angular distance from the north celestial pole.*

The following are the laws of the diurnal motion:

I. *Every star in the heavens appears to describe a circle around the pole as a centre in consequence of the diurnal motion.*

II. *The greater the star's north-polar-distance the larger is the circle.*

III. *All the stars describe their diurnal orbits in the same period of time, which is the time required for the earth to turn once on its axis* (twenty-four hours).

These laws are true of the thousands of stars visible to the naked eye, and of the millions upon millions seen by the telescope.

The circle which a star appears to describe in the sky in consequence of the diurnal motion of the earth is called the *diurnal orbit* of that star (an orbit is a path in the sky).

These laws are proved by observation. The student can satisfy himself of their correctness on any clear night.

If the star's north-polar-distance is less than the altitude of the pole, the circle which the star describes will not meet the horizon at all, and the star will therefore neither rise nor set, but will simply perform an apparent diurnal

revolution round the pole. Such stars are shown in Fig. 25. The apparent diurnal motion of the stars is in the direction shown by the arrows in the cut. Below the north pole the stars appear to move from left to right, west to east ; above the pole they appear to move from east to west.

The circle within which the stars neither rise nor set is called *the circle of perpetual apparition.* Within it the

FIG. 28.—THE STARS OF THE DIPPER;
as they appear at different times during their daily revolution round the pole.

stars perpetually appear—are visible. The radius of this circle is equal to the altitude of the pole above the horizon or to the north-polar-distance of the north point of the horizon.

When a photographic camera is directed to the north pole of the heavens at night and an exposure of about 12 hours is given the developed plate will look like Fig. 29.

The plate has remained stationary; the stars have in 12 hours moved one-half round their diurnal orbits. In moving they have left "trails" on the plate. Each trail is an arc of a circle, and the centre of all these circles is

Fig. 29.

From a photograph of the motion of the stars near the north pole of the heavens. The exposure-time was 12 hours. The bright trail nearest the pole was made by Polaris.

the same. It is the north celestial pole. If the camera had been directed to the equator the trails of the stars passing across the plate would have been straight lines.

If the student is a photographer, he should try these experiments for himself, using the longest-focus lens that he can obtain.

We have now to inquire *why* do the stars rise and set according to these laws. What explanations can be given of their motions? Of all the possible explanations, which is

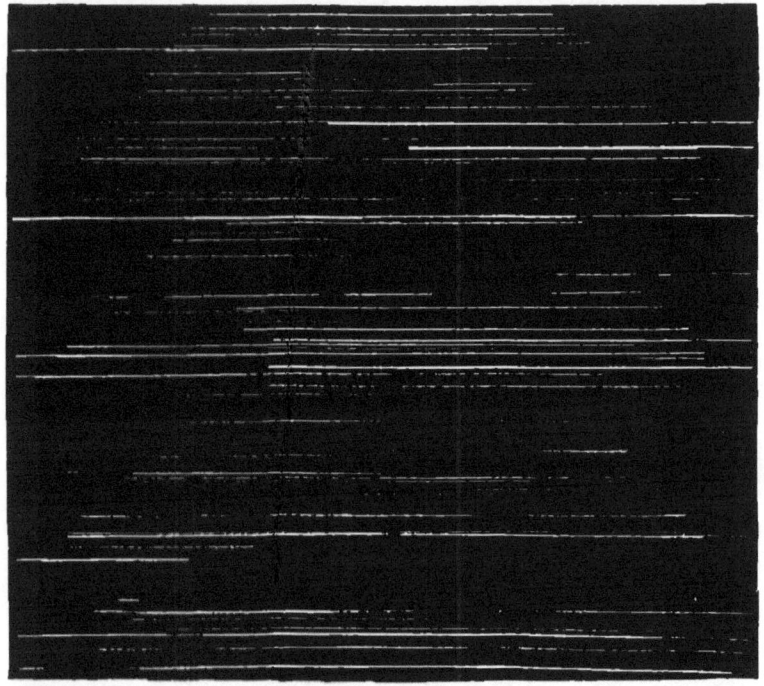

FIG. 30.

From a photograph of the trails of stars near the celestial equator.

the right one? It is possible to explain the rising and setting of the stars in several ways. Let us give three such ways.

(*A.*) The Earth and the observer are at rest and each and every star has a particular motion of its own, each star moving at just such a rate as actually to move completely round the Earth back to its starting-point in 24 hours. There are at least a hundred million stars, in all possible situations. It is incredible that each one of them has a special rate of motion of its own—just as a railway train has its own rate of motion—and that the 100,000,000 motions are so nicely regulated as to obey the laws of the diurnal motion exactly. This explanation is too complicated. It must be rejected.

(*B.*) All the stars are set in a huge sphere above us ; all of them are at the same distance from us; the sphere itself turns round the Earth once in 24 hours, while the Earth and the observer remain at rest. This was the explanation given by the ancients and it was a perfectly good explanation so long as it was not known that the stars were situated at very different distances from us; so long as it was not known that some stars were comparatively near and some much further off. As soon as we know this one fact it is impossible to suppose the stars to be set all in *one* sphere. There would need to be a sphere for each star (since no two stars are at exactly the same distance from us). Moreover the planets (*Venus, Jupiter*, etc.) and the comets, are sometimes at one distance from us and sometimes at another. So that the explanation adopted by the ancients must also be given up, since the planets and comets rise and set like the stars.

(*C.*) The simplest explanation possible is that the stars are fixed and do not move at all ; that the whole Earth with the observer on its surface revolves round an axis once every 24 hours; so that the actual turning of the Earth from west to east makes the stars (and the planets and comets) appear to move from east to west—from rising to setting. This is the true explanation. It is not true because it is the simplest ; nor is there any one simple and conclusive proof of its truth. It is true because it completely and thoroughly explains every single one of millions and millions of cases—some of them very different from others. There are some rather complicated proofs of it, but no simple ones suitable to be given here. We must accept it as true because it explains completely and thoroughly *every* case that has arisen in the past and because there are millions and millions of such cases. Or, let us say that we will accept it as true until we come to some case which is not explained by it.

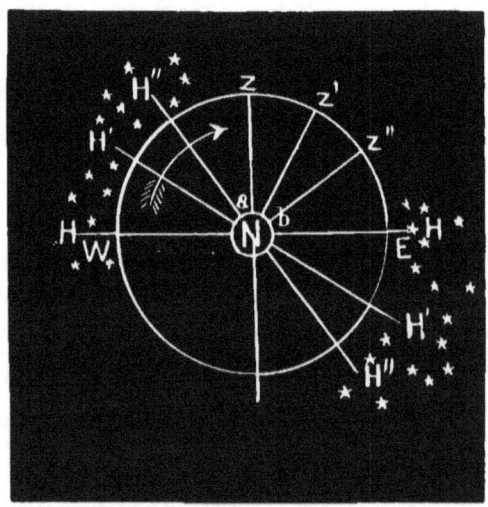

Fig. 31.

The real motion of the horizon of an observer among the stars makes them appear to rise and set.

The observer on the Earth is unconscious of its rotation, and the celestial sphere appears to him to revolve from east to west around the Earth, while the Earth appears to remain at rest. The case is much the same as if he were on a steamer which was turning round, and as if he saw the harbor-shores, the ships, and the houses apparently turning in an opposite direction.

Fig. 31 is intended to explain the apparent diurnal motion of the stars which is caused by the real rotation of the Earth on its axis. The little circle N is the Earth, seen as it would be by a spectator very far away. The circle WZE is one of the circles of the celestial sphere. W is towards the west and E towards the east. The Earth revolves from west to east in the direction of the arrow. Suppose a to be the situation of an observer on the Earth. Z will be his zenith in the heavens. HH will be his horizon (since it is a plane through the centre of the Earth perpendicular to the line joining his zenith and nadir). After a while the observer will have been carried onwards by the rotation of the Earth and his zenith will be at Z'. His horizon will have moved to HH'. It will have moved *below* all the stars in the space HEH', and these stars will have " risen "— they will have come above his horizon. His horizon will have moved *above* all the stars in the space HWH' and these stars will have " set "—they will have sunk below his horizon.

It is really the horizon that moves and the stars that are at rest; but in common language we say that one group of stars has risen above his horizon, and that the second group has set. A little later the observer on the rotating Earth will be at the point b; his zenith will be at Z' and his horizon at $H''H''$. His horizon will have sunk *below* a new group of stars in the east (and these stars will have "risen"); and his horizon will have moved *above* a group of stars in the west (and this group will have " set ").

The zenith of an observer moves once round the celestial sphere each day. His horizon (which is perpendicular to the line joining his zenith and nadir) moves once round the celestial sphere each day, likewise. Therefore, stars in the east rise, culminate (come to their greatest altitude), and set daily. This is the apparent diurnal motion of the stars, and it is explained by the actual motion of the Earth on its axis.

Before leaving this figure one important thing must be noticed. Suppose there are *two* observers on the Earth, one at a and one at b. Their zeniths would be at Z and at Z'' on the celestial sphere at some instant. Their horizons would be, at this instant, HH and $H'H''$. The observer to the eastward (b) would see a whole group of stars that are yet invisible to the other observer further west (a). That is, an observer at Greenwich at ten o'clock at night (for example) will see groups of stars then invisible to an observer at Washington. The horizon of the Washington observer has not yet moved below them; they have not yet risen to him. If the Washington observer waits for several hours these groups will, by and by, rise. But the Greenwich observer always sees stars rise before they have risen at Washington.

— What is the *diurnal* motion of the stars? Describe the course of a southern star from its rising to its setting. At what point does such a star attain its greatest altitude above the horizon? What number will express the altitude (in degrees, for instance) of a star when it is rising? What is the point of culmination of a star? The word culmination is often used to express a *time* as well as a definite point in the sky—what time? How can stakes set in the ground be used to demonstrate the diurnal motion of the stars? Is the motion of the stars from rising to setting uniform? How do you know? The southern stars all rise and set. What stars do not rise and set? What stars, then, are always above the observer's horizon? The north-polar-distance of every star that never sets must be less than the altitude of—what point? Make a sketch of the seven stars of the Great Bear. Which two are the pointers? Where would *Polaris* be in this sketch? Hold the paper on which the sketch is made between the thumb and finger of your left hand with *Polaris* covered by your thumb. Now turn the paper round slowly, taking hold of the outer edges of it. If you face the north while doing this you will see that you are imitating, by a model, the actual diurnal motions of the northern stars. Define the north pole of the heavens. In which direction (west to east, or east to west) do such stars move when they are *above* the pole? When they are *below* below the pole? How do they move (up or down?) when they are furthest east? Furthest west?

Define in a brief and accurate phrase the north-polar-distance in stars?

Give the three *laws* of the diurnal motion. I. Every star in the heavens ————. II. The greater the star's N.P.D. ———— III. All the stars describe their diurnal *orbits* in the same ————, which is the ————? What is the diurnal *orbit* of a star? How can you know that these laws are true? What is the circle of perpetual apparition? Why is it so called?

The foregoing laws, I, II, III, are true, as we know from observation. These are the appearances. What is the real cause of these appearances? How do we know that the stars are not actually set in a huge sphere above our heads, and that this sphere does not turn around the fixed Earth once every day? (motions of planets, comets, etc.) The Earth turns on its axis once in 24 hours—do you feel it turning? If the Earth turns, and the observer stays at one place (say in New York) on its surface, does he move in space? If the observer moves round a circle every day, will his zenith move on the surface of the celestial sphere? his nadir? Will his horizon move among the stars? When his horizon moves below a group of stars in the east, those stars will ———— ? When his horizon moves above a group of stars in the west those stars will ———— ?

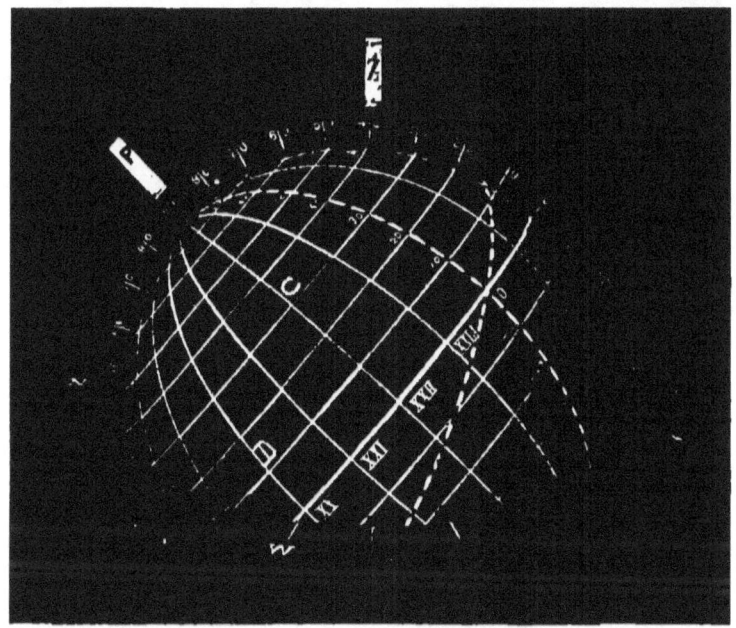

Fɪɢ. 32.—Pᴀʀᴛ ᴏғ ᴀ Cᴇʟᴇsᴛɪᴀʟ Gʟᴏʙᴇ:
Showing the principal circles of the celestial sphere.

In this figure Z is the zenith of the observer, and NWS his horizon. P is the north celestial pole, and XX, XXI . . . O, I . . . the celestial equator. O is the vernal equinox. All stars on the *hour circle* of II hours are on the celestial meridian of the observer (PZS). The star C (whose $R.A. = 22^h$) is 4 hours west of the meridian; the star D ($R.A. = 20^h$) is 6^h west—nearly to the western horizon.

In Fig. 33 Z, P, NWS, etc., have the same meaning as in Fig. 32. In fact, the picture represents the same globe *after* it has been turned one hour towards the west. The stars C and D are in the same places *on the celestial sphere* as before, but C is now 5^h

west of the meridian, and D is just setting 7ʰ west of the meridian. In Fig. 32 A and B (whose right ascensions are 2ʰ) were on the celestial meridian of the observer; here they are 1ʰ west of the meridian.

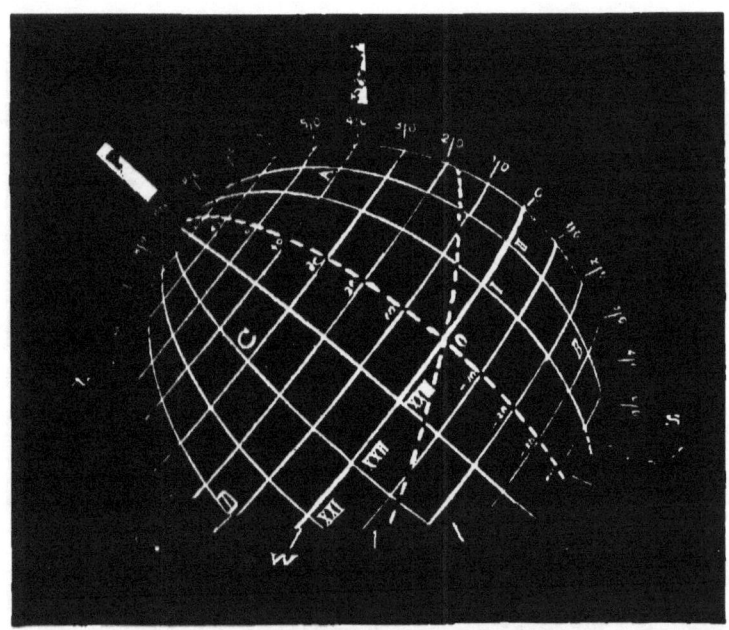

FIG. 33.—PART OF A GLOBE:
Showing the principal circles of the celestial sphere.

CHAPTER IV

THE DIURNAL MOTION TO OBSERVERS IN DIFFERENT LATITUDES, ETC.

12. The Latitude of an Observer on the Earth.—*The altitude of the celestial pole above the horizon of any place on the Earth's surface is equal to the latitude of that place.*

Let L be a place on the Earth $PEpQ$, Pp being the Earth's axis and EQ its equator. Z is the zenith of the place, and HR its *sensible* horizon. Its celestial or rational

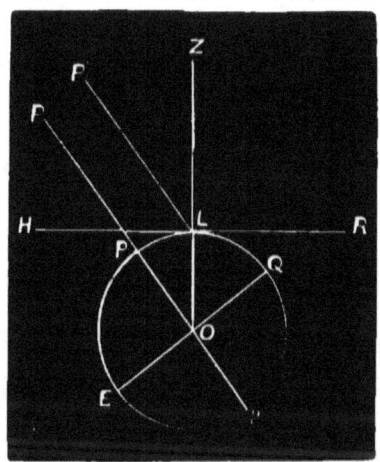

FIG. 34.

horizon would be represented by a line through O parallel to HR. LOQ is the latitude of L according to ordinary geographical definitions; *i.e.*, it is the angular distance of L from the Earth's equator. Prolong OP indefinitely to P' and draw LP'' parallel to it. P' and P''

are points on the celestial sphere infinitely distant from L. In fact they appear as *one* point; since the dimensions of the Earth are vanishingly small compared with the radius of the celestial sphere.* We have then to prove that $LOQ = P''LH$.

POQ and ZLH are right angles, and therefore equal. $ZLP'' = ZOP'$ by construction. Hence $ZLH - ZLP'' = P''LH = POQ - ZOP' = LOQ$, or the latitude of the point L is measured by either of the equal angles LOQ or $P''LH$.

In Geography, which deals only with the Earth, it is convenient to define the latitude of an observer anywhere on the surface to be the angular distance of the point where he stands from the terrestrial equator. The latitude of an observer at L is LOQ.

In Astronomy, which deals chiefly with the heavens, it is convenient to define *the latitude of an observer* anywhere on the Earth's surface to be *the altitude of his celestial pole above his horizon.* The latitude of an observer at L is $P''LH =$ the altitude of the pole; or we might say, the latitude of an observer is the N.P.D. of the north point of his horizon (if he is in the northern hemisphere). The latitude of an observer at L is $P''LH$ in Fig. 34.

It is often more convenient, in Astronomy, to define the latitude of an observer by describing the place of his zenith on the celestial sphere—and to say, *the latitude of an observer* anywhere on the Earth's surface *is the declination of his zenith.*

Fig. 35 represents the celestial sphere $HZRN$. The Earth is a point at the centre of the circle. Some observer on the Earth has a zenith Z, a nadir N, a horizon HR. P is the pole of the heavens and E a point of the celestial equator.

---

* Two lines drawn from the star *Polaris* to the points L and O make an angle with each other of less than $\frac{1}{500000}$th of $1''$.

In the figure *PH* measures the latitude of the observer, because *PH* is the north-polar-distance of the north-point of his horizon. *Z* is his zenith, *EZ* is the declination of his zenith (it is the angular distance of *Z* from the celestial equator).

Now the arc *PH* = the arc *EZ* because the arc *ZH* is 90°, and *PH* = 90° − *PZ*; moreover, the arc *PE* is 90°, and *EZ* = 90° − *PZ*. Therefore *PH* (the observer's latitude) is measured by *EZ* (the declination of his zenith).

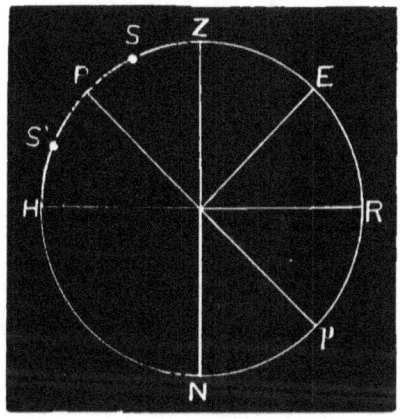

FIG. 35.

The latitude of an observer is measured by the declination of his Zenith.

— In Fig. 12 the latitude of the observer is measured either by (*NP*) *H* or by *QZ*.

In Fig. 16 the latitude of the observer is measured either by the angle *PON* or by the angle *COZ* (or by the arcs *PN* and *CZ*).

In Fig. 36 the latitude of the observer whose zenith is *Z* is the elevation of the north pole of the heavens (*P*) above his horizon (*NWS*) = 40° ; it is measured by the declination of his zenith (*Z*) = 40°.

— Define the latitude of an observer on the Earth according to Geography. Define the latitude of an observer on the Earth according to Astronomy in three ways : I. The altitude of the North Pole above the observer's horizon is the ——— of the observer. II.

The *N.P.D.* of the north point of an observer's horizon is the
———— of the observer.   III. The declination of an observer's zenith
is the ———— of that observer.

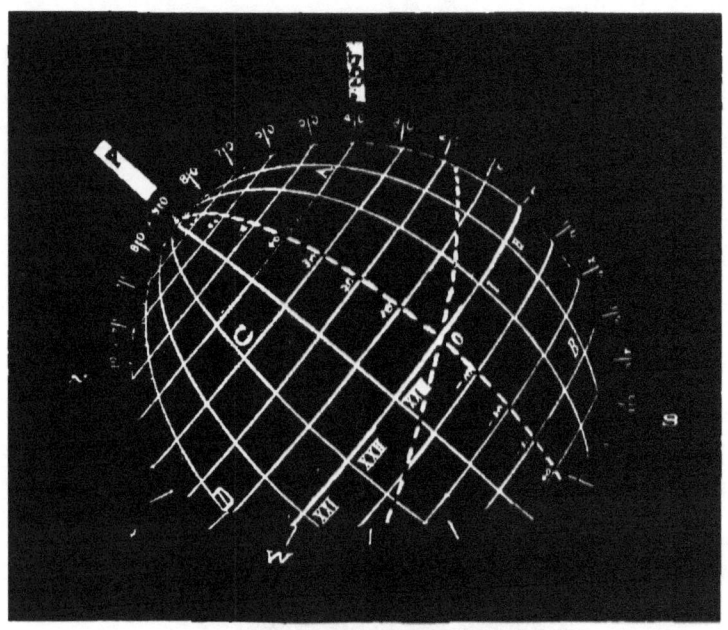

Fig. 36.

So far we have only spoken of observers in the northern
hemisphere of the Earth.   The northern hemisphere is
the most important to us, because all the more intelligent
nations of the globe lived in it for centuries and all astronomy was perfected there.   Later on, our definitions will
be extended to cover all cases.

13. **The Horizon of an Observer Changes as He Moves
from Place to place on the Earth.**—The theorem that has
just been written is easily proved.   As the observer travels
from place to place on the Earth his zenith moves on the
celestial sphere.   It is the point directly over his head,

His horizon is the plane always perpendicular to the line joining his zenith and nadir. As this line moves with the motion of the observer his horizon must move.

It is so important to understand just how the horizon of an observer moves and just how the appearances of his sky are changed, that it is well worth while to take space to consider several cases.

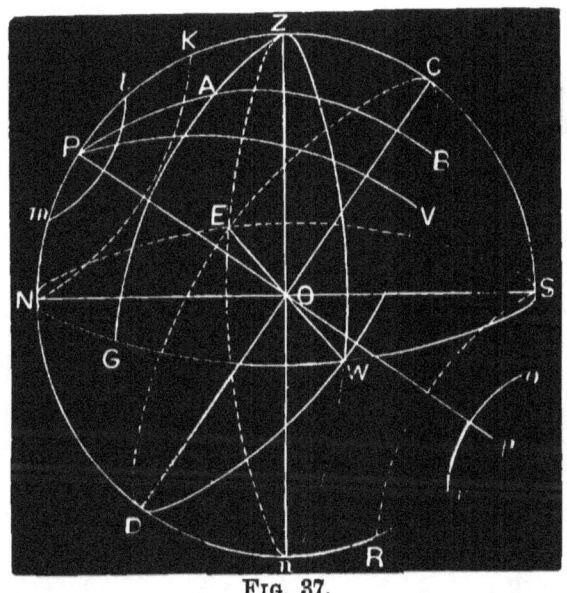

Fig. 37.

The circles of a celestial sphere for an observer in north latitude *PN* or *CZ*.

The student must pay particular attention to this figure. When he understands just what it means he has mastered all the more important theorems of spherical astronomy. The large circle stands for the celestial sphere. The Earth is a point at *O*. *P* is the north pole of the heavens (and *p* the south pole), and hence *DWCE* must be the celestial equator (since its plane is perpendicular to the line joining the poles). The celestial sphere is full of stars.

Now let us suppose there is an observer on the Earth (*O*) at some point in the northern hemisphere. If he is in the northern hemisphere his zenith *must* be somewhere between *C* and *P*. Let us suppose that the observer is on the parallel of 34° north latitude, say on the parallel of Wilmington, N. C., or of Los Angeles, California. His latitude is 34° then, and his zenith must be at *Z*, just 34° north of *C*. His nadir must be at *n;* his horizon must be *NS*. Suppose that we are looking at the celestial sphere, as drawn in the figure, from a point outside of it and west of it. *W* will be his *west* point; *E* his *east* point; the line *EW* is drawn so that it looks (in perspective) perpendicular to *NS*, the observer's north and south line.

The Earth will turn round once a day on the axis joining the poles *P* and *p*. The stars in the celestial sphere will appear to rise above his eastern horizon *NES;* they will culminate on his meridian *NZS;* they will set below his western horizon *NWS*. A star which rises at *E* will culminate at *C* and set at *W*. If he could see below his horizon this star would seem to him to move from *W* to *D* and then from *D* to *E* again. The interval of time between two successive risings would be 24 hours. Some stars in the north would never set. All of them would lie within the circle of perpetual apparition *KN*. *lm* is the diurnal orbit of a *circumpolar* star. Some stars would never rise to this observer. His horizon would hide them. All the stars further south than the circle *SR*, (the circle of perpetual occultation) would never be seen. A star near the south pole would have a diurnal orbit like *or*.

The student should notice that a part of this drawing is quite independent of the situation of the observer. We can draw the celestial sphere, the celestial poles, the equator, the earth, and they will be the same for any and every observer; they will be the same whether any observer exists or not. But the instant we imagine an observer on the earth—anywhere on the earth—his zenith is fixed. It *must* be at a point on the celestial sphere distant from the celestial equator by an arc equal to the observer's latitude. So soon as the zenith is fixed a horizon is fixed. As soon as the horizon is fixed we know that *some* stars will never rise above it, and that *some* stars will never set below it. If we draw the celestial sphere as it is for any particular observer we shall be able to say just how the stars will appear to move for him; just what stars he can see, and just what others he can never see.

The student should exercise himself in making diagrams of the celestial sphere for observers in different latitudes. Let him make such a diagram, placing the observer's zenith (Z) at K in the last figure, and another placing the observer's zenith at l.

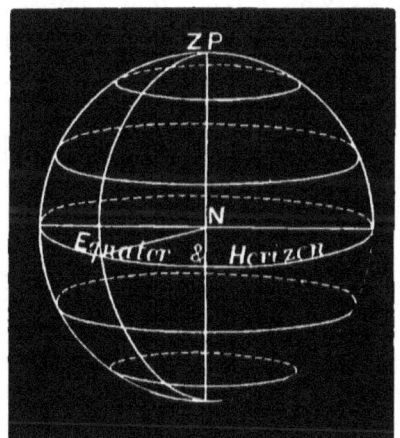

FIG. 38.

The circles of the celestial sphere and the diurnal motions of the stars as they appear to an observer at the north pole of the earth.

The Diurnal Motion of Stars as Seen by an Observer at the North Pole of the Earth.—An observer at the north pole of the Earth is in terrestrial latitude 90°; the altitude of the north celestial pole above his horizon will be 90°.

His zenith and the north celestial pole will coincide.   The star *Polaris* will be neatly at his zenith.

Fig. 38 shows the celestial sphere as it would appear to an observer at the north pole of the Earth.   The zenith of the observer will be exactly overhead, of course, and the pole will coincide with his zenith.   His horizon and the celestial equator will coincide, therefore.   As all the stars perform their diurnal revolutions in circles parallel to the celestial equator, no matter what the latitude, in this particular latitude they will revolve parallel to the *horizon*. None of the stars of the southern half of the celestial sphere will be visible at all.   All the stars of the northern hemisphere will be constantly visible.   They will not rise and set, but they will revolve in diurnal orbits parallel to the horizon.

Arctic explorers who travel from temperate regions towards the north find the north celestial pole constantly higher and higher above their horizon.   When they are in latitude 50°, the altitude of the pole (of the star *Polaris*) will be 50°; when they are in latitude 70°, the altitude of *Polaris* will be 70°; if they reach the pole of the Earth, the altitude of *Polaris* will be 90°.

The student may know that from March to September of every year the Sun is north of the celestial equator (in north declination) ; and that from September to March the Sun is south of the celestial equator (in south declination). From March to September, then, the Sun is a star of the northern hemisphere ; from September to March the Sun is a southern star. An observer at the north pole of the Earth sees all the northern stars revolve in diurnal orbits parallel to his horizon, and he will thus have the Sun above the horizon for six entire months, and for the next six months he will not see the Sun at all. An observer at the south pole of the Earth will have the Sun constantly above his horizon from September to March; constantly below it from March to September. The Fig. 39 will illustrate the diurnal orbit of the Sun to an observer at the north pole of the Earth. The Sun is at the point *O* (near *W*) on March 22, and from March to June travels every day about 1° along the lowest broken line — — — — of the figure. The Sun is on the hour circle *I* on April 6, on *II* on April 22, on *III* (near *E*) on May 8, on *IV* on May 23 (and always on the dotted curve). The student should trace out in the picture the diurnal orbits of the Sun on the dates just given.

The Diurnal Motion of Stars as Seen by an Observer at the Earth's Equator.—If the observer is at any point on

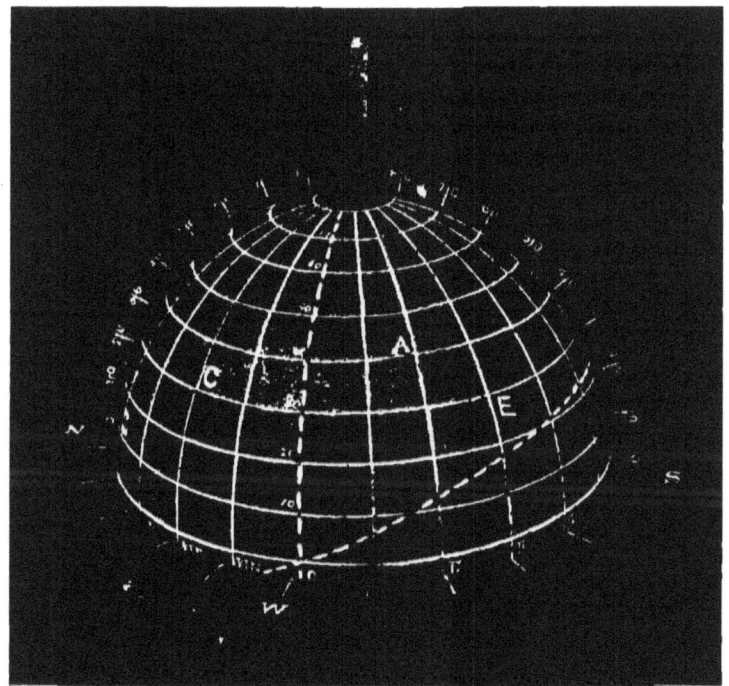

Fig. 39.

A globe so set as to show the circles of the celestial sphere for an observer at the north pole of the earth.

the Earth's equator his terrestrial latitude will be 0°; the elevation of the north celestial pole above his horizon will be 0°; the star *Polaris* will be in his horizon.

Fig. 40 shows the celestial sphere as it appears to an

observer on the Earth's equator. The zenith of the observer is in the celestial equator. The latitude of the observer is 0° and hence the altitude of the north celestial pole (of *Polaris*) is 0°; that is, the north and south celestial poles are in his horizon. All the stars appear to move in their diurnal orbits parallel to the celestial equator, no matter what may be the observer's latitude. In this case they will all appear to revolve in circles perpendicular to the horizon. All the stars of the sky, those in both halves

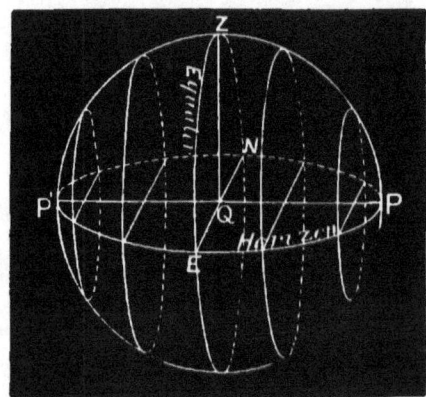

Fig. 40.

The circles of the celestial sphere and the diurnal motions of the stars as they appear to an observer on the earth's equator.

of the celestial sphere, will be visible, for all of them will rise, every day, above the eastern horizon and will pass across the sky and set below the western horizon. Every star will be above the horizon exactly half a day—12 hours.

In Fig. 41 the diurnal paths of all stars are perpendicular to the horizon, and every star is 12ʰ above and 12ʰ below it. Stars whose right-ascension is 6ʰ are on the meridian in the picture The star *E* is 3ʰ, the stars *A*, *B*, are 4ʰ west of the meridian. The vernal equinox (*O*) is 6ʰ west.

The *ecliptic* (the path of the Sun) is marked on the northern celestial hemisphere by a broken line — — — — from *O* towards *E*, etc. The *Sun* is at *O* on March 22 ; on the hour-circle I, April 6 ; on II, April 22 ; on III, May 8 ; on IV, May 23 (and always on the dotted curve). The student should trace out the diurnal orbits of the Sun for the dates just given. It is clear that the Sun will cross the celestial meridian of an observer at the Earth's equator *north* of his zenith when the Sun is in north declination (March to September), and south of it whenever the Sun is in south declination In our latitudes the Sun is never seen north of the zenith, as may be seen by inspecting Fig. 33, where the dotted line is the Sun's path.

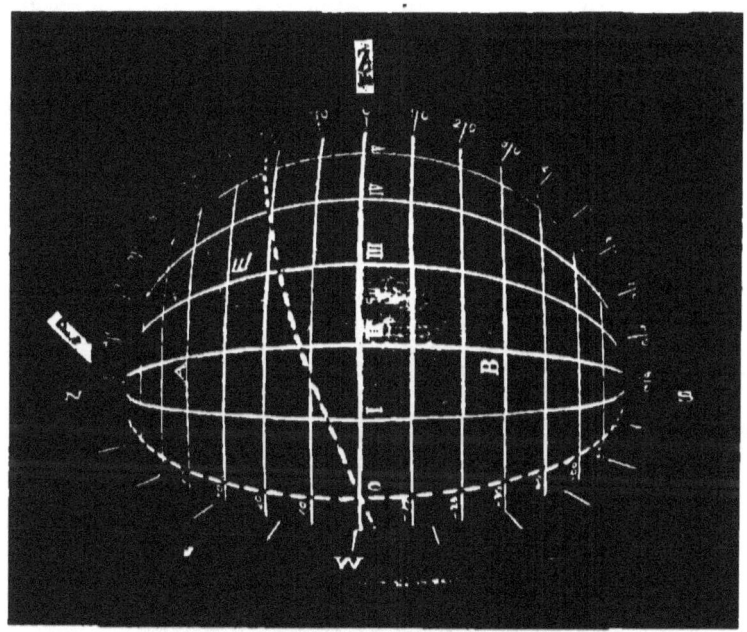

Fig. 41.

A globe so set as to show the circles of the celestial sphere for an observer at the earth's equator. *Z* is his zenith ; *P* the north celestial pole ; NWS his horizon.

If now the observer travels southward from the equator, the south pole will, in its turn, become elevated above his horizon, and in the southern hemisphere appearances will be reproduced that have been already described for the northern, except that the direction of the motion will, in

one respect, be different. The heavenly bodies will still
rise in the east and set in the west, but those near the
celestial equator will pass north of the zenith of the observer instead of south of it, as in our latitudes. The sun,
instead of moving from left to right, there moves from
right to left. In the northern hemisphere of the Earth
we have to face to the south to see the sun ; while in the
southern hemisphere we have to face to the north to see it.

If the observer travels west or east on a parallel of latitude of the Earth's surface, his zenith will still remain at
the same angular distance from the north pole as before
(since his terrestrial latitude remains unchanged), and as
the phenomena caused by the diurnal motion at any place
depend only upon the altitude of the elevated pole at that
place, these will not be changed except as to the times of
their occurrence.

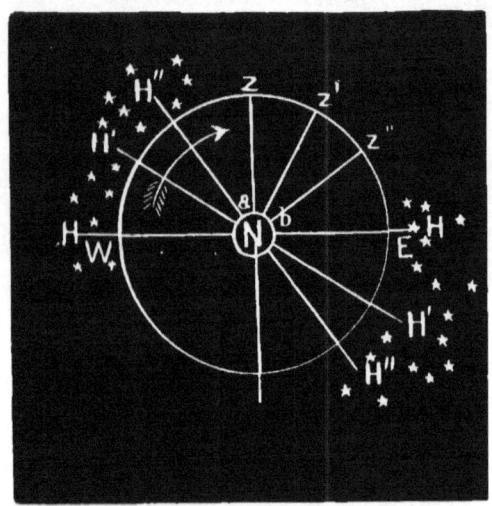

FIG. 42.

The risings of the stars to an observer on the earth are earlier the
farther east he is. East is in the direction of the arrow, since the earth
revolves from west to east.

A star that appears to pass through the zenith of his first station will also appear to pass through the zenith of the second (since each star remains at a constant angular distance from the pole), but later in time, since it has to pass through the zenith of every place between the two stations. The horizons of the two stations will intercept different portions of the celestial sphere at any one instant, but the Earth's rotation will present the same portions successively, and in the same order, at both. An observer at *b* (east of *a*) will see the same stars rise earlier than an observer at *a*. (See Fig. 42.)

Change of the Position of the Zenith of an Observer by the Diurnal Motion.—If the student has mastered what has gone before he can solve any questions relating to the diurnal motion. The following presentation of these questions will be found useful in relation to problems of longitude and time, that are to be considered shortly.

In Figure 43 *nesq* is the Earth ; *NESQ* is the celestial sphere. An observer at *n* will have his zenith at *NP*, and his horizon will coincide with the celestial equator. The stars will appear to revolve parallel to his horizon (the celestial equator), as we have seen. If the observer is at *s*, his zenith is at *SP*. If the observer is in 45° north latitude (the latitude of Minneapolis), his zenith will be at *Z* in the figure. The Earth revolves on its axis once daily, and the observer will be carried round a circle. His zenith (*Z*) will move round a circle of the celestial sphere (*ML*) corresponding to the parallel of 45° on the Earth. If the observer is on the earth's equator at *q*, his zenith will be at *Q*, and it will move round the circle *EQ* of the celestial sphere once daily. If the observer is at 45° *south* latitude on the Earth, his zenith will be at *S*, and the zenith will move round a circle of the celestial sphere (*SO*) once daily, and so on. Thus, for each parallel of latitude on the Earth we have a corresponding circle on the celestial sphere (a parallel of declination), and each of these latter circles has its poles at the celestial poles.

Not only are there circles of the celestial sphere that correspond to parallels of latitude on the Earth, but there are also celestial meridians which correspond to the various terrestrial meridians. The plane of the meridian of any place contains the zenith of that place

and the two celestial poles. It cuts from the earth's surface the terrestrial meridian, and from the celestial sphere that great circle
which we have defined as the celestial meridian.

To fix the ideas, let us suppose an observer at some one point of the
Earth's surface. A north and south line on the Earth at that point
is the visible representative of his terrestrial meridian. A plane
through the centre of the Earth and that line contains his zenith, and

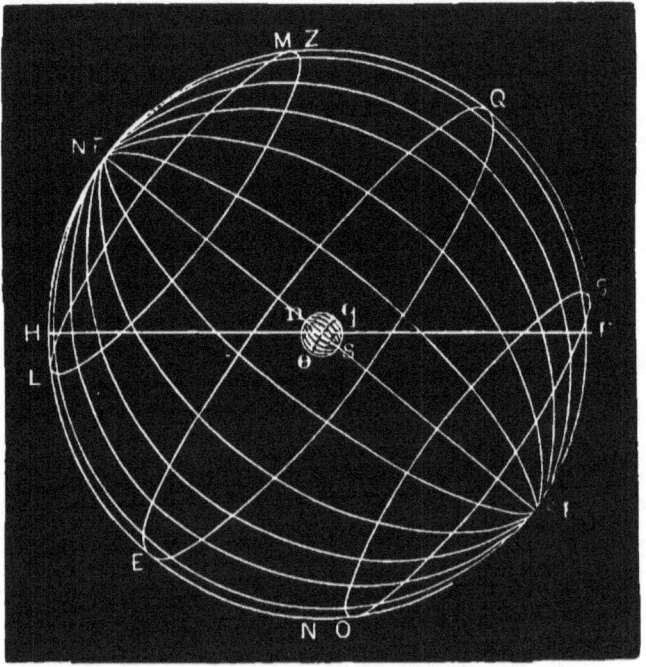

FIG. 43.

The change of the position of the observer's zenith on the celestial sphere
due to the diurnal motion.

cuts from the celestial sphere the celestial meridian. As the Earth
rotates on its axis his zenith moves round the celestial sphere in a parallel, as *ZL* in the last figure.

Suppose that the east point is in front of the picture, the west
point being behind it. Then as the Earth rotates the zenith *Z* will
move along the line *ZL* from *Z* towards *L*. The celestial meridian
always contains the celestial poles and the point *Z*, wherever it may

be. Hence, the arcs of great circles joining *N.P.* and *S.P.* in the figure are representatives of the celestial meridian of this observer, at different times during the period of the Earth's rotation. They have been drawn to represent the places of the meridian at intervals of 1 hour. That is, 12 of them are drawn to represent 12 consecutive positions of the meridian during a semi-revolution of the Earth.

In this time *Z* moves from *Z* to *L*. In the next semi-revolution *Z* moves from *L* to *Z*, along the other half of the parallel *ZL*. In 24 hours the zenith *Z* of the observer has moved from *Z* to *L* and from *L* back to *Z* again. The celestial meridian has also swept across the heavens from the position *N.P.*, *Z*, *Q*, *S*, *S.P.*, through every intermediate position to *N.P.*, *L*, *E*, *O*, *S.P*, and from this last position back to *N.P.*, *Z*, *Q*, *S*, *S.P.* The terrestrial meridian of the observer has been under it all the time.

This real revolution of the celestial meridian is incessantly repeated with every revolution of the Earth. The sky is studded with stars all over the sphere. The celestial meridian of any place approaches these various stars from the west, passes them, and leaves them.

This is the *real* state of things. *Apparently* the observer is fixed. His terrestrial and celestial meridians seem to him to be fixed, not only with reference to himself, as they are, but to be fixed in space. The stars appear to him to approach his celestial meridian from the east, to pass it, and to move away from it towards the west. When a star crosses the celestial meridian it is said to *culminate*. The passage of the star across the meridian is called the *transit* of that star. This phenomenon takes place successively for each observer on the Earth.

Suppose two observers, A and B, A being one hour (15°) east of B in longitude. This means that the angular distance of their terrestrial meridians is 15° (see page 28). From what we have just learned it follows that their celestial meridians are also 15° apart. When B's meridian is *N.P.*, *Z*, *Q*, *R*, *S.P.*, A's will be the first one (in the figure) beyond it ; when B's meridian has moved to this first position, A's will be in the second, and so on, always 15° (one hour) in advance. A group of stars that has just come to A's meridian will not pass B's for an hour. When they are on B's meridian they will be one hour west of A's, and so on. A's zenith is always one hour west of B's. The same stars successively rise, culminate, and set to each observer (A and B), but the phenomena will be presented earlier to the eastern observer.

If the student has access to a celestial globe all the prob-

lems that have been considered in this chapter can be
quickly solved by its use.

In Figure 44 *Z* is the zenith, *N* the nadir, and *W* the west point
of the observer. *P* is the north celestial pole, X, XI, . . . XIV, XV,
. . . the celestial equator. The dotted line from *P* through XII to
the south celestial pole is the hour-circle of 12 hours. The dotted
line inclined to the equator by an angle of 23° is the sun's path—the
ecliptic. Stars whose right-ascension are 17^h are on the observer's
celestial meridian.

The star *K* (R.A. = 13^h, Decl. = + 20°) is 4^h west of the meridian ; the star *R* (R.A. = 10^h, Decl. = + 30°) is just setting ; the
stars north of Decl. + 50° are circumpolar—they never set.

— Prove that as an observer moves from place to place his horizon must change. If an observer is in the northern hemisphere of
the Earth his zenith is in the northern half of the celestial sphere.
Prove it by a diagram. What is a circumpolar star ? Draw a diagram representing the celestial sphere with its poles, its equator.
Now, suppose an observer on the Earth in 30° north latitude ;
where will his zenith be on the diagram ? Draw a circle to show
what stars will always be above his horizon. Suppose an observer
in 86° north latitude (the highest latitude reached by NANSEN in
1895) ; where will his zenith be ? Draw circles to show how the
stars appeared to move in their diurnal orbits to NANSEN. The horizon of an observer in some latitude is the same as the celestial equator—in what latitude ? An observer at the north pole of the Earth
would have the Sun constantly above his horizon for six months—
prove it. All the stars are successively visible to an observer on the
Earth's equator—prove it.

The Celestial Globe.—A celestial globe is a globe marked
with the lines and circles of the celestial sphere—the celestial poles, the celestial equator, the celestial meridians and
parallels, etc., and with the principal stars, each one in its
proper right-ascension and declination. The Figs. 32, 33,
39, 41, and 44 represent such a globe with the stars omitted. Every school should own a celestial globe, because all
the problems of spherical astronomy can be simply explained or illustrated by its use. In text-books we are
obliged to use diagrams. They are necessarily drawn on a

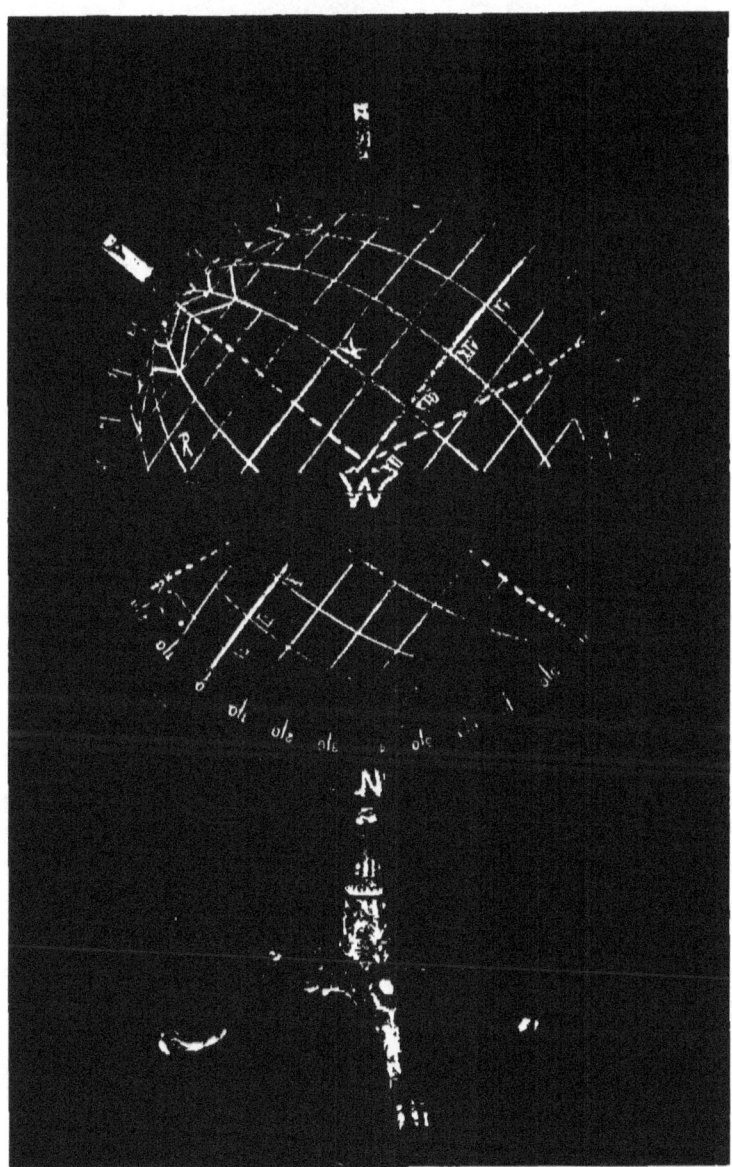

FIG. 44.

View of a globe showing the circles of the celestial sphere for an observer in 40° north latitude (the latitude of Philadelphia, Columbus, O., Quincy, Ill., Denver, etc.).

flat surface, and the student has to imagine the spherical surface. The school-globe shows the surface as it really is.

The celestial globe must be set so that the elevation of the north celestial pole (if the observer lives in the northern hemisphere) above the horizon is the same as the latitude of the observer. (His latitude can be taken from any good map.) Then the celestial globe will represent his celestial sphere just as it really is, when the line *NS* is placed north and south, *N* to the north. Any one of the problems of this chapter can be illustrated by turning the celestial globe about the axis. For instance, let the student point out the circumpolar stars, those that never rise and set to him. Let him take a star a little further south and turn the globe till the star is at the eastern horizon—just rising. By turning the globe slowly he will see exactly how this particular star moves in its apparent diurnal orbit from rising to culmination, and from culmination to setting. Let him particularly notice how its altitude increases from zero at rising to a maximum at culmination; and how it decreases from culmination to zero at setting.

After he has studied the diurnal motion of one star, let him choose another one and trace *its* course from rising to setting. He should study, in this way, the diurnal motions of stars in all parts of the sky. If he has his globe by him while he is observing the real stars in the sky, the globe will help him to understand quickly, in a few minutes, motions that the real stars require 24 hours to make. Other problems can be, and should be, studied in the same way.

CHAPTER V

CO-ORDINATES—SIDEREAL AND SOLAR TIME.

14. Systems of Co-ordinates to define the Place of a Star in the Celestial Sphere.—Let us now briefly consider some of the ways in which the position of a star in the celestial sphere may be described. Many of them are already familiar.

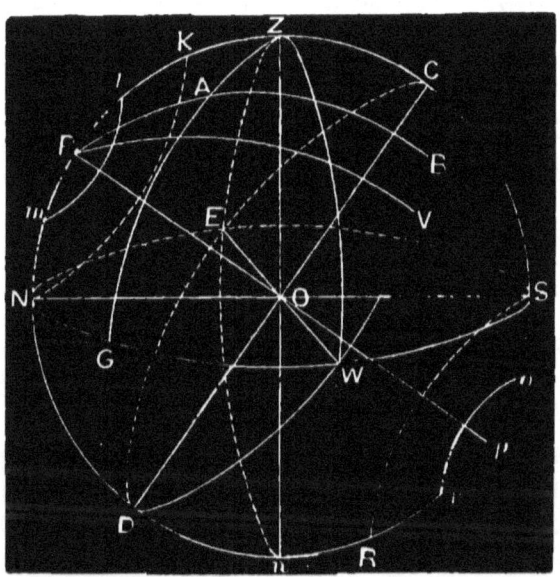

Fig. 45.—Systems of Co-ordinates on the Celestial Sphere.

Any great circles of the celestial sphere which pass through the two celestial poles are called *hour-circles*. Each hour-circle is the *celestial* meridian of some place on the Earth.

77

The hour-circle of any particular star is that one which passes through the star at the time. As the Earth revolves, different hour-circles, or celestial meridians, come to the star, pass over it, and move away towards the east.

In Fig. 45 let O be the position of the Earth in the centre of the celestial sphere $NZSD$. Let Z be the zenith of the observer at a given instant, and P, p, the celestial poles. By definition $PZSpnNP$ is his celestial meridian. NS is the horizon of the observer at the instant chosen. PON is his latitude. If P is the north pole, he is in latitude 34° north, because the angle $PON = 34°$.

$ECWD$ is the celestial equator; E and W are the east and west points. The Earth is turning from W to E. The celestial meridian, which at the instant chosen in the picture contains PZp, was in the position PV about three hours *earlier.*

PC, PB, PV, PD are parts of hour-circles. If A is a star, PB is the hour-circle passing through that star. As the Earth turns PB turns with it (towards the east), and directly PB will have moved away from A towards the top of the picture, and soon the hour-circle PV will pass through the star A. When it does so, PV will be the hour-circle of the star A. At the instant chosen for making the picture PB is its hour-circle.

We are now seeking for ways of defining the position of a star, of any star, on the celestial sphere. We define the position of a place on the Earth by giving its latitude and longitude. These two angles are called the *co-ordinates* of this place. Co-ordinates are angles which, taken together, determine the position of a point. If we say that the longitude of a city is 77° and that its latitude is 38° 53′ N., we know that this city is Washington. These two numbers determine its position. The place of this city is described by them and no other city can be meant.

To describe and determine the place of a star on the celestial sphere we may employ several different pairs of co-ordinates. Those spoken of here will all be needed in what is to follow.

North-polar-distance and Hour-angle. — The north-polar-distance (N.P.D.) of the star A is PA. *The hour-*

angle of a star is the angular distance between the celes-
tial meridian of the observer and the hour-circle passing
through that star. The hour-angle is counted from the
meridian *towards the west* from 0° to 360° (or from 0ʰ to
24ʰ). The hour-angle of a star at A at the instant chosen
for making the picture is ZPB. The hour-angle of a star
at K is 0°. The hour-angle of a star at V is ZPV; of a
star at D is $ZPD = 180° = 12^h$; and so on.

The hour-angle is *measured* by the arc of the celestial

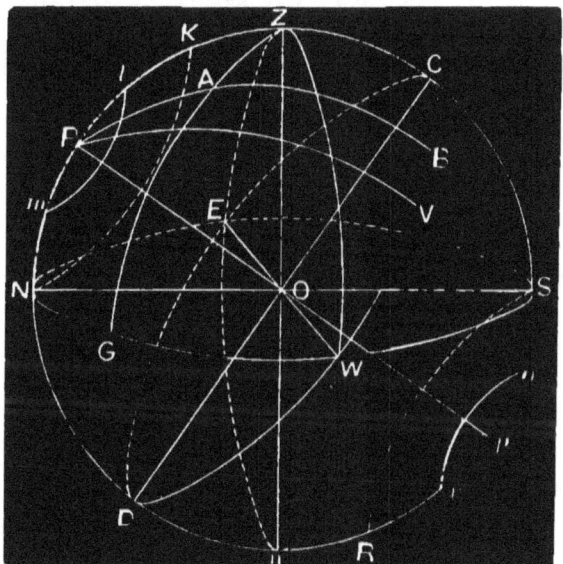

Fɪɢ. 45 *bis.*

equator between the celestial meridian of the observer and
the foot of the hour-circle through the star. The arc CB
is the measure of the angle ZPB. Knowing the two co-
ordinates PA and CB the place of the star A is described
and determined.

North-polar-distance and Right-ascension.—The north-
polar-distance of the star A is PA, measured along the
hour-circle PB. Let us choose some fixed point V on the

equator to measure our other co-ordinate from, and let us always measure it on the equator *towards the east* from 0° to 360° (from 0^h to 24^h). That is, from V through B, C, E, D, W, successively.

VB is the *right-ascension* of A. *The right-ascension of a star is the angular distance of the foot of the hour-circle through the star from the* vernal equinox, *measured on the celestial equator, towards the east.*

Exactly what the *vernal equinox* is we shall find out later on; for the present it is sufficient to define it as a certain fixed point on the celestial equator.*

If we have the right-ascension and north-polar-distance (R.A. and N.P.D.) of a star, we can point it out. Thus VB and PA define the position of A.

The right-ascension of the star K is VC. Of a star at E it is VCE; of a star at D it is $VCED$; of a star at W it is $VCEDW$; and so on.

Right-ascension and Declination.—It is sometimes convenient to use in place of the north-polar-distance of a star its *declination*.

The declination of a star is its angular distance north or south of the celestial equator.

The declination of A is BA, which is 90° *minus* PA.

The relation between N.P.D. and δ is

$$\text{N.P.D.} = 90° - \delta; \quad \delta = 90° - \text{N.P.D.}$$

North declinations are $+$; south declinations are $-$, just as geographical latitudes are $+$ (north) and $-$ (south).

Altitude and Azimuth.—A vertical plane with respect to any observer is a plane that contains his vertical line. It must pass through his zenith and nadir, and must be perpendicular to his horizon. A vertical plane cuts the celestial sphere in a *vertical circle*.

---

* It is, in fact, that point at which the Sun passes the celestial equator in moving from the southern half of the heavens to the northern half. The Sun is south of the celestial equator from September 22 to March 21 and north of it from March 21 to September 22.

As soon as we imagine an observer to be at any point on the Earth's surface his horizon is at once fixed ; his zenith and nadir are also fixed. From his zenith radiate a number of vertical circles that cut the celestial horizon perpendicularly, and unite again at his nadir.

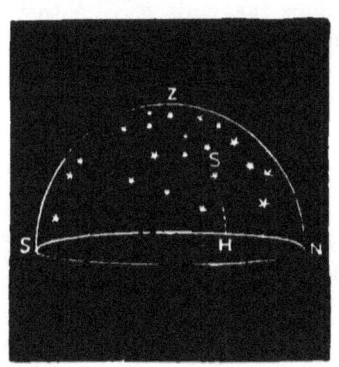

Some one of these vertical circles will pass through any and every star visible to this observer.

The altitude of a heavenly body is its angular elevation above the plane of the horizon measured on a vertical circle through the star.

The zenith distance of a star is its angular distance from the zenith measured on a vertical circle.

Fig. 46.

In the figure, *ZS* is the zenith distance (ζ) of *S*, and *HS* (*a*) is its altitude. *ZSH* is an arc of a vertical circle.

$$ZSH = a + \zeta = 90°; \quad \zeta = 90° - \alpha; \quad \alpha = 90° - \zeta.$$

The azimuth of a star is the angular distance from the point where the vertical circle through the star meets the horizon from the north (or south) point of the horizon. NH or SH is the azimuth of *S* in Fig. 46. The *prime-vertical* of an observer is that one of his vertical circles that passes through his east and west points. The *azimuth* of a star on the prime-vertical is 90°.

Co-ordinates of a Star.—In what has gone before we have described various ways of expressing the apparent positions of stars on the surface of the celestial sphere. That one most commonly used in Astronomy is to give the right-ascension and north-polar-distance (or declination) of the star. The apparent position of the star on the celestial sphere is fixed by these two co-ordinates just as the position of a place on the Earth is fixed by its two co-ordinates, latitude and longitude.

If the student has a celestial globe he can set it so as to make the preceding definitions very clear. The north pole of the globe must be above the horizon of the globe by an angle equal to the latitude.

In the figure Z is the observer's zenith, as before. The star A has the following co-ordinates: R.A. $= 2^h$, hour-angle 1^h west, Decl. $= + 40°$, $N.P.D. = 50°$, zenith distance $=$ the arc ZA, altitude $= 90° - ZA$, azimuth, the arc measured on the horizon SWN from S through W to to the foot of a vertical circle from Z through A; the azimuth of A is something more than $90°$. The student should point out the corresponding co-ordinates for the stars B, C, and D.

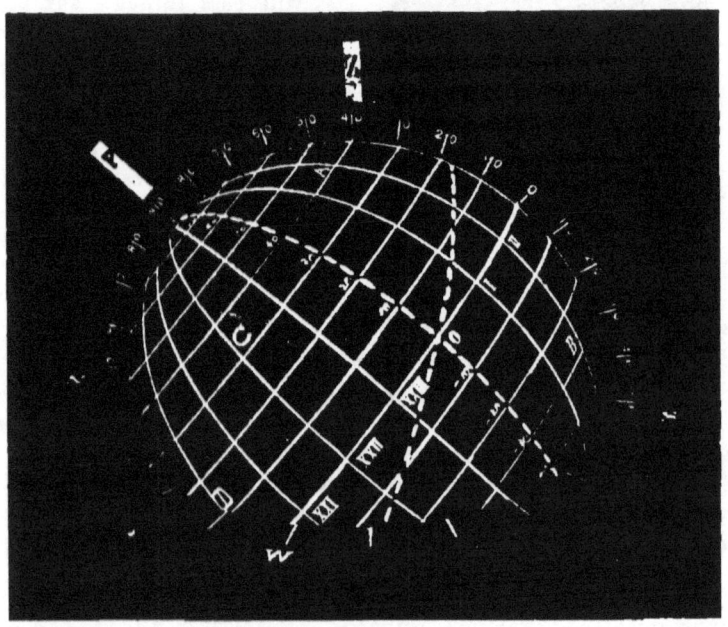

Fig. 47.

A globe showing the circles of the celestial sphere as they appear to an observer in 40° north latitude.

Students must try to realize the circles that have been described in the book as they actually exist in the sky. They are in the sky first; and in the book only to explain the appearances in the sky. On a starlit night let him first find the north celestial pole (near the star *Polaris*). All hour-circles pass through this point. Next he must find his zenith. All vertical circles pass through this point. The great circle in the sky that passes through the north pole of the heavens and his own zenith is his own celestial meridian. Let him trace it out in the sky from the north point of his horizon to the south point; and imagine it extending completely round the earth as a great circle. Let him choose a star a little to the west of his meridian and decide : 1st. What is the N.P.D. of this star? 2d. What is its hour-angle? Next he should select a star far to the west, and decide what *its* N.P.D. and hour-angle are. Then he should take a star a little to the east of his meridian and decide the same points for this star. A little practice of this sort will make all the circles of the sky quite familiar.

— Define hour-circles of the celestial sphere. What is the hour-circle of a star? Does a star have different hour-circles at different instants? What are the two co-ordinates that determine the position of a point on the surface of the Earth? What pairs of co-ordinates may be used to determine and describe the position of a star on the celestial sphere? Define the hour-angle of a star. What is the measure of the hour-angle on the celestial equator? Define the right-ascension of a star. Hour-angles are counted from the celestial meridian of a place towards the—— ? The right-ascension of a star is counted, on the celestial equator, towards the—— ?

15. Measurement of Time; Sidereal Time; Solar Time; Mean Solar Time—SIDEREAL TIME.—The Earth rotates uniformly on its axis and it makes one complete revolution in a *sidereal day.*

A sidereal day is the interval of time required for the Earth to make one complete revolution on its axis, or, what is the same thing, it is the interval between two successive transits of the same star over the celestial meridian of a place on the Earth. A sidereal day = 24 sidereal hours. A sidereal hour = 60 sidereal minutes. A sidereal minute

= 60 sidereal seconds. In a sidereal day the earth turns through 360°, so that

$$24 \text{ hours} = 360°; \text{ also,}$$
$$1 \text{ hour} = 15°; 1° = 4 \text{ minutes.}$$
$$1 \text{ minute} = 15'; 1' = 4 \text{ seconds.}$$
$$1 \text{ second} = 15''; 1'' = 0.066 \text{ second.}$$

When a star is on the celestial meridian of any place its hour-angle is zero, by definition (see page 79). It is then at its transit or culmination.

As the Earth rotates, the meridian moves away (eastwardly) from this star, whose hour-angle continually increases from 0° to 360°, or from 0 hours to 24 hours. Sidereal time can then be directly measured by the hour-angle of any star in the heavens which is on the meridian at an instant we agree to call sidereal 0 hours. When this star has an hour-angle of 90°, the sidereal time is 6 hours; when the star has an hour-angle of 180° (and is again on the meridian, but invisible unless it is a circumpolar star), it is 12 hours ; when its hour-angle is 270°, the sidereal time is 18 hours ; and, finally, when the star reaches the upper meridian again, it is 24 hours or 0 hours. (See Fig. 48, where $ECWD$ is the apparent diurnal path of a star in the equator. It is on the meridian at C.)

Instead of choosing a *star* as the determining point whose transit marks sidereal 0 hours, it is found more convenient to select that point in the sky from which the right ascensions of stars are counted—the vernal equinox—the point V in Fig. 48. *The sidereal time at any instant is measured by the hour-angle of the vernal equinox.* The fundamental theorem of sidereal time is: *The hour-angle of the vernal equinox, or the sidereal time, is equal to the right-ascension of the meridian;* that is, $CV = VC$.

To avoid continual reference to the stars, we set a clock so that its hands shall mark 0 hours 0 minutes 0 seconds

at the instant the vernal equinox is on the celestial meridian of the place; and the clock is regulated so that exactly
24 hours of its time elapses during one revolution of the
Earth on its axis.

In this figure *PZCS* is the celestial meridian of the observer whose
zenith is *Z.* *V* is the vernal equinox. It is that point on the celestial sphere from which right-ascensions are counted. We shall soon
see how to determine it.

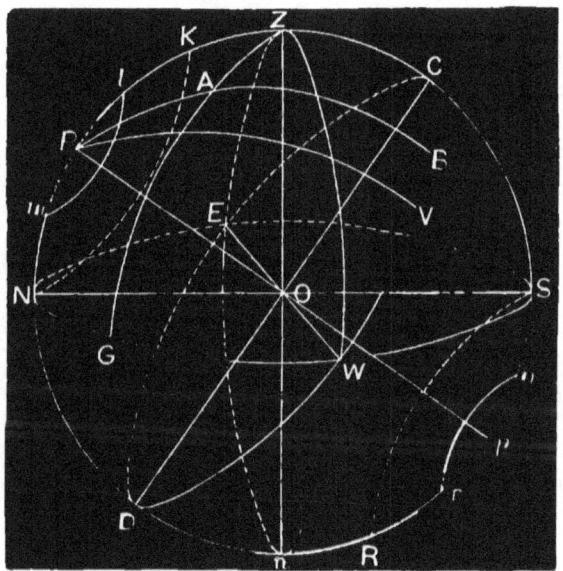

Fig. 48.—Measurement of Sidereal Time.

Suppose that there were a very bright star exactly at V. (There is
no star exactly at the vernal equinox.) Such a star would rise (at *E*);
culminate (at *C*); and set (at *W*). When it is on the celestial meridian of the observer its hour-angle is 0ʰ 0ᵐ 0ˢ (at *C*). Two hours
later the star *V* will have moved 30° to the westward, towards setting. Its hour-angle *ZPB* will then be 2ʰ. The sidereal time of the
observer whose zenith is *Z* will then be 2ʰ. Six hours after its culmination (at *C*) the star *V* will have moved to *W* and its hour-angle
will be 6ʰ. The sidereal time of the particular observer whose zenith

is Z will then be 6ʰ. When V has moved to D, the sidereal time will be 12ʰ. When V has moved to E, the sidereal time will be 18ʰ. When V has moved to C the sidereal time will be 24ʰ (or 0ʰ again) and a new sidereal day will begin ; and so on forever.

When the hour-angle of V is 2ʰ and the vernal equinox is at B, the right-ascension of the celestial meridian (of the

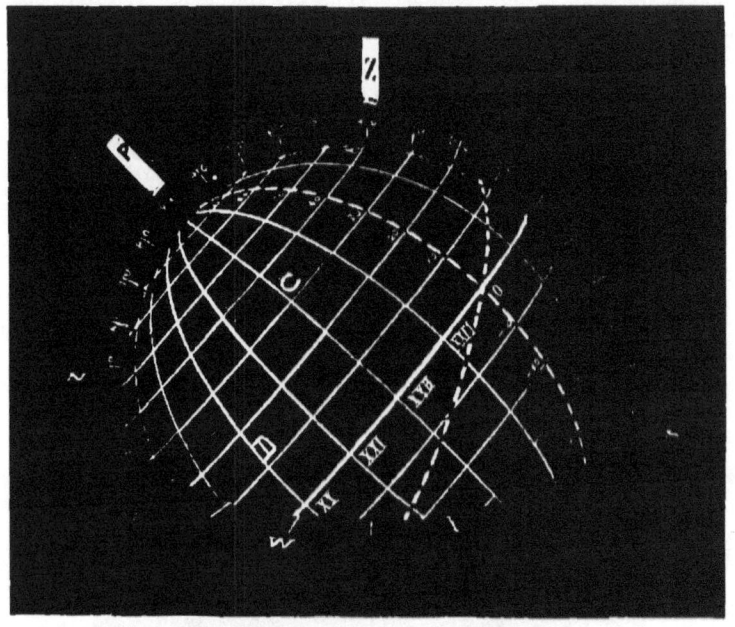

Fig. 49.

The hour-angle of the vernal equinox, O, in this figure is 2 hours west. The sidereal time is therefore 2 hours. The R.A. of the observer's meridian is 2 hours.

point C) is 2ʰ. The right-ascension of any star on the meridian at that instant must be 2 hours. Speaking generally, when the vernal equinox is anywhere (as at V in Fig. 48) the right-ascension of the celestial meridian (of the point C) in the figure will be VC. The sidereal time is the angle ZPV measured by the arc CV. The right-ascension of the meridian is *VC.* The right-ascension of any star on the meridian at that instant will be *VC.*

Conversely—if a star *C* is on the celestial meridian of a place at any instant the right-ascension of that star is expressed by the same number of degrees (or of hours) as the hour-angle of the vernal equinox or as the sidereal time.

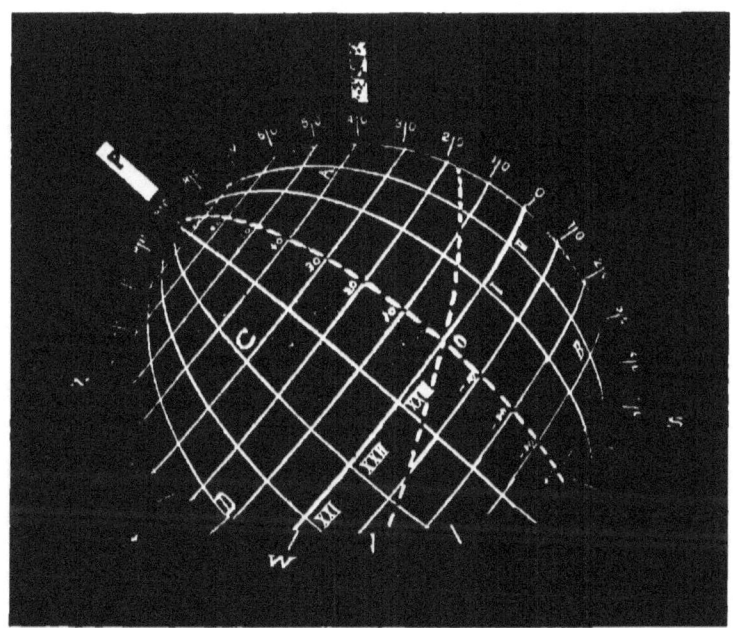

FIG. 50.

The hour-angle of the vernal equinox, *O,* in this figure is 3 hours west. The sidereal time is therefore 3 hours. The R. A. of the observer's meridian is 3 hours.

Suppose then that we had a catalogue of the right-ascensions of stars like this—and we have such catalogues. See Table V for a specimen of the sort:

The R. A. of the star *Aldebaran* is 4^h 30^m
" " " " " " *Sirius* is 6^h 41^m
" " " " " " *Regulus* is 10^h 3^m
" " " " " " *Spica* is 13^h 20^m
" " " " " " *Arcturus* is 14^h 11^m
" " " " " " *Vega* is 18^h 34^m
" " " " " " *Fomalhaut* is 22^h 52^m

Suppose further that we had a way of knowing when a star was on our celestial meridian, that is, exactly south of us (and we have such a way, as will soon be seen), then if an observer noticed that *Sirius* was on his celestial meridian at a certain instant he would know that the sidereal time at that instant must be 6^h 41^m. (For the R.A. of *Sirius* is 6^h 41^m and this is the R.A. of the meridian, and this is equal to the hour-angle of the vernal equinox; and, finally, this is

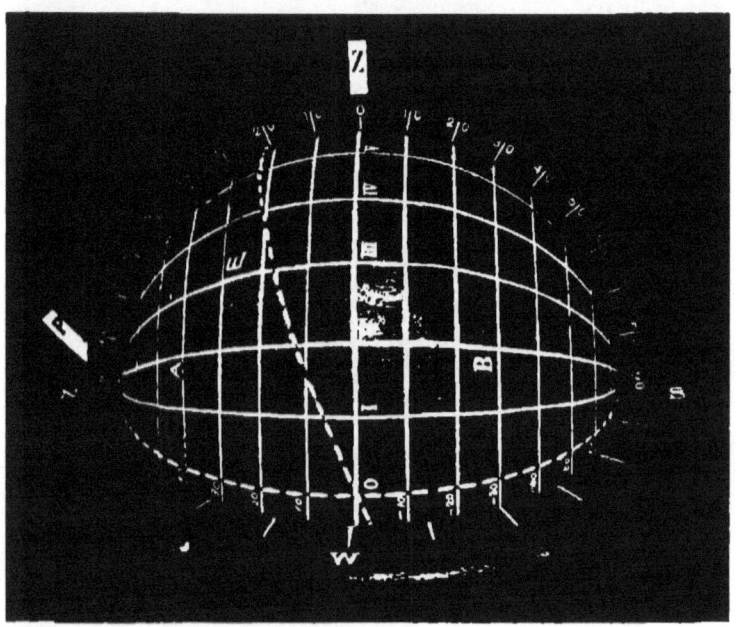

Fig. 51.

The hour-angle of the vernal equinox, *O*, in this figure is 6 hours west. The sidereal time is therefore 6 hours. The R.A of the observer's meridian is 6 hours.

the sidereal time at that instant). If the star *Fomalhaut* is on the celestial meridian of an observer at another instant, the sidereal time at that instant must be 22^h 52^m, and so on. The sidereal clock must show on its dial 6^h 41^m when *Sirius* is on the meridian ; and it must show 22^h 52^m when *Fomalhaut* is on the meridian, and so on. As soon as we know the right-ascension of one star we can set the hands of the sidereal clock correctly. When *Sirius* is on the meridian on

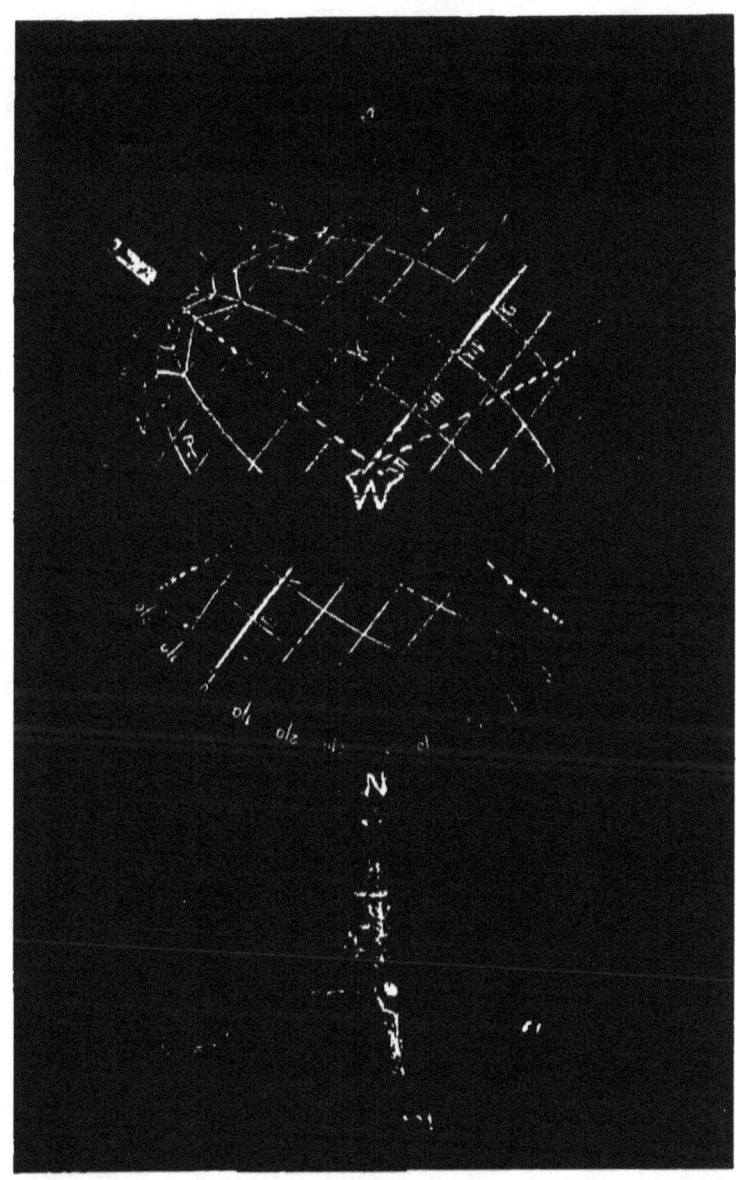

FIG. 52.

The hour-angle of the vernal equinox in this figure is 17 hours. The sidereal time is therefore 17 hours. The R.A. of the observer's meridian is 17 hours.

Monday they must point to 6^h 41^m. When *Sirius* comes to the meridian on Tuesday they must again mark 6^h 41^m. And it is just the same for other stars. Any star whose right-ascension is known will enable us to set the hands of the sidereal clock correctly as soon as we know the direction of our meridian in space. The hour-hand of the clock must move over 24^h every day, from one transit of the star till the next succeeding transit.

Solar Time.—Time measured by the hour-angle of the sun is called *true* (or *apparent*) solar time. *An apparent solar day is the interval of time between two consecutive transits of the Sun over the celestial meridian.* The instant of the transit of the Sun over the meridian of any place is the *apparent noon* of that place, or local apparent noon.

When the Sun's hour-angle is 12 hours or 180°, it is local apparent midnight.

The ordinary sun-dial marks apparent solar time. As a matter of fact, apparent solar days are not equal. In intervals of time that are really equal the hour-angle of the true Sun changes by quantities that are not quite equal. The reason for this will be fully explained later. Hence our clocks are not made to keep this kind of time.

Mean Solar Time.—A modified kind of solar time is therefore used, called *mean solar time*. This is the time kept by ordinary watches and clocks. It is sometimes called civil time, because it regulates our civil affairs. *Mean solar time is measured by the hour-angle of the mean Sun*, a fictitious body which is imagined to move uniformly in the equator. We have tables that give us the position of this imaginary body at any and every instant, just as catalogues of stars give us the right-ascensions of stars. We may therefore speak of the transit of the mean Sun as if it were a bright shining point in the sky. *A mean solar day is the interval of time between two consecutive transits of the mean Sun over the celestial meridian.* Mean noon at any place is the instant when the mean Sun is on the celestial meridian of that place (at *C* in Fig. 48). Twelve hours after local mean noon is local mean midnight. The mean sun is then at *D* in Fig. 48. The mean solar day is divided into 24 hours of 60 minutes each.

Astronomers begin the mean solar day at noon and count round to 24 hours. It happens to be convenient for them to do so. In ordinary life the *civil day* is supposed to begin at midnight, and is divided into two periods of 12 hours each. When the mean Sun is at *D*, in Fig. 48, it is midnight (12ʰ) of Sunday—Monday begins. When the mean Sun is at *C*, it is mean noon (12ʰ) of Monday. When the mean Sun has again reached *D* it is midnight (12ʰ)—Tuesday begins, and so on. It is more convenient, in ordinary life, to change the date—the day—at midnight, when most persons are asleep.

Everything that is here said about the measurement of time can be clearly illustrated by the use of a celestial globe. Set the globe to correspond to the observer's latitude. The vernal equinox is marked on every globe. Place the vernal equinox on the meridian of the observer. It is now sidereal 0ʰ. Rotate the globe slowly to the west. The hour angle of the vernal equinox measures the sidereal time. Trace the course of the equinox throughout a whole revolution ; that is, throughout a sidereal day.

Again, suppose the sun to be in north declination 15°, and in R.A. 2ʰ 31ᵐ (its approximate position on May 1 of each year). Find this point on the globe (see Fig. 50), and trace the sun's course from rising to setting, and to rising again ; that is, throughout 24ʰ. You will see that the sun rises north of the east point on May 1 and reaches a high altitude at noon for observers in the northern hemisphere of the Earth.

Again, suppose the Sun to be in south declination 15°, and in R.A. 14ʰ 34ᵐ, its approximate position on November 3 of each year (see Fig. 52). Find this point on the globe, and trace the Sun's course from rising to setting, and to rising again. You will see that the Sun rises south of the east point on November 3, and that its altitude at noon is considerably less in November than in May.

The student should also try to realize all these explanations regarding time by conceiving the appearances in the sky. On a starlit night he should face southwards and he will see some star on his celestial meridian. If the right ascension of that star is 3^h 24^m 16.93^s then, at that instant, the sidereal time is 3^h 24^m 16.93^s; a second later it is 3^h 24^m 17.93^s; an hour later still it is 4^h 24^m 17.93^s, and so on. Let him trace out in the sky the position of the celestial equator. The vernal equinox must be *west* of his meridian by an arc of 3^h 24^m, etc., or of $51°$. Let him fix in his mind a point of the equator $51°$ west of the meridian. The vernal equinox is there. In an hour it will be $15°$ further to the west; in two hours it will be $30°$ further, and so on. In 24 hours it will have made the circuit of the sky and have returned to its former place once more.

The same kind of exercises should be gone through with in the daytime, so as to realize the motions of the mean Sun. The mean Sun is never very far away from the true Sun. At noon the Sun is due south, on the celestial meridian. At 2 P.M. the hour-angle of the mean Sun is 2^h; at 3 P.M. it is 3^h; at midnight it is 12^h.

— Define a sidereal day. What is the measure of the sidereal time at any instant? When the vernal equinox is on the celestial meridian of a place, what is the sidereal time at that instant? What is the relation between the sidereal time at any instant and the right ascension of the meridian at that instant? Draw a diagram that will show that relation. If a star whose R.A. is 6^h 41^m is on the celestial meridian of a place at a certain instant, what is the sidereal time of that place at that instant? If you knew that the R A. of *Sirius* was 6^h 41^m, how could you set the hands of a clock so as to mark the correct sidereal time? What is true solar time? What kind of time is marked by a sun-dial? How is mean solar time measured? Is the mean Sun a body that really exists? Is there any objection to imagining such a body to exist in the sky, and to supposing that it has motions from rising and setting like the stars? What is a mean solar day? Define the instant of mean noon. How many hours in a mean solar day? In civil life we divide a mean solar day into —— groups of —— hours each. If you have a celestial globe use it so as to illus-

trate what you have learned about different kinds of time. Stand up
and imagine yourself out of doors on a starlit night. Point at your
zenith (*Z*). Point out your horizon. Point out the north celestial
pole (*P*) (it is at an altitude equal to your latitude). Point out
the celestial equator. Choose some point of the equator to be the
vernal equinox *V*. What is the hour-angle of *V*? (Answer: It is
ZP V—point out this angle.) In an hour from now where will *V* be?
in two hours? in 24 hours? Why does *V* have different positions
in the sky at different instants? In speaking of sidereal time we
refer everything to *V* = the vernal equinox. Now, suppose that instead of considering the motions of *V* you think of the motions of the
true Sun. Describe those motions as well as you know them, and say
what the apparent solar time is. Do the same things for the mean
Sun. Do you now thoroughly understand that the hour-angle of the
mean Sun is measured by the motion of the hour-hand of your watch?
The hands of your watch point to 4 P.M. What event took place 4
hours ago (supposing your watch to be keeping local mean solar
time)?

CHAPTER VI.

16. Time—Terrestrial Longitudes.— We have seen that time may be reckoned in at least three ways. The natural unit of time is the day.

A *sidereal day* is the time required for the Earth to turn once on its axis; it is measured by the interval between two successive transits of the same *star* (*sidereus* is the Latin for a star or a group of stars) over the same celestial meridian.

A *solar day* is the interval of time between two successive transits of the true Sun over the same celestial meridian. It is longer than a sidereal day, because the Sun appears to be constantly moving eastwards among the stars (as we shall soon see), so that if the Sun has the same right-ascension as the star *Sirius* on Monday noon, by

East   West

Monday   Tuesday

Tuesday noon it will have moved about a degree to the east of *Sirius*. Therefore *Sirius* will come to the celestial meridian on Tuesday a little earlier than the Sun, and hence the solar day will be a little longer than the sidereal day. The eastward motion of the true Sun in right-ascension is not uniform, so that intervals of time that are really equal are not measured by *equal* angular motions of the true Sun. The true Sun moves in the *ecliptic*—not in the celestial equator. Hence a " mean Sun " has been

94

invented, as it were. *The mean Sun is an imaginary point*—like a star—*moving uniformly along the celestial equator so as to make one complete circuit of the heavens in a year.*

A *mean solar day* is the interval of time between two successive transits of the mean Sun over the same celestial meridian. As the mean Sun moves eastwards among the stars, a mean solar day is longer than a sidereal day. The exact relation is:

$$\text{1 sidereal day} = 0.997 \text{ mean solar day,}$$
$$\text{24 sidereal hours} = 23^h\ 56^m\ 4^s.091 \text{ mean solar time,}$$
$$\text{1 mean solar day} = 1.003 \text{ sidereal days,}$$
$$\text{24 mean solar hours} = 24^h\ 3^m\ 56^s.555 \text{ sidereal time,}$$

and

$$366.24222 \text{ sidereal days} = 365.24222 \text{ mean solar days.}$$

Local Time.—When the mean Sun is on the celestial meridian of any place, as Boston, it is mean noon at Boston. When the mean Sun is on the celestial meridian of St. Louis, it is mean noon at St. Louis. St. Louis being west of Boston, and the Earth rotating from west to east, the local noon of Boston occurs earlier than the local noon at St. Louis. The local sidereal time at Boston at any given instant is expressed by a larger *number* than the local sidereal time of St. Louis at that instant.

The sidereal time of mean noon can be calculated beforehand (as we shall see) and is given in the astronomical ephemeris (the *Nautical Almanac*, so called) for every day of the year. We can thus determine the local mean solar time when we know the sidereal time. In what precedes we have shown (page 84) how to set and regulate a sidereal clock. A mean-solar clock can be regulated by comparing it with a sidereal time-piece as well as by direct observation of the Sun. After the student understands the construction and use of astronomical instruments we shall return to this matter of time and show exactly how the mean solar time of our clocks and watches is determined.

Terrestrial Longitudes.—Owing to the rotation of the Earth, there is no such fixed correspondence between meridians on the Earth and meridians on the celestial sphere as there is between latitude on the Earth and declination in the heavens. The observer can always determine his latitude by finding the declination of his zenith, but he cannot find his longitude from the right-ascension of his zenith with the same facility, because that right-ascension is constantly changing.

Consider the plane of the meridian of a place extended out to the celestial sphere so as to mark out on the latter the celestial meridian of the place. Take two such places, Washington and San Francisco, for example; then there will be two such celestial meridians cutting the celestial sphere so as to make an angle of about forty-five degrees with each other in this case.

Let the observer imagine himself at San Francisco. His celestial meridian is over his head, at rest with reference to him, though it is moving among the stars. Let him conceive the meridian of Washington to be visible on the celestial sphere, and to extend from the pole over toward his southeast horizon so as to pass about forty-five degrees east of his own meridian. It would appear to him to be at rest, although really both his own meridian and that of Washington are moving in consequence of the Earth's rotation.

The stars in their courses will first pass the meridian of Washington, and about three hours later they will pass his own meridian. Now it is evident that if he can determine the interval which a star requires to pass from the meridian of Washington to that of his own place, he will at once have the difference of longitude of the two places by turning the interval of time into degrees, at the rate of 15° to each hour.

The difference of longitude between any two places depends upon the angular distance of the terrestrial (or celestial) meridians of these two places, and not upon the motion of the star or sun which is used to determine this angular difference, and hence the longitude of a place is the same whether expressed as the difference of two sidereal or of two solar times. The longitude of Washington west from Greenwich is 5^h 8^m or $77°$, and this is in fact the ratio of the angular distance of the meridian of Washington from that of Greenwich, to 24 hours or $360°$. The angle between the two meridians is $\frac{77}{360}$ of 24 hours, or of a whole circumference.

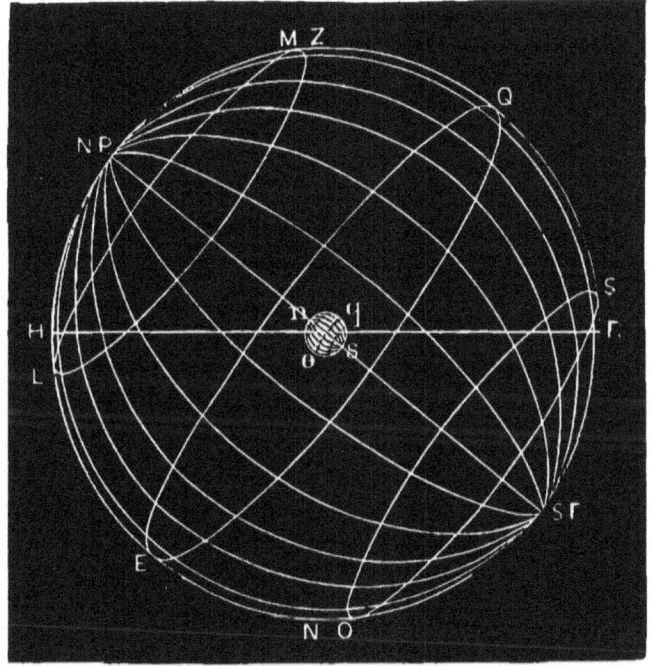

Fig. 53.—Relation between Terrestrial Meridians and Celestial Meridians.

Every observer on the earth has a terrestrial meridian on which he stands and a celestial meridian over his head. The latter passes through the celestial poles and the observer's zenith.

The difference of longitude of any two places on the Earth is measured by the difference of their simultaneous local times.

If two stations on the Earth (say Greenwich and Washington) have sidereal time-pieces set and regulated properly to the two local times, we shall know the difference of longitude of the two places as soon as we can compare the two time-pieces. The dials will differ by the difference of longitude.

One way to determine the longitude is actually to carry the Washington time-piece over to Greenwich and to compare its dial with that of the Greenwich time-piece. When the Greenwich time-piece marks 5^h 8^m P.M. the Washington time-piece will mark 0^h (noon). We cannot transport pendulum clocks by sea and keep them running, so that the Washington time-piece referred to must be a chronometer, which is nothing but a large and perfect watch kept going by the motive power of a coiled spring.

A much better way of comparing the two time-pieces is to send the beats of a clock by telegraph from one station to the other. It is possible to arrange things so that an observer at Greenwich can make a signal that can be observed at Washington. If Greenwich sends a signal at 5^h 8^m P.M., Washington will note the face of the standard clock when it is received, and the Washington local time will be 0^h (noon). A Greenwich signal sent at 6^h 8^m local Greenwich time, will be received at Washington at 1^h, and so on. This is the theory of the method now universally employed for exact determinations of longitude. It was first employed by our Coast and Geodetic Survey between Baltimore and Washington in 1844, and it was called "the American method."

It is of vital importance to seamen to be able to determine the longitude of their vessels. The voyage between Liverpool and New York is made weekly by scores of steamers, and the safety of the voyage depends upon the certainty with which the captain can mark the longitude and latitude of his vessel upon the chart.

The method used by a sailor is this: with a sextant (see Chapter VII) the local time of the ship's position is determined by an observation of the · Sun. That is, on a given day he can set his watch so that its hands point to twelve at *local* mean noon. He carries on his ship a chronometer which is regulated to Greenwich mean time. Its hands always point to the Greenwich hour, minute, and second. Suppose that when the ship's time is 0^h (noon) the Greenwich time is $3^h 20^m$. The ship is *west* of Greenwich $3^h 20^m = 50°$. The difference of simultaneous local times measures the difference of longitude. ˙Hence the ship is somewhere on the terrestrial meridian of 50° west of Greenwich. If the altitude of the pole-star is measured, the latitude of the ship is also known. Suppose the altitude of the pole-star above the horizon to be 45°. The ship is then in the regular track of vessels bound for Liverpool. Observations like this are made every day.

When the steamer *Faraday* was laying the direct cable from Europe to America she obtained her longitude every day by comparing her ship's time (found by observation on board) with the Greenwich time telegraphed along the cable and received at the end of it which she had on her deck.

From the National Observatory at Washington the beats of a clock are sent out by telegraph along the lines of railway every day at Washington noon ; at every railway station and telegraph office the telegraph sounder beats the seconds of the Washington clock. Any one who can set his watch to the local time of his station (by making observations of the sun at his own station), and who can compare it with the signals of the Washington clock, can determine for himself the difference of the simultaneous local times of Washington and of his station, and thus his own longitude east or west from Washington.

Standard Time in the United States.—In a country of small area, it is practicable to use the local time of its capital city all over the country. Greenwich time (nearly the same as London time) is the standard time of the whole of

England. The case is not quite the same in a country of wide extent in longitude. San Francisco is about 3^{h} west of Washington, and it would be inconvenient to use Washington local time in San Francisco.

The matter was regulated in 1883 by the railways of the United States and Canada, which adopted the system now in use. By this system the continent was divided into four sections, each 15° (one hour) of longitude in width (from east to west). Each section extended south from the Arctic Ocean to Central America and the Gulf. In each section a central meridian was chosen, and the local time of that meridian was taken for the standard time of all the cities and towns of that section. The meridians chosen as central were:

I. The meridian of 75° W. from Greenwich (it passes west of Albany and east of Philadelphia).

II. The meridian of 90° W. from Greenwich (it passes east of St. Louis and nearly through New Orleans).

III. The meridian of 105° W. from Greenwich (it passes a little to the west of Denver).

IV. The meridian of 120° W. from Greenwich (it passes a little west of Virginia City and of Santa Barbara).

The local time of the 75th meridian was called Eastern Time ;
"   "   "   "   " 90th   "   "   " Central Time ;
"   "   "   "   " 105th   "   "   " Mountain Time ;
"   "   "   "   " 120th   "   "   " Pacific Time.

Greenwich time is 5 hours later than Eastern time ;
"   " " 6 "   "   " Central time ;
"   " " 7 "   "   " Mountain time ;
"   " " 8 "   "   " Pacific time.

Eastern time is used throughout the New England States, Pennsylvania, New Jersey, Delaware, the Virginias, and in the greater portion of the Carolinas east of the Blue Ridge.

Central time is used in Florida and Georgia and in the Central States, including Texas, most of Kansas and Nebraska, and in the eastern half of the two Dakotas,

Mountain time is used in the group of States about the Rocky Mountains, including most of Arizona, Utah, Idaho, and Montana.

Pacific time is used in the Pacific States.

Throughout the United States and Canada every watch and clock running on standard time should show the same minute and second. The hour hands alone should differ. Standard time is Greenwich time, so far as the minutes and seconds are concerned, with an arbitrary change of whole hours in the different sections. All time-pieces in England show Greenwich time. The chronometers of most ships on the Atlantic run on Greenwich time. All time-pieces in the United States run on Greenwich time so far as the minutes and seconds are concerned; the only difference is a difference in the whole hour. The chronometers of most ships in the Pacific Ocean run on Greenwich time, with no change in the hour.

The standard time of the Hawaiian Islands will probably be that of the 150th meridian west of Greenwich (10 hours slower than Greenwich time); that of the Philippine Islands will probably be the local time of the 120th meridian *east* of Greenwich (8 hours faster than Greenwich time). Cape Colony (Cape of Good Hope) time is 1^h 30^m fast of Greenwich time, and Natal time is 2^h fast The time of West Australia is 8^h, of Japan and South Australia 9^h, of Victoria and Queensland 10^h, and of New Zealand 11^h 30^m fast of Greenwich time. On the Continent of Europe, Belgium and Holland use Greenwich time unchanged, while Norway, Sweden, Denmark, Austria, and Italy employ a standard time 1^h fast of Greenwich time. France still holds to the meridian of Paris as standard, and French time is 9^m 21^s faster than Greenwich time. The system of standard time is so convenient that it will eventually be extended to all civilized countries, in all likelihood.

Change of the Day to an Observer travelling round the Earth.—Suppose an observer to be at Greenwich. When the mean Sun crosses his celestial meridian it is noon. Let us say it is Monday noon. When the mean Sun next crosses his celestial meridian it is Tuesday noon, and so on. Whenever the mean Sun crosses the meridian of any observer anywhere on the Earth it is noon for him. If he is east of Greenwich the Sun crosses his celestial meridian before it reaches the Greenwich meridian, and his time is *later* than the Greenwich time. If he is west of Greenwich the Sun does not cross his celestial meridian until after it has crossed that of Greenwich, and the Greenwich time is later.

Suppose a traveller to set out from Greenwich carrying a watch with him that shows not only the Greenwich hour and minute, but also the day. It would be easy to have a watch made with a day-hand that went forward one number (of days) every time the hour-hand marked another 24 hours elapsed. Suppose this observer to carry a card also, on which he makes a mark, thus | *every time the Sun crosses his celestial meridian.* He makes a mark for every one of his noons. Suppose him to travel eastwards round the globe.

When he comes to Sicily (15° = 1 hour of longitude east of Greenwich) the local time will be 1 P.M. of Monday, when his watch shows noon of Monday. At Alexandria in Egypt (30° = 2 hours of longitude east of Greenwich) the local time will be 2 P.M. when his watch shows noon, and the day will be the same as the Greenwich day.

If he goes to the Fiji Islands (180° = 12 hours of longitude east of Greenwich) he will find the date *later* there than the date he carries with him in his watch. The local time at Fiji will be 12 hours later than his. It will be Monday midnight (and thus the beginning of Tuesday) when his watch marks Monday noon. This is natural enough. He is travelling eastwards and the Sun crosses these eastern meridians before it crosses that of Greenwich. When he reaches St. Louis (270° = 18 hours of longitude east of Greenwich) the date there would be, *on the same principle,* 18 hours later than the Greenwich date. When his watch marks Monday noon the people there might call the time 18 hours later ; that is, Tuesday 6 A.M. (12^h (noon) $+ 18^h = 30^h$, and $30^h - 24^h = 6^h$). But in fact they call the day Monday instead of Tuesday, though they call the hour corresponding to Greenwich noon 6 A.M. Instead of reckoning their time to be 18 hours *more* (later) than Greenwich time, they reckon it to be 6 hours *less* (earlier). The 18 hours more that they fail to count at all and the 6 hours less make up 24 hours = 1 day. The traveller has thus gained a day on his journey.

When he finally arrives at Greenwich again his watch agrees

with the Greenwich reckoning as to hours and minutes. The day-hand of the watch shows that he has been away for 100 days (let us say), but his card shows 101 marks on it. The Sun has somehow passed his celestial meridian once more than the number of days elapsed. To make the name of his day agree with the name of the day used in Hawaii, the United States, and England he has to drop one day. How is it that he has gained a whole day in travelling eastwards round the Earth?

When the Sun crosses the celestial meridian of an observer it is noon for him. If the observer stays at one spot on the Earth the Earth itself, in turning on its axis eastwardly, brings his celestial meridian to and past the Sun daily. If the observer travels round the Earth towards the east to meet the Sun his own travels will move his celestial meridian eastward a little every day. The Sun will pass his meridian 101 times if he has himself gone round the Earth in 100 days. One hundred of the transits of the Sun will be due to the rotation of the Earth on its axis. One of them will be due to his own circumnavigation of the globe.

If instead of going eastwards the observer (with his watch and his card) should travel westwards round the globe he would find the local time at Washington five hours *less* (earlier) than the Greenwich time. At St. Louis the local time would be six hours *less* (earlier). At San Francisco it would be eight hours *less* (earlier). When his watch marks Greenwich noon of Monday the people of San Francisco will call the date 4 A.M. of Monday—eight hours *less* (earlier) than Greenwich.

When he reaches India or Germany he will find his Monday is not called Monday but Tuesday. When he returns to Greenwich he will find that his reckoning agrees with the Greenwich reckoning in every respect but one. His watch will show the Greenwich hour and minute exactly. His watch shows that he has been absent for 100 days, let us say. But his card shows that he has had only 99 noons. In going round the world to the westward, away from the Sun, he has lost one whole day. If he had remained in Greenwich the Earth's rotation would have brought his celestial meridian to the Sun and past it 100 times. But in his journey westward he has carried his celestial meridian with him and moved it away from the Sun. The Earth has turned round 100 times during his absence, but the Sun has only crossed his (travelling) meridian 99 times. Thus he has lost a day by travelling completely round the Earth westwards—away from sunrise. If he had travelled towards sunrise—eastwards—he would have gained a day, as we have just seen.

The Earth turns round just 100 times in a certain interval of time, and there is never any trouble in keeping the account. Those persons who stay in one place (as at Greenwich) have simply to count the number of transits of the Sun over their celestial meridian. Those persons who travel *westwards* must *add* a day when they cross the meridian of Fiji (180° from Greenwich). Those persons who travel *eastwards* must *subtract* a day at this meridian, which is called the international date-line (meaning change-of-date line).

When Alaska was transferred from Russia to the United States it was found that one day had to be dropped. The Russian settlers had brought their Asiatic date with them, while we were using a reckoning less by one day because our count was brought from Europe.

Ships in the Pacific Ocean passing the meridian of 180° *add* a day going *westwards* and *subtract* a day going *eastwards*.

It is to be noted that the place where the change of date is made depends upon civil convenience and not upon astronomical necessity. The traveller must necessarily change his date *somewhere* on his journey round the world. It is convenient for trade that two adjacent countries should have the same day-names; so that the date-line in actual use deflects slightly from the 180th meridian. All Asia is to the west of this line; all America, including the Aleutian Islands, is east of it. Samoa is east of it, but the Tonga group and Chatham Island are west of it.

— Define a sidereal day, a so'ar day, a mean-solar day. Which of the three is the shorter? Why is a sidereal day shorter than a mean solar day? What is *local* time? What measures the difference of longitude between two places on the Earth? Describe how to determine the difference of longitude between Boston and San Francisco by the transportation of chronometers—by the comparison of clocks by telegraph. How does a sailor determine his longitude from Greenwich at sea? Give an account of standard time as employed in the United States. Into how many sections is the country divided? Name the four kinds of time employed. Four watches keeping the

standard time of San Francisco, Denver, St. Louis, and Philadelphia are laid side by side :—How will their standard times differ?
How will their minutes and seconds compare with Greenwich time?
What time is used by most ships? *Change of the Day.* When is it
noon to any observer? If the observer is E. of Greenwich does his
noon occur earlier or later than the noon of Greenwich? Explain
why it is that an observer travelling completely round the Earth to
the eastwards—towards sunrise—gains a day ; and why an observer
travelling completely round the Earth westwards away from sunrise
loses a day.

17. Methods of Determining the Latitude of a
Place on the Earth. **Latitude from Circumpolar
Stars.**—In the figure suppose Z to be the zenith of the
observer, $HZRN$ his meridian, P the north pole, HR his
horizon. Suppose S and S' to be the two points where
a circumpolar star crosses the meridian, as it moves around

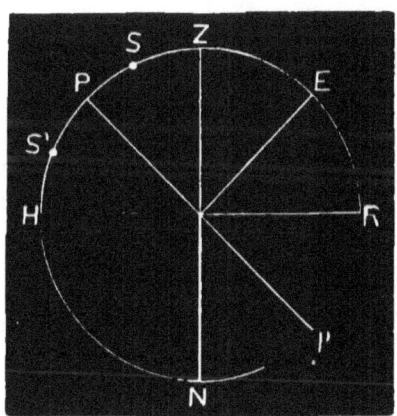

Fig. 54.

The latitude of a place on the earth can be determined by measuring
the zenith distances of a circumpolar star at its two culminations.

the pole in its apparent diurnal orbit. $PS = PS'$ in the
star's north-polar-distance, and $PH = \phi =$ the latitude
of the observer.

$$\frac{ZS + ZS'}{2} = ZP = 90° - \phi.$$

Therefore $\phi = 90° - \left\{ \dfrac{ZS + ZS'}{2} \right\}.$

ZS and ZS' can be measured by the sextant or by the meridian-circle, as will be explained in the next chapter. Granted that these arcs can be measured, it is plain that the latitude of a place is known as soon as they are known.

Latitude by the Meridian Altitude of the Sun or of a Star.—In the figure Z is the observer's zenith, P the pole,

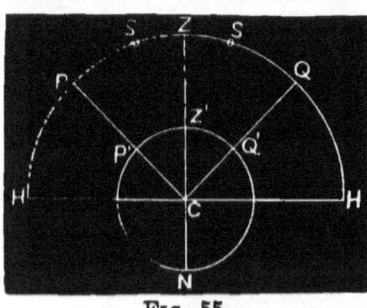

Fig. 55.

The latitude of a place on the earth (of a ship at sea) can be determined by measuring the meridian altitude of the sun (or of a star).

HH the horizon, PZH the observer's meridian, Q a point of the celestial equator. The star S is on the meridian (and just at its *greatest* altitude at that instant). Its altitude HS can be measured by one of the instruments described in the next chapter. ZS is therefore known, for $ZS = 90°$ $- HS$. QS is the declination of the Sun (or of a star), and QS is given in the Nautical Almanac.

$ZS + QS = QZ =$ the declination of the observer's zenith, or

$\zeta + \delta = \phi =$ the latitude of the observer.

If the star (or Sun) S' culminates north of the zenith at S'

$$QS' - ZS' = QZ,$$

or

$$\delta - \zeta = \phi.$$

This is the method uniformly used at sea, where the

meridian altitude of the Sun is measured every day with the sextant. The meridian altitudes of stars are often measured at sea, by night, to determine the latitude.

—Explain how to determine the latitude of a place on the Earth by measuring the zenith distances of a circumpolar star at its upper and at its lower culmination. Draw a diagram to illustrate the method. Explain how to determine the latitude of a place on the Earth by measuring the meridian altitude of the Sun.

18. Parallaxes of the Heavenly Bodies.—The apparent position of a body (a planet, for instance) on the celestial sphere remains the same as long as the observer is fixed. If the observer changes his place and the planet remains in the same position, the apparent position of the planet will change. The change in the apparent position of a planet due to a change in the position of the observer is called the

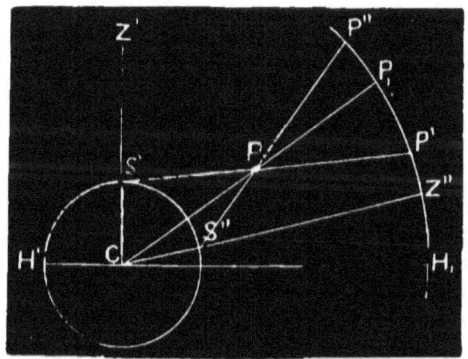

FIG. 56.—PARALLAX.

Change in the apparent position of a star due to a change in the place of the observer.

parallax of the planet. To show how this is let *CH′* be the Earth, *C* being its centre. *S′* and *S″* are the places of two observers on the surface. *Z′* and *Z″* are their zeniths in the celestial sphere *H, P″*. *P* is a planet. (*P* is drawn near to the Earth to save space in the figure. If it were drawn at its proper proportional distance for the

Moon, which is the nearest celestial body to the Earth (240,000 miles distant), the drawing would show P more than two feet distant from C.)

S' will see P in the apparent position P'. S'' will see P in the apparent position P''. That is, two different observers will see the same object in two different apparent positions. If the observer S' moves along the surface directly to S'', the apparent position of P on the celestial sphere will appear to move from P' to P''. This change is due to the *parallax* of P.

If the observers S' and S'' could go to the centre of the Earth (C) they would both see the planet P in the position P_1.

Astronomical observations made by observers at points on the Earth's surface (as at Greenwich and Washington) are corrected, therefore, by calculation, so as to reduce them to what they would have been had the observers been situated at the centre of the Earth, from which point the planet would be seen always in one position on the celestial sphere.

The student can try an experiment in the classroom that will illustrate what parallax is (See Fig. 57). Let him set up a pointer somewhere in the middle of the room and look at it from a point near the south-west corner of the room I. The line joining his eye and the pointer will meet the opposite wall in a point 1. One of his classmates under his direction should mark the point 1. Now let the observer go to another station, II. He will see the pointer projected against the opposite wall at 2, and this point should be marked also. If he goes to III the pointer will be seen projected at 3, and so on. The change in the *apparent* position of the pointer on the opposite wall due to the change in the observer's place is the *parallax* of the pointer. The *real* position of the pointer has not changed at all.

While the observer has moved from 1 to III the apparent position of the pointer has moved from 1 to 3. Any one who is making a railway journey can find many examples of parallactic changes of apparent position by fixing his eye on points in the landscape. They will appear to move relatively to each other as the observer moves.

In Fig. 58 suppose that C represents the Sun, around which the Earth S' moves in the nearly circular orbit S' S'' H'. $S'C$ is no longer 4000 miles as in the last example, but it is 93,000,000 miles. Suppose P to be a star. When the Earth is in the position S' the

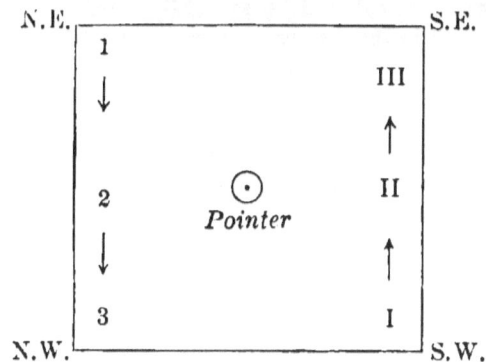

FIG. 57.

To illustrate the parallax of a body.

star will be projected on the celestial sphere at P'; when the Earth has moved to S'', the star will be projected on the celestial sphere at P''. While the Earth is moving from S' to S'' the star P will appear to move from P' to P''. It will not really move in space at all, but

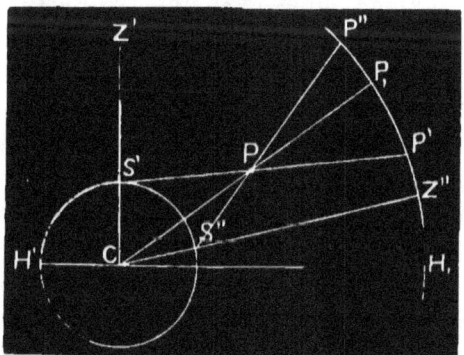

FIG. 58.—THE ANNUAL PARALLAX OF A STAR.

its apparent position on the celestial sphere will appear to move because the observer moves. If the observer were at the Sun (C) instead of on the Earth (at S') he would see the star at P_1; if the observer S'' were at the Sun (C) he, also, would see the star at P_1.

Observations made at different points of the Earth's orbit (at different times of the year, that is) are reduced, by calculation, to what they would have been if the observer had made them from the Sun instead of from the Earth.

One important point should be especially noted here. If the distance of P from C, in the last figure, *increases* the changes in its positions P', P'' due to changes in the position of the observer (S', S'' etc.) will be *less* and *less*. The student can prove this by drawing the figure three times, making the small circle and the points S', S'' the same in each figure. In the first drawing let him make $CP = 1$ inch, in the second make $CP = 2$ inches, in the third make $CP = 3$ inches. The greater the distance of a body from the observer, the less the change in the body's apparent position due to a given change in the observer's place.

The Moon is 240,000 miles away from the Earth. An observer at Greenwich will see the Moon projected on the celestial sphere in a place quite different from the Moon's place as seen from the Cape of Good Hope. *Jupiter* is over 400,000,000 miles away from the Earth. Observers at Greenwich and at the Cape of Good Hope will see it at different apparent positions on the celestial sphere, but these positions will not be very far apart. *Sirius* is over 200,000,000,000,000 miles away from the Earth. Observers at Greenwich and at the Cape of Good Hope will see it in the same position. That is, we have no telescopes that will measure its exceedingly small change of place. An observer at Greenwich looking at *Sirius* in January will see it in a position on the celestial sphere only a very little different from the place in which the same observer will see it in July. Yet the observer has travelled half round the Earth's orbit meanwhile, and his place in July is about 186,000,000 miles distant from his place in January. (The distance from the Earth to the Sun is about 93,000,000, and twice that is 186,000,000.) It is clear that if we can *measure* the amount of displacement of the Moon, of *Jupiter*, of *Sirius*, due to a known change in the observer's place, there must be a way to calculate how far off these bodies are to suffer the observed changes in their apparent positions.

— What is the parallax of a star (or of the Sun, or of a planet)? To what point of the Earth are observations made on its surface reduced? Why are they so reduced? Describe a simple experiment to illustrate parallactic changes. Is there a change in the apparent position of stars due to the revolution of the Earth round its orbit? Draw a figure to illustrate this. To what point within the Earth's orbit are observations reduced to avoid such parallactic changes? Prove by three drawings that the further a star is from the observer the less are its parallactic changes due to a given change in the observer's place.

CHAPTER VII.

ASTRONOMICAL INSTRUMENTS.

19. Astronomical Instruments — Telescopes.—Celestial Photography—The Nautical Almanac.—The instruments of astronomy are *telescopes* that enable us to see faint stars which otherwise we should not see at all; or *telescopes and circles combined*, that enable us to measure angles; or *timepieces* (chronometers and clocks) that enable us to measure intervals of time with exactness; *spectroscopes*, that enable us to analyze the light from a heavenly body and to say what chemical substances it is made of, etc. All these instruments have been gradually perfected until most of them are now extremely accurate, but many of them had very humble beginnings.

Clocks.—The first timepieces were sun-dials,* water-clocks, etc. The ancients noticed that the shadow of an obelisk moved during the day. When the Sun was rising in the east the shadow of an obelisk lay opposite to the Sun towards the west. As the Sun rose higher in the sky and moved towards the meridian the shadow moved towards the north and grew shorter. When the Sun was exactly south of the obelisk (on the meridian due south of the observer and at its greatest altitude) the shadow lay exactly to the north and it was the shortest. As the Sun drew towards the west the shadow moved towards the east and

* We know that a Sun-dial was set up in Rome B.C. 263. PLAUTUS speaks of a slave who complained of Sun-dials and the new-fangled hours. In old time, he says, he used to eat when he was hungry ; now the time when he gets his meals depends on the Sun !

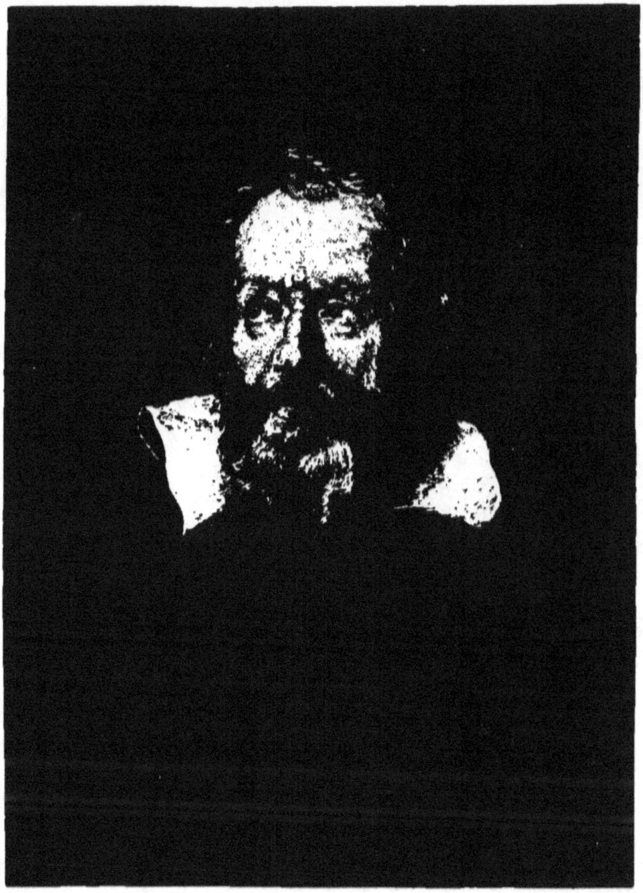

FIG. 59.—GALILEO.
Born 1564; died 1642.

grew longer; and as the Sun was setting in the west the shadow pointed towards the east. A circle was traced on the ground round the obelisk and the north point of the circle was marked. When the shadow fell at this point the Sun was due south at noon and the day was half over. This was the first timepiece. By dividing the circle into smaller parts the day was likewise divided into parts. Some of the churches in Italy have sun-dials laid out on their floors so that a spot of sunlight admitted through the south wall traverses an arc divided into hours and minutes.

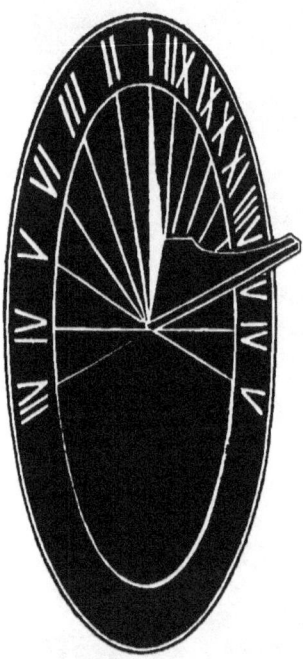

Fig. 60.—A Sun dial.

The student should set up a vertical pole and trace a circle around it and divide the circle into parts, using his watch to get the hour marks. The circular dial of Fig. 60 is horizontal and XII is towards the north.

It was not easy, in ancient times, to mark the places on the dial that corresponded to the hours and to the smaller divisions of time. These were often counted by water-clocks or sand-clocks, in which water or sand poured from a box through a hole in the bottom. The lowering of the upper surface of the water or sand marked the passage of time. The common hour-glass is a sand-clock. Candles were marked by lines at equal intervals and equal intervals of time were counted by the burning of equal lengths of wax. The student can construct timepieces in this way and he can test their accuracy by a watch or clock.

Galileo noticed about the year 1600 that a given pendulum always made its swings in equal times no matter whether it swung through large arcs or small ones. A long pendulum swung slowly; a short pendulum swung faster; but each pendulum had its own time of swinging and it always swung in that time. A pendulum about $39\frac{1}{10}$ inches long made a swing in one second (from its lowest point to its lowest point again in one second). It made 86,400 vibrations in a mean solar day.* Intervals of time could now be accurately divided.

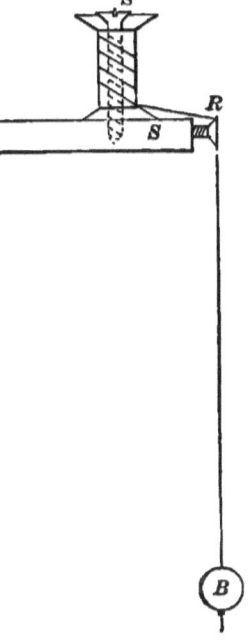

The student should make a pendulum for himself. A very good method is described in Allen's Laboratory Physics as follows:

Near *S*, which may be the edge of a table or shelf, is screwed a spool *S'*. The screw is "set up" until the spool turns with considerable friction. A string is wound around the spool and is held in place by passing through the slot of another screw, *R*, inserted horizontally in the edge of the support. The lower end of the string passes through a hole in a ball *B*, which forms the pendulum-bob. The length of the pendulum may be varied by turning the spool so as to wind or unwind the string. Small adjustments are best made by gently turning the spool.

FIG. 61.—A HOME-MADE PENDULUM WHOSE LENGTH CAN BE READILY VARIED.

Many improvements have been made in pendulum-clocks since they were first invented by HUYGHENS (pronounced hī'genz) in 1657, and they are now extraordinarily accurate. Chronometers are merely very perfect watches. Their motive force is a coiled spring, and they can be transported by sea or land while they are running, which is not true of clocks, of course.

* $60 \times 60 \times 24 = 86,400.$

Circles.—Angles can be measured by circles divided to degrees, etc.   If the arc $S'S'$ is so divided and if it has a radial bar ES' that can be moved around a pin at the centre of the circle at E, the angle between any two stars can be measured in the following way:

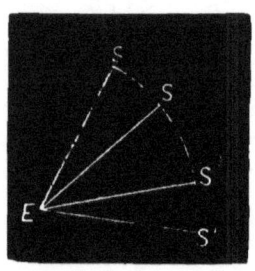

1st. Place the circle so that its plane passes through the two stars S' and S' when the eye is at E.

2d. Point the bar at S' and read the divisions on the circle— as 10° 5', for example.   The eye will still be at E, of course.

3d. Point the bar at S' and read the circle—as 22° 11'.

FIG. 62. — MEASUREMENT OF ANGLES BY A CIRCLE (OR BY A PART OF A CIRCLE).

The angle between the two stars $S'ES'$ is 12° 6', the difference of the two readings.   In the figure the angle $S'ES'$ is about 12°; $S'ES'$ is about 22°; $S'ES'$ is about 30°; $S'ES'$ is about 64°.

Before the telescope was invented the bar ES' was provided with sights like the sights on a rifle.   One sight was at E (the place of the eye), the other at the further end of the bar.   The unavoidable error of directing such a bar to a star is about 1' of arc, so that the positions of stars before the telescope was invented were liable to errors of 1' or so. The eye cannot detect a change of direction less than about one minute of arc.   The bar and its sights are nowadays replaced by a telescope, and the positions of stars determined by such a combination of a circle and a telescope are affected by errors of less than 1''.   The precision is more than 60 times greater.

The student will do well to make a half-circle in the following way: Cut a half-circle 8¼ inches in diameter out of a piece of thick hard pasteboard, leaving a knob or projection about 1 inch square at *C*. Through this knob bore a hole with an awl at the exact centre of the circle. Order from Keuffel & Esser, opticians, No. 127 Fulton street, New York city, a paper circle, 8 inches in diameter, divided to 30'. It is No. 1296 of their catalogue. It can be sent by mail and will cost 20 cents. Cut the paper-circle in two along a diameter and fasten it to the pasteboard, making the centre of the paper-circle coincide with the centre of the pasteboard circle. Make a narrow flat light wooden arm for the index-arm, like Fig. 64: *A* is the centre of the

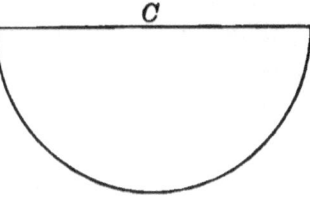

FIG. 63.—A HALF CIRCLE.

circle. The arm must revolve about a pin (or a rivet) at *A*. *B* and *C* are the sights. Two common pins will do. *D* is an index mark, or pointer, drawn on the arm. All angles are read from this mark. *a, b, c, d,* are four divisions of the paper circle. If $a = 17°$, $b = 18°$, $c = 19°$, $d = 20°$, then the reading of the pointer is 18¼ degrees. In using the circle the eye must be at *A*; the observer looks along the

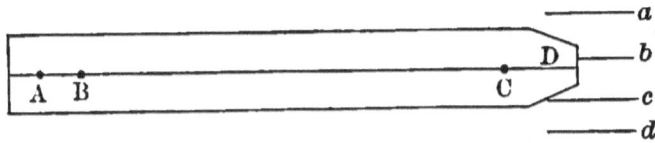

FIG. 64.—INDEX ARM FOR A DIVIDED CIRCLE.

sights *BC* and moves the arm till the sights and the star are in the same line. To measure the angle between two stars the plane of the circle must be put in the plane of the eye and of the two stars and *kept there.* To measure the altitude of the celestial pole (the latitude of the observer) the plane of the circle must be vertical. Two readings must be made: 1st, when the index arm is horizontal (a level will show this) and 2d, when the arm points to Polaris. A light plumb line suspended from the centre of the circle will mark the vertical direction, so that zenith distances can be measured.

Invention of the Telescope.—The first telescope used in astronomy was invented by GALILEO in 1609.* It was like a long single-barreled opera-glass. The best of GALILEO'S telescopes magnified only about 30 times; but this was

* Eleven years before the Pilgrims landed at Plymouth. Probably no one of them had even heard of this invention.

enough to explain many things that had been mysteries for two thousand years. The Moon's face was very well shown in GALILEO's instruments and the mountains of the Moon were then discovered. The Milky Way was shown to consist of closely crowded stars. If the student will look at the Moon's face and at the Milky Way with a common opera-glass (which magnifies about 3 times) he will see far more than with the eye. The true shapes of the planets *Venus* and *Mercury* were made out for the first time. It was seen that they had *phases* like the Moon (they were sometimes crescent, sometimes full, etc.), and this discovery, more than any other, helped to overthrow the theory of PTOLEMY that the Earth was the centre of the universe, and to establish the theory of COPERNICUS, that the centre of our system was the Sun, not the Earth.

GALILEO discovered four satellites of *Jupiter* also and showed, in this way, that "the seven planets" (Sun, Moon, *Mercury*, *Venus*, *Mars*, *Jupiter*, *Saturn*) were seven in number, not because of some mystic law, but simply because the other bodies of the system happened to be too faint to be seen with the unassisted eye.

FIG. 65.—A DOUBLE - CONVEX LENS OF GLASS.

Seven had been a mystical number since the times of PYTHAGORAS. There were seven planets, seven days of the week, seven wise men of Greece, seven cardinal virtues, seven deadly sins, seven notes of music in the octave, etc. Men regarded this number as if it were sacred in itself; and they were not willing to believe their own eyes when more than seven heavenly bodies were shown to them. The greatest value of GALILEO's discovery was precisely its demonstration that men *must* accept a scientific fact when it is proved; and that Nature was governed by laws of a different kind from the fanciful analogies of the imagination. From the time of GALILEO men began to think about Nature in a new way and the discoveries of his telescope are, for that reason, the most important scientific discoveries ever made.

Construction of the Telescope.—Long before the time of GALILEO glass lenses had been used for spectacles. The Emperor Nero (died A.D. 68) is said to have employed such a lens. It was found that a double-convex lens made out of glass not only collected light, but that if it was held in a proper position it magnified the object looked at. The ordinary hand reading-glass is a familiar example of this fact.

Figure 66 shows the way in which the reading-glass

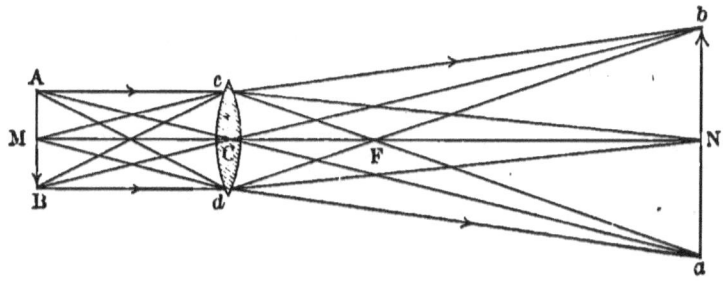

FIG. 66.
The reading-glass *C* magnifies an object *AB* to the size *ab*.

magnifies. *AMB* is an object viewed by a reading-glass *C*. From every point of the object *AB* rays of light issue, and they go in *every* direction. (The proof of this fact is that no matter where you stand you can still see *AB*; and if you see it there must be rays that come from *AB* and reach your eye.) The bundle of rays that comes from the point *A* and falls on the reading-glass *C* is *cAd*. No other rays from *A* fall on the glass. These pass through the glass and come to a *focus* at *a*; *a* is the *image* of the point *A* of the object. The point *B* of the object is sending out rays in every direction. Some of them fall on the glass—

namely the bundle *cBd*. This bundle of rays passes
through the glass and comes to a *focus* at *b*; *b* is the
image of the point *B* of the object. The point *M* of the
object is giving out rays in every direction. Only those
that fall on the glass can pass through it—namely the
bundle of rays *cMd*. This bundle of rays passes through
the glass and comes to a *focus* at *N*. *N* is the *image* of
the point *M* of the object. *Every* point of the object sends
out rays, and bundles of rays from every such point pass
through the glass and each such bundle comes to a *focus*
somewhere on the line *ab* and forms an *image* of the corresponding point of the object. All these separate images,
taken together, make one image, a picture, of the object.
ab is the image, the picture, of *AB*.

Now suppose that with a second hand-glass you should
look at the image *ab* just as you looked at the object *AB*
with the first hand-glass. If the second glass is held in a
proper position you can magnify the image *ab* just as the
object *AB* was originally magnified. *A combination of
the two or more lenses to make a magnified image is a telescope.* GALILEO's invention was the use of two lenses in
combination.

All *refracting telescopes* (telescopes in which rays of light
from the object are bent—refracted—by the telescope so as
to form an image) consist essentially of two lenses. The
first lens (that one nearest the star) is made as large as possible so as to collect as much light as possible. All the
bundles of rays that fall upon it are bent—refracted—by
this lens and brought to a *focus;* and together they make
an image—a picture—of the object. This first lens is
called *the object-lens* (or the object-glass). Its sole use is
to collect as many rays from the object as possible and to
form them into an image—a picture—at the focus. If
you should hold a piece of ground-glass at the focus of a
telescope you would see a small picture on the glass—a pic-

ture of the Sun, of the Moon, of a star, according as the telescope was pointed to the Sun, the Moon, or a star. If you should put a photographic plate at the focus you could make a photographic negative of the Sun, the Moon, a star.

The second lens (it is called the eyepiece) is used to magnify the image formed by the object-lens. Every telescope is provided with several eyepieces. Some of these magnify more than others. If a powerful eyepiece is used the telescope may magnify 1000 times. If one of the less powerful is employed it may magnify 100 times. You can change the magnifying power of a telescope by changing the eyepiece, therefore; and there is not much point to the common question: "How much does this telescope magnify?" The answer is "it depends upon what eyepiece you are using." The tube of a telescope is chiefly for the purpose of keeping the object-glass and the eyepiece at the right distance apart.

It is found that single lenses of glass give imperfect images of objects. The images from single lenses are somewhat distorted and they are bordered with fringes of color. A few experiments with a common reading-glass will prove this. Much of the imperfection can be avoided by making the object-glasses of telescopes out of two lenses of different kinds of glass close together, as in Fig. 67. The light from the star first falls on a lens of crown-glass and after passing through

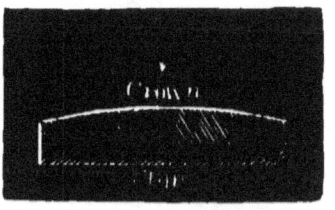

FIG. 67.—THE ACHROMATIC OBJECT-GLASS.

it falls on a lens of flint-glass. The two lenses act like a common convex lens in bringing the rays to a focus to form an achromatic or colorless image. The image from such an object-glass is much more perfect than that formed by a single lens. Eyepieces, also, are made of two or more

lenses. The telescopes now in use are practically as perfect as they can be made from the glass we now have.

Light-gathering Power of a Telescope.—It is not merely
by magnifying that the telescope assists vision, but also by
increasing the quantity of light received from any object—
from a star, for example. When the unaided eye looks at
any object, the retina can only receive so many rays as
fall upon the pupil of the eye. The eye is itself a little
telescopic lens whose image is received on the sensitive retina. By the use of the telescope it is evident that as many
rays can be brought to the retina as fall on the entire object-glass. The pupil of the human eye has a diameter of
about one fifth of an inch, and by the use of the telescope
it is virtually increased *in surface* in the ratio of the square
of the diameter of the objective to the square of one fifth
of an inch; that is, in the ratio of the *surface* of the objective to the *surface* of the pupil of the eye. Thus, with
a two-inch aperture to our telescope, the number of rays
collected is one hundred times as great as the number collected with the naked eye, because

$$(.2)^2 : (2)^2 = .04 : 4.0$$
$$= 1 : 100.$$

With a 5-inch object-glass the ratio is					625 to 1
" 10 "	"	"	"		2,500 to 1
" 15 "	"	"	"		5,625 to 1
" 20 "	"	"	"		10,000 to 1
" 26 "	"	"	"		16,900 to 1
" 36 "	"	"	"		32,400 to 1

When a minute object, like a small star, is viewed, it is
necessary that a certain number of rays should fall on the
retina in order that the star may be visible at all. It is
therefore plain that the use of the telescope enables an observer to see much fainter stars than he could detect with
the naked eye, and also to see faint objects much better

than by unaided vision alone. Thus, with a 36-inch telescope we may see stars so minute that it would require the
collective light of many thousands to be visible to the unaided eye.

Reflecting Telescopes.—One of the essential parts of a refracting
telescope is the object-glass, which brings all the incident rays from
an object to one focus, forming there an image of that object. In
reflecting telescopes (reflectors) the objective is a mirror of speculum
metal or silvered glass ground to the shape of a paraboloid. Fig.
63 shows the action of such a mirror on a bundle of parallel rays,

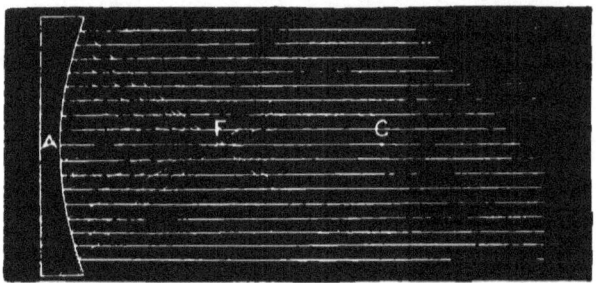

FIG. 68.—THEORY OF THE REFLECTING TELESCOPE.

which, after impinging on it, are brought by reflection to one focus
F. The image formed at this focus can be viewed with an eyepiece,
as in the case of the refracting telescope.

The eyepieces used with such a mirror are of the kind already described. In the figure the eyepiece would have to be placed to the
right of the point *F*, and the observer's head would thus interfere
with the incident light. Various devices have been proposed to rem-
edy this inconvenience, of which the most simple is to interpose a
small plane mirror, which is inclined 45° to the line *AC*, just to the
left of *F*. This mirror will reflect the rays which are moving towards
the focus *F* (downwards on the page) to another focus outside of the
main beam of rays. At this second focus the eyepiece is placed and
the observer looks into it in a direction perpendicular to *AC* (upwards on the page). See Fig. 69.

— Name some of the instruments used in astronomy. *Sun-dial.*
Describe the motion of the shadow of an obelisk from sunrise to noon,
from noon to sunset. At what time in the day is the shadow of the
obelisk the shortest? Prove it by a drawing. At what instant of

the day does its shadow point due north? Say how you could make
a sun-dial with a pole and a common watch. *Water-clocks.* Tell
what they were. *Pendulums.* How can you make a pendulum that
swings in a second of time? *Divided circles.* Say how you could make
one. Describe how to use it in measuring the angle between two stars
(the vertex of the angle is at the eye). *Telescopes.* When did GALILEO
construct his first telescope? Draw a diagram to show how a common reading-glass forms an *image* of an *object* at a *focus.* Define a

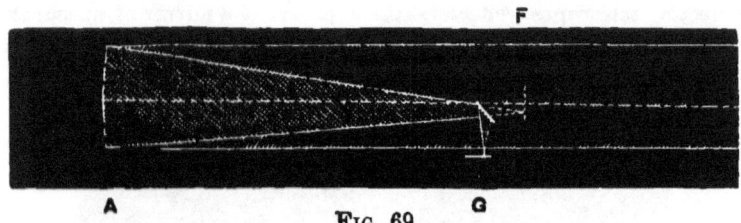

Fig. 69.

This figure shows the way in which the rays of light move in a reflecting
telescope. They come from a star as a beam of light and cover the whole
of the curved mirror at the bottom of the tube (*A*). This mirror reflects
them towards a focus (like *F* in the preceding figure). Before the rays
reach the focus, they fall on a small flat mirror which turns them at right
angles to their former direction and they come to a new focus (*G*) outside
of the telescope-tube. Here the eyepiece is placed.

telescope. Exactly what was Galileo's invention? What is a *refracting telescope?* What is an *object-glass?* an *eye-piece?* What is
the sole purpose of the object-glass? Why then is it an advantage
to make it as large as may be? What is the sole purpose of the eyepiece? What is the answer to the question "How much does this
telescope magnify?" Draw a diagram of a *reflecting-telescope.*

20. The Transit Instrument.—The *Transit Instrument*
is used to observe the transits of stars over the celestial
meridian. The times of these transits are noted by the
sidereal clock, which is an indispensable adjunct of the
transit instrument. It stands near it so that the dial of
the clock can be seen and so that the beats of the pendulum can be heard every second. A skilled observer can
estimate the time to the nearest tenth of a second. The
first transit-instrument was invented in the XVII century.

The transit instrument consists essentially of a telescope *TT* fastened to an axis *VV* at right angles to it. The ends of this axis ter-

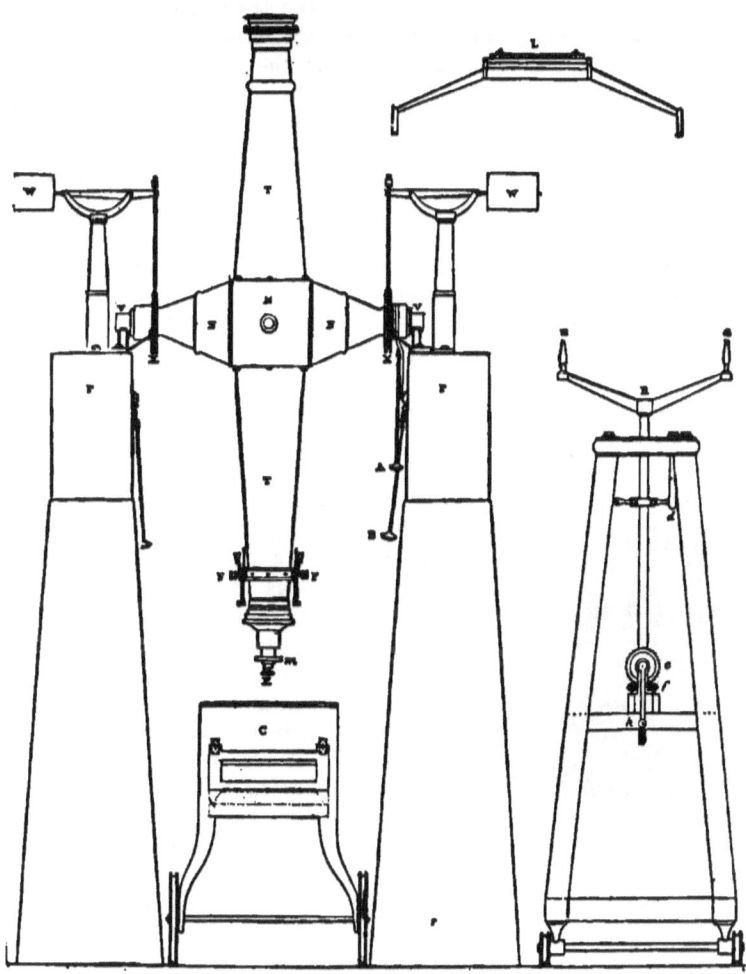

FIG. 70.—A TRANSIT-INSTRUMENT.

minate in accurately cylindrical pivots which rest in metallic bearings
VV which are shaped like the letter Y, and hence called the Ys.
The object-glass of the telescope is at the upper end of the tube in
the drawing. The eyepiece is at *E.* The telescope can be moved
so as to point to any point in the celestial meridian—to the zenith,
the south point of the horizon, the nadir, the north point, the celestial pole.

The Ys are fastened to two pillars of stone, brick, or iron. Two
counterpoises *WW* are connected with the axis as in the plate, so as
to take a large portion of the weight of the axis and telescope from
the Ys, and thus to diminish the friction upon them and to render
the rotation about *VV* more easy and regular. The line *VV* is
placed accurately level; and also perpendicular to the meridian, or in
the east and west line. The plate gives the form of transit used in
permanent observatories, and shows the observing chair *C,* the re-
versing carriage *R,* and the level *L.* The arms of the latter have
Ys, which can be placed over the pivots *VV.*

The *reticle* is a network of fine spider-lines placed in the focus of
the objective.

In Fig. 71 the circle represents the field of view of a transit as seen
through the eyepiece. The seven vertical lines, I, II, III, IV, V,

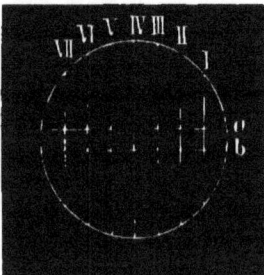

FIG. 71.—SPIDER-LINES
IN THE FOCUS OF A
TELESCOPE.

VI, VII, are seven fine spider-lines tightly
stretched across a hole in a metal plate,
and so adjusted as to be perpendicular to
the direction of a star's apparent diurnal
motion. The horizontal wires, *guide-wires,*
a and *b,* mark the centre of the field. A
star will move across the field of view
parallel to the lines *ab* and will cross the
lines I to VII in succession. The field of
view is illuminated at night by a lamp
which causes the field to appear bright.
The wires are dark against a bright ground.
The *line of sight* is a line joining the centre
of the object-glass and the central one, IV, of the seven vertical
wires.

The axis *VV* is horizontal; it lies east and west. When
TT is rotated about *VV* the line of sight marks out the
celestial meridian of the place on the sphere.

How the Transit-instrument is Used in Observation.—It is pointed
at the place where a star is about to cross the meridian in its course

from rising to setting. As soon as the star enters the field the telescope is slightly moved so that the star will cross between the lines *a* and *b*. As the star crosses each spider-line, I to VII, the exact time of its transit over each line is noted. The average of these seven times gives the time the star crossed the middle line IV. (Seven observations are better than one, and this is why seven lines are used.) Let us call this time *T*. It will be a number giving hours, minutes, seconds and fractions of seconds, as 10^h 25^m $37^s.22$ for example. *T* is then the time *by the sidereal clock* when the star was on the meridian. When a star is on the celestial meridian of a place the sidereal time is equal to the right-ascension of the star. (See page 88.) Suppose the right-ascension of the star that we have observed to be known and to be R. A. $= 10^h$ 25^m $36^s.18$. This number is the sidereal time at the instant of the transit of the star. But the clock time was 10^h 25^m $37^s.22$. Hence the clock is too fast by $1^s.04$.

By observing the time (T) when a star of *known* right-ascension (R.A.) crosses the meridian we can determine the correction of the clock. The clock *should* mark a sidereal time equal to R.A. It *does* mark a time T. Hence its correction is R.A. $- T$, because,

$$T + (\text{R.A.} - T) = \text{R.A.} = \text{the sidereal time.}$$

In this way we can set and regulate the sidereal clock, so that its dial marks the exact sidereal time at any and every instant. (In practice we do not move the hands but allow for its errors.) Table V, at the end of the book, gives a list of the R.A. of a number of stars.

Now suppose the sidereal clock to be correct and the times of transit T^1, T^2, T^3, etc., of stars of *unknown* right-ascension to be recorded.

Then $T^1 =$ the R.A. of the first star,
$T^2 =$ " " " " second star,
$T^3 =$ " " " " third star, and so on.

The right-ascension of any and every unknown star can be determined as soon as we have the clock correction. It

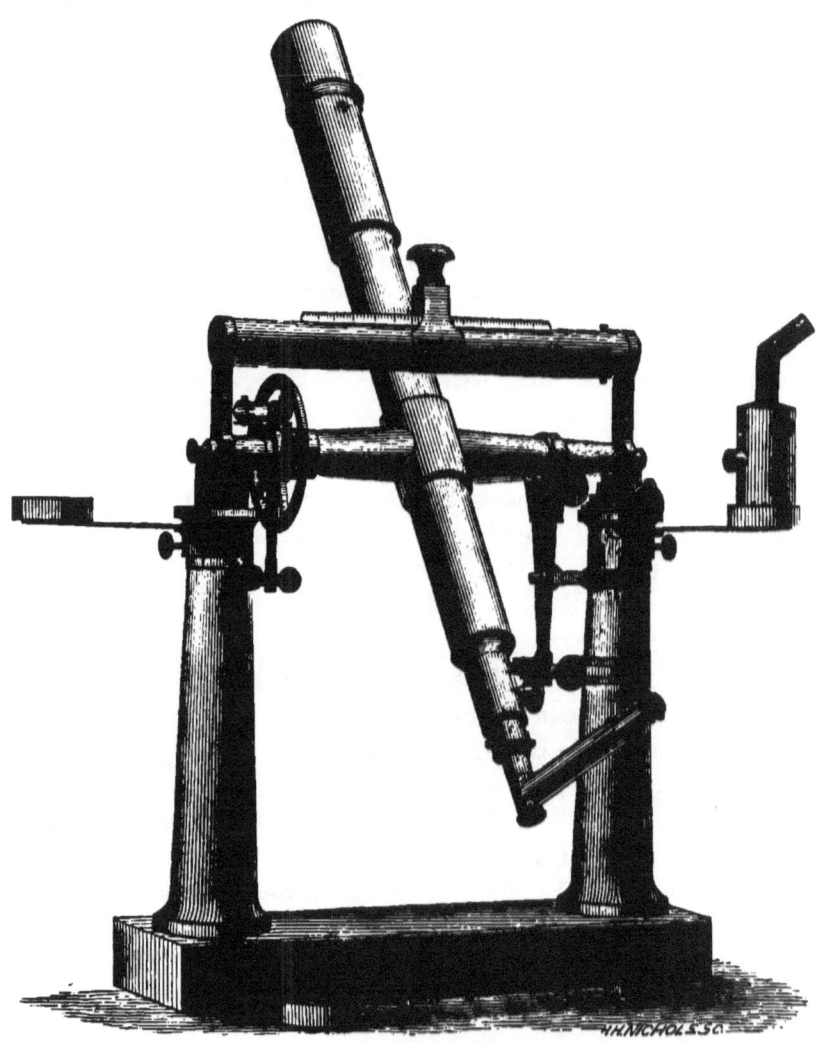

FIG. 72.—A SMALL TRANSIT-INSTRUMENT.
The length of the telescope of this instrument is about two feet.

is in this way that the transit instrument is employed to
determine the right ascensions of unknown stars.

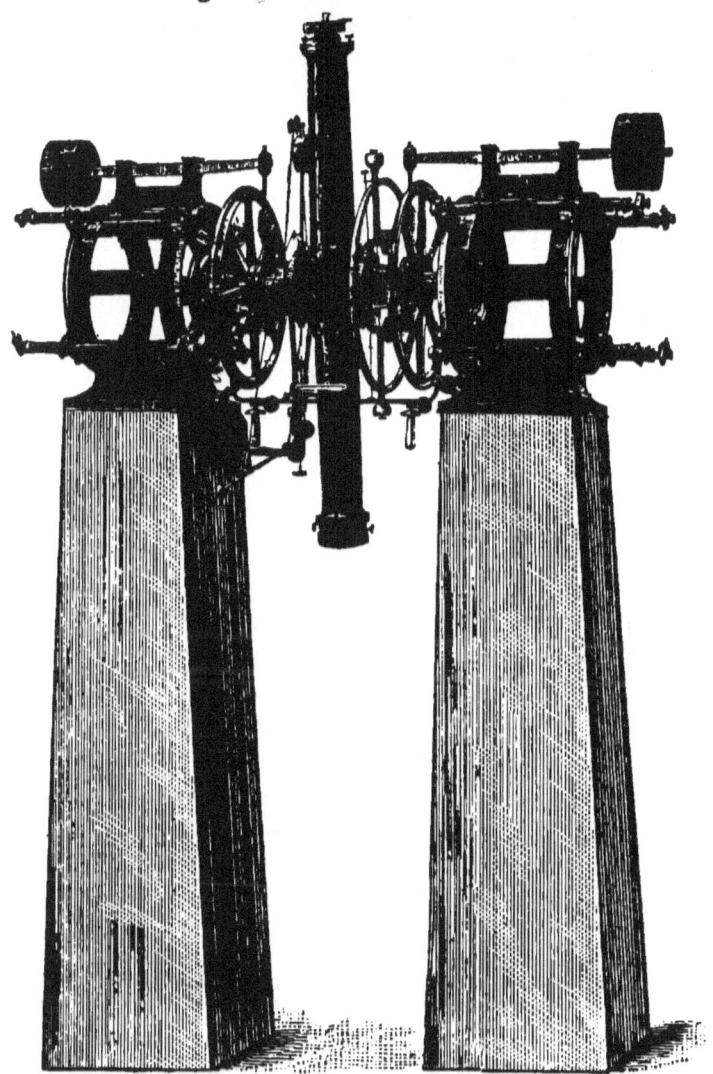

FIG. 73.—A MERIDIAN-CIRCLE.

The Meridian-circle.—The meridian-circle (or transit-
circle) is a combination of the transit-instrument with a

circle (or two circles) fastened to its axis. With the transit-instrument we can determine the right-ascensions of stars; with the circle we can measure their declinations.

The picture shows a meridian-circle. Its telescope is pointed downwards and the eyepiece is at its upper end. The instrument differs from the transit in having two finely divided circles. Each of these circles is read by four long horizontal microscopes. The *axis* of the instrument is made level by a hanging-level which is shown in the cut. The level is, of course, removed when observations of stars are made. Meridian-circles were first made in the XIX century.

Such an instrument can be used as a transit-instrument precisely as has been described. Its circle can be used to determine the declinations of stars.

The telescope is moved (so as to trace out the meridian) by turning the horizontal axis (*V V*, *NN*, in Fig. 70). As the axis turns the circles turn with it. The angle through which they turn can be determined by noticing how many degrees, minutes, and seconds, °, ', ", have turned past the microscopes. In the same room with the meridian-circle and a few feet south of it there is a small horizontal telescope. It has a level which rests on top of it, and it can be made exactly horizontal. If we point the telescope of the meridian-circle at the small horizontal telescope (see the diagram) the meridian-circle telescope will be horizon-

Observer's ⎰ Telescope of the meridian- ⟫⟶   ⟵⟪ Horizontal telescope
eye.   ⎱ circle pointing south.   pointing north.

FIG. 74.—To DETERMINE THE READING OF A MERIDIAN-CIRCLE WHEN IT IS POINTED HORIZONTALLY.

tal when it sees directly down the tube of the horizontal telescope. The circle must now be read. Suppose its reading in °, ', " to be *H*. This reading *H* is called the horizontal point. In practice it is more usual to determine the nadir point instead of the horizontal point *H*, but it is a little simpler for the student to consider the horizontal point as the starting-point.

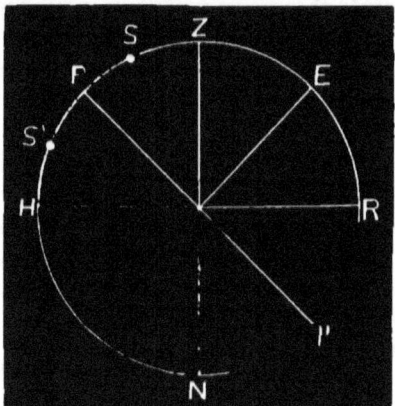

FIG. 75.—THEORY OF THE MERIDIAN-CIRCLE.

In the figure *HR* is the observer's horizon, *Z* his zenith, *PZR* his meridian, *P* the pole, *E* a point of the equator, *S* and *S'* the two points where a circumpolar star crosses his meridian.

When the telescope is pointed south, at *R*, and is horizontal, the circle-reading is *H*. Let us suppose *H* is equal to 180° 0' 0''. If the telescope is pointed to *Z* the reading will be 90° 0' 0'', because the zenith is 90° from the horizon. If the telescope is pointed to the point *H* (the north point of the horizon) the reading will be 0° 0' 0''. If it is pointed to *N* the reading will be 270° 0' 0''. We need to know the reading for the polar point *P*, and for the equator point *E*. The star *Polaris* is not *exactly* at the North Pole, though it is near it, and so we have no direct way of pointing at the pole. If we know the latitude of the observer measured by the arc *HP*, and it is ϕ, then the polar reading *P* will be ϕ; and the equator reading *E* will be 90° + ϕ (because the arc *PE* is 90°).

If we do *not* know the latitude ϕ we must point the telescope at a star *S* when it is crossing the meridian and determine its zenith distance *ZS*; and twelve hours later we must again point the telescope at the same star, when it is crossing the meridian again (at *S'*), and determine the zenith distance *ZS'*. Then (as has already been proved on page 106),

The latitude of the observer = $\phi = 90° - \left\{ \dfrac{ZS + ZS'}{2} \right\}$

Thus, whether the latitude of the observer is known or unknown, we can determine the reading of the circle when the telescope is pointed to any one of the points R, E, Z, P, H.

The latitude of the Lick Observatory is $37°$ $20'$ $24'' = \phi$. Its meridian-circle would then have the following readings:

For the	north-point	(H in the figure)	=	$0°$	$0'$	$0''$
"	solar-point	(P ")	=	$37°$	$20'$	$24''$
"	zenith-point	(Z ")	=	$90°$	$0'$	$0''$
"	equator-point	(E ")	=	$127°$	$20'$	$24''$
"	south-point	(R ")	=	$180°$	$0'$	$0''$
"	nadir-point	(N ")	=	$270°$	$0'$	$0''$

If the telescope was pointed to a star S as it crossed the meridian, and if the circle reading for S was $57°$ $40'$ $36''$, the north-polar distance of S would be $20°$ $20'$ $12''$, and its declination would be $69°$ $39'$ $48''$. Its zenith distance north would be $32°$ $19'$ $24''$.

Model of a Meridian circle.—The student will do well to make a simple model of a meridian-circle out of wood. Let him take a piece of wood (planed on all its sides) about a foot long and exactly square, and whittle the ends of it till they are nearly cylindrical. This will serve as the axis. Perpendicular to the axis at its middle point he should nail on a flat piece of wood, about two feet long, to stand for the telescope. One end of this last piece should be marked "object-glass" and the other end "eyepiece." One pasteboard circle 8 inches in diameter should be prepared and a paper circle divided to 30' (see page 117) should be neatly fastened to this. A square hole should be cut in the circle, exactly at its centre, and the circle fitted to the axis and fastened securely to it. Two wooden boxes at the right distance apart will serve for piers. On the top of the piers Ys, sawed out of wood, must be fastened to receive the pivots of the axis.

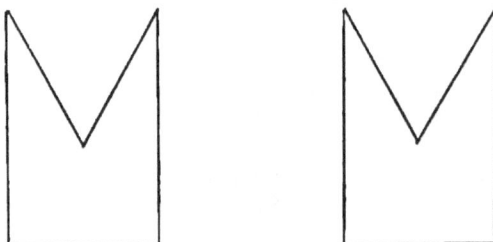

Fig. 76.—Ys of a Meridian-circle.

The line joining the *Ys* should be east and west. A pointer must be fastened to the pier, so that it will just touch the divisions of the circle as they are moved past it. It will be convenient to make this pointer of rather stiff copper wire bent to the proper shape and filed to a point at the index end. With a model of this sort the whole process of observing with the meridian-circle will be very clear.

The telescope of a transit-instrument or of a meridian-circle can only move in one plane, namely in the plane of the celestial meridian. As the axis is turned the telescope traces out the celestial meridian in the sky. Stars can only be seen with these instruments at the moments when they are crossing the meridian of the observer. For a couple of minutes at that time a star is seen moving across the field of view of the telescope. For the rest of the 24 hours (until the next transit) the star cannot be seen. This arrangement is convenient if the object is to determine the star's *position*—its right-ascension and its declination. It is very inconvenient if we desire to examine the star (or planet) carefully to determine whether it is a double star, whether it is surrounded by a nebula, whether its brightness is changing, and so on. Comets, for example, are very seldom seen far away from the Sun and therefore are seldom on the meridian during the dark hours. Hence they are not often observable by transit-instruments.

Equatorial Mountings for Telescopes.—For such careful examinations of the physical appearances of stars and comets we need to have the telescope mounted on a stand so contrived that we can keep the star in the field of view of the telescope for hours at a time. We wish to be able to point at a star when it is rising in the east and to follow it as long as it is above the horizon, if desirable. A mounting for a telescope that will permit it to be pointed to any star above the horizon is called an *equatorial mounting*. Before we describe the forms of such mountings that are actually in use let us see if we can make the principles on which they must be devised clear.

Suppose we had a very large globe like the one shown in Fig. 44 *bis.* Suppose the observer and the eye piece of the telescope were in the centre of such a globe and that the object-glass was set in a hole cut through the surface of the globe at some point (any point) of the equator. It is clear that the observer could see any star *in the equator* so long as it was above the horizon, because he would simply have to turn the globe (and the telescope with it) until it pointed to the star and then to move the globe slowly to the west so as to follow the star as it moved from rising towards setting. Such a mounting as this would do for a star in the equator and for no other star; but it would do for all stars in the equator.

If the object-glass were placed at some point (any point) in the parallel of 15° north declination, then all stars in *that* parallel could be viewed so long as they were above the horizon by rotating the globe, as before, about its axis that points to the north pole. The same thing would be true for stars on the other parallels of 30°, 45°, 60°. It is plain that the mounting we want must have a *polar axis* like that of the globe, so that when the telescope is once pointed at a star that star can be kept in view from its rising to its setting by simply rotating the polar axis. It is also plain that the desired mounting must be so contrived that the telescope can be set to any and every declination. Such a mounting would be used:

1st. By setting the telescope to the declination of the star we wished to examine:

2d. By following that star as long as we pleased by rotating the mounting about its *polar* axis.

If *OP* in Fig. 77 were the polar axis of the telescope and if the telescope were set on the stars *A, B, C, D,* in succession, these stars could be followed from rising to setting.

FIG. 78a. — THE 36-INCH REFRACTOR OF THE LICK OBS[ERVATORY]
UNIVERSITY OF CALIFORNIA.

The lines drawn in the different cones *A, B, C, D,* represent different positions of the telescope. The circles *A, B, C, D,* are different parallels of declination. Suppose then that (in the diagram Figure 78) *TT* is a telescope mounted on an axis *DL* so that *TT* can be revolved about the axis *DL* so as to point to any *declination ;* and further suppose that *DL* and *TT* together can be rotated about the axis *SN* which is pointed to the north pole of the heavens.

The large pictures (Figs. 78*a*, 80, 81) show a telescope mounted as in the diagram (Fig. 78). The telescope is parallel to the polar axis.

If we moved the upper end of the telescope *TT* towards the east to point at another star in another declination such a telescope would look as in Fig. 81. If we moved the upper end of the telescope *TT* towards the south to point at another star such a telescope would look as in Figure 78*a*, where the tube is pointing towards a star south of the zenith, but north of the equator and not very far from the meridian. In the figure (78*a*) the polar axis (on top of the pier) is pointing to the north pole of the heavens. The north end of the axis is the highest. The *declination axis* is fastened to the end of the polar axis, and the telescope is fastened to one end of the declination axis. By taking hold of the eye-end of the telescope it can be pointed to any desired declination whatever—it can be made to point south (horizontally), to the zenith (vertically), or to the pole (as in Fig. 80). After it is pointed to the desired *declination* the polar axis can be rotated in its bearings (about the line *NS* in figure 78) so that the telescope sees the desired *star.* The star can be followed from rising to setting by slowly rotating the telescope and declination axis (together) towards the west.

If we point such a telescope to a star when it is rising (doing this by rotating the telescope first about its declination axis and then about the polar axis), we can, by simply rotating the whole apparatus on the polar axis, cause the telescope to trace out on the celestial sphere the apparent diurnal path which this star will follow from rising to setting. In most telescopes of the sort a driving-clock is arranged to turn the telescope round the polar axis at the same rate at which the earth itself turns about its own axis of rotation—at the rate at which all stars move from rising to setting. Hence such a telescope once pointed at a star will continue to point at it so long as the driving-clock is in operation, thus enabling the astronomer to

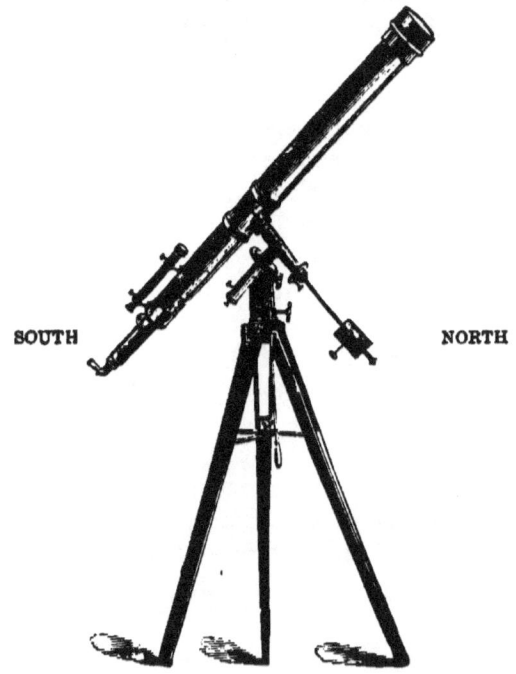

SOUTH   NORTH

FIG. 79.—A SMALL EQUATORIAL TELESCOPE MOUNTED ON A PORTABLE STAND.

make an examination or observation of it for as long a time as is required. If we place a photographic plate in the focus of a suitable objective mounted equatorially we can obtain a long-exposure picture of the star-groups to which it is directed, and so on.

The student should make a model of the essential parts of an equatorial mounting out of wood. The model should have a *polar axis NS* capable of being turned round the line *NS;* a *declination*

FIG. 80.—AN EQUATORIAL TELESCOPE POINTED TOWARDS THE POLE.

FIG. 81.—AN EQUATORIAL TELESCOPE POINTED AT A STAR IN
THE NORTH-EASTERN REGION OF THE SKY.

axis DL capable of being turned round the head of the polar axis *N;* a long stick *TT* to stand for a telescope (mark the object-glass end of it). The whole should be mounted on a box so that *NS* lies in a north and south line, and so that the line *NS* makes an angle with the horizon equal to the latitude of the observer. A surveyor's theodolite becomes an equatorial when its horizontal circle is tilted up into the plane of the celestial equator.

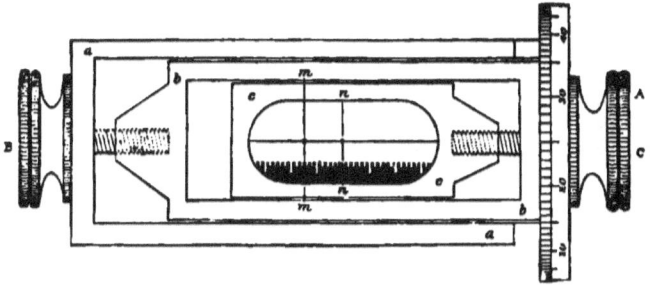

Fig. 82.—The Micrometer.

An apparatus used in connection with a telescope for measuring small angular distances.

The Micrometer.—A telescope on an equatorial mounting is very suitable for long-continued observations, such as the examination of the surface of a planet during the greater part of a night, but in order to fully utilize it, some means of measuring must be provided. The equatorial cannot be used to measure large arcs with exactness —such an arc as the difference of declination of two stars several degrees apart. When it is provided with a micrometer it is exactly fitted to measure small distances with great precision—such a distance as that between two stars separated by a few minutes of arc, for example.

The principle of the micrometer is illustrated in figure 82. A metal box is fitted with two slides *b* and *c* and with two accurate screws *A* and *B*. The screw *A* has a head divided into 100 parts. A hole is cut in each of the slides. A spider-line, *n*, is stretched across the hole in the slide moved by the screw *A*, and a spider-line *m* is stretched across the hole in the slide moved by the screw *B*.

The micrometer is fastened to the end of the telescope, at right angles to its axis, so that the lines *m* and *n* are in the focus of the telescope, thus :

FIG. 83.

OP is the object-glass of a telescope whose focus is *F*; *AB* is the micrometer.

When the screw *A* is moved the spider-line *n* moves, and the line *m* moves with the motion of the screw *B*. The oval hole in Fig. 82 represents the field of view of the telescope. The observer sees the two spider-lines *m* and *n*, a fixed spider-line at right angles to them, a comb-scale at the bottom of the field and whatever stars the tele-scope is viewing. One complete revolution of the screw *A* moves the line *n* from one tooth of the comb-scale to the next tooth and whole revolutions of *A* are counted in this way. Fractions of a revolution are counted on the divided head of screw *A* as its divisions move past a fixed index or pointer.

Suppose that it is desired to measure the distance between two stars *S* and *T* that are visible in the field of view. During these measures the telescope is driven by the clock so as to follow the stars as they move from rising towards setting.

$$S \qquad\qquad T$$
$$* \qquad\qquad *$$

FIG. 84.

The micrometer is moved so that its long fixed spider-line passes through *S* and *T* thus :

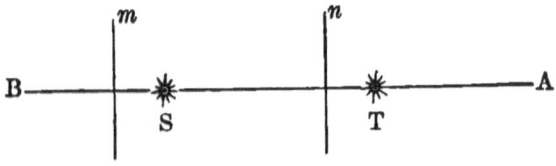

FIG. 85.

The lines m and n will appear as in the figure 85. The screw B is then moved until the line m passes through S and the screw A is moved till the line n passes through T, thus:

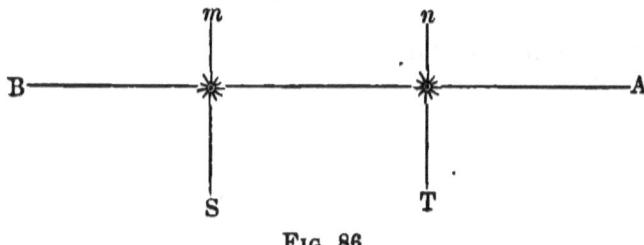

FIG. 86.

The "reading" of the screw A is then taken. Suppose it to be 21 whole revolutions (read on the comb-scale) and $\frac{57}{100}$ of a revolution (read on the divided head—the mark 57 being opposite to the index). The screw A is then moved (B remaining as before) until the line n exactly coincides with the line m, and a second "reading" of A is made. Suppose it to be 9 whole revolutions (from the scale) and $\frac{33}{100}$ (from the index). The distance between the two stars S and T is evidently $ST = 21^r.57 - 9^r.33 = 12^r.24$. If one whole revolution of the screw is known and equal to $11''.07$ then the distance $ST = 12.24 \times 11.07 = 135''.50$.

When the value of one revolution of the screw is known in seconds of arc all distances measured in revolutions and parts can be reduced to arc. *The value of one revolution in arc* is determined once for all by placing the lines m and n perpendicular to the direction of the diurnal motion of a star and at a known distance—say 50 revolutions—apart, thus:

FIG. 87.

If the telescope is kept in a fixed position the star, by its diurnal motion, will move across the field of view in the direction of the arrow. The exact times of its transits over n and m are observed.

Suppose that it requires 6ᵐ 9.ˢ0 of sidereal time to pass from the line *n* to the line *m*.

$$6^m\ 9^s = 369^s = 553''.5 \text{ because } 1^s = 15'' \text{ (see page 84).}$$

Fifty revolutions of the screw = 533″.5, therefore, and 1 revolution = 11″.07.

The relative position of two stars *A* and *B* is not completely defined when we know their distance apart and nothing more. We need to know the angle that the line joining them makes with the celestial meridian (or with the parallel). To determine this the micrometer is attached to a *position-circle*, so that the micrometer-box can be rotated in a plane perpendicular to the axis of the telescope. To measure the *position-angle* of two stars the telescope is kept in a fixed

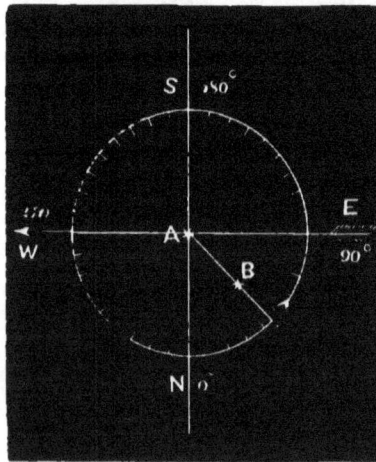

position and the micrometer-box is turned until one of the stars moves by its diurnal motion along the spider-line *m*. The circle is then "read." Suppose its "reading" to be 90°. The direction of the parallel (*EW*) is then 90° to 270°; of the celestial meridian (*NS*) 0° to 180°. The telescope is then pointed at *A* and moved by the driving clock so that *A* remains at the middle of the field. The micrometer-box is turned until the spider-line *m* passes through the two stars *A* and *B* (see the figure) and the circle is again read. Suppose

Fig. 88.—MEASUREMENT OF THE   the reading to be 46°. This is
POSITION ANGLE OF TWO   the measure of the angle *NAB*
STARS *A* AND *B*.   —of the angle that the line join-

ing the two stars makes with the celestial meridian passing through *A*. When we know the position-angle and the distance of two stars we know all that can be known about their relative situation.

The diameters of planets can be measured with the micrometer.

Photography.—If we put a photographic plate in the focus of the telescope instead of a micrometer, and if we give the proper exposure (the telescope being moved by the driving-clock) we shall have on the plate a photograph of all the stars in the field.

If we stop the clock and allow a star to move by its diurnal motion across part of the field of view it will leave a "trail" from the

FIG. 89.

east to the west side of the plate. After the plate is developed, we shall have a map of all the stars and can measure their

$W \longleftarrow \text{—————————————} E$

position-angles one from another, at leisure, and in the daytime. Their distance apart can be measured in inches and fractions of an inch. The value of one inch on the plate expressed in seconds of arc can be determined once for all by observing transits of a star over two pencil lines ruled on a ground-glass plate in the focus one inch apart. It is clear that a photographic plate will give us *first*, a map of all the stars in the field ; *second*, the means of measuring their precise relative positions just as measures with the micrometer will do. One great advantage of the photographic method over visual measures with the micrometer is that the plate gives a permanent record, so that the actual micrometric measurements can be made at leisure and repeated as often as necessary. Another marked advantage is that *many* pairs of stars are photographed at one exposure, whereas only one pair can be observed at one time by the eye.

Celestial Photography.—Photographs of the Sun, Moon, Planets, Stars, Comets, and Nebulæ can be made with telescopes specially constructed for photography, and these photographs can be subsequently studied under microscopes, just as if the object itself were visible. The intervals of clear sky can be utilized to obtain the photographs, and they can be measured when the sky is cloudy. A great saving of time is thus practicable. A second great advantage of the photographic plate in Astronomy is that the exposures can be made as long as desired. Objects can be registered in this way that are too faint to be seen with the eye using the same telescope. The eye soon becomes fatigued with the extreme attention required for astronomical observing. The photographic plate is not subject to fatigue. It has certain disadvantages that need not be discussed here, and the plate will never supersede the eye. On the other hand, it has already been of immense importance in Practical Astronomy and is destined to be employed in many new ways. Some of its applications are mentioned in Part II. of this book.

The Sextant.—The sextant is a portable instrument universally

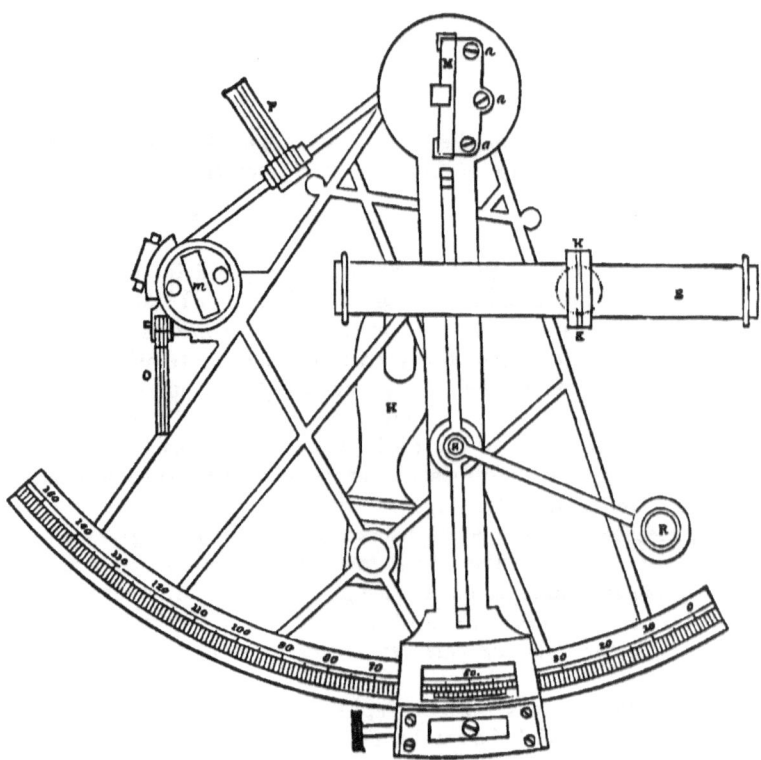

FIG. 90.—THE SEXTANT.

The radius of its divided circle is usually from 6 to 10 inches.

used by navigators at sea. It was invented by SIR ISAAC NEWTON, and quite independently by THOMAS GODFREY, a sea-captain of Philadelphia. The figure shows its general appearance. Its purpose is to measure the *altitude* of a star (or of the Sun). It consists essentially of a divided circle ; of a movable index arm *SM* which carries a mirror *M* (called the index-glass) firmly fastened to it ; of another mirror *m* (called the horizon-glass) fastened to the frame of the instrument ; and of a small telescope *E*. It is held by a handle *H*. When altitudes are measured, the plane of the instrument is vertical.

The instrument is used daily at sea to measure the altitude of the Sun. The chronometer-time at which the altitude is measured is noted. The method of making the observation is to point the telescope *E* at the sea-horizon, which will appear like a horizontal line across its field of view, thus :

The rays from the Sun strike the index-glass *A* (or *M* in Fig. 90), and are reflected from it. By moving the index-arm (the glass moves with it) the *reflected* rays from the Sun (*AB*) may be made to

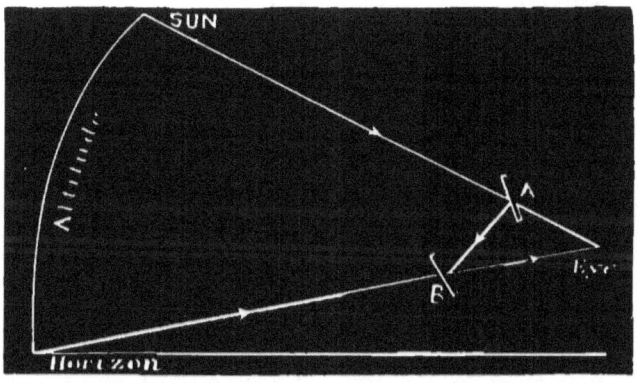

Fig. 91.—Theory of the Sextant.

fall on the horizon-glass *B* (or *m* in Fig. 90). When the index-arm has been moved so that the image of the Sun (⊙) appears to touch the horizon ———⊙——— the index-arm reads the altitude of the Sun on the divided circle.

The altitude of the Sun is also measured daily at apparent noon, that is when the Sun is highest, by every navigator to obtain his *latitude*.

In the figure *Z'* is an observer on the Earth *CP'Z'Q'*, *Z* is his zenith, *HH* his horizon, *P* is the celestial pole, *PZH* his celestial meridian, *Q* a point of the celestial equator. *S* is the Sun on his meridian. The altitude of the Sun *HS* is measured by the sextant. 90° — *HS* = *ZS*, and *ZS* is thus a known arc. The declination of the Sun at that instant is *QS*. It is a known quantity because it can be taken from tables in the *Nautical Almanac* that have been calculated

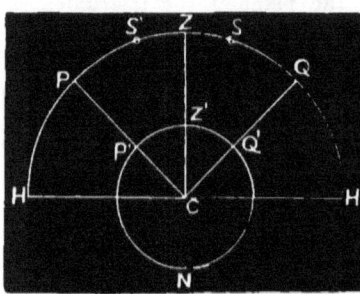

beforehand. *QZ* = the declination of the observer's zenith = his latitude = *ZS* + *QS* = the sum of two known arcs. If the Sun is on the meridian north of the observer's zenith, as it may be in certain latitudes, *QZ* = the observer's latitude = *QS'* — *ZS'* = the Sun's declination (a known quantity) *minus* the Sun's zenith distance (which is known as soon as *HS'*, the altitude, has been measured with the sextant). Thus the ship's latitude is determined.

FIG. 92.—THE LATITUDE OF AN OBSERVER DETERMINED BY MEASURING THE MERIDIAN ALTITUDE OF THE SUN.

The altitude of the Sun is measured daily in the morning (or afternoon, or both) to determine the ship's *longitude*, or rather to determine the local mean time of the ship's position. If we know that the local mean time of the ship is *T* at the instant that the Greenwich time is *G* the west longitude of the ship will be *G* — *T* (= the difference of the simultaneous local times). The Greenwich time is always known, on the ship, from the dial of the Greenwich chronometer that she carries. The local time of the ship is calculated from the triangle *ZPA* as soon as the Sun's altitude has been measured.

In figure 93 *PZS* is the celestial sphere, *O* the place of the Earth, *Z* the zenith of an observer, *NS* his horizon, *E* his east point, *A* the place of the Sun in the afternoon, *BA* the Sun's declination, *PA* the Sun's north polar distance, *GA* the Sun's altitude, *ZA* the Sun's zenith distance. The angle *ZPA* is the local apparent solar time because it is the hour-angle of the Sun (see page 90). We wish to determine *ZPA*. In the triangle *ZPA*, *PA* is known (it is 90° *minus* the Sun's declination which is given in the *Nautical Almanac*); *ZP* is known (it is 90° *minus* the latitude *PN*); *ZA* is known (it is 90° *minus* the Sun's altitude which has been measured by the sextant). Hence every part of the triangle is known and the angle *ZPA* (expressed in hours, minutes and seconds, not in degrees, etc.) corrected for the difference between *mean* and *apparent* solar time gives the local time of the ship = *T*. If *G* is the Greenwich time (from the

Greenwich chronometer) at that instant, the ship's west longitude is $G - T$, a known quantity.

Thus a little instrument that can be held in the hand enables the navigator to determine his position on the Earth's surface with considerable accuracy and in a very few minutes. Sextant observations at sea will give the position of a ship to within a mile or so.

— Make a sketch of the *transit instrument* and name the important parts—the telescope, the axis, the Ys, the piers. When the in-

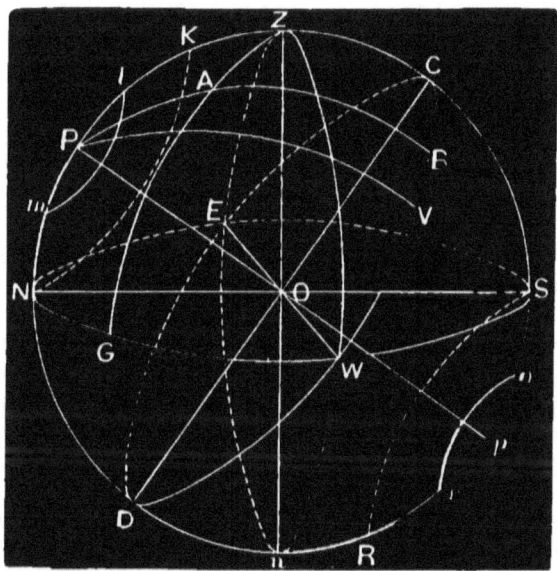

Fig. 93 —The Local Time of an Observer Determined by Measuring the Altitude of the Sun.

strument is revolved, what circle of the celestial sphere does it trace out? If a star of known R.A. $= A$ crosses the meridian at a clock time T, what is the correction of the clock? If the sidereal clock is correct, and a star of unknown R.A. crosses the meridian at a time B, what is the R.A. of this star?

Make a sketch of the important parts of the *meridian-circle*, and name the parts. How may the horizontal-point H of the circle be determined? Suppose H to be known, what is the reading for the zenith-point Z? for the nadir? Suppose the latitude of the observer $(= \phi)$ to be known also, what is the reading for the polar point P?

for the equator-point *E?* Describe how a model of a meridian-circle can be made. For what purpose are transit instruments and meridian-circles used? Describe the *equatorial mounting* for telescopes, and say what its advantages are. Draw a diagram of such a mounting. Explain the construction of a micrometer. How is it used to determine the angular distance of two stars—their position-angle? How is the value of one revolution of the micrometer determined in arc? Explain how a photograph of a group of stars is made. What are some of the advantages of photographic methods of observation? With the *sextant* the altitude of the Sun (or of a star) can be measured. How is the *latitude* of a ship at sea determined? the *longitude* of the ship?

The Nautical Almanac.—The governments of the United States, Great Britain, France, Germany, and other countries issue annually a *Nautical Almanac* for the use of navigators and others. Copies of the *Nautical Almanac* can be purchased through book-dealers. The Almanac contains :

Tables of the R.A. and Decl. of the Sun, Moon, and Planets for every day in the year.

Tables of the R. A. and Decl. of all the brighter stars.

Tables of all eclipses of the Sun, Moon, and of the satellites of Jupiter, as well as many other data of importance to the astronomer and the navigator.

To give the student a better idea of the *Nautical Almanac* a small portion of one its pages for the year 1882 is here printed. (See page 151.)

The third column shows the R. A. of the Sun's centre at Greenwich mean noon of each day. The fourth column shows the hourly change of this quantity (9.815 on Feb. 12). At Greenwich 0 hours, on Feb. 12, the sun's R. A. was 21ʰ 44ᵐ 10ˢ.80. Washington is 5ʰ 8ᵐ (5ʰ.13) west of Greenwich. At Washington mean noon, on the 12th, the Greenwich mean time was 5ʰ.13. 9.815 × 5.13 is 50ˢ.35. This is to be *added* since the R. A. is increasing. The sun's R. A. at Washington mean noon, on Feb. 12, is therefore 21ʰ 45ᵐ 1ˢ.15. A similar process will give the sun's declination for Washington mean noon. In the same manner, the R. A. and Dec. of the sun for *any* place whose longitude is known can be found.

The column ''Equation of Time'' gives the quantity to be subtracted from the Greenwich mean solar time to obtain the Greenwich apparent solar time (see page 90). Thus, for Feb. 1, the Greenwich mean time of Greenwich mean noon is 0ʰ 0ᵐ 0ˢ. The true sun crossed the Greenwich meridian (apparent noon) 13ᵐ 51ˢ.34 *earlier* than this, that is at 23ʰ 46ᵐ 08ˢ.66 on the preceding day ; i.e. Jan. 31. Having the apparent solar-time by observation (see page 148) the mean solar time can be found from this table.

Again, when it was 0ʰ 0ᵐ 0ˢ of Greenwich mean time on Feb. 10, it was 21ʰ 21ᵐ 50ˢ.70 of Greenwich local sidereal time (see the last

FEBRUARY, 1882—AT GREENWICH MEAN NOON.

Day of the week.	Day of the month.	The Sun's				Equation of time to be substracted from mean time.	Diff. for 1 hr.	Sidereal time or right-ascension of mean sun.
		Apparent right-ascension.	Diff. for 1 hour.	Apparent declination.	Diff. for 1 hour.			
		H. M. S.	S.	° ′ ″	″	M. S.	S.	H. M. S.
Wed.	1	21 0 13.01	101.75	S 17 2 22.4	+42.82	13 51.34	0.318	20 46 21.70
Thur.	2	21 4 16.84	10.141	16 45 5.4	43.57	13 58.58	0.284	20 50 18.26
Fri.	3	21 8 19.82	10.107	16 27 30.9	44.30	14 5.01	0.250	20 54 14.81
Sat.	4	21 12 21.98	10.073	16 9 39.2	+44.99	14 10.61	0.216	20 58 11.37
Sun.	5	21 16 23.33	10.040	15 51 30.8	45.69	14 15.41	0.183	21 2 7.92
Mon.	6	21 20 23.89	10.007	15 33 6.1	46.36	14 19.40	0.150	21 6 4.48
Tues.	7	21 24 23.63	9.974	15 14 25.4	+47.03	14 22.60	0.117	21 10 1.03
Wed.	8	21 28 22.60	9.941	14 55 29.1	47.66	14 25.01	0.084	21 13 57.59
Thur.	9	21 32 20.79	9.909	14 36 17.7	48.28	14 26.65	0.052	21 17 54.14
Fri.	10	21 36 18.21	9.877	14 16 51.6	48.88	14 27.51	0.020	21 21 50.70
Sat.	11	21 40 14.88	9.846	13 57 11.2	49.47	14 27.63	0.011	21 25 47.25
Sun.	12	21 44 10.80	9.815	13 37 16.9	50.03	14 26.99	0.042	21 29 43.81

column of the table). Having the sidereal time by observation (see page 127), the corresponding mean solar time can be found from this table.

How to Establish a True North and South Line.—In order to set the hands of a sidereal timepiece correctly we must make them indicate the hours, minutes, and seconds of any star's right-ascension at the instant that star is crossing the observer's meridian. In order to make the timepiece keep sidereal time correctly we must regulate it so that the hands go through 24ʰ 0ᵐ 0ˢ in the interval between two successive transits of the same star across the meridian. To make these observations, we need to know the direction of the meridian, and to mark it permanently.

For students who cannot own a transit instrument it is convenient to mark the meridian by two plumb-lines, *A* and *B*, one due north of the other, thus:

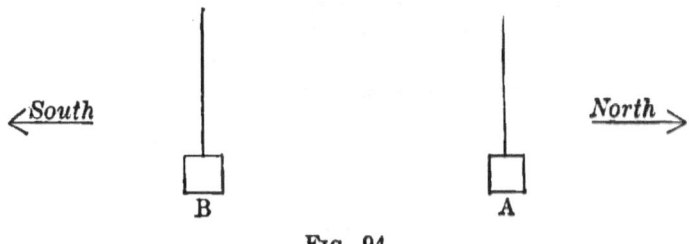

FIG. 94.

The plumb-lines can be made out of good fishing-line ; the plumb-bobs out of bits of lead. To prevent them from swinging in the wind it is a good plan to keep the bobs immersed in pails of water. The lines can be suspended from nails driven into walls, trees, etc. The meridian-line should be marked in a place where a good view of the whole meridian from north to south can be commanded.

The problem is to place the plumb-lines in a true north and south line. There are several ways of doing this. The following process

FIG. 95.—URSA MAJOR.

Zeta (ζ) Ursæ majoris is the middle star of the handle of the Dipper.

is as simple as any. Mark on the ground a line in the direction of the needle of a common compass. This will be approximately north and south. At the north end of this line choose a place for the northern plumb-line *A* and hang it there. Ten or fifteen feet south of *A* suspend the second plumb-bob *B* from a framework of wood that can be moved east or west, if necessary. *A* is always to hang in the place first chosen. *B* is to be moved east or west until the right place is found and then it is to remain there always. The line joining *A* and *B* (after *B* is placed correctly) is the meridian line of the observer.

The plumb-line *B* is placed correctly when *both* plumb-lines seem to pass through the two stars Polaris and Zeta (ζ) *Ursæ majoris* at the same time.

The right-ascensions of these two stars differ by 12 hours. When Polaris is crossing the meridian from east to west (upper culmination) ζ *Ursæ majoris* is crossing the meridian from west to east (lower culmination). A line joining them at this instant is a celestial meridian. If we move the plumb-line *B* until *both* plumb-lines *A* and *B* pass through both stars then the line joining *A* and *B* must be in the plane of the celestial meridian.

The stars will be approaching their culminations

about 11 P.M.	Oct. 20,		about 8 P.M.	Dec. 5,
" 10 "	Nov. 5,		" 7 "	Dec. 20,
" 9 "	Nov. 20,		" 6 "	Jan. 5,
	about 5 P.M.	Jan. 20,		

and these are the hours to prepare to observe them.

The observation consists in moving the support of the plumb-line *B* (the southern plumb-line) slowly and gently east or west until both stars seem to be on the two plumb-lines at the same time, as in Fig. 96. When they are so let both plumb-lines rest, and see if the stars stay on the two lines for a few minutes. If they do, both lines are in the right position. If they do not, move the southern plumb-line *B* slightly. After the plumb-line *B* has been put in the right position its place must be marked; and the next morning its nail can be permanently fixed. It will be well to test the meridian-line, so determined, by another night's observations. Finally, a meridian-line can be established by this process; and whenever the observer wishes he can observe the transit of any celestial body over the two plumb-lines and note the hour, minute, and second by his sidereal time piece.* In order to see the plumb-lines in a dark night he should chalk them well, or paint them white. If this is not enough they can be illuminated by the light of a lantern placed behind his back (so as not to interfere with his seeing the stars).

FIG. 96.

* A cheap watch, regulated to run on sidereal time, is a great convenience in making astronomical observations.

CHAPTER VIII.

APPARENT MOTION OF THE SUN TO AN OBSERVER ON THE EARTH—THE SEASONS.

21. Apparent Motion of the Sun to an Observer on the Earth.—Long before the Christian era the ancients knew that there were two classes of bodies to be seen in the sky. The *stars*—the first class—rose and set, to be sure; but they were always in the same relative position. They kept their configurations. They were fixed. One star did not move away from others. The stars of *Ursa Major* shown in Fig. 1 kept their relative positions— their grouping—century after century. There was another class of celestial bodies which the ancients called *planets* or wandering stars. Some of them (*Mercury*, *Venus*, *Mars*, *Jupiter*, *Saturn*) looked exactly like stars to the naked eye, but they moved among the fixed stars, sometimes being near to one fixed star, then leaving it and moving near another star. You can easily observe such motions as these for yourself. *Mars* or *Jupiter* moves among the fixed stars with a motion that is quite obvious if you regularly observe its place (and make a sketch of the stars near by). The Moon moves quite rapidly among the stars.

The Sun also moves among the stars, but as the stars are not visible in the daytime, it is necessary to observe the Sun at sunrise and at sunset in order to prove to yourself that it is moving. The ancients understood this fact very well and they had mapped the path of the Sun among the stars quite accurately. You can do the same thing by observing the Sun at sunrise and sunset each

154

day and by marking down on a celestial globe, every day, the position of the Sun. If you continued this process for a year you would find that the Sun had apparently made a complete circuit of the heavens.

If the Sun were near to a bright star on Jan. 1 (so that the Sun and the star rose and set at the same time) you would see that the Sun moved eastwards so as to set *later* than the star on Jan. 2. It would set still later than the star on Jan. 3, and so on. In July it would set about 12 hours later than the star. In half a year the Sun has moved away from the star by half the circuit of the heavens. In the next January the Sun would be near the same star again so as to set at the same time with it. The Sun then has, in the year, made a complete circuit of the heavens. The ancients proved this and you can prove it for yourself if you will give a year to the demonstration. The year is measured by the time required for the Sun to make this circuit.

The explanation of the apparent motion of the Sun is to be found in the real motion of the Earth. The Earth moves round the Sun in a nearly circular *orbit* (path) and completes one revolution in about 365¼ days, one year.

In Fig. 97 let *S* represent the Sun, *ABCD* the orbit of the Earth around it, and *EFGH* the sphere of the fixed stars. This sphere is infinitely larger than the circle *ABCD*. Suppose now that 1, 2, 3, 4, 5, 6 are a number of consecutive positions of the Earth in its orbit. A line 1*S* drawn from the Sun to the Earth in any given position is called the *radius-vector* of the Earth. Suppose this line extended so as to meet the celestial sphere in the point 1′. It is evident that to an observer on the Earth at 1 the Sun will appear projected on the celestial sphere at 1′; when the earth reaches 2 the Sun will appear at 2′, and so on. In other words, as the Earth revolves around the Sun, the latter will seem to perform a revolution among the fixed stars. The stars do not seem to move because they are at such enormous distances that a change of the Earth's place from 1 to 6, or from *A* to *C*, makes almost no change in the *direction* of lines joining the Earth and any star. In space the lines *HA, HC, HD, HB* are *almost* (though not quite) parallel.

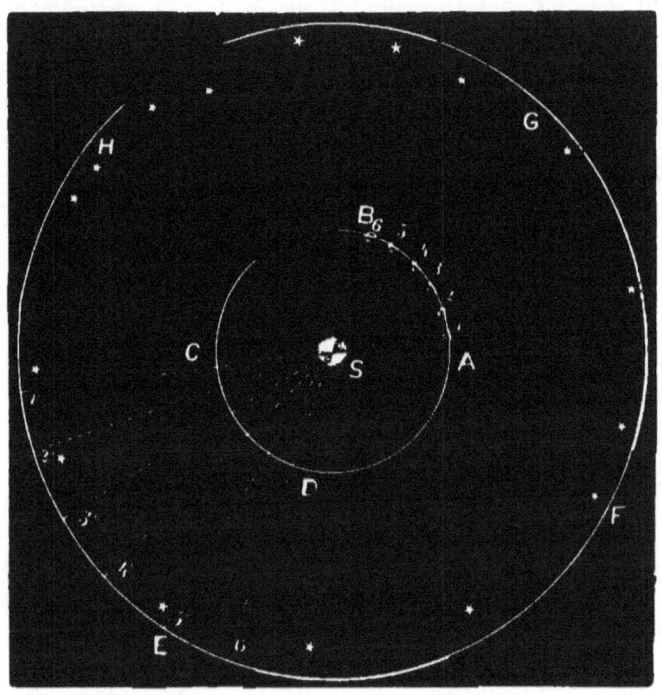

Fig. 97.—The Annual Revolution of the Earth about the Sun, in the Orbit *ABCD*.

The diameter of this orbit is about 186,000,000 miles.

The apparent places of the Sun (1', 2', 3', 4', 5', 6', etc.) can be defined in the sky by their right-ascensions and declinations, or by their distances from the stars there situated. The right-ascensions and declinations of these stars are known (or if they are not known they can be determined by observation).

It is plain that an observer on the Sun would see the Earth projected at points on the celestial sphere exactly opposite to the corresponding points of the Sun's apparent path viewed from the Earth. Moreover, if the Earth moves more rapidly in some portions of its orbit than in others (as it does) the Sun will appear to move more rapidly

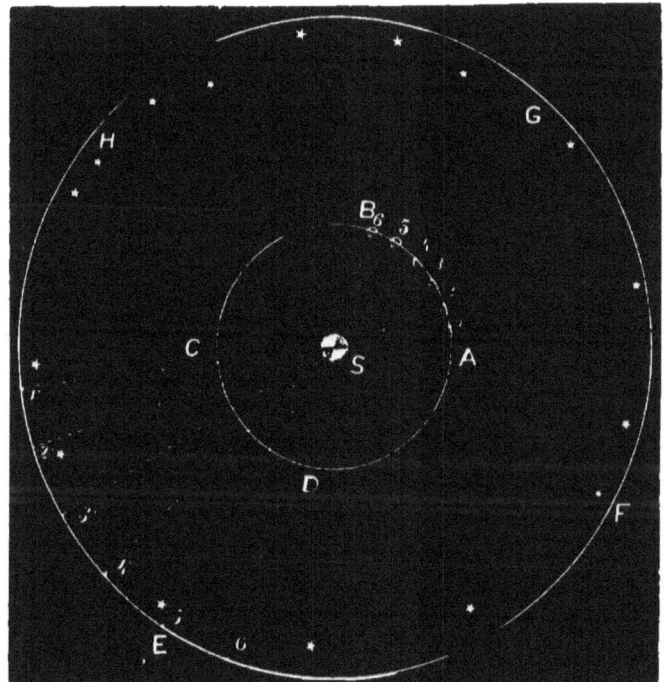

FIG. 98.—THE REVOLUTION OF THE EARTH IN ITS ORBIT ABOUT THE SUN.

among the stars in consequence. The two motions must accurately correspond one with the other. The apparent motion of the Sun in the heavens is a precise measure of the real motion of the Earth in its orbit.

The *radius-vector* of the Earth (the line joining Earth and Sun) describes a plane surface as the Earth moves.

In the figure this is the plane of the paper.   In space this
plane is called the plane of the *ecliptic*.   This plane will
cut the celestial sphere in a great circle; and the Sun will
appear to move in this circle.   The circle is called *the
ecliptic*.   The plane of the ecliptic divides the celestial
sphere into two equal parts.   A *sidereal year* is the interval
of time required for the Sun to make the circuit of the sky
from one star back to the same star again; or, it is the
interval of time required for the Earth to go once around
its orbit.

When the earth is at 1 in the figure the Sun will appear
to be at 1', near some star, as drawn.   Now by the *diurnal*
motion of the Earth the Sun is made to rise, to culminate,
and to set successively to every observer on the Earth.
This star being near the Sun rises, culminates, and sets with
him; it is on the meridian of any place at the local noon
of that place (and is therefore not visible except in a telescope since we cannot see stars in the daytime with the
naked eye).   The star on the right-hand side of the figure,
near the line *CS1* prolonged, is nearly opposite to the Sun.
When the Sun is rising at any place, that star will be
setting; when the Sun is on the meridian of the place, that
star is on the lower meridian; when the sun is setting, that
star is rising.   It is about 180° from the Sun.

Now suppose the Earth to move to 2.   The Sun will be
seen at 2', near the star there marked.   2' is *east* of 1'; the
Sun appears to move *among the stars* (in consequence of
the earth's *annual* motion) from west to east.   The star
near 2' will rise, culminate, and set with the Sun to every
observer on the Earth.   Like things are true of the Sun
in each of its successive apparent positions 3', 4', 5', 6', etc.

The student should here notice how our notions of the
direction East and West have arisen.   In the first place
men noticed that the Sun rose in one part of the sky
(which they named East) and set in another (West).

Secondly, it was found that these risings and settings were caused by the daily rotation of the Earth on its axis and that if the stars appeared to move from east to west the Earth must really turn from west to east. The Sun appears to move, in consequence of the Earth's *annual* motion, from west to east among the stars (from 1' towards 6' in the figure).

The Earth moves around its circle *ABCD* in the same direction that the Sun appears to move around *its* circle *FGHE*. Draw an arrow outside of *FGHE* parallel to 1', 2', 3', 4', 5', 6', with the point near 6' and the feather near 1'. Draw another arrow outside of *ABCD* with the point near *D* and the feather near *C*. These arrows are parallel. Hence the Earth moves *in its orbit* from west to east. Or, suppose *ABCD* and *FGHE* to be two watch-dials and *SA* and *SE* to be the hands. When *SA* points to the top of its dial (*ABCD*) its next movement is towards the left (in the figure). When *SE* points to the top of its dial (*FGHE*) *its* next movement is towards the left, likewise. As the Sun is observed to move from west to east *among the stars*, the Earth must also move from west to east *in its orbit*.

The apparent position of a body as seen from the Earth is called its *geocentric place*. The apparent position of a body as seen from the sun is called its *heliocentric place*.

In the last figure, suppose the Sun to be at *S*, and the Earth at 4. 4' is the *geocentric* place of the Sun, and *G* is the *heliocentric* place of the Earth.

THE SUN'S APPARENT PATH.

It is evident that if the apparent path of the Sun lay in the equator, it would, during the entire year, rise exactly in the east and set in the west, and would always cross the meridian at the same altitude (see page 68). The days would always be twelve hours long, for the same reason that a star in the equator is always twelve hours above the horizon and twelve hours below it. But we know that this is not the case. The Sun is sometimes north of the equator and sometimes south of it, and therefore it has a motion in declination.

The Sun was observed with a meridian-circle and a sidereal clock at the moment of transit over the meridian of Washington on March 19, 1879. Its position was found to be

Right-ascension, $23^h 55^m 23^s$; Declination, $0° 30'$ south.

The observation was repeated on the 20th and following days, and the results were:

March 20, R.A. $23^h 59^m \ 2^s$; Dec. $0° \ 6'$ South.
" 21, " $0^h \ 2^m 40^s$; " $0° 17'$ North.
" 22, " $0^h \ 6^m 19^s$; " $0° 41'$ "

If we lay these positions down on a chart, we shall find them to be as in Fig. 99, the centre of the Sun being south of the equator in the first two positions, and north of it in the last two. Joining the successive positions by a line, we shall have a representation of a small portion of the apparent path of the Sun on the celestial sphere, or of the *ecliptic.*

It is clear that the Sun crossed the equator on the afternoon of March 20, 1879, and therefore that the equator and ecliptic intersect at the point where the Sun was at that time. This point is called the *vernal equinox,* the first word indicating the season, while the second expresses the equality of the nights and days which occurs when the Sun is on the equator.

If similar observations are made at any place on the Earth in any year it will be found that the Sun moves along the ecliptic from the southern hemisphere into the northern hemisphere about March 20 of each and every year; and the point where the ecliptic crosses the equator—

the vernal equinox—can be determined by observation. The declination of this point is zero (because it is on the equator) and its right-ascension is also zero (because right-ascensions are counted from the vernal equinox). From

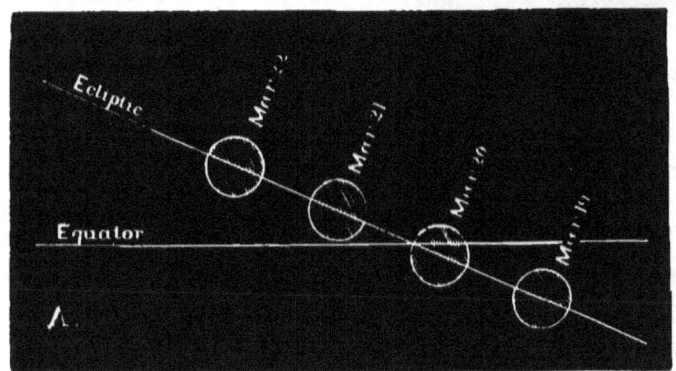

Fig. 99.—The Sun Crossing the Equator.

March to September the Sun is in the northern hemisphere. Figs. 49, 50, 51, 52 have the ecliptic marked upon them, and the student should point out the places of the Sun for the beginning of each month of the year (so far as is possible) on each figure. (See the next paragraph.)

Here for example are the positions of the Sun for the first day of every month of the year 1898 at Greenwich mean noon:

1898	Jan. 1	R. A	=	$18^h\ 49^m$	*Decl.* =	South	23°
South	Feb. 1		=	$21^h\ 1^m$	=	"	17°
	Mar. 1		=	$22^h\ 50^m$	=	"	7°
	Apr. 1		=	$0^h\ 43^m$	=	North	5°
	May 1		=	$2^h\ 35^m$	=	"	15°
North	June 1		=	$4^h\ 38^m$	=	"	22°
	July 1		=	$6^h\ 42^m$	=	"	23°
	Aug. 1		=	$8^h\ 47^m$	=	"	18°
	Sept. 1		=	$10^h\ 43^m$	=	"	8°
	Oct. 1		=	$12^h\ 31^m$	=	South	3°
South	Nov. 1		=	$14^h\ 27^m$	=	"	15°
	Dec. 1		=	$16^h\ 31^m$	=	"	22°

On June 21, 1898, the Sun had its greatest *northern* declination = + 23° 27'; on December 22, 1898, the Sun had its greatest *southern* declination = − 23° 27'.

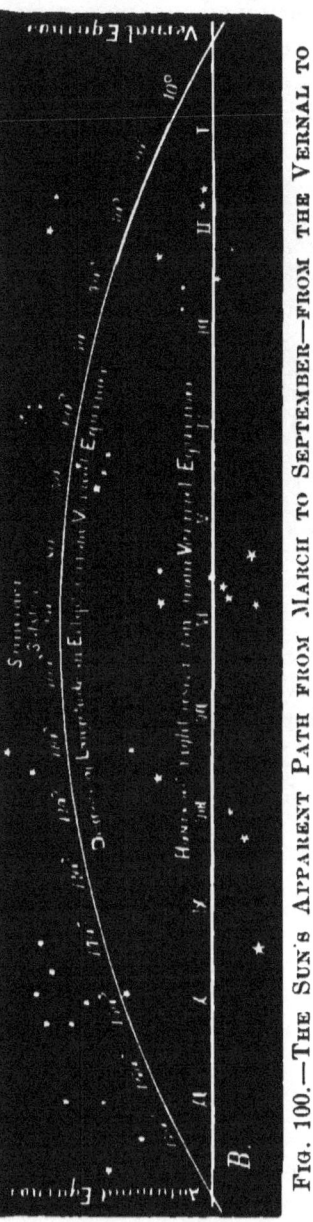

FIG. 100.—THE SUN'S APPARENT PATH FROM MARCH TO SEPTEMBER—FROM THE VERNAL TO THE AUTUMNAL EQUINOX.

If the right-ascensions and declinations of the Sun during the months from March to September are laid down on a map we shall have a diagram like Fig. 100. The straight line represents the celestial equator. The vernal equinox is at the right-hand side of the picture. The right-ascension of the vernal equinox is *zero*, and the *hours* of right-ascension are marked I, II, . . . X, XI. These numbers *increase* as you go *eastwards;* hence the point XI is east of the point II.

The Sun crosses the equator (going northwards) at the vernal equinox in the month of March. It continues to move north until June 21, when it reaches its greatest *northern* declination (23° 27′). For several days at this time the Sun moves very little in declination and seems (so far as its motion in declination is concerned) to stand still. For this reason the ancients called the Sun's place about June 21 the summer *solstice* (Latin *sol* = the Sun, *sistere* = to cause to stand still). Its right-ascension is VI hours.

From June 21 to September 22 the Sun remains north
of the equator, but its declination grows less and less
during these months. Finally on September 23 the Sun
crosses the equator once more going southwards at a point
called the *autumnal equinox.* Its declination is then zero
(because it is on the equator) and its right-ascension is XII
hours (because it is 180° distant from the vernal equinox,

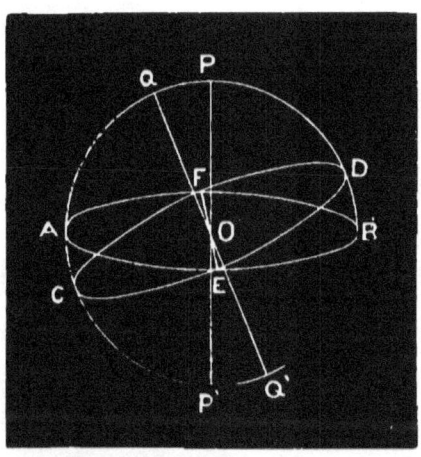

Fig. 101.—The Celestial Sphere with the Equator (*AB*)
and the Ecliptic (*CD*).

P is the north pole of the celestial equator ; *Q* is the north pole of the
Sun's apparent path, the ecliptic.

the zero of right-ascensions). After September 22 and
until the succeeding March the Sun is in the southern half
of the celestial sphere. Its south declination continually
increases until December 22, when it is 23° South, in right-
ascension XVIII hours. This point is the *winter solstice.*
From the winter solstice to the vernal equinox the Sun is
moving northwards (in declination) and always eastwards
(in right-ascension) along the ecliptic. Finally in the
succeeding March the Sun again crosses the equator at the
vernal equinox (R.A. = 0ʰ, Decl. = 0°). The point *D* of

the last figure is the summer solstice; the point *C* is the winter solstice.

The ecliptic, as well as the equator, is marked on all globes; and the annual motion of the Sun can be illustrated by tracing out the Sun's path day by day. It requires about 365 days for the Sun to move around the 360° of the ecliptic. Hence the Sun moves eastward

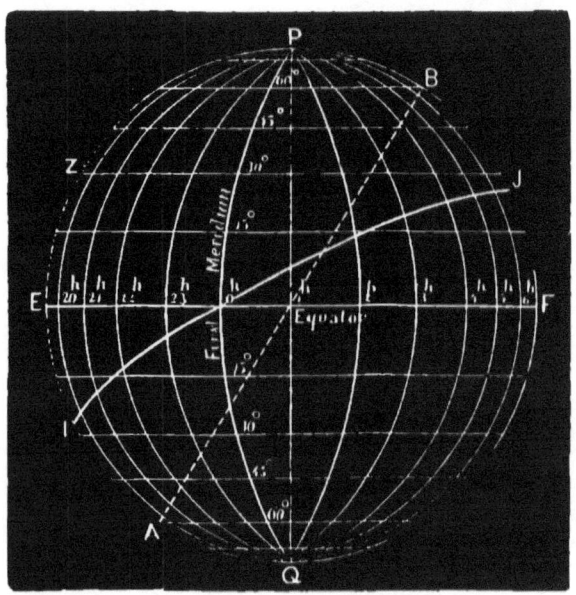

FIG. 102.—THE CELESTIAL SPHERE.
EF is the celestial equator, *IJ* the ecliptic.

among the stars about 1° per day. The Sun's *angular* diameter is about half a degree. Therefore the Sun moves each day about two of its own diameters.

The *celestial latitude* of a star is its angular distance north or south of the *ecliptic*. The *celestial longitude* of a star is its angular distance from the vernal equinox, measured on the *ecliptic* eastwards from the equinox. The degrees of celestial longitude for half the year are marked on Fig. 100.

The *sidereal year* was defined (page 158) as the interval of time between two successive returns of the Sun to the same *star*. Its length is 365 days, 6 hours, 9 minutes, 9.3 seconds.

The *astronomical year* (the year as commonly used) is the interval between two successive returns of the Sun to the same equinox. Its length is 365 days, 5 hours, 48 minutes, 46 seconds. It is shorter than the sidereal year

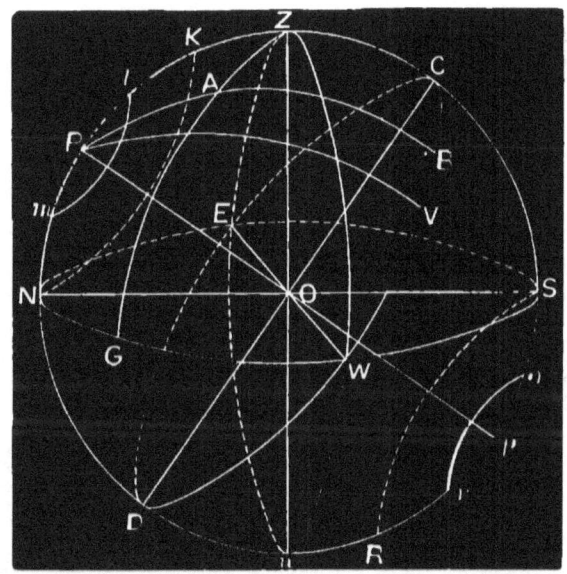

FIG. 103.—THE CELESTIAL SPHERE AS IT APPEARS TO AN OBSERVER IN 34° NORTH LATITUDE ($PON = 34°$).

The ecliptic is not drawn on this figure.

because the equinoctial points are not fixed (as the stars are) but move slowly. This will be explained more fully later on.

Length of the Day at Different Seasons of the Year.— The length of time that any star is above the horizon of an observer depends *first* on the observer's latitude, and

second on the star's declination. We have just seen that
the Sun's declination is about 23° south on January 1, 5°
north on April 1, 23° north on July 1, 3° south on
October 1.

To every observer the Sun will be above the horizon for
different periods at different times of the year. The
summer days will be the longest and the winter days the
shortest.

Figure 103 represents the celestial sphere to an observer
in 34° north latitude. On January 1 the Sun (Decl. =
south 23°) will cross his meridian 23° south of the point *C*
(nearly half way from *C* to *S*), and will describe a diurnal
orbit parallel to *CWD* (the equator). It will remain above
the horizon a short time. The night will be longer than
the daylight hours. On March 20 the Sun will be at *V*
(the vernal equinox). It will cross the meridian at *C* and
will remain above the horizon (*NS*) twelve hours. The
days and nights will be equal. On July 1 the Sun is in
declination 23° north and will cross the meridian 11° south
of *Z* (*CZ* = 34°; 34° − 23° = 11°). The daylight hours
will be long.

By constructing such a diagram for his own latitude and by marking the place of the sun for different days of the year the student
can say, beforehand, just what the apparent diurnal path of the sun
will be for any day in any year. A celestial globe set for his latitude
will show the same things. He should notice that the sun rises north
of his east point in the summer ; in the east point at the equinoxes ;
south of the east point in the winter. The sun's diurnal path at the
equinoxes of March and September is the celestial equator, at the winter
solstice it is the *tropic of Capricorn* ; at the summer solstice it is the
tropic of Cancer. These tropics are circles of the celestial sphere
drawn parallel to the equator, one (*Cancer*) 23¼° north of it, the other
(*Capricorn*) 23¼° south of it. They are called *tropics* because the Sun
there *turns* from going north (or south) in declination and begins to
go south (or north). They are marked on all globes. The regions
of the earth between the latitudes 23¼° north and south are called the
tropics.

If the observer is on the equator of the Earth, all the days and nights of the whole year will be equal, no matter what the Sun's declination may be. (See Fig. 105.)

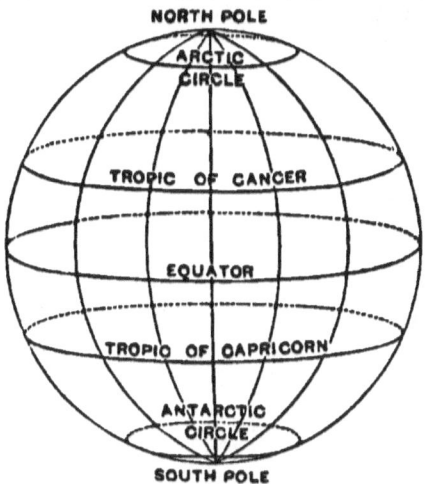

FIG. 104.—THE CIRCLES OF THE EARTH.

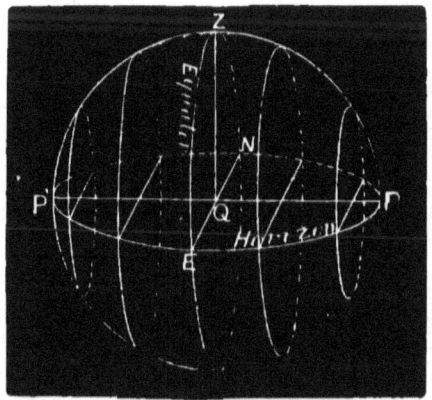

FIG. 105.—THE CELESTIAL SPHERE AS IT APPEARS TO AN OBSERVER ON THE EARTH'S EQUATOR.

All the stars (and the Sun) are always above the horizon 12 hours and below it 12 hours. The days and nights are all equal.

The following little table will be found useful and interesting.

The Approximate Time of Sunrise for Observers between 30° and 48° of North Latitude.

N. B.—The column of the table headed with the observer's latitude is the one to be consulted.

N. B —The approximate time of sunset is as many hours *after* noon as the time of sunrise is *before* it. For instance on May 1 in latitude 44° the sun rises at 4ʰ 51ᵐ A.M. i.e. 7ʰ 9ᵐ before noon. The approximate time of sunset on that day is therefore 7ʰ 9ᵐ P.M.

Latitude.	30°	32°	34°	36°	38°	40°	42°	44°	46°	48°
Date.	h. m.	h. m.	h. m.	h. m.	h. m.	h. m.	h. m.	h. m.	h. m.	h. m.
Jan. 1......	6 56	7 0	7 5	7 10	7 16	7 22	7 29	7 36	7 43	7 51
11.....	6 57	7 1	7 5	7 10	7 16	7 21	7 27	7 33	7 40	7 47
21.. ...	6 56	7 0	7 3	7 7	7 12	7 18	7 23	7 28	7 34	7 41
Feb. 1.....	6 50	6 54	6 57	7 1	7 5	7 9	7 13	7 18	7 23	7 28
11.....	6 41	6 47	6 50	6 52	6 55	6 58	7 1	7 5	7 9	7 14
21.....	6 34	6 36	6 39	6 41	6 44	6 46	6 49	6 51	6 53	6 57
Mar. 1......	6 27	6 28	6 29	6 31	6 33	6 34	6 36	6 38	6 40	6 42
11.....	6 14	6 15	6 16	6 16	6 17	6 17	6 18	6 19	6 20	6 21
21......	6 2	6 2	6 1	6 1	6 1	6 1	6 1	6 0	6 0	6 0
Apr. 1......	5 49	5 48	5 47	5 46	5 45	5 44	5 43	5 42	5 41	5 39
11.....	5 37	5 35	5 34	5 33	5 31	5 29	5 26	5 24	5 22	5 19
21.....	5 27	5 24	5 22	5 20	5 17	5 14	5 11	5 8	5 4	5 0
May 1......	5 17	5 14	5 11	5 7	5 3	5 0	4 56	4 51	4 46	4 41
11.. ...	5 9	5 5	5 1	4 57	4 52	4 48	4 43	4 38	4 33	4 27
21.....	5 3	4 58	4 58	4 49	4 44	4 39	4 33	4 27	4 20	4 13
June 1.. ...	4 58	4 53	4 48	4 43	4 38	4 32	4 25	4 18	4 11	4 3
11.....	4 56	4 52	4 47	4 41	4 35	4 30	4 23	4 15	4 8	3 59
21.....	4 59	4 54	4 48	4 42	4 36	4 30	4 23	4 15	4 8	3 58
July 1......	5 2	4 56	4 51	4 45	4 39	4 34	4 27	4 19	4 12	4 4
11.....	5 6	5 2	4 57	4 51	4 45	4 40	4 34	4 27	4 19	4 11
21.....	5 12	5 7	5 2	4 58	4 53	4 48	4 42	4 36	4 29	4 22
Aug. 1.....	5 18	5 14	5 10	5 6	5 2	4 57	4 52	4 47	4 42	4 35
11......	5 24	5 21	5 17	5 14	5 10	5 7	5 2	4 57	4 53	4 47
21.....	5 30	5 28	5 25	5 23	5 20	5 17	5 13	5 10	5 6	5 2
Sept. 1.....	5 36	5 34	5 32	5 31	5 29	5 27	5 25	5 23	5 21	5 18
11.....	5 42	5 41	5 40	5 39	5 38	5 37	5 35	5 34	5 33	5 31
21.. ...	5 47	5 47	5 47	5 47	5 46	5 46	5 45	5 45	5 45	5 44
Oct. 1.....	5 54	5 54	5 55	5 55	5 55	5 56	5 57	5 58	5 59	6 0
11.....	6 0	6 1	6 2	6 3	6 5	6 7	6 8	6 10	6 12	6 14
21.....	6 6	6 9	6 11	6 13	6 16	6 18	6 21	6 23	6 25	6 28
Nov. 1	6 14	6 17	6 21	6 24	6 26	6 29	6 33	6 37	6 41	6 45
11.. ...	6 22	6 25	6 29	6 33	6 37	6 41	6 45	6 50	6 55	7 1
21.....	6 30	6 34	6 38	6 42	6 47	6 52	6 57	7 3	7 10	7 17
Dec. 1.. ...	6 38	6 43	6 47	6 52	6 57	7 2	7 8	7 15	7 22	7 29
11......	6 46	6 51	6 56	7 1	7 7	7 12	7 18	7 25	7 33	7 41
21......	6 53	6 58	7 3	7 8	7 13	7 19	7 26	7 33	7 40	7 48

If the observer is at the Earth's north pole the Sun would be continuously above his horizon so long as the Sun was in the northern half of the celestial sphere, that is, from March to September; and continuously below his horizon from September to March. An observer at the south pole of the Earth has daylight continuously from September to March and continuous darkness from March to September.

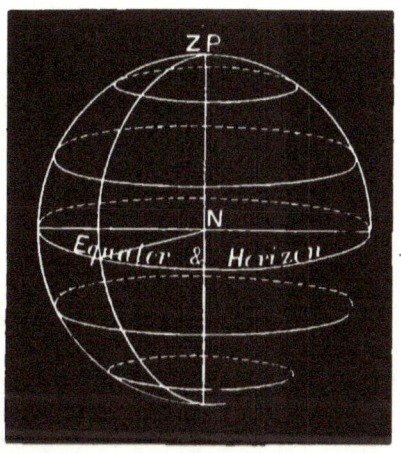

FIG. 106.—THE CELESTIAL SPHERE AS IT WOULD APPEAR TO AN OBSERVER AT THE NORTH POLE OF THE EARTH.

The Sun would be above the horizon all the time from March 20 to September 22. The day would be six months long. The sun would be below the horizon all the time from September 22 to March 20. The night would also be six months long.

The Zodiac and the Signs of the Zodiac.—The zodiac is a belt in the heavens, extending some 8° on each side of the ecliptic, and therefore about 16° wide (see figure 50). The planets known to the ancients are always seen within this belt. At a very early day the zodiac was mapped out into twelve regions known as the *signs of the zodiac*, the names of which have been handed down to the present time. Each of these regions was supposed to be the seat of a constellation or group of stars. Commencing at the vernal equinox, the first thirty degrees of the ecliptic through which the Sun passed, or the region among the stars in which it was found during the month following, was called the sign *Aries.* The next thirty degrees was called the sign *Taurus*, and so on. The names of the signs in order are:

Spring signs.	1. ♈ Aries.	The sun enters the sign	*Aries*, March 20.			
	2. ♉ Taurus.	"	"	"	*Taurus*, April 20.	
	3. ♊ Gemini.	"	"	"	*Gemini*, May 20.	
Summer signs.	4. ♋ Cancer.	"	"	"	*Cancer*, June 21.	
	5. ♌ Leo.	"	"	"	*Leo*, July 22.	
	6. ♍ Virgo.	"	"	"	*Virgo*, August 22.	
Autumn signs.	7. ♎ Libra.	"	"	"	*Libra*, September 22.	
	8. ♏ Scorpius.	"	"	"	*Scorpius*, October 23.	
	9. ♐ Sagittarius.	"	"	"	*Sagittarius*, Nov. 23.	
Winter signs.	10. ♑ Capricornus.	"	"	"	*Capricornus*, Dec. 21.	
	11. ♒ Aquarius.	"	"	"	*Aquarius*, Jan. 20.	
	12. ♓ Pisces.	"	"	"	*Pisces*, February 19.	

Each of the signs of the zodiac coincides roughly with a constellation in the heavens; and thus there are twelve constellations called by the names of these signs, but the signs and the constellations no longer accurately correspond as they formerly did. Although the Sun now crosses the equator and enters the *sign* Aries on the 20th of March, he does not reach the *constellation* Aries until nearly a month later. This arises from the precession of the equinoxes, to be explained hereafter.

— Why are the stars *fixed?* Are the planets *fixed?* Which way does the sun move among the stars—eastwards or westwards? How long does it take the sun to make a complete circuit of the heavens? What is the reason that the sun appears to move among the stars? What is the earth's *radius-vector?* What is the plane of the ecliptic? What is a *sidereal year?* Describe the way in which our notions of the directions east and west have arisen. The stars in their diurnal orbits rise in the—— The earth turns on its axis from——to—— The sun moves from——to—— among the stars. The earth moves in its real orbit in the same *direction* that the sun moves in its apparent path, from——to—— therefore. What is the *geocentric* or the *heliocentric place* of a body? What is the *vernal equinox?* the *autumnal equinox?* the *winter solstice?* the *summer solstice?* Why are these points called solstices? How long is the sun in the northern half of the celestial sphere? About how far does the sun move in the sky each day? What is an *astronomical year?* Why are our winter days shorter than our days in summer? How long is a summer day to an observer at the earth's north pole? How long is a day to an observer at the earth's equator? What is the *Zodiac?* What are the *signs of the Zodiac?*

22. Obliquity of the Ecliptic.—The obliquity of the ecliptic is the angle between the plane of the ecliptic and the plane of the celestial equator. It is the angle between the planes *DOC* and *AOB* in the figure. It is measured

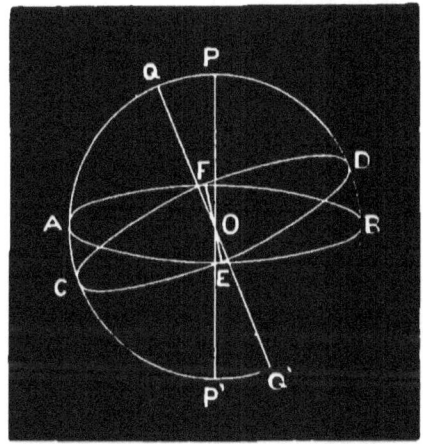

FIG. 107.—OBLIQUITY OF THE ECLIPTIC.
AB is the celestial equator, *CD* is the ecliptic.

by the arc *DB* or *AC*. *DB* is the Sun's greatest northern declination; *AC* is the Sun's greatest southern declination. As soon as we have measured either of these (with a meridian-circle, for example) the obliquity is known. It is about $23\frac{1}{2}°$. It was determined by the ancient astronomers quite accurately by observing the shadow of an obelisk at the times of the summer and winter solstices. At the summer solstice the Sun has its greatest north declination, and therefore its meridian altitude on that day is a maximum. Its meridian altitude on the day of the winter solstice is a minimum.

If *AB* is an obelisk and the line *Bd* is a north and south line, and if the Sun is on the line *Ad* on December 22 and on *Aj* on June 21, then the shadow of the obelisk will be *Bj* in June (the shortest shadow of the year) and *Bd* in December (the longest meridian shadow of the year) and *Bm* at the equinoxes. The angle *dAj* can be measured. It is equal to *twice* the obliquity and *mAB* measures the

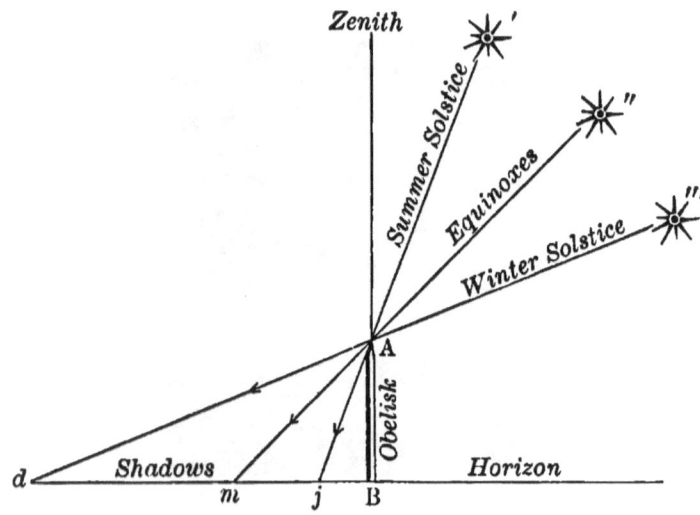

FIG. 108.—THE OBLIQUITY OF THE ECLIPTIC—
determined by the shadow of an obelisk at a place whose latitude is 45° N.

latitude of the place, as the student can readily prove for himself.

The Cause of the Seasons on the Earth.—In each and every year we, who live in the temperate zones of the Earth, witness the coming of spring, of summer, of autumn, of winter. They come and go in a cycle of a year, and the cause of the change of seasons must therefore depend on the Earth's annual revolution in its orbit. The

different seasons are marked by changes in the quantity of
heat received from the Sun. In the summer the altitude
of the Sun is high and the days are long. In the winter
the altitude of the Sun is not so high and the days are
shorter. The difference between the heat of summer and
winter depends chiefly on the differences named. The
Earth revolves about the Sun in an orbit which is very
nearly a circle, so that the change of seasons does not
depend on the varying distance of the Earth from the Sun.
As a matter of fact the Earth is somewhat nearer to the
Sun in January than it is in July.

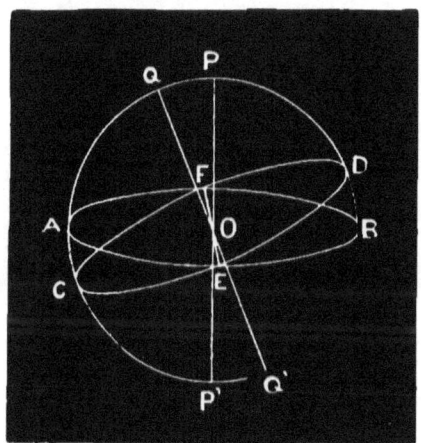

Fig. 109.—The Ecliptic, *CD*, and the Celestial Equator,
AB, with their poles, *Q* and *P*.

The Sun's apparent motion is in the ecliptic *CD*. The
vernal equinox is at *E*, the summer solstice at *D*, the
autumnal equinox at *F*, the winter solstice at *C*. The arc
$BD = AC = 23\frac{1}{2}°$, the obliquity of the ecliptic.

The Sun's North-polar distance at *E* is 90°;
" " " " " *D* " $66\frac{1}{2}°$;
" " " " " *F* " 90°;
" " " " " *C* " $113\frac{1}{2}°$.

In Fig. 110 the oval line represents the path of the Earth
in its annual revolution about the Sun in the ecliptic. The
line *NS* in each picture of the Earth represents the Earth's
axis, *N* its north end. The Earth's axis is always directed
to a point very near to the star *Polaris* at all times of the
year, that is, wherever the Earth may be in her orbit.
Hence the four lines *NS* are drawn parallel to each other.

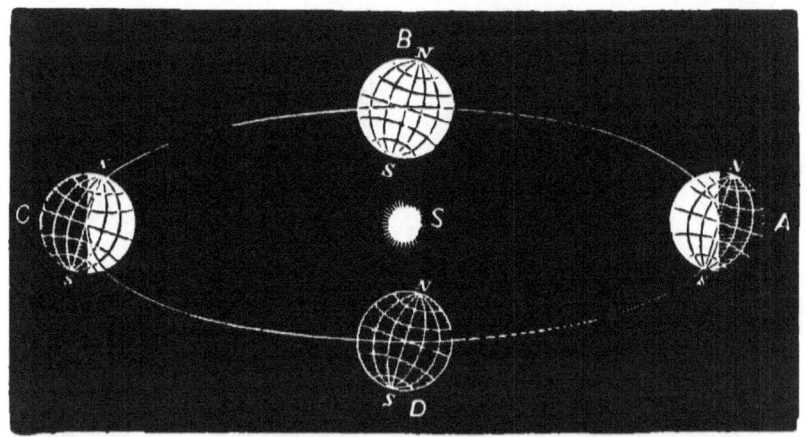

FIG. 110.—THE SEASONS.

The Earth is shown in four positions in its orbit. *A* = the winter solstice; *B* = the vernal equinox; *C* = the summer solstice; *D* = the autumnal equinox. The orbit of the Earth is nearly a circle. It is much
foreshortened in the picture.

The Earth's axis is perpendicular to the celestial equator,
but it is inclined to the ecliptic by an angle of $23\frac{1}{2}°$, and
it has been so drawn.

If the student will join the centre of the Sun (S) with
the centre of the Earth in each one of the four positions
drawn he will see that, as has been said,

The Sun's N.P.D. at *A* (winter solstice)   is $113\frac{1}{2}°$;
"   "   "   " *B* (vernal equinox)   is $90°$;
"   "   "   " *C* (summer solstice)   is $66\frac{1}{2}°$;
"   "   "   " *D* (autumnal equinox) is $90°$.

He can also prove that the Sun's *altitude* to any observer in the northern hemisphere is greater in summer than in winter by drawing the horizon of an observer on the same parallel of the Earth at *A* and at *C*.

The Sun shines on one half of the Earth only—namely on that half which is turned toward him. This hemisphere is left bright in each of the figures *ABCD*. The other half of the sphere is dark. Consider the picture at

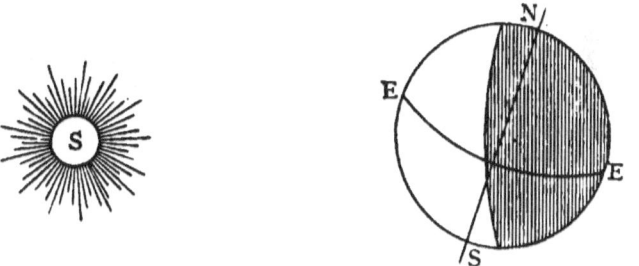

Fig. 111.—A. The Earth at the Winter Solstice.

A (winter solstice) and remember that the Earth is turning on its axis every 24 hours. Every observer on the Earth, in any latitude, is carried round his parallel of latitude by the Earth's rotation once in every 24 hours. The parallels

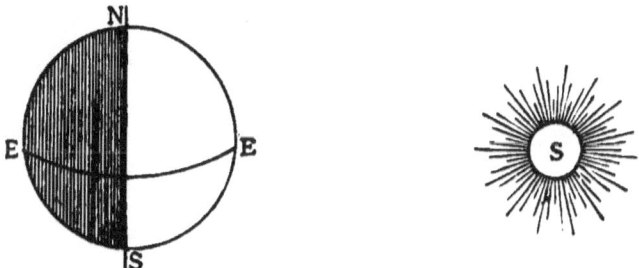

Fig. 112.—B. The Earth at the Vernal Equinox.

of latitude are drawn in the picture. A person near *N* will remain in darkness during the whole 24 hours. A person anywhere in the northern hemisphere of the Earth will be *less* than half the time in the light, *more* than half the time in darkness. The Sun will be less than half the time above his horizon. The daylight hours will be shorter than the hours of darkness. This is the time of winter in the northern hemisphere of the Earth.

Take, next, the Earth at the vernal equinox *B.* Half

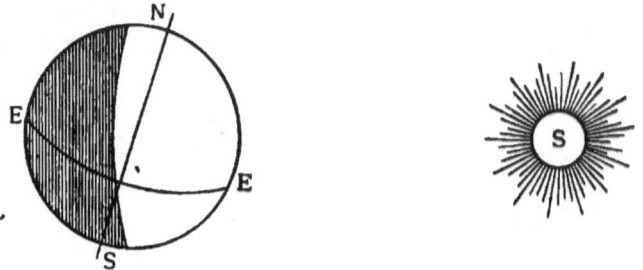

FIG. 113.—C. THE EARTH AT THE SUMMER SOLSTICE.

of the Earth is lighted by the Sun, and the Sun's rays just reach the two poles *N* and *S.* The days and nights are equal. At the summer solstice *C* an observer at the Earth's north pole has perpetual day; and the Sun is above the horizon of every person in the northern hemi-

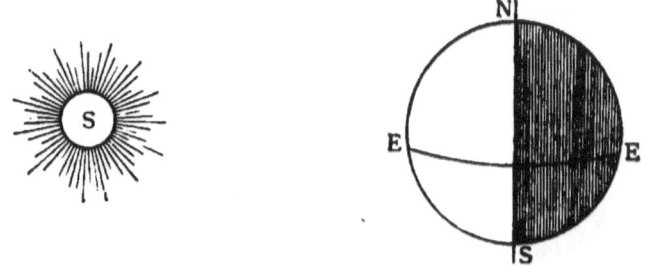

FIG. 114.—D. THE EARTH AT THE AUTUMNAL EQUINOX.

sphere for more than half the 24 hours. The days are longer than the nights. At the autumnal equinox, *D,* the circumstances are like those at the vernal equinox.

The foregoing explanation of Fig. 110 illustrates the dependence of the seasons upon the length of time that the Sun is above the horizon. The altitude of the Sun above the horizon also plays an important part in producing the change of the seasons. (See Fig. 115).

In the figure a beam of sunshine having the cross-section *ABCD* strikes the soil *cbDA* at an angle *h*. It is clear that the area *cbDA* is greater than the area *ABCD*. The amount of heat in the sunbeam is always the same. This con-stant amount of heat is dis-tributed over a larger surface according as the altitude of the Sun is less. Hence in a winter's day, when the Sun even at noon is low, each square mile of soil receives less heat than it receives in summer, when the Sun is high.

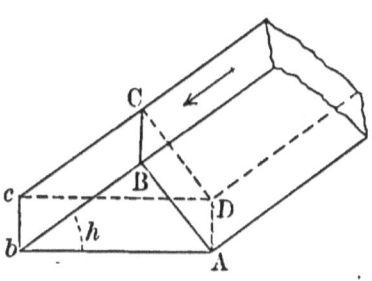

Fig. 115.—The Effect of the Sun's Elevation on the Amount of Heat Imparted to the Soil.

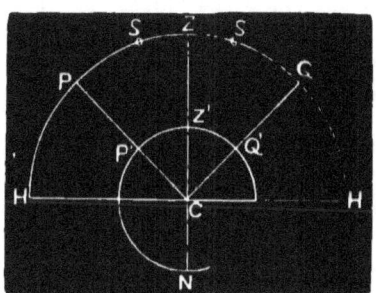

Fig. 116.—The Meridian Altitude of the Sun at S is Equal to $(90° - \phi + \delta)$; $HS = HQ + QS$.

At a place on the Earth whose latitude is $45°$ ($= \phi$) the meridian-altitude of the Sun is 45° on March 20 (90° − 45° + 0°);

" 68½° " June 21 (90° − 45° + 23½°);

" 45° " September 22 (90° − 45° + 0°);

" 21½° " December 22 (90° − 45° − 23½°).

Therefore the Sun's rays are inclined to the soil at very different angles at different dates, and the amount of heat received per square mile varies. Not only is less heat per square mile received in December than in June, but it is received for a shorter period. In latitude 45° the Sun is above the horizon for about 15½ hours on June 21 (see the table on page 168), while on December 22 it is above the horizon for a little more than 8½ hours. There are two reasons, then, for the change of seasons: *first,* the duration of sunshine is longer at some dates than at others, *second* the amount of the Sun's heat received per square mile per hour is greater at some dates than at others.

— The student should take a pin and put it on the various parallels of latitude in the four diagrams *ABCD*, Fig. 110. The rotation of the Earth carries an observer round his own parallel of latitude. The pictures show whether the observer is more or less than 12 hours in the light of the Sun—whether his days are longer or shorter than his nights. They also show how the altitude of the Sun varies at different seasons of the year. Notice that an observer on the Earth's equator always has days and nights of equal length, no matter what the season of the year. Prove that the Sun is always in the zenith to some observer in the Earth's torrid zone.

What is the obliquity of the ecliptic? How many degrees is it? Show how it can be determined by observing the lengths of the shadow of an obelisk. What are the two causes of the change of seasons on the Earth?

CHAPTER IX.

THE APPARENT AND REAL MOTIONS OF THE PLANETS —KEPLER'S LAWS.

23. The Apparent Motions of the Planets to an Observer on the Earth—Their Real Motions in Their Orbits.—The apparent motions of the planets were studied by the ancients by mapping down their positions among the fixed stars from night to night. The same process can be followed to-day by any one who will give the time to it. The place of the planet must be fixed by observation each night, with reference to stars near it, and then this place must be transferred to a star-map, like those printed at the end of this book, for instance. A curved line joining the different apparent positions of the planet on different nights will represent its apparent path.

Astronomers, who are provided with accurate instruments such as meridian-circles, fix the positions of the planets by determining their right-ascensions and declinations every night. By platting these positions on a map they obtain a representation of the apparent orbit with great accuracy.

Something of the same sort can be done by the student with much simpler instruments. He needs only a common watch and a straight ruler some three feet long, together with a star-map. Suppose that he wishes to determine the place of the planet *Mars* (♂). The first step is to identify the planet in the sky, by its brightness, its place, or by its motion. He then selects two bright stars not very far away from it (let us call them *A* and *B* for convenience).

Holding up the ruler so that its edge passes through the two stars, he notices that it passes very nearly through the planet, which

Fig. 117.—Copernicus.
Born 1473, died 1543.

is, however, let us say, a little to the west of the line. On the star-map he must find the two stars *A* and *B*. Suppose that they are *α* and *β Aurigæ* (between the numbers 105° and 120° at the top of Plate II). A dot must now be put on the map in the proper position

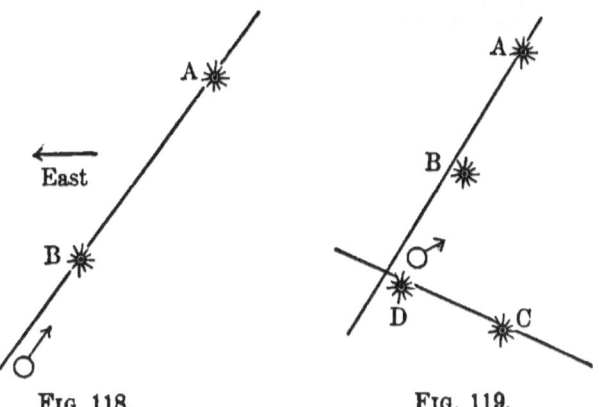

FIG. 118.   FIG. 119.

to represent the place of the planet; and the dot must be numbered (1). In his note-book opposite 1 the observer must write the year, the month, the day, and the hour of observation thus:

1. 1899, February 27, 9ʰ P.M.

The place of the planet is much more accurately fixed if the observer makes allineations with four stars, thus:

C might be *δ Aurigæ* on Plate II and *D* a star given but unnamed there.

On succeeding nights other positions of the planet can be obtained in the same way, and its apparent path can be had by joining the different positions. The times of each observation are to be noted. The positions of other planets as *Mercury*, *Venus*, *Jupiter*, and *Saturn* can also be studied from night to night, and their apparent paths fixed in like manner. Observations of this kind, if continued long enough, will give the apparent paths of the different planets in the sky. The courses of the Sun and Moon can be studied in the same manner, except that observations of the Sun must be made near the times of sunset and sunrise, because it is only at these times that stars are visible near it.

If such observations are made the student can discover for himself what the ancients knew very well, namely, that there are heavenly bodies with apparent motions of three very different kinds. The Sun and Moon have apparent motions of one kind. If we mark down the positions of the Sun day by day upon a star-chart, they will all fall into a regular circle which marks out the ecliptic, and its motion is always towards the east. The monthly course of the Moon is found to be of the same nature; and although its motion is by no means uniform in a month, it is always towards the east, and always along or very near a certain great circle.

Venus and *Mercury* have motions of a different kind. The apparent motion of these bodies is an oscillating one on each side of the Sun. If we watch for the appearance of one of these planets after sunset from evening to evening, we shall by and by see it appear above the *western* horizon. Night after night it will be farther and farther from the Sun until it attains a certain maximum distance; then it will appear to return towards the Sun again, and for a while it will be lost in its rays. A few days later it will reappear to the west of the Sun, and thereafter be visible in the *eastern* horizon before sunrise. In the case of *Mercury* the time required for one complete oscillation back and forth is about four months; and in the case of *Venus* it is more than a year and a half.

The third class comprises *Mars, Jupiter*, and *Saturn*. The general or average motion of these planets is towards the east, a complete revolution around the celestial sphere being performed in two years in the case of *Mars*, 12 years in the case of *Jupiter*, and 30 years in that of *Saturn*. But, instead of moving uniformly forward, they seem to have a swinging motion; first, they move forward or toward the east through a pretty long arc, then backward or westward through a short one, then forward through a longer one, etc. It is by the excess of the longer arcs over the shorter ones that the circuit of the heavens is made.

Observations of the planets will show that each one of them has an apparent motion like those just described. The problem is to discover the real cause of these observed motions.

The general motion of the Sun, Moon, and planets among the stars being towards the east, observed motions

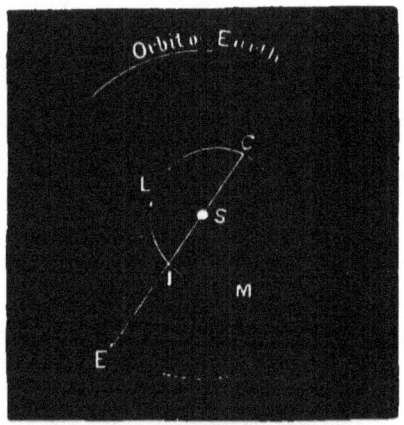

FIG. 120.

If *S* is the Sun, *E* the Earth, *CLM* the orbit of an inferior planet, then the planet is in inferior conjunction at *I*, at superior conjunction at *C*, at its greatest elongation from the Sun at *L* and *M*.

in this direction are called *direct;* motions towards the west are called *retrograde.* During the periods between direct and retrograde motion the planets will for a short time appear stationary.

The planets *Venus* and *Mercury* are said to be at greatest *elongation* when at their greatest angular distance from the Sun.

An inferior planet is said to be in *conjunction* with the Sun when both planet and Sun are in the same direction as seen from the Earth. It is in inferior conjunction when it is between the Sun and Earth; in superior conjunction when the Sun is between the Earth and the planet. A superior planet is said to be in *opposition* to the Sun when the planet is directly opposite in direction to the Sun as seen from the Earth.

Arrangements and Motions of the Planets of the Solar System.—The Sun is the centre of the solar system and all

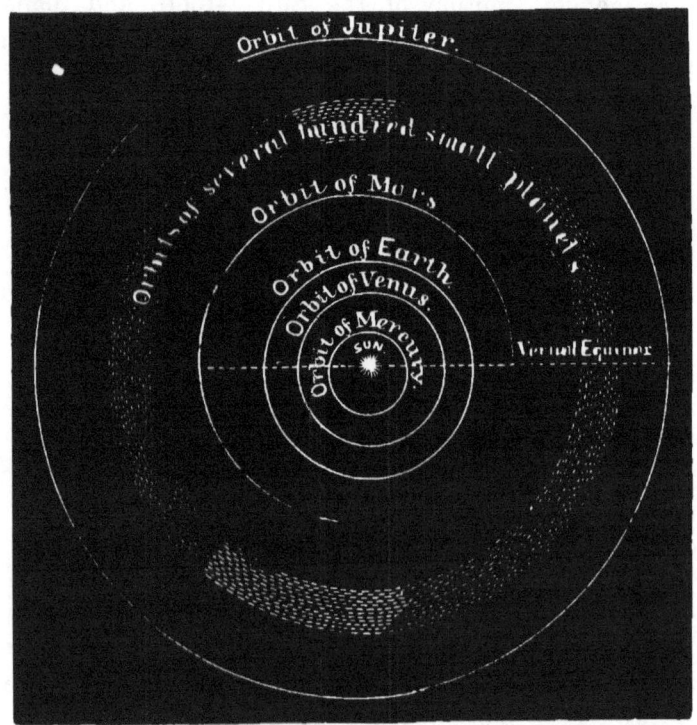

FIG. 121.—THE ORBITS OF MERCURY, VENUS, THE EARTH, MARS, AND JUPITER.

The distance from the Sun to the Earth is 93,000,000 miles ; from the Sun to Jupiter is 481,000,000 miles ; the other distances are in proportion.

the planets revolve about the Sun. Some of the planets have satellites or moons that revolve about the planet while the planet itself revolves about the Sun. Our own Moon is such a satellite. The orbits of the planets are all nearly, but not exactly, in the same plane, namely, in the plane of the Earth's orbit—the ecliptic.

NAME.	SYMBOL.	Distance from the Sun.*	Sidereal Period of Revolution.
Group of Planets each about the size of the Earth. { Mercury Venus.. Earth .. Mars ...	☿ ♀ ⊕ ♂	0.39 0.72 1.00 1.52	88 days = 3 months ⊥. 225 " = 7½ " 365¼ " = 12 " 687 " = 22½ "
The Small Planets...	..	About 2.65	3 to 8 years.
Groups of very large Planets. { Jupiter.. Saturn.. Uranus. Neptune	♃ ♄ ♅ ♆	5.20 9.54 19.18 30.05	11 9⁄10 years. 29½ " 84 " 164 1⁄10 "

* The distance of the Earth = 1.00 = 93,000,000 miles.

The planets *Mercury* and *Venus* which, as seen from the earth, never appear to recede very far from the Sun, are in reality those which revolve inside the orbit of the Earth. The planets *Mars, Jupiter,* and *Saturn* are more distant from the Sun than the Earth is. *Uranus* and *Neptune* are planets generally invisible except in the telescope, and their orbits are outside of that of *Saturn.* On the scale of Fig. 121 the orbit of *Neptune,* the outermost planet, would be more than thirty inches in diameter.

Inferior planets are those whose orbits lie inside that of the Earth, as *Mercury* and *Venus.*

Superior planets are those whose orbits lie outside that of the Earth, as *Mars, Jupiter, Saturn,* etc. The ancient astronomers gave these names and they have been retained in use, although they now have little significance.

The farther a planet is situated from the Sun the slower is its motion in its orbit. Therefore, as we go outwards from the Sun, the periods of revolution are longer, for the double reason that the planet has a larger orbit to describe and moves more slowly in its orbit. The Earth moves 18½ miles per second in its orbit, while *Saturn* moves but 6 miles per second.

An observer on the Sun at *S* would see the Earth along the lines *S* 1, *S* 2, *S* 3, etc. If these lines are prolonged (to the *right* hand in the figure) the Earth would seem, to an observer on the Sun, to move eastwardly among the

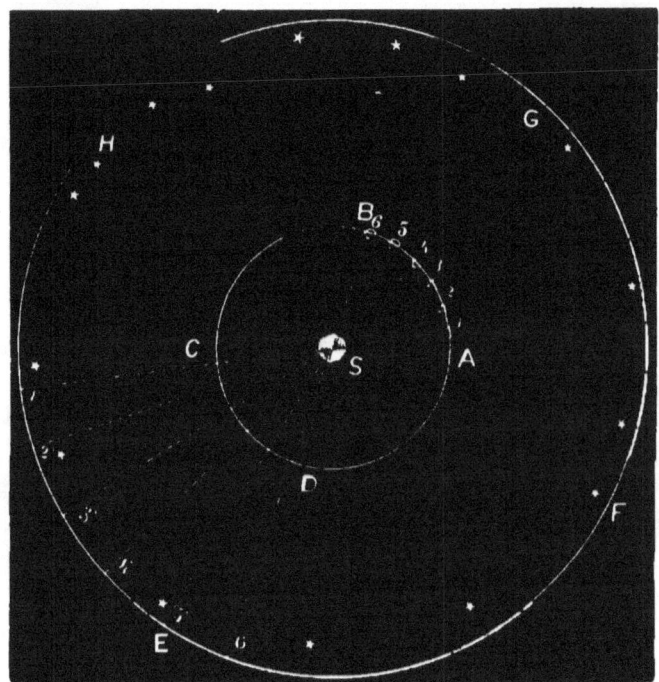

Fig. 122.—The Motion of the Earth in Its Orbit—It is Direct Motion.

stars (see page 158). The real motion of the Earth seen from the Sun is direct. We have proved on page 159 that the apparent motion of the Sun is always direct also. The plane of the Earth's orbit—the ecliptic—is the plane in which all the other planets revolve very nearly. It is to the slower motion of the outer planets that the occasional apparent retrograde motion of the planets is due, as may be seen by studying Fig. 123. The apparent position of a planet, as seen from the Earth, is determined by the line joining the Earth and planet. We see the planet along this line. Supposing this line to be continued so as

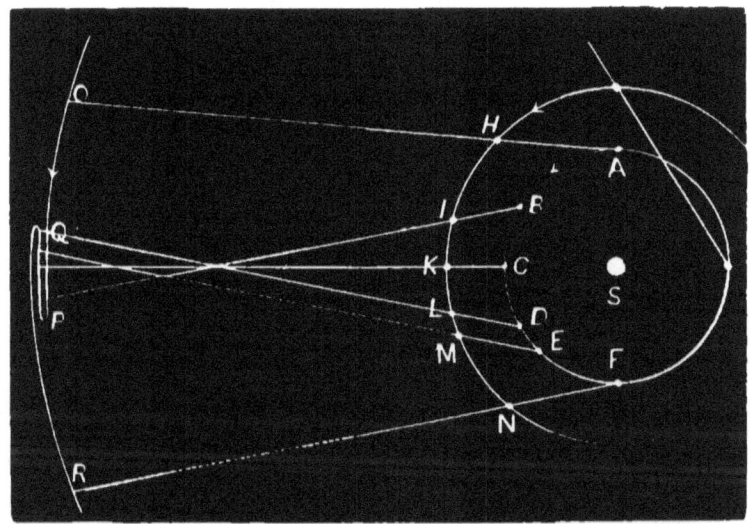

FIG. 123.

The apparent motion of a superior planet, as seen from the Earth, is sometimes direct and sometimes retrograde. The motion is always retrograde when the planet is nearest the Earth, always direct when the planet is farthest from the Earth.

to intersect the celestial sphere, the apparent motion of the planet will be defined by the motion of the point in which the line meets the celestial sphere. If this motion is towards the east the motion of the planet is *direct;* if this motion is towards the west, the motion of the planet is *retrograde.*

Let us consider the case of one of the superior planets. Its orbit is outside of the Earth's orbit. Its motion in its orbit is slower than the Earth's motion in its orbit. Let *S* be the Sun, *ABCDEF* the orbit of the Earth and *HIKLMN* the orbit of a superior planet—*Mars*, for example. The real motion of *Mars* is direct. It moves round its orbit in the direction of the arrow, just as the Earth moves round its orbit in the direction marked. In both cases the real motion is from west to east.

When the Earth is at *A*, *Mars* is at *H*
"   "   "   " *B*,   "   " *I*
"   "   "   " *C*,   "   " *K*
"   "   "   " *D*,   "   " *L*
"   "   "   " *E*,   "   " *M*
"   "   "   " *F*,   "   " *N*

As the Earth moves faster than *Mars* the arcs *AB*, *BC*, *CD*, *DE*, *EF* correspond to greater angles at *S* than do the arcs *HI*, *IK*, *KL*, *LM*, *MN*.

When the Earth is at *A* and *Mars* at *H*, an observer on the Earth will see *Mars* along the line *AH*. This line meets the celestial sphere at *O*. *Mars* will then appear to be projected among the stars near *O*. When the Earth is at *B* and *Mars* at *I*, the planet will be viewed along the line *BP* and it will be seen on the celestial sphere among the stars near *P*. While the Earth is moving in its orbit from *A* to *B* *Mars* will appear to move (eastwards) among the stars from *O* to *P*. Its apparent motion is in the same direction as the Earth's real motion. When the Earth is at *C* and *Mars* at *K* the planet will be seen along the line *CK* (prolonged). Its apparent place among the stars will be slightly *to the west* of *P*—it will appear to have moved backwards—its apparent motion is, at this time, *retrograde*.

When the Earth is at *C* *Mars* is in *opposition* to the Sun. The Sun and *Mars* are seen from the Earth in opposite directions. The apparent motion of all superior planets at the time of opposition is retrograde.

While the Earth is moving from *C* to *D* in its orbit, *Mars* is moving from *K* to *L* in its orbit, and the apparent position of *Mars* on the celestial sphere is moving *to the west*—in a retrograde direction. As the Earth moves from *D* to *E* *Mars* moves from *L* to *M* and the planet is seen along the lines *DL* and *EM* prolonged. These lines are parallel. They meet the celestial sphere in the same group of stars. The planet, therefore, seems to stay in the same position among the stars. It appears to be *stationary* just after opposition, while the Earth is moving from *D* to *E*.

As the Earth moves from *D* to *F* *Mars* moves in its orbit from *L* to *N*. Its apparent place on the celestial sphere among the stars changes from *Q* to *R*. Its apparent motion is again direct—towards the East. It is in this way that a superior planet—one whose orbit is outside of the Earth's orbit—moves around the celestial sphere. Its general motion is eastwardly through long arcs. Near opposition its apparent motion is retrograde and, for a period, it is stationary. It does not then change its place with reference to stars near it.

The student can study the apparent motion of a superior planet near *conjunction*, or of an inferior planet by constructing suitable diagrams like the foregoing.

The superior planets (*Mars, Jupiter, Saturn*, etc.) make the whole circuit of the sky in long forward arcs with short loops of retrogression. The inferior planets (*Mercury* and *Venus*) do not make the circuit of the sky. They oscillate on either side of the Sun, never going very far away from it. When they are west of the Sun they rise before him and are *morning stars*. When they are east of the Sun they set after the Sun and are *evening stars*. If *Venus* is an evening star she will approach the Sun nearer and nearer and set nearer and nearer to the time of sunset. By and by she approaches so closely as to be lost in his rays (at inferior conjunction—*KCS* in Fig. 123, where *K* is now the Earth and *C Venus*). In a few days she has passed the Sun going westwards and rises before him as a morning star. The apparent motion of all planets is retrograde when they are nearest to the Earth and direct when they are farthest from us.

The apparent motions of all the planets visible to the naked eye were perfectly familiar to the ancient astronomers, as has been said. The positions of the planets had been observed by them for centuries. But the *reasons* for these complex movements were not known. It was everywhere believed that the Earth was the centre of the Universe and that the Sun, the Moon, the stars, and all the planets were made for the sole benefit of mankind. All the explanations of the ancient philosophers started with the assumption that the Earth was the centre of the Universe and that the Sun and all the planets revolved around it. No one thought of questioning this proposition. It was everywhere believed.

PTOLEMY of Alexandria in Egypt worked out a theory of the Universe on this scheme about A.D. 140. It was a very ingenious system and it explained observed appearances fairly well so long as the observations were not very accurate.

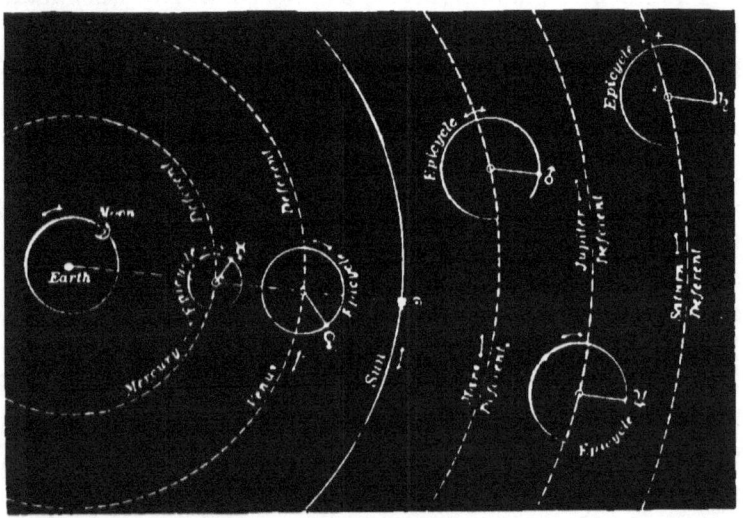

FIG. 124.—THE SYSTEM OF THE WORLD ACCORDING TO PTOLEMY.

Each planet was supposed to move round the circumference of a small circle called its *epicycle* (see the cut), while the centre of the epicycle moved around a larger circle called the *deferent*. By taking the epicycles and the deferents of suitable sizes a very fair representation of the apparent motions of the Sun and planets was made.

The swinging motions of *Mercury* and *Venus* on each side of the Sun were explained by their motions around their epicycles, which would make them appear alternately east and west of the Sun if their epicycles moved round their deferents at the same rate that the Sun moved (see the cut). The retrogradations of the superior planets— *Mars, Jupiter,* and *Saturn*—were explicable in a similar fashion.

It is not necessary to go into details in this matter because PTOLEMY'S explanation of the Universe is not the correct one. Still the student should know something of a theory which was believed by every one from the first centuries of our Christian era until COPERNICUS proposed the true explanation. It was not until COPERNICUS had made long-continued observations on his own account and had given his whole life to solving the problem that it was known that the Sun and not the Earth was the centre of the planetary motions. He proposed this explanation in 1543, but it was not generally accepted until the discoveries of GALILEO (1610), about three centuries ago.

The theory of PTOLEMY accounted pretty well for the facts known in his time. It represented the apparent motion of the planets as he observed them. But the observations of the Arabian astronomers in Spain (A.D. 762 to 1492) and of TYCHO BRAHE (pronounced Tee-ko Brä-hee) in Denmark about 1580, and especially the revelations of GALILEO'S telescope, made PTOLEMY'S explanation impossible. It was not long before it was found that even the system proposed by COPERNICUS was not entirely satisfactory. It was certain that the Sun and not the Earth was the centre of the planetary motions, as he had said. But accurate observations soon made it equally certain that the planets did not revolve in *circular* orbits. They revolved about the Sun in orbits nearly but not quite circular, in curves like ovals. They certainly did not revolve in circles.

From the time of COPERNICUS (1543) till that of

KEPLER (about 1630) the whole question of the true system of the Universe was in debate. The circular orbits introduced by COPERNICUS also required a complex system of epicycles to account for some of the observed motions of the planets, and with every increase in accuracy of observation new devices had to be introduced into the system to account for the new phenomena observed. In short, the system of COPERNICUS accounted for so many facts (as the stations and retrogradations of the planets) that it could not be rejected, and had so many difficulties that without modification it could not be accepted.

— Describe how the place of a planet may be fixed, among the fixed stars, by simple observations. If such observations are made for long periods the apparent paths of the Sun and planets become known.—In what apparent paths do the Sun and Moon move? *Mercury* and *Venus?* The superior planets? Define the inferior conjunction of *Venus*—the superior conjunction of *Mercury*—the opposition of *Jupiter.* Define the inferior planets—the superior planets. Define direct motion—retrograde. What was the theory of the Universe proposed by PTOLEMY in A.D. 140? How long did men hold the belief that the Earth was the centre about which the planets revolved? Who proposed the *heliocentric* theory of the solar system? At what date? What was the shape of the orbits of all the planets in this theory?

24. Kepler's Laws of Planetary Motion.—KEPLER (born 1571, died 1630) was a genius of the first order. He had a thorough acquaintance with the old systems of astronomy and a thorough belief in the essential accuracy of the Copernican system, whose fundamental theorem was that the Sun and not the Earth was the centre of our system. He lived at the same time with GALILEO, who was the first person to observe the heavenly bodies with a telescope of his own invention, and he had the benefit of accurate observations of the planets made by TYCHO BRAHE. The opportunity for determining the true laws of the motions of the planets existed then as it never had before; and fortunately he was able, through labors of which it is difficult to form an idea to-day, to reach a true solution.

The Periodic Time of a Planet.—The time of revolution of a planet in its orbit round the Sun (its *periodic time*) is

FIG. 125.—JOHN KEPLER,
Born 1571, died 1630.

determined by continuous observations of the planet's course among the stars.

The periodic times (the sidereal periods) of the planets were known to KEPLER from the observations of the ancient astronomers.

Mercury revolved about the Sun in about 88 days = 0.24 yrs.
Venus   "   "   "   "   "   225 " = 0.62 "
Earth   "   "   "   "   "   365 " = 1.00 "
Mars   "   "   "   "   "   687 " = 1.88 "
Jupiter   "   "   "   "   "   4333 " = 11.86 "
Saturn   "   "   "   "   " 10,759 " = 29.46 "

The Relative Distances of Planets from the Sun.—
KEPLER had no way of determining the absolute distance
of each planet from the Sun (its distance in miles), but if
the distance of the Earth from the Sun was taken as the
unit (1.000) he could determine the distances of the other
planets in terms of this unit in the following way:

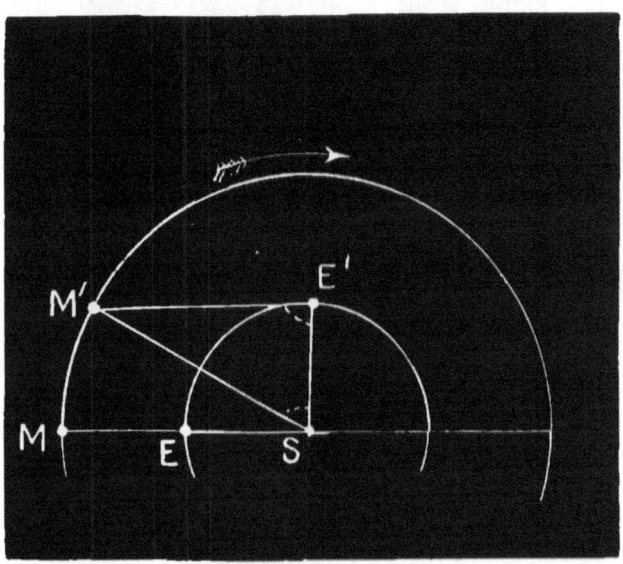

FIG. 126.—METHOD OF DETERMINING HOW MUCH GREATER THE
DISTANCE OF MARS FROM THE SUN IS THAN THE DISTANCE OF
THE EARTH FROM THE SUN.

In the figure let *S* be the Sun, *EE'* the orbit of the earth, and *MM*
the orbit of *Mars*. When the Earth is at *E* and *Mars* at *M* the planet
is in *opposition*, i.e., it is seen from the Earth in a direction exactly
opposite to the Sun. It is on the meridian of the observer exactly at
midnight. After a hundred days, for example, *Mars* will have

moved to M' and the Earth will have moved to E'. The observer will then see the Sun in the direction E' to S; he will see *Mars* in the direction E' to M'. At this time the angle $M'E'S$ can be *measured* with a divided circle, and it therefore is a known angle. The angle ESE' is known, because we can calculate through what angle the Earth will move in 100 days, since we know that it moves through 360° in 365¼ days. The angle MSM' is likewise known, since we can calculate through what angle *Mars* will move in 100 days, because we know that *Mars* moves through 360° in 687 days. The angle $M'SE$ is therefore known because $ESE' - MSM' = M'SE'$. Hence in the triangle $M'SE'$ we know the two angles marked in the diagram. $E'SM'$ is measured, $M'SE'$ is calculated. The angle $SM'E' = 180° - \{E'SM' + M'E'S\}$ because in any plane triangle the sum of the angles is 180°. Hence in this triangle we can determine all three angles. We can therefore construct a triangle *of the right shape.* If we assume the Earth's distance SE' to be 1.000 we can determine the distance of *Mars* in terms of that unit. If KEPLER had known the distance SE' in miles (as it is known nowadays) then he could have determined the absolute distance, SM', of *Mars.* As it was, he could say that if the Earth's distance, SE', was called 1.000 then the distance of *Mars*, SM', must be 1.52.

At different points of the Earth's orbit the corresponding distances of *Mars* were determined. The same thing was done for the other planets at different points of their orbits. KEPLER found that if the mean distance of the Earth from the Sun was called 1.000 then the mean distances for all the planets were:

For *Mercury*, $a_1 = 0.3871$;   for *Mars*, $a_4 = 1.5237$;
"   *Venus*, $a_2 = 0.7233$;   "   *Jupiter*, $a_5 = 5.2028$;
"   *Earth*, $a_3 = 1.000$;   "   *Saturn*, $a_6 = 9.5388$.

The radius-vector of a planet is the line that joins it to the Sun.

KEPLER made thousands and thousands of such calculations and determined the radius-vector of *Mars* from the Sun at all points in its orbit, assuming that the Earth's average (mean) distance was 1.000. He could therefore make a map of the orbit of *Mars* as in the following figure.

In the figure *S* is the place of the Sun. At some date
Mars was somewhere along the line *SP* (*Mars* was in a
certain known celestial longitude). If the distance of the
Earth from the Sun was taken as the unit then the dis-

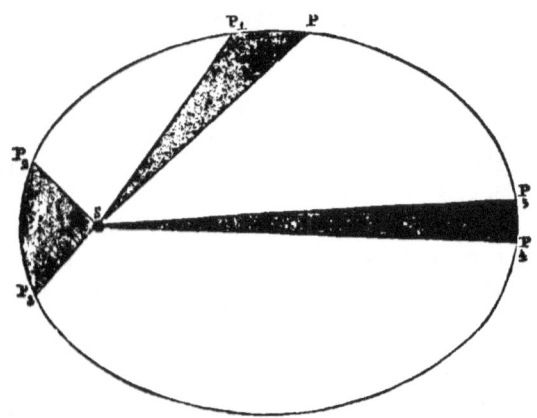

Fɪɢ 127.—Tʜᴇ Oʀʙɪᴛ ᴏғ ᴀ Pʟᴀɴᴇᴛ, *P*, ᴀʙᴏᴜᴛ ᴛʜᴇ Sᴜɴ, *S*.

tance of *Mars* was known in terms of that unit. *Mars* was
at the point *P*. At a later time *Mars* was somewhere along
the radius-vector SP_1, which was in the right longitude.
Calculation showed that *Mars* was at the point P_1. At
other times *Mars* lay somewhere along the radii-vectores
SP_2, SP_3, SP_4, SP_5. Calculation showed that the planet
was at the points P_2, P_3, P_4, P_5. The curved line joining
all these points was the visible representation of the orbit
of *Mars*. The curve P_1 . . . P_5 was the true shape of
the orbit. Nothing was known of the size of the orbit
except that it was so and so many times larger than the
Earth's; but at any rate its true shape was known. It
was not a circle; it was something like an oval.*

KEPLER'S next problem was to determine what kind of

* The real orbit of *Mars* is very nearly a circle and the oval of this
figure has been exaggerated purposely. The curve that *Mars*
describes is not exactly circular, but it is much less oval than
Fig. 127.

a curve the orbit of *Mars* really was. It was not a circle
at any rate. He tried all kinds of curves and finally discovered that *Mars*, like every other planet, moved around
the Sun in an *ellipse* and that the Sun was not at the
centre of the ellipse, but at one of the *foci*.

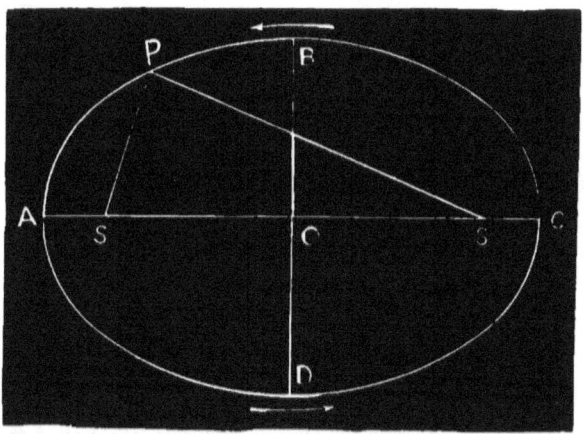

FIG 128.—AN ELLIPSE.

*An ellipse is a curve such that the sum of the distances
of every point of the curve from two fixed points (the foci)
is a constant quantity.*

The student should draw a number of ellipses for practice. Drive
two tacks into a board at S and S'. Tie a string at S' and the other
end of the string at S. Let the length of the string be $SP + PS'$·
Put a pencil at the point P and move the pencil round the curve,
always keeping the string stretched tight. Wherever the pencil P
may be the length SP *plus* the length $S'P$ is a constant quantity.
For every point of the curve $SP + S'P = $ a constant. Take a string
of a different length to start with and tie it to S and S' and you will
get an ellipse of a different shape. Put the tacks S and S' nearer
together and the ellipse will be of another shape, but it will still be
an ellipse.

$ADCP$ is an ellipse ; S and S' are the foci. By the definition of
an ellipse $SP + PS' = AC$, and this is true for every point. S is
the focus occupied by the Sun, "the filled focus." AS is the *least
distance* of the planet from the Sun, its *perihelion distance;* and A

is the *perihelion*, that point nearest the Sun.   *C* is the *aphelion*, the point farthest from the Sun.   *SA, SD, SC, SB, SP* are radii vectores at different parts of the orbit.   *AC* is the *major axis* of the orbit = 2*a*.

The major axis of the orbit is twice the *mean distance* of the planet from the Sun, *a*.   *BD* is the *minor axis*, 2*b*.   The ratio of *OS* to *OA* is called the *eccentricity* of the ellipse.   By the definition of the ellipse, again, $BS + BS' = AC = 2a$; and $BS = BS' = a$. $\overline{BS}^2 = \overline{BO}^2 + \overline{OS}^2$, or $OS = \sqrt{a^2 - b^2}$.   The eccentricity of the ellipse is

$$\frac{OS}{OA} = \frac{\sqrt{a^2 - b^2}}{a}$$

After years of laborious calculation KEPLER discovered three laws governing the motion of the planets.   (The student should memorize these laws.)

The first law of KEPLER is—

I. Each planet moves around the Sun in an ellipse, having the Sun at one of its foci.

Suppose the planet to be at the points P, P_1, P_2, P_3, P_4, etc., at the times T, T_1, T_2, T_3, T_4, etc., in Fig. 129.

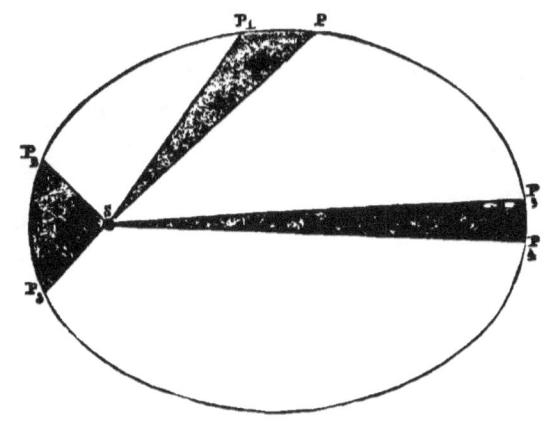

Fig. 129.—KEPLER'S SECOND LAW.

Suppose the intervals of *time* $T_1 - T$, $T_2 - T_2$, $T_4 - T_4$ to be equal.   KEPLER computed the areas of the surfaces PSP_1, P_2SP_3, P_4SP_4 and found that these areas were equal also, and that this was true for each and every planet in every part of its orbit. The second law of KEPLER is—

II. The radius-vector of each planet describes equal areas in equal times.

These two laws are true for each planet moving in its own ellipse about the Sun.

For a long time KEPLER sought for some law which should connect the motion of one planet in *its* ellipse with the motion of another planet in *its* ellipse. Finally he found such a relation between the *mean distances* of the different planets and their *periodic times.*

His third law is:

III. The squares of the periodic times of the planets are proportional to the cubes of their mean distances from the Sun.

That is, if T_1, T_2, T_3, etc., are the periodic times of the different planets whose mean distances are a_1, a_2, a_3, etc., then

$$T_1^2 : T_2^2 = a_1^3 : a_2^3;$$
$$T_2^2 : T_3^2 = a_2^3 : a_3^3;$$
etc.   etc.

If T_3 and a_3 are the periodic time and the mean distance of the Earth and if T_3 ($= 1$ year) be taken as the unit of time and a_3 ($= 1.000$) be taken as the unit of distance, then for any other planet whose periodic time is T and mean distance a

T^2 (its periodic time) $: 1 = a^3$ (the cube of its mean dist.)$: 1$.

But the periodic time of each planet was already known from observation (see page 193); hence its mean distance can be determined because

$$a^3 = T^2 \quad \text{or} \quad a = (T^2)^{\frac{1}{3}}.$$

If, in the last equation, we substitute the values of the periodic time of each planet in succession, expressed in

years and decimals of a year, we shall obtain the value of
a, its mean distance from the Sun, expressed in terms of
the Earth's mean distance = 1.000.

For *Mercury*, $T_1 =$ 0.24 years and $a_1 =$ 0.39
" *Venus*, $T_2 =$ 0.62 " " $a_2 =$ 0.72
" *Earth*, $T_3 =$ 1.00 " " $a_3 =$ 1.00
" *Mars*, $T_4 =$ 1.88 " " $a_4 =$ 1.52
" *Jupiter*, $T_5 =$ 11.86 " " $a_5 =$ 5.20
" *Saturn*, $T_6 =$ 29.46 " " $a_6 =$ 9.54

KEPLER'S laws are true for the *satellites* as well as for
the planets. *Mars* has two satellites, *Phobos* and *Deimos*,
that revolve in ellipses in periods T' and T'' at mean distances a' and a''. In their ellipses the line joining the
satellite to *Mars* sweeps over equal areas in equal times ;
and $(T')^2 : (T'')^2 = (a')^3 : (a'')^3$.

KEPLER'S three laws give the dimensions of the orbits of
every planet in terms of the Earth's distance = 1.00.
They do not explain why it is that the planets follow these
orbits (this was not known until the time of NEWTON), but
they enable us to calculate just where any planet will be in
its orbit at any time.

For instance, suppose that *Mars* was at the place P at the time T
and we wished to know where it will be at the time T'. The whole
area of the ellipse is swept over by the radius-vector of *Mars* in 1.88
years. We can calculate how much of an area will be swept over in
the time $T' - T$. Then we can calculate what the angle at S of the
sector PSP' must be to give this sector the calculated area. A line
drawn from S to P' making the calculated angle with SP will intersect the orbit at the point P'. The planet will be at the point P' (in
a known celestial longitude) at the time T''.

Elements of a Planet's Orbit.—When we know a and b (the major and
minor semi-axes) for any orbit, the shape and size of the orbit is
known.

Knowing a we also know T, the periodic time; in fact a is found
from T by KEPLER'S law III.

If we also know the planet's celestial longitude (L) at a given epoch, say December 31st, 1850, we have all the *elements* necessary for finding the place of the planet *in its orbit* at any time, as has just been explained.

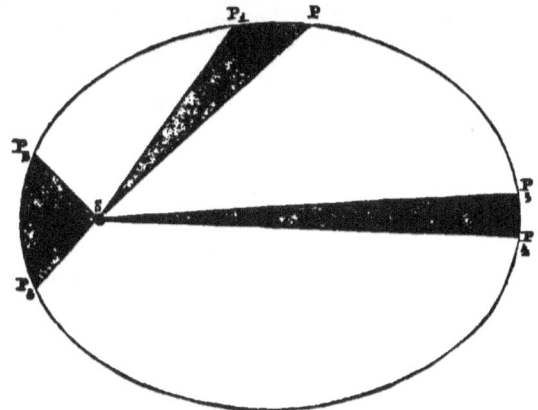

FIG. 130.—TO CALCULATE THE PLACE OF A PLANET IN ITS ORBIT AT ANY FUTURE TIME.

The orbit lies in a certain plane ; this plane intersects the plane of the ecliptic at a certain angle, which we call the *inclination i.* Knowing *i*, the plane of the planet's orbit is fixed. The plane of the orbit intersects the plane of the ecliptic in a line, the *line of the nodes.* Half of the planet's orbit lies below (south of) the plane of the ecliptic and half above. As the planet moves in its orbit it must pass through the plane of the ecliptic twice for every revolution. The point where it passes through the ecliptic going from the south half to the north half of its orbit is the *ascending node;* the point where it passes through the ecliptic going from north to south is the *descending node* of the planet's orbit. If we have only the *inclination* given, the orbit of the planet may lie anywhere in the plane whose angle with the ecliptic is *i*. If we fix the place of the nodes, or of one of them, the orbit is thus fixed in its plane. This we do by giving the (celestial) longitude of the ascending node ☊.

Now everything is known except the relation of the planet's orbit to the sun. This is fixed by the *longitude of the perihelion,* or *P.*

Thus the *elements* of a planet's orbit are :

i, the *inclination* to the ecliptic, which fixes the plane of the planet's orbit;

☊, the *longitude of the node,* which fixes the position of the line of intersection of the orbit and the ecliptic;

P, the *longitude of the perihelion*, which fixes the position of the major axis of the planet's orbit with relation to the Sun, and hence in space;

a and *e*, the *mean distance* and *eccentricity* of the orbit, which fix the shape and size of the orbit (see page 198);

T and *M*, the *periodic time* and the *longitude at the epoch*, which enable the place of the planet in its orbit, and hence in space, to be fixed at any future or past time.

The elements of the older planets of the solar system are now known with great accuracy, and their positions for two or three centuries past or future can be *predicted* with a close approximation to the accuracy with which these positions can be observed.

Moreover it was proved by two great French astronomers (LA-GRANGE and LAPLACE) about a hundred years ago that all the planets would always continue to revolve in or near the plane of the ecliptic; that the eccentricity of each orbit might vary within narrow limits, but could never depart widely from its present value, and finally that the mean-distances of the planets would always remain the same as now. The Earth, for example, will always remain at the same *average* distance from the Sun as now, though by a change in the eccentricity its least and greatest distances from the Sun may be slightly greater or less than at present. Hence there can never be any great changes in the seasons of the Earth due to a change in its distance from the Sun.

If the mean-distances of the planets remain essentially unchanged their periodic times will also remain unchanged, by the 3d law of KEPLER, so long as we consider the planets as rigid solids.

— What is a planet's *periodic-time?* How can the *relative* distances of the planets from the Sun be determined ? What are the three laws of planetary motion discovered by KEPLER? Define an ellipse. Do KEPLER's laws explain *why* the planets move in elliptic orbits? why their radii-vectores describe equal areas in equal times? why for any two planets $T^2 : T_1^2 = a^3 : a_1^2$? What are the *elements* of a planet's orbit?

CHAPTER X.

UNIVERSAL GRAVITATION.

25. The Discoveries of Sir ISAAC NEWTON.—Before the time of Sir ISAAC NEWTON very little was known of the laws that govern the motion of bodies on the Earth. A stone dropped from the hand falls to the ground. Why? NEWTON's answer was that the Earth attracted the stone downwards somewhat as a magnet attracts iron to itself. The Earth itself was made up of stones and soil. Why did not the stone attract the Earth upwards? NEWTON's answer was that the stone did, in fact, attract the Earth. But as the Earth had a mass of millions of tons and the stone a mass of only a few pounds the motion of the Earth upwards towards the stone was very small compared to the motion of the stone downwards to the Earth. It was too small to be appreciable—but the Earth moved nevertheless. The attraction was in proportion to the attracting mass, he said.

Each particle of a huge mass, like that of the Earth, would attract the stone, and the whole of the Earth's attraction would be the sum of all the particular attractions. The stone would also attract each one of the Earth's particles, but as they were all joined together it could move no one of them without moving them all. If the Earth attracted a stone near its surface why should it not attract the Moon in the sky? The Moon would be attracted less because it was distant, but it would certainly be attracted, he said. There were reasons for believing

203

that attractions grew less in proportion to the *square* of the distance, not in proportion to the simple distance.

His reasoning was something like this: We see that there is a force acting all over the Earth by which all bodies are drawn towards its centre. This force is called *gravity*. It extends to the tops not only of the highest buildings, but of the highest mountains. How much higher does it

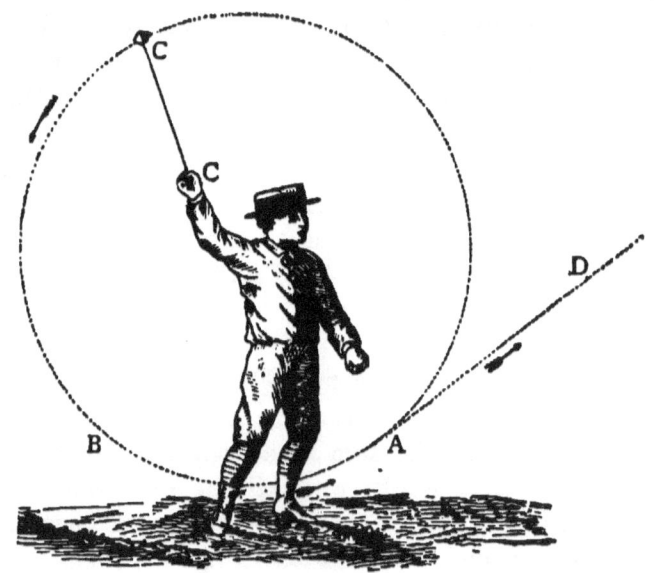

Fig. 131.

A stone in a sling is whirled round in the direction of the arrows in the circle *CBA*. At *A* the string breaks and the stone flies away in the tangent *AD*. It would move away in that direction forever if the Earth did not attract it downwards.

extend ? Why should it not extend to the Moon ? If it does, the Moon would tend to drop towards the Earth, just as a stone thrown from the hand drops. As the Moon moves round the Earth in her monthly course, there must be some force drawing her towards the Earth; else she would fly entirely away in a straight line just as a stone thrown from a sling would fly away in a straight line if the

FIG. 132.—SIR ISAAC NEWTON.
Born 1642; died 1727.

205

Earth did not attract it. Why should not the force which makes the stone fall be the same force which keeps the Moon in her orbit ?

To answer this question, it was necessary to calculate the intensity of the force which would keep the Moon herself in her orbit, and to compare it with the intensity of gravity at the Earth's surface. It had long been known that the distance of the Moon was about sixty radii of the Earth. If this force diminished as the inverse square of the distance, then at the Moon it would be only $\frac{1}{3600}$ as great as at the Earth's surface.

Experiments at the Earth's surface had proved that a body fell 16 feet in a second of time. The Moon in her orbit ought then to fall towards the Earth (that is, ought to bend away from a straight line) by $\frac{1}{3600}$ part of 16 feet in each and every second, or the Moon should bend away from a straight line (a tangent to her orbit) by about $\frac{1}{19}$ part of an inch every second. Now the size of the Moon's orbit was known and its curvature was known. It was found that the orbit of the Moon did, in fact, deflect from the tangent to the orbit by $\frac{1}{19}$ part of an inch per second. NEWTON proved this point by calculation, and from that time forward he felt sure that the force that kept the Moon in its orbit about the Earth was a force of the same kind as the *gravity* that made a stone fall to the Earth, and that it was this very same force that kept all the planets in their orbits about the Sun.

To prove that his idea was right it was necessary to prove that *if* the Sun attracted the planets just as the Earth attracted the Moon the laws of KEPLER would be a necessary consequence. NEWTON made such a proof. He proved strictly and mathematically that any two bodies which attracted each other in proportion to their masses and inversely as the square of their distances apart would obey laws like those of KEPLER. If one of the bodies was very large (like the Sun) and the other much smaller (like one of the planets) then it necessarily followed from the single law of gravitation that:

I. The planet would revolve about the Sun in an ellipse (or in one of a set of curves of the same sort). II. The radius-vector of the planet would describe equal areas in equal times. And he further proved that if there were two planets in the system the following law would be very nearly true: III. The squares of their periodic times would be proportional to the cubes of their mean distances from the Sun. These are the three laws which KEPLER deduced from observation. All the planets in the solar system obey these laws. All the planets obey the law of gravitation therefore.

KEPLER's laws were proved to be true by observation. NEWTON showed that *if* any planet moved about the sun so that its radius-vector described equal areas in equal times *then* the planet obeyed a force that was directed always to the sun as a centre of force. *If* the path of any planet was an ellipse (or if it were a parabola or hyperbola) *then* the central force must vary inversely as the square of the distance, and could vary in no other way. *If* all the planets were bound together (as they are) by KEPLER's third law, *then* all the planets are acted on by one and the same kind of force. The amount of force acting on any planet depends on its distance from the Sun and on the mass of the Sun. Observations fixed the length of each planet's year and its distance from the Sun.

From these data the mass of the Sun could be calculated in terms of the Earth's mass. Not only were these things true for all the planets ; they governed the motions of satellites about their primary planet. The Moon revolves about its primary, the Earth, in obedience to its attraction ; but it is likewise attracted by the Sun and hence its orbit is perturbed. NEWTON calculated perturbations of the Moon's motion that had been known as facts of observation since the time of HIPPARCHUS, and others that had been observed by TYCHO BRAHE and FLAMSTEED, and he accounted for all these observed facts by his theory. He also calculated some of the perturbations of the path of one planet by the attraction of other planets.

Up to NEWTON's day the motions of comets had been simply mysterious. He showed that they moved according to KEPLER's laws, *usually* in parabolas, not in ellipses. He calculated the shape that a rotating fluid mass should assume and from this deduced the figure of the Earth. He showed that it was a spheroid, not a sphere, and proved that the precession of the equinoxes, observed as a fact by HIPPARCHUS, and unexplained since his time, was a mere result of the spheroidal shape of the Earth. The Tides—another mystery— were explained by NEWTON as a result of the Moon's attraction of the waters of the Ocean.

His discoveries in pure mathematics are only second in importance to his discoveries in celestial mechanics. The binomial theorem was discovered by him (it is engraved on his tomb in Westminster Abbey). The Differential Calculus is his invention. He made most important discoveries in optics also.

The epigram of the English poet POPE expresses the feeling of awed amazement with which the men of his own time regarded this mighty genius :

> *Nature and Nature's laws lay hid in Night :*
> *God said let Newton be—and all was Light.*

Let us see what NEWTON thought of himself. Towards the end of his life he said, " I know not what the world will think of my labors, but to myself it seems that I have been but as a child playing on the seashore ; now finding some pebble rather more polished and now some shell rather more agreeably variegated than another, while the immense ocean of Truth extended itself, unexplored, beyond me."

In science his name is venerated and honored by all those who can appreciate his marvellous genius. His greatest effect on Mankind has been to set before them a new path for their thoughts to follow. Since his day men have a new view-of-the-world, and his discoveries have influenced the thoughts, beliefs, and ideals of men and nations as powerfully and as effectively as those of PLATO, ARISTOTLE, CO-PERNICUS, and GALILEO. We should not now think as we all do if our thoughts did not run in channels first opened by him.

All the motions of all the bodies in the solar system were deduced by NEWTON from one single law—the law of Universal Gravitation. The discoveries of PTOLEMY, of COPERNICUS, of KEPLER, and of all other astronomers were nothing but special cases of one universal law. PTOLEMY and other great astronomers before his time had mapped out the apparent courses of the planets in the sky with diligence and with accuracy. COPERNICUS had shown that these apparent paths were described because the real centre of the motion was the Sun. KEPLER had proved that the paths of the planets about the Sun were not circles as COPERNICUS supposed, but ellipses; and he gave the laws according to which the planets moved in their real orbits.

NEWTON started with the simple fact of gravity (Latin *gravitas* = heaviness). He said a body is heavy because the Earth attracts it. The Earth (like every mass) attracts all other bodies in the Universe, the nearer bodies more, the distant bodies less. The attraction is directly proportional to the mass; it is inversely proportional to the square of the distance. If this law is true everywhere (as experiment proves it to be true on the Earth) then all KEPLER'S laws are a necessary consequence of it. One single law accounts for every motion in the solar system. Probably this law accounts for all the motions of the stars also.

The student should memorize the law of universal gravitation in the form that NEWTON gave to it—as follows:

Every particle of matter in the universe attracts every other particle with a force directly as the masses of the two particles and inversely as the square of the distance between them.

To thoroughly understand the discoveries of NEWTON it is necessary to study *Mechanics* or the science that treats of the action of forces on bodies. This science requires a mathematical treatment too difficult and too long to be given here. After the Mechanics of terrestrial bodies is understood it must be applied to the special case of the heavenly bodies—*Celestial Mechanics*. Only the barest outline of NEWTON'S achievements can be given in this place. The following paragraphs may help the student to understand the nature of the questions involved.

If we represent by m and m' the masses of two attracting bodies, we may conceive the body m to be composed of m particles, and the other body to be composed of m' particles. Let us conceive that each particle of one body attracts each particle of the other with a force that varies as $\frac{1}{r^2}$. Then every particle of m will be attracted by each of the m' particles of the other, and therefore the attractive force on each of the m particles will vary as $\frac{m'}{r^2}$. Each of the m particles being equally subject to this attraction, the total attractive force between the two bodies will vary as $\frac{m\,m'}{r^2}$.

Each of the two masses attracts the other by a force varying as $\frac{m\,m'}{r^2}$.

If a straight stiff rod whose length was r could be slipped in between the two masses m and m', the pressure on either end of

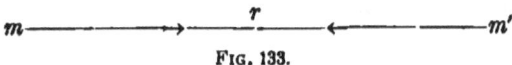

FIG. 133.

the rod would be the same. It would be a pressure proportional to $\frac{m\,m'}{r^2}$.

When a given force acts upon a body, it will produce less motion the larger the body is, the *accelerating* force being proportional to the total attracting force divided by the mass of the body moved. Therefore the accelerating force which acts on the body m', and which determines the amount of motion, will be $\frac{m}{r^2}$; and conversely the accelerating force acting on the body m will be represented by the fraction $\frac{m'}{r^2}$. If m is very large (as in the case of the Sun) and if m' is relatively small (as in the case of a planet), the motion of the planet will be determined by the Sun's accelerating force while the Sun will be but little affected by the accelerating force of the planet.

It makes no difference at all of what substances m and m' are made up. A mass of gas (as a comet) attracts in proportion to its quantity of matter, just as a mass of lead attracts in proportion to *its* quantity of matter.

It is in this respect, especially, that the force of gravitation differs from a force like magnetism. A magnet will attract iron but not wood. But both wood and iron are heavy.

The attraction of a spherical body on a particle outside of itself is the same as if the whole mass of the spherical body were concentrated at its centre. We may treat the problems of Celestial Mechanics as if the Sun and all the planets were mere points, the whole mass of each body being concentrated at their centres. The attraction of the Earth for bodies on its surface is the same as if the earth were a mere point, its whole mass being concentrated at its centre.

A word may be said on the variation of forces inversely as the square of the distance. Suppose we take the force of gravitation. At a distance of *one* radius of the Earth from the Earth's centre (at the Earth's surface) let us call its intensity *one ;* at a distance of two radii (some 4000 miles above the Earth's surface therefore) it will be $\frac{1}{4}$; at a distance of 3 radii it will be $\frac{1}{9}$; and so on.

$$\text{Distances} = 1, 2, 3, 4, 5, 6, \ldots 100 \ldots 1000$$
$$\text{Forces} = 1, \tfrac{1}{4}, \tfrac{1}{9}, \tfrac{1}{16}, \tfrac{1}{25}, \tfrac{1}{36}, \cdots \tfrac{1}{10000}, \cdots \tfrac{1}{1000000}$$

An excellent practical example of a quantity that varies inversely as the square of the distance may be had by watching the headlight of a train-car as it approaches you. When it is five blocks off the intensity of the light is $\frac{1}{25}$th, four blocks off $\frac{1}{16}$th, three blocks $\frac{1}{9}$, two blocks $\frac{1}{4}$ of the intensity at a distance of a block. Gravitation varies according to a similar law.

Gravitating force seems to go out from every particle of matter in the Universe in all directions somewhat as rays of light stream out in all directions from a lamp. It streams out in straight lines. Whatever is in its way is attracted. If a planet is there it attracts the planet. If nothing is there no attraction is exerted on empty space. The rays of gravitation (so to speak) pass directly through a body and a second body beyond it is attracted just as if the first body were not there. There is no gravitational shadow, as it were.

A ——————————— B ——————— C

If A were a lamp and B and C two screens, the screen B would be lighted and the screen C would be in shadow. But if A is a heavy body it will attract a body at B and another body C beyond it just as if B were not there.

Moreover, the storehouse of gravitational attraction in a heavy body is never exhausted. The sun attracts a planet at a certain distance just as much in July as in the preceding January, just as much in 1907 as in 1620.

It requires *time* for the light of the Sun to travel across the space that separates it from the Earth. A beam of light leaves the Sun and does not arrive at the Earth for 8^m 19^s, it does not arrive at *Jupiter* for 43^m 15^s. It takes these times to pass over the intervening spaces. But the gravitating effect of the Sun traverses these spaces *instantaneously*, so far as we now know. When gravitation is con-sidered in this way, as a force inherent in a body, as sourness is in-herent in a fruit, a recital of its properties sounds like a fairy-tale. The explanation of gravitation is not yet known. This force, like the force of magnetism and other forces, is a mystery. When its ex-planation comes to be known it will probably be found that a heavy body must not be considered to be in *empty* space, but in a space filled with some substance like the ether which transmits light. The body influences the ether and sets up strains and stresses within it. These stresses are transmitted in all directions with immense (prob-ably not infinitely great) velocities. When these stresses meet a second body they act upon it to produce the phenomena of gravita-tion.

A word may also be said as to the intensity of the force of gravi-tation. The popular notion is that gravitation is a very powerful force. This is because we live on an earth which is very large in comparison to our own size, and to the sizes of objects that we use in our daily life. In reality gravitation may be called a feeble force compared to such a force as the expansion of water when it freezes and bursts the stout pipes in which it is contained. Two masses M and M', each weighing 415,000 tons, a mile apart, attract each other with a force of one pound. Imagine two huge cubes of iron, each weighing 415,000 tons. If at a mile's distance they only exert a force of one pound we must decide that the force of gravitation is feeble rather than powerful. If M and M' were two miles apart their mu-tual attraction would be only four ounces. If M was doubled in size, their attraction at one mile's distance would be two pounds; if both M and M' were doubled their attraction would be four pounds, and so on. These effects one would call small rather than large.

The discoveries of NEWTON in relation to the force of gravitation that binds the planets together and that determines every circum-stance of every motion of everything on the Earth lead to conclu-sions like those just set down. What the true nature of this force is we do not know any more than we know the true nature of the forces of chemical affinity and the like. No doubt a complete under-standing of it will some day be reached, and what now seems mar-vellous will then be simple. There is no doubt that the motions of every particle on the Earth and of every planet in the solar system are obedient to this law. The simple proof is that the motions of planets, comets, and of many stars have been calculated beforehand on this theory and that observation has subsequently verified the predictions. The pages of the Nautical Almanac (see page 150) are

nothing but a series of such predictions that are afterwards verified
over and over again in the minutest particular. The place that a
planet will occupy in the sky a century hence can be predicted
nearly as accurately as the planet can then be observed. Not only
this, but the paths of thousands of projectiles to be fired from cannon have been calculated beforehand, and these predictions have been
subsequently verified by experiment. Every swing of a pendulum
and every fall of a heavy body is obedient to this law, and in thousands and thousands of similar cases the law has been accurately
verified by experiment.

Mutual Actions of the Planets — Perturbations.—KEPLER's laws
would be accurately followed in any system of only two heavy
bodies, as the Sun and any one planet, *Mars* for example. If a third
body exists, the Earth for instance, it will attract the Sun and also
Mars. The Sun and *Mars* will likewise attract the Earth. The
motion of *Mars* about the Sun will not be exactly the same in a system of three bodies as in a system of two.
The mass of the Sun is so very much
greater than the mass of the Earth that
Mars will travel in an orbit almost the
same as its undisturbed orbit—almost, but
not quite. The Earth will produce slight
disturbances—*perturbations* they are called
—in the orbit of *Mars*, and these perturbations can be exactly calculated from NEW-
TON's law. The orbit of the Earth will
also be perturbed by *Mars*.

Each of the planets will act on every
one of the other planets to alter its motion.
These disturbances in the solar system are
small, because the Sun's mass is so very
large compared to the mass of the disturbing body. Even *Jupiter*, the largest
of the planets, has a mass less than $\frac{1}{1000}$ of
the Sun's mass.

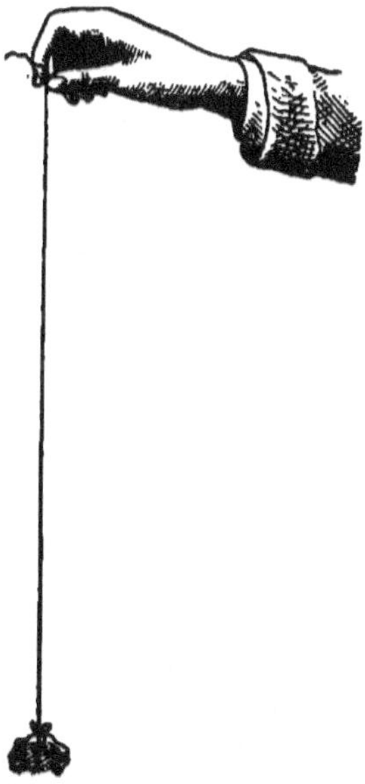

The Vertical Line.—The direction
up and down, the vertical direction, is
defined for any observer by the line

FIG. 134.—A PENDULUM
AT REST HANGS VER-
TICALLY.

in which a pendulum at rest hangs. The pendulum is attracted by the whole Earth and if the Earth were a sphere
it would always point to the Earth's centre. As the Earth

is a spheroid (its meridians being ellipses and not circles)
a pendulum at rest at any point of the Earth's surface does
not point *exactly* to the centre, although its direction is

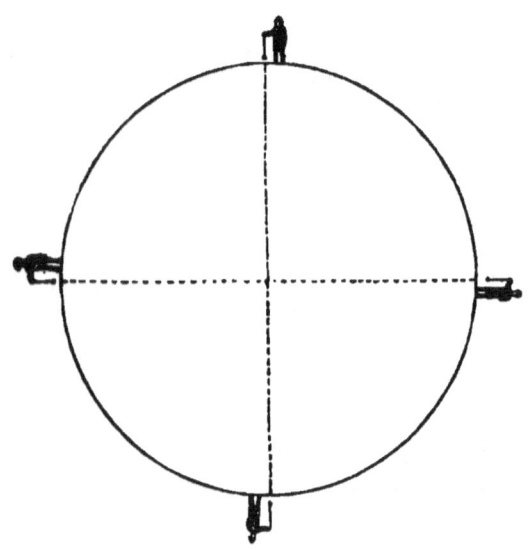

Fig. 135.—A Pendulum at Rest on a Spherical Earth
    Points nearly to the Centre of the Earth.

never far from that of the Earth's radius.   (The radius of
the Earth and the pendulum never make an angle of more
than 12' of arc—a fifth of a degree—with each other.)

The zenith of an observer may now be defined as that
point over his head where a pendulum at rest at his station
would meet the celestial sphere if the pendulum were indefinitely long.   A pendulum at rest always lies in the line
of joining an observer's zenith and nadir.

Remarks on the Theory of Gravitation.

The real nature of the discovery of Newton is frequently
misunderstood.   Gravitation is sometimes spoken of as if
it were a theory of Newton's, now very generally received,

but still liable to be ultimately rejected as a great many other theories have been.

NEWTON did not discover any *new* force, but only showed that the motions of the heavenly bodies could be accounted for by a force which we all know to exist. Gravitation is the force which makes all bodies here at the surface of the Earth tend to fall downward; and if any one wishes to subvert the theory of gravitation, he must begin by proving that this force does not exist. This no one would think of doing. What NEWTON did was to show that this force, which, before his time, had been recognized only as acting on the surface of the Earth, really extended to the heavens, and that it resided not only in the Earth itself, but in the heavenly bodies also, and in each particle of matter, wherever situated. To put the matter in a terse form, what NEWTON discovered was not *gravitation*, but the *universality* of gravitation.

— What was the principal work of PTOLEMY and his predecessors? What was the discovery of COPERNICUS? What was KEPLER's discovery? What was the greatest discovery of NEWTON? Give NEWTON's law of universal gravitation in his own words. Did NEWTON discover gravitation? What, in fine, was his discovery? Define the zenith of an observer—his nadir.

CHAPTER XI.

THE MOTIONS AND PHASES OF THE MOON.

26. The Moon makes the circuit of the heavens once in each (lunar) month. She revolves in a nearly circular orbit around the Earth (not the Sun) at a mean distance of 240,000 miles. At certain times the new Moon, a slender crescent, is seen in the west near the setting Sun. On each succeeding evening we see her further to the east, so that in two weeks she is exactly opposite the Sun, rising in the east as he sets in the west. Continuing her course two weeks more, she has approached the Sun from the west, and is once more lost in his rays. At the end of twenty-nine or thirty days, we see her again emerging as new Moon, and her circuit is complete. The Sun has been apparently moving towards the east among the stars during the whole month at the rate of 1° daily (see page 165), so that during the interval from one new Moon to the next the Moon has to make a complete circuit relatively to the stars, and to move forward some 30° further to overtake the Sun. The revolution of the Moon *among the stars* is performed in about 27⅓ days, so that if the Moon is very near some star on March 1, for example, we shall find her in the same position relative to the star on March 28.

The Moon's revolution relative to the stars is performed in 27⅓ days; relative to the Sun in 29½ days. Her periodic time in her orbit about the Earth is 27⅓ days therefore.

Phases of the Moon.—The Moon is an opaque body and is formed of materials something like the rocks and soils of

216

the Earth. Like the planets, she does not shine by her own
light, but by the light of the Sun, which is reflected from
her surface much as sunlight would be reflected from a
rough mirror. As the Moon, like the Earth, is a sphere,
only half of her globe can be illuminated at a time—namely,
that half turned towards the Sun.

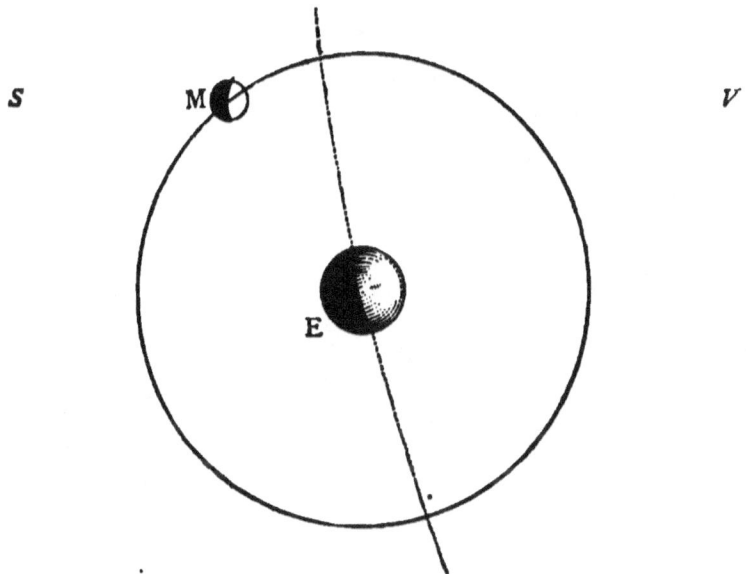

Fig. 136.—The Moon (*M*) in her Orbit Round the Earth (*E*).

Half of each body is illuminated by the Sun. The Sun is not shown in
the drawing. If it were to be inserted it would have to be on the right-
hand side of the picture about thirty-five feet distant from *E*.

We can see only half of the Moon—namely, that half that
is turned toward us. An eye at *S* (on the left-hand side
of the page) could see half of the Moon if it were illuminated. But as the dark side is turned toward *S* an eye
placed there would see nothing. No light would come to
it. An eye at *V* would see the Moon as a bright circle.
The half turned toward *V* is fully illuminated.

In this figure the central globe is the Earth; the circle around it represents the orbit of the Moon. The rays of the Sun fall on both Earth and Moon from the right, the

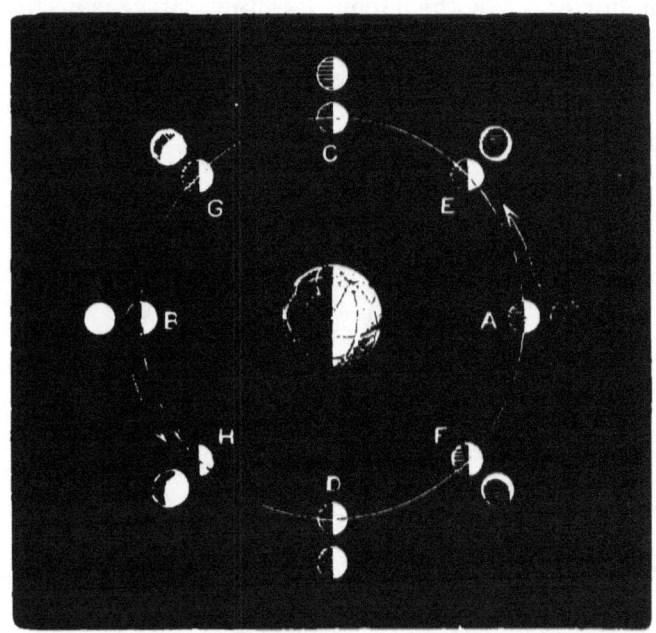

Fig. 137.—The Phases of the Moon Explained.

Sun being some thirty feet away (on the scale of the drawing) in the line *BA*. For the present purpose we suppose both Earth and Sun to be at rest and the Moon to move round her orbit in the direction of the arrows. Eight positions of the Moon are shown around the orbit at *A*, *E*, *C*, etc., and the right-hand hemisphere of the Moon is illuminated in each position. Outside of these eight positions are eight pictures showing how the Moon looks as seen from the Earth in each position.

At *A* it is " new Moon," the Moon being nearly between the Earth and the Sun. Its dark hemisphere is then turned towards the Earth, so that it is entirely invisible. The Sun and Moon then rise and set together. They are in the same direction in space.

At E the observer on the Earth sees about a fourth of the illuminated hemisphere, which looks like a crescent, as shown in the outside figure. In this position a great deal of light is reflected from the Earth to the Moon and back again from the Moon to the Earth, so that the part of the Moon's face not illuminated by the Sun shines with a grayish light. At C the Moon is in her *first quarter*. The Moon is on the meridian about 6 P.M. She is about 90° (6 hours) east of the Sun. When the Sun is setting the Moon is therefore near the meridian. At G three-fourths of the hemisphere that is illuminated by the Sun is visible to the observer; and at B the whole of it is visible. The Moon at B is exactly opposite to the Sun and it is then "full Moon." The full Moon rises at sunset. As the Moon moves to H, D, F, the phases change in a reverse order to those of the first half of the month.

The Tides.—The phenomena of the tides are familiar to those who live near the seashore. Twice a day the waters of the ocean rise high on the beach. Twice a day they recede outwards. The first "high tide" occurs at any place (speaking generally) about the time when the Moon is on the meridian of that place. About six hours later comes "low tide"; about twelve hours after the first "high tide" comes a second "high tide," and finally, about six hours after this a second "low tide." The Moon revolves about the Earth once in about 25ʰ (not 24ʰ), for it is moving eastwards among the stars nearly 15° daily.

In figure 138 suppose O to be the centre of the Earth and m a place on its surface. Suppose, for simplicity, that the whole Earth is surrounded by a shallow shell of water. There is a high tide at m when the Moon (M) is on the meridian of m. Let us see why this is so. The Earth is attracting the Moon, and by its attraction the Moon is kept in her orbit.

The Moon moves towards the Earth a little every second.

The Moon likewise attracts every particle of the earth, solid and fluid alike. The fluid particles nearest M (at m) are perfectly free to move, and they are therefore heaped up into a kind of a wave whose crest is at *m.* The particles of water near *m″* and *m‴* are drawn towards *m.* The Moon at *M* also attracts the solid body of

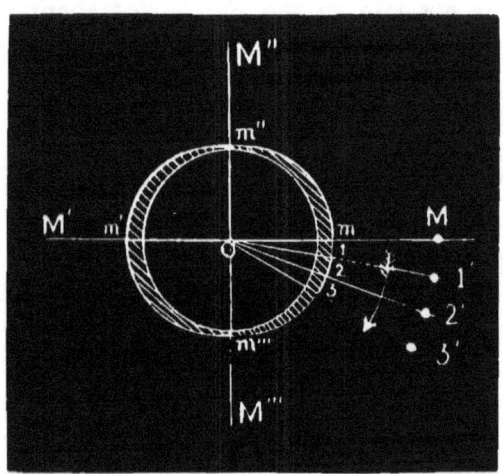

FIG. 138.—THE TIDES OF THE OCEAN ARE PRODUCED BY THE MOON'S ATTRACTION.

the Earth with a force that is inversely proportional to the square of the distance *MO*—to $\dfrac{1}{(MO)^2}$—and the Earth moves towards the Moon a little every second. The Moon also attracts the fluid particles near *m′,* in the further hemisphere of the Earth, with a force proportional to $\dfrac{1}{(Mm')^2}$. If they were a solid separate from the main body of the Earth, they would move less than the rest of the Earth, because they are less attracted, being more distant.

The Moon at *M* attracts the solid Earth as a whole, more than it attracts the waters of the distant hemisphere *m″m′m‴.* The solid Earth, which must move as a whole, moves towards *M* in consequence of its attraction more than the waters of the distant hemisphere, which are therefore left behind as it were, heaped up into a kind of wave whose crest is at *m′* opposite to the moon *M.* The shape of the *tidal ellipsoid* is shown by the shaded area in the figure.

When the moon is at *M* on the meridian of a place at *m,* the tidal ellipsoid is as drawn. There is high tide at *m,* low tide at a place 90° distant (*m″*), high tide at *m′,* low tide again at *m‴.* Whenever the moon is on the meridian of any place such an ellipsoid is formed. As the Moon moves round the earth each day from rising to setting, this ellipsoid moves with it.

In an hour the moon will have moved to 1' and the crest of the wave to 1. The tide will be high at 1 and falling at m. As the moon moves by the diurnal motion to 2', 3', M''', M', the crest will move with it. When the moon is at M''' it is low water at m and m'. When the moon is at M', it is again high water at m; and so on.

If we suppose M to be the sun, a similar set of *solar* tides will be produced every 24 hours. The actual tide is produced by the super-position of the solar and lunar tides.

The foregoing explanation relates to an Earth covered by an ocean of uniform depth. To fit it to the facts as they are a thousand cir-cumstances must be taken into account which depend on the modify-ing effects of continents and islands, of deep and shallow seas, of currents and winds. Practically the time of high tide at any station is predicted in the "Tide-Tables" by adding to the time of the Moon's transit over the meridian a quantity that is determined from observation and not from theory.

— Describe the changes of the shape of the Moon's disk from new moon to the next new moon. Does the Moon shine by her own light? What part of the globe of the Moon is illuminated by the Sun? About what time does the new moon rise? the full moon?

CHAPTER XII.

ECLIPSES OF THE SUN AND MOON

27. The Earth's Shadow—the Moon's Shadow—Lunar Eclipses—Solar Eclipses—Occultations of Stars by the Moon.—A point of light L sends out rays in every direction. If an opaque disk VO is interposed in the path of some of these rays it will form a shadow on the side furthest from the light. All the space between the lines

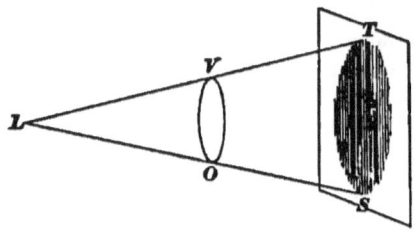

Fig. 139.—The Shadow of a Disk VO Formed by a Point of Light L and Projected on a Screen TS.

LV, LO, and other lines drawn from the point L to the borders of VO will be dark. The region $VOST$ is dark and it is called the shadow of VO. If the source of light is not a mere point the shadow is not so simple. The candle-flame AB shines on the sphere DC and illuminates one-half of it. The region to the right of the sphere and between the lines BDS' and ACS receives no light at all. If a screen is interposed the shadow is shown quite black at $S'S$. None of the region to the right of the sphere between the lines AP' and BP is fully illuminated. Some of the candle-flame is cut off from every part of this region

222

by the sphere. Let the student mark a point half way from S to P (call it a). From a draw a line tangent to the sphere near C and prolong it till it meets the candle-

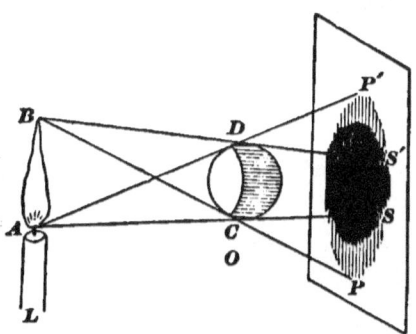

Fig. 140.—The Shadow—Umbra and Penumbra—of a Sphere
Formed by a Candle.

flame (at a point that we may call b). Draw also the line aA. The point a is illuminated by part of the flame (the part between b and A) and it receives no light from the part of the flame between b and B. It is impossible to draw a straight line through a that will meet the flame between b and B unless such a line passes through the sphere DC. The region $DS'SC$ is the *umbra* of the shadow; the region $DP'S'$, CSP, etc., is the *penumbra.* If the shadow is received on a screen the circle SS' is often called the *umbra* and the ring $PSP'S'$ the *penumbra.*

The Shadow of the Earth.—In figure 141 S is the Sun, E the Earth. The cone BVB' is the *umbra;* that part of the cone $BFB'F'$ which is not *umbra* is the *penumbra.*

Dimensions of the Earth's Shadow.—Let us investigate the distance EV from the centre of the Earth to the vertex of the shadow. The triangles VEB and VSD are similar, having a right angle at B and at D. Hence

$$VE : EB = VS : SD = ES : (SD - EB).$$

So if we put

$l = VE$, the length of the shadow measured from the centre of the Earth,

$r = ES$, the radius-vector of the Earth, = 92,900,000 miles,

$R = SD$, the radius of the Sun,   =   433,000   " ,

$\rho = EB$ the radius of the Earth,   =   4000   " ,

we have

$$l = VE = \frac{ES \times EB}{SD - EB} = \frac{r\rho}{R - \rho}.$$

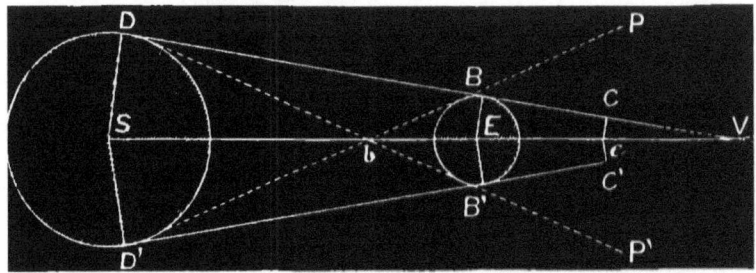

Fig. 141.—Dimensions of the Shadow of the Earth.

That is, l is expressed in terms of known quantities, and thus is known.

Its length is about 866,000 miles.

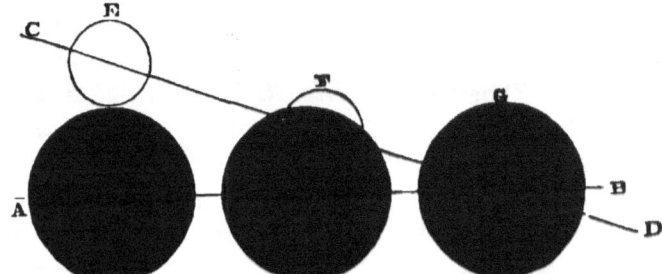

Fig. 142.—AB is the Ecliptic; CD is the Moon's Orbit.

The three dark circles on AB are three positions of the Earth's shadow. Sometimes the Moon is totally eclipsed as at G, sometimes partially eclipsed as at F, sometimes she just escapes eclipse as at E.

Eclipses of the Moon.—The mean distance of the Moon from the Earth is about 238,000 miles and the Moon often passes through the Earth's shadow-cone (EV). While the Moon is within that cone none of the light of the Sun can reach her surface and she is said to be eclipsed.

·If the Moon moved exactly in the plane of the ecliptic she would pass through the Earth's shadow-cone at every full Moon (for it is at full Moon that the Sun and Moon are on opposite sides of the Earth) and would be totally eclipsed once every lunar month. The Moon's orbit is, however, inclined to the ecliptic at an angle of about 5°, and therefore she often escapes eclipse, as is shown by the diagram. As a matter of fact it is very seldom that more than two lunar eclipses occur in any calendar year.

Eclipses of the Moon are calculated beforehand and the phases are printed in the almanac. Supposing the Moon to be moving around the Earth from below upward in figure 141, its advancing edge first meets the boundary $B'P'$ of the penumbra. The time of this ocurrence is given in the almanac as that of *Moon entering penumbra.* A small portion of the sunlight is then cut off from the advancing edge of the Moon, and this amount constantly increases until the edge reaches the boundary $B'V$ of the shadow. The eye can scarcely detect any diminution in the brilliancy of the Moon until she has almost touched the boundary of the true shadow. The observer must not, therefore, expect to detect the coming eclipse until very nearly the time given in the almanac as that of *Moon entering shadow.* As the Moon enters the true shadow the advancing portion of the lunar disk will be entirely lost to view. It takes the Moon about an hour to move over a distance equal to her own diameter, so that if the eclipse is nearly central the whole Moon will be immersed in the shadow about an hour after she first strikes it. This is the time of beginning of *total eclipse.* So long as only a moderate portion of the Moon's disk is in the shadow, that portion will be entirely invisible, but if the eclipse becomes total the whole disk of the Moon will nearly always be visible, shining with a red coppery light.

This is owing to the refraction of the Sun's rays by the lower strata of the Earth's atmosphere. We shall see hereafter that if a ray of light DB (see Fig. 141) passes from the Sun to the Earth, so as just to graze the latter, it is bent by refraction more than a degree out of its course. At the distance of the Moon the whole shadow of the Earth is filled with this refracted light. Some of it is reflected back to the Earth, and as it has passed twice through the Earth's atmosphere the light is red for the same reason that the light of the setting Sun is red.

The Moon may remain enveloped in the shadow of the Earth during a period ranging from a few minutes to nearly two hours, according to the distance at which she passes from the axis of the shadow and the velocity of her angular motion. When she leaves the shadow, the phases which we have described occur in reverse order.

It very often happens that the Moon passes through the penumbra of the Earth's shadow without touching the shadow at all. The diminution of light in such cases is scarcely perceptible unless the Moon at least grazes the edge of the shadow.

Eclipses of the Sun.—The shadow of the Earth falling upon the Moon cuts off the Sun's light from it and causes a lunar eclipse. The shadow of the Moon falling on a part of the Earth cuts off the light of the Sun from all observers in that region of the Earth and causes a solar eclipse.

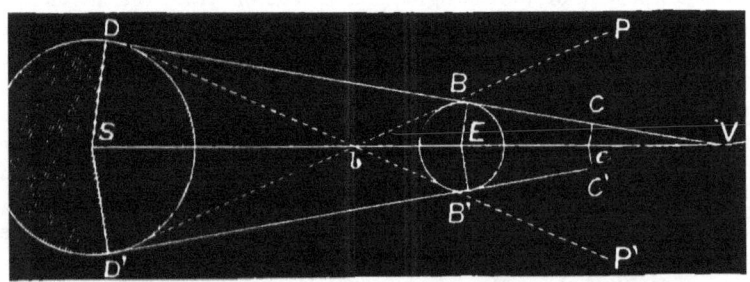

Fig. 143.—Dimensions of the Shadow of the Moon.

In this figure let S represent the Sun, as before, and let E represent the Moon. The cone BVB' is now the umbra of the Moon's shadow. We wish to know the length of the Moon's shadow VE. By a method similar to that given on page 224, using accurate values of the different quantities, it is found that VE at new Moon is about 232,000 miles. The average distance of the centre of the Moon from the centre of the Earth is about 239,000 miles (or from the centre of the Moon to the *surface* of the Earth about 235,000 miles), and hence generally the Moon's shadow will not quite reach to the Earth's surface and generally there will be no solar eclipse at new Moon. If the Moon's orbit were a circle with a radius of 239,000 miles we should have no solar eclipses at all. It is, however, an ellipse, and at favorable times (that is when the Moon's shadow is long enough and when it points at the Earth) the Moon's shadow may reach the Earth and even beyond it. At such times the Sun's light will be cut off from all observers on the Earth within the shadow and a solar eclipse will occur. The conditions at such favorable times are illustrated by the figure.

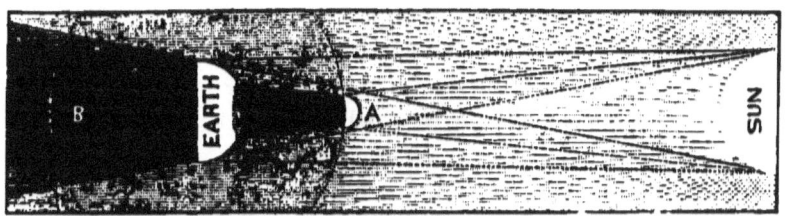

FIG. 144.

The Sun is eclipsed to all observers on the Earth within the shadow of the new moon (*A*). The full Moon is eclipsed whenever it passes through the Earth's shadow (*B*).

It is clear that all observers on the Earth within the umbra of the Moon's shadow at *A* cannot see the Sun at all. To them the Sun will be totally eclipsed. Observers on the Earth within the penumbra of the Moon's shadow (see the figure) will see a part of the Sun only. To such observers the Sun will be partially eclipsed.

The diameter of the Moon's umbra at the surface of the Earth is seldom more than 160 miles. It is usually much less. Observers within this umbra see a *total solar eclipse*. As the Moon moves in its orbit at the rate of over 2000 miles per hour (which is about twice the velocity of a cannon-ball) the shadow moves correspondingly. It sweeps

over the surface of the Earth in a curved line or belt. The
observers within this belt see the total eclipse one after
another. At any one place the totality *cannot* last more
than 8 minutes and it usually lasts much less than this.

At the total solar eclipse of July, 1878, for example, the shadow of
the Moon travelled diagonally across North America from Behring's
Straits through Alaska west of the Rocky Mountains of British Co-
lumbia and entered the United States not far east of Vancouver.
From thence the shadow crossed Washington, Idaho, the south-
western part of Wyoming, the State of Colorado (near Denver), the
State of Texas, and, curving across the Gulf of Mexico, traversed
Cuba. The duration of totality was about 3 minutes near Vancouver, about 2½ minutes near Galveston. The shadow-path of the
total solar eclipse of May 28, 1900, is described in Chapter XVI.

In order to see a total eclipse an observer must station
himself beforehand at some point of the Earth's surface
over which the shadow is to pass. These points are generally calculated some years in advance, in the astronomical
ephemerides.

Eclipses of the Sun are useful to astronomy because
during an eclipse the Sun's light is cut off from the Earth's
atmosphere and we have a short period of darkness during
which the surroundings of the Sun can be examined with
the spectroscope or with the photographic camera. Great
discoveries have been made at these times, as we shall see.
Eclipses are useful to history and to chronology because they
afford a precise means of fixing dates. Total solar eclipses
are so impressive (see Chapter XVI for a description of the
phenomena) that they are often recorded in ancient annals.
Calculation can fix the date at which such an event was
visible, and thus render a service to chronology. Lunar
eclipses are often serviceable in the same way.

There is another way of looking at the problem of solar
eclipses which is worth attention. An observer on the
Earth sees the Sun as a bright circle in the sky. The
apparent angular diameter of the Sun (the angle between

two lines drawn from the observer's eye to the upper edge
and to the lower edge of the Sun, respectively) is greatest
when the Earth is nearest to the Sun, least when the Earth
is farthest away. In the same way the apparent angular
diameter of the Moon to an observer on the Earth is
greatest when the Moon is nearest, least when the Moon is
furthest away.

These apparent angular diameters have been measured
and the results of observation are given in the following
little table:

	Greatest.	Least.	Average.
Apparent diameters of the Moon ...	33′ 33″	29′ 24″	31′ 08″
Apparent diameters of the Sun.....	32′ 33″	31′ 28″	32′ 00″

If at any new Moon the centres of the Sun, Moon, and
Earth are in a straight line, an eclipse will occur. If the

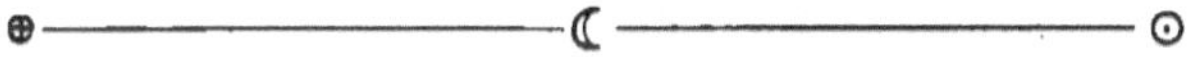

FIG. 145.

angular diameter of the Moon is *less* than that of the Sun
we shall have an *annular eclipse* of the Sun. When the
centre of the Moon just covers the centre of the Sun the
appearance will be like figure 146. As the Sun at this time
has a larger angular diameter it will appear, at the moment
of central eclipse, like a bright ring round the dark
(unilluminated) body of the Moon. The Moon will move
across the disk of the Sun from west towards east and the
ring will only endure for a short time.

If the centres of the Earth, Sun, and Moon are in a
straight line at any new Moon, and if at that time the
apparent angular diameter of the Moon is *greater* than that
of the Sun there will be a total eclipse of the Sun.

If at the time of new Moon the Moon does not pass centrally across the Sun's disk, but above the centre or below it, there may be a total eclipse (or an annular eclipse), but usually there will only be a partial eclipse. Only a part of the Sun's disk will be covered in such a case.

There are more eclipses of the Sun than of the Moon. A year never passes without at least two of the former, and sometimes five or six, while there are rarely more than two eclipses of the Moon, and in many years none at all. But at any one place on the Earth more eclipses of the Moon than of the Sun will be seen. The reason of this is that an eclipse of the Moon is visible over the entire hemisphere of the Earth on which the Moon is shining, and as it lasts several hours, observers who are not in this hemisphere at the beginning of the eclipse may, by the Earth's rotation, be brought into it before it ends. Thus the eclipse will usually be seen over more than half the Earth's surface. But each eclipse of the Sun can be seen over only so small a part of the Earth's surface, and while there are many more solar eclipses than lunar for the whole Earth taken together, fewer are visible at any one station.

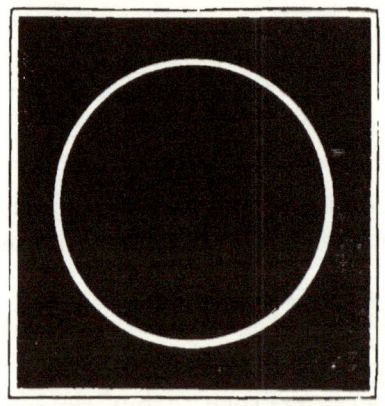

Fig. 146.—The Dark Body of the Moon Projected on the Disk of the Sun at the Middle of an Annular Eclipse.

Occultation of Stars by the Moon.—Since all the bodies of the solar system are nearer than the fixed stars, it is evident that they must from time to time pass between us and the stars. The planets are, however, so small that such a passage is of very rare occurrence. But the Moon is so large and her angular motion so rapid that she passes over some star visible to the naked eye every few days. Such phenomena are termed *occultations of stars by the Moon.*

The *Nautical Almanac* contains predictions of all occultations, These predictions are obtained by calculating the Moon's path on the celestial sphere and by noticing what bright stars (or planets) her disk will cover to observers at different stations on the Earth.

— What is a shadow? its umbra? penumbra? Draw a diagram showing the shadow of the Earth cast by the Sun. Point out the umbra and the penumbra of this shadow. What is the cause of a lunar eclipse? Why do we not have lunar eclipses at every full moon—once a month? What is the color of the totally eclipsed moon? Why does it have this color? What is the cause of a solar eclipse? Why do we not have solar eclipses at every new moon? (Answer: because in the first place the Moon's shadow is often too short to reach the surface of the Earth and also because it often does not at new Moon point at the Earth, but above the Earth or below it.)

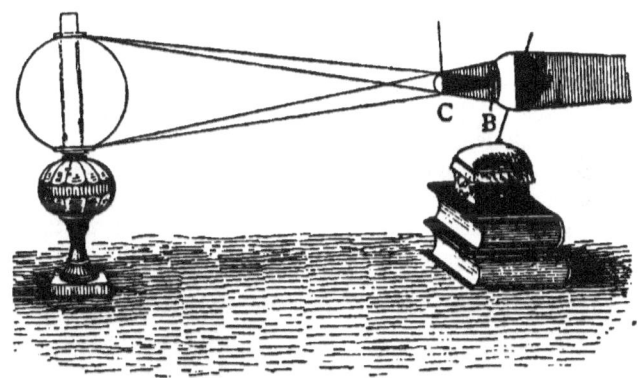

Fig. 147.—A Schoolroom Experiment to Illustrate a Solar Eclipse.

The room must be darkened. The lamp should have a ground glass or an opal globe to represent the circle of the Sun's disk. An orange (*B*) fastened to a pincushion by a knitting-needle may stand for the Earth. A golf-ball suspended by a string (*C*) may stand for the Moon. By placing *C* on the other side of *B* the circumstances of a lunar eclipse may be illustrated.

What is a partial eclipse of the Moon? of the Sun? a total eclipse of the Moon? of the Sun? an annular eclipse of the Sun? Why can there never be an annular eclipse of the Moon? What is an *occultation?* Longfellow has a poem, "The Occultation of Orion." Could the Moon cover a whole constellation?

CHAPTER XIII.

THE EARTH.

28. Astronomy has to do with the Earth as a planet. Physical Geography treats of the Earth without considering its relation to the other bodies of the solar system. But our only means of understanding the conditions on other planets is to be found in a comparison of these conditions with circumstances on the Earth. For this reason it is convenient to recall some of the facts taught by Physical Geography and to group them with others derived from Astronomy.

The Earth's average distance from the Sun is about 92,800,000 miles. Its least distance (in December) is 91,250,000 miles; its greatest distance (in June) is 94,500,000 miles. The seasons on the Earth depend chiefly on the north-polar distance of the Sun and not on the Earth's proximity to it. The Earth revolves on its axis once in 24 (sidereal) hours. By its rotation an observer at the equator is carried round at the rate of more than 1000 miles per hour. It was a favorite argument of the men of the Middle Ages against the theory that the earth was in rotation that so great a velocity as this could not possibly fail to be remarked. If the rotation were not uniform and regular the argument would be convincing.

The Earth travels around the circumference of its orbit once in 365 days, at the rate of about 66,000 miles per hour, at the rate of about 18½ miles per second.

Figure of the Earth.—PTOLEMY taught in the *Almagest* (A.D. 140) that the Earth was a sphere. Five hundred years before his time ARISTOTLE had proved the same thing, and before ARISTOTLE there were philosophers who held the same opinion. PTOLEMY maintained that the

232

Earth was rounded in an east-to-west direction because the Sun, Moon, and stars do not rise and set at the same moment to all observers, but at different moments. The Earth was rounded in a north and south direction because new stars appeared above the southern horizon as men travelled southwards, or above the northern horizon as they travelled northwards.

It was well known in his time that a journey of a few hundred miles to the north or south would change the horizon of an o' server so that new stars became visible. Such short journeys could not produce such results on a globe of *very* large size. The voyage of MAGELLAN at the beginning of the sixteenth century first established in all men's minds the fact that the Earth was a spherical body.

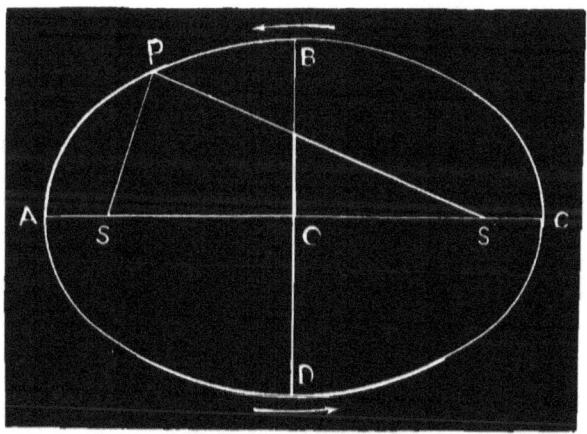

FIG. 148.—AN ELLIPSE.
$AC = 2a$ is the major axis; $BD = 2b$ is the minor axis

The popular opinion for many centuries was that the Earth was a flat disk everywhere surrounded by water.

The Earth is not a sphere, but a spheroid. If it is cut by *meridian* planes (through the poles) the curves cut out of its surface are *ellipses*, not circles.

If an ellipse is revolved about the axis BD the resulting solid is a spheroid. The Earth's meridian is very little different from a circle. The minor axis, the line joining the two poles, is the axis of rotation.

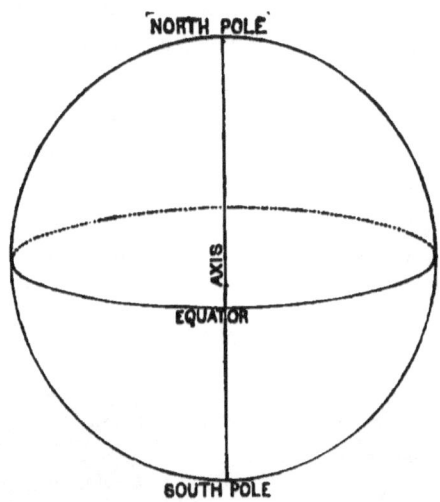

FIG. 149.—THE EARTH—ITS AXIS, ITS POLES, ITS EQUATOR.

Its equatorial semi-diameter $= a = 20,926,202$ feet,
                                          $= 3963.296$ miles,
                                          $= 6,378,190$ metres.

Its polar semi-diameter $= b = 20,854,895$ feet,
                                          $= 3949.790$ miles,
                                          $= 6,356,456$ metres.

The equatorial diameter $= 2a = 7926\ 6$ miles,
    "   polar   " $= 2b = 7899\ 6$ "
                                          $=$ about $500,000,000$ inches.

The circumference of the equator $= 24,899$ miles,
    "   "   "   a meridian $= 24,856$ "
                                          $= 40,000,000$ metres.

A railway train travelling a mile a minute would require 17 days and nights of continuous travel to go once around the Earth.

The area of the whole Earth is about 197,000,000 square miles.
    "   "   "   " dry land   "   "   50,000,000   "   "   .

So that the area of the Earth is more than fifty times that of the United States. We shall see that the planets *Jupiter*, *Saturn*, *Uranus*, and *Neptune* are, each one of them, far larger than the Earth ; and the Sun is immensely larger. Its diameter is 866,400 miles.

Geodetic Surveys.—Since it is practically impossible to measure around or through the Earth, the figure and the size of our planet has to be found by combining measure- ments on its surface with astronomical observations. Even a measurement on the Earth's surface made in the usual way of surveyors would be impracticable, owing to the in- tervention of mountains, rivers, forests, and other natural obstacles. The method of triangulation is therefore uni- versally adopted for measurements extending over large areas.

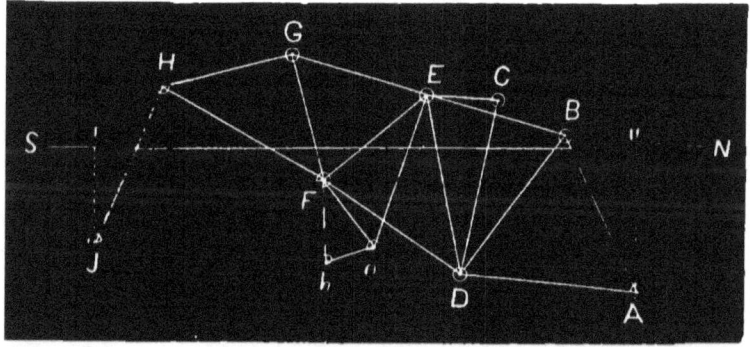

Fig. 150.—A Part of the French Triangulation near Paris.

Triangulation is executed in the following way: Two points, *a* and *b*, a few miles apart, are selected as the extremities of a base-line. They must be so chosen that their distance apart can be accurately measured; the intervening ground should therefore be as level and free from obstruction as possible. One or more elevated points, *EF*, etc., must be visible from one or both ends of the base-line. The directions of these points relative to the meridian are accurately observed from each end of the base, as is also the direction *ab* of the base-line itself. Suppose *F* to be a point visible from each end of the base, then in the triangle *abF* we have the length *ab* determined by actual measurement, and the angles at *a* and *b* determined by observations. With these data the lengths of the sides *aF* and *bF* are determined by a simple computation.

The observer then transports his instruments to *F*, and determines in succession the direction of the elevated points or hills *DEGHJ*, etc. He next goes in succession to each of these hills, and determines the direction of all the others which are visible from it. Thus a network of triangles is formed, of which all the angles are observed, while the sides are successively calculated from the first base. For instance, we have just shown how the side *aF* is calculated; this forms a base for the triangle *EFa*, the two remaining sides of which are computed. The side *EF* forms the base of the triangle *GEF*, the sides of which are calculated, etc.

Chains of triangles have thus been measured in Russia and Sweden from the Danube to the Arctic Ocean, in England and France from the Hebrides to the Sahara, in this country down nearly our entire Atlantic coast and along the great lakes, and through shorter distances in many other countries. An east and west line has been measured by the Coast Survey from the Atlantic to the Pacific Ocean.

Suppose that we take two stations, *a* and *j*, Fig. 150, situated north and south of each other, determine the latitude of each, and calculate the distance between them by means of triangles, as in the figure. It is evident that by dividing the distance between them by the difference of latitude in degrees we shall have the length of one degree of latitude. Then if the Earth were a sphere, we should at once have its circumference by multiplying the length of one degree by 360. It is thus found that the length of 1 degree is a little more than 111 kilometres, or between 69 and 70 English statute miles. Its circumference is therefore about 40,000 kilometres, and its diameter between 12,000 and 13,000.* (25,000 and 8000 miles.)

The general surface of the Earth is found to be rather smooth. The highest mountain is about 5¼ miles high; the deepest ocean is about 5¼ miles deep. Eleven miles covers the range of height and depth. The *average* elevation of the continents above the sea-level is about 2000 feet. The *average* depth of the ocean is about 12,000 feet.

---

* When the metric system was originally designed by the French, it was intended that the kilometre should be $\frac{1}{10000}$ of the distance from the pole of the Earth to the equator. This would make a degree of the meridian equal, on the average, to 111¼ kilometres. But the metre actually adopted is nearly $\frac{1}{100}$ of an inch too short.

Mass and Density of the Earth.

The *mass* of a body is *the quantity of matter it contains.* It is measured by the product of its *volume* (V) by its density (D)

$M = V . D.$ For another body $M' = V' \cdot D'$.

For equal volumes $V = V'$ and $M : M' = D : D'$.

That is, the densities of equal volumes of two substances are proportional to the masses of the substances, to the quantity of matter in them. For example, copper is of greater density than water because a cubic foot of copper contains more matter than a cubic foot of water. The density of pure water at about 39° Fahr. is taken as the unit-density. The unit-volume may be taken as a cubic foot. The unit-mass will then be that of a cubic foot of pure water at 39° Fahr.

The weight of a body is the force with which it is attracted to the centre of the Earth. A body of mass m is attracted by the Earth's mass M by $\frac{Mm}{r^2}$, where r is the distance Mm. (See page 210.) The weight w of m is then $\frac{Mm}{r^2}$. The weight w' of any other body m' is $w' = \frac{Mm'}{r'^2}$. If the bodies are at the same place on the Earth $r = r'$ and $w : w' = m : m'$, or *the weights of bodies at the same place on the Earth are proportional to their masses.* It is easy to measure the relative weights of two bodies by balancing them in scales against certain pieces of metal. Hence by weighing two bodies of weights w and w' we can determine the ratio of their masses m and m'. If m is a cubic foot of water, m' is the absolute mass of the other substance.

The weight of a body m due to the Earth's attraction is $\frac{Mm}{r^2}$. If the body is at the pole of the Earth $r = 7899.6$ miles. If it is at the equator $r = 7926.6$ miles. Its weight will therefore be greater at the pole than at the equator. If we wish to weigh out a certain quantity of gunpowder in Greenland we may balance it against a piece of metal that we call an ounce. If we take the gunpowder to Peru it will " weigh " less because it will there be

further from the Earth's centre.   But it will still balance
the ounce in Peru, because that also is less attracted by the
Earth in precisely the same proportion.   A piece of iron a
cubic foot in volume "weighs" less in a balloon than at
the Earth's surface.   In practical life no note need be
taken of the differences of the Earth's attraction at different latitudes.   But in Astronomy these differences of attraction due to differences of distance must be taken into
account.   The attraction of the Earth for the Moon is
different at different times because the Moon is sometimes
near the Earth, sometimes further away.

The density of pure water at about 39° Fahr. is taken as the unit-
density.   For equal volumes of any two substances $M : M' = D : D'$
or, their densities are proportional to their masses.   At the same
place on the Earth $W : W' = M : M'$ or, their weights are also proportional to their masses, hence

$$W : W' = D : D'.$$

If one of these substances is pure water (W', D') we have
$D = \dfrac{W \cdot D'}{W'}$ and we can determine D, the density of any substance,
as copper, by weighing it against an equal volume of water.   In
this way the densities of all substances on the Earth have been
determined.

The surface-rocks of the Earth are about $2\frac{1}{4}$ times as dense as
water, and volcanic lavas deep down in the Earth are about 3 times
as dense.   The deeper the origin of the rocks the denser they are,
because they are subject to greater pressures.   We can determine
the density of any single specimen of rock that can be brought to
the surface.   We can get no specimens of rock from depths greater
than a few miles.   How then shall we determine the average density
of the whole Earth?

*To determine the density of the Earth we must find how much matter
it must contain in order to attract bodies on its surface with forces
equal to their observed weights, that is, with such intensity that at the
equator a body shall fall nearly five metres (about 16 feet) in a second.
To find this we must know the relation between the mass of a body and
its attractive force.   This relation can be found by measuring the
attraction of a body of known mass.*

We may measure the attraction of a body of known mass in the following ingenious way. In Fig. 151 *HIKL* is a cube of lead 1 metre on each edge. Two holes are bored through the cube at *DF* and *EG*. A pair of scales *ABC* has its scale-pans *DE* connected by fine wires to other scale-pans *FG*, below the block. Suppose the pans empty and everything at rest.

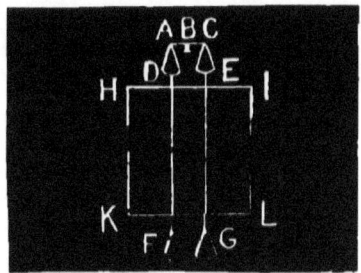

FIG. 151 — EXPERIMENT TO DETERMINE THE DENSITY OF THE EARTH.

I. Put a weight *W* in *D*, and balance the scales by weights in *G*. At *D* the total attraction on *W* is the attraction of the Earth *plus* the attraction of the block, while at *G* we have the attraction of the Earth (downwards) *minus* the attraction of the block (upwards); hence

The weight in *D* + (attraction of the block) = The weights in *G* − (attraction of the block), whence

(1)   Weights in *G* = weight in *D* + 2 (attraction of block).

II. Put the weight *W* in *F*, and balance the scales by weights in *E*. At *F* the total attraction is earth *minus* block, and at *E* it is earth *plus* block.

The weight in *F* − (attraction of the block) = The weights in *E* + (attraction of the block), whence

(2)   Weights in *E* = weight in *F* − 2 (attraction of block).

Subtract equation (2) from (1), remembering that the (weight in *D*) = (weight in *F*).

Weights in *G* − weights in *E* = 4 (attraction of block),

after small corrections have been applied for the difference of height of *D*, *E*, *F*, *G*, etc.

The attraction of this block, which has a known mass in kilogrammes (or pounds), is thus known, and hence *the general relation between mass in kilogrammes (or pounds) and attractions.*

The *attraction* of the Earth is known. It is such as to cause bodies to have their observed weights. Hence the *mass* of the Earth becomes known. The *volume* of the Earth is known from geodetic surveys. The *density* of the whole Earth is therefore known from the equation $D = \dfrac{M}{V}$.

The density of the Earth is about $5\frac{1}{2}$ times that of water,

" " " copper " " $8\frac{1}{2}$ " " " " ,

" " " clay " " 2 " " " " .

The *mass* of the Earth is 6,000,000,000,000,000,000,000 tons.

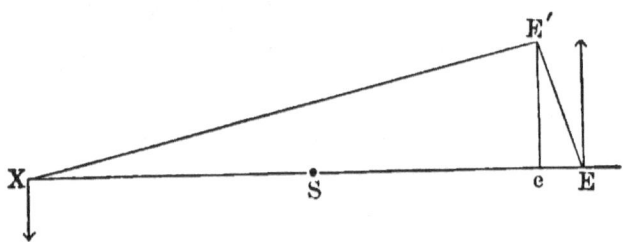

FIG. 152.

Determination of the Mass of the Earth in Terms of the Mass of the Sun.—The mass of the Earth expressed in tons or pounds is known The mass of the Earth in fractions of the Sun's mass ($= 1.0$) can be determined by calculating how far the Earth is deflected by the Sun's attraction each second, as she travels in her orbit. Her motion *along* her orbit is $18\frac{1}{4}$ miles per second (because the circumference of her orbit is 584,600,000 miles and because it is traversed in a sidereal year of 365^{d} 9^{h} 9^{m} 9^{s}). (Fig. 152.) Her deflection from a straight line each second is $\frac{18}{100}$ of an inch, as may be proved from the foregoing diagram, in which E is the place of the Earth at the beginning of a second, E' its place at the end of the second, EE' the orbit of the Earth, S the place of the Sun, X another point of the Earth's orbit, Ee the Earth's fall towards the Sun in a second.

In the two right triangles $XE'E$ and $EE'e$ we have $EX : EE' = EE' : Ee$, or (twice 93,000,000) : $18\frac{1}{4} = 18\frac{1}{4} : Ee$, whence $Ee = 0.01$ of a foot, approximately.

The mass of the Sun at 93,000,000 miles causes the Earth to move towards his centre 0.01 foot. If the Sun were 4000 miles from the Earth his attraction would be greater in the proportion of $[93,000,000]^{2}$ to $[4000]^{2}$ or as 8,650,000,000,000,000 to 16,000,000 or as 540,500,000 to 1. If the Sun were at a distance of only 4000 miles from the Earth (or from any heavy body) the body would fall in a second 540,500,000 times $\frac{1}{100}$ of a foot or 5,405,000 feet. The Earth makes a heavy body at its surface (4000 miles from its centre) fall $16\frac{1}{10}$ feet in a second. Hence

Mass of Sun : Mass of Earth = 5,405,000 feet : 16.1 feet,

or as 335,000 to 1. If the exact values of all the quantities are employed instead of the approximate ones used above the value of the Earth's Mass (Sun's Mass = 1.0) is $\frac{1}{315470}$.

Constitution of the Earth.—The body of the Earth is made up of layers of rocks of different density arranged in shells like the coats of an onion. The outer layers are the least dense; the inner layers (those subject to the greatest pressures) are the most dense. The Earth is composed of various substances, some simple (elements) like iron, some compound like clay. There are about 70 or 80 elementary substances (gold, iron, carbon, oxygen, hydrogen, etc.), and it is noteworthy that nearly all of these elements are known to exist in the Sun, and that many of them are known to exist in the stars. It is probable that the Sun, the Earth, and all the planets are made out of the same elements and that the amazing differences between them are chiefly due to differences in their temperature.

The temperature of the solid crust of the Earth increases as we go downwards at the rate of about 1° Fahr. for every 55 or 60 feet, or about 90° per mile. At the depth of 10 miles the temperature is about 900°; at the depth of 30 miles about 2700°, and so on. Iron melts at the surface of the Earth (where it is free from great pressure) at about 3000°. If the substances in the Earth's interior were free from pressure the interior would be a fluid mass, and there would be great tides in this interior ocean. Astronomical observations show that there are no such tides, whence it follows that the interior of the Earth is, on the whole, solid. There are many reservoirs of melted rocks (lavas) no doubt in the neighborhood of volcanoes, but on the whole the Earth is solid and about as stiff as a globe of steel. The spheroidal shape of the Earth seems to show that it once was in a fluid condition, for a rotating mass of fluid will take the form of a spheroid. It will be flattened at the poles. Its meridians will be ellipses. This is the shape, not only of the Earth, but of all the planets,

All the heat of the Earth comes to it from the Sun. The Sun sends its heat out in all directions along every possible line that can be drawn from the Sun outwards. The Sun would warm the whole interior surface of a sphere 93,000,000 miles in diameter just as much as it now warms the Earth which occupies one small point of such a sphere. So far as mankind is concerned all the heat that does not fall on the Earth is lost. The Earth receives only the minutest fraction of it (not more than $\frac{1}{2000000000}$).

Atmosphere of the Earth.—The Earth is surrounded by an ocean of water in which the attractions of the Sun and Moon produce tides. It is likewise surrounded by an ocean of air, and in this atmosphere slight tides are also observed. The effect of the atmosphere on the *climates* of the Earth is most important, and it is treated in works on *Meteorology.*

Astronomy is chiefly concerned with the effects of the Earth's atmosphere in producing a refraction (a bending) of the rays of light that reach us from the stars so that we do not see them quite in their true directions. The atmosphere of the Earth surrounds it to a height of a hundred miles or more. Its heavier layers are nearest the Earth's surface. Even at a height of 3 or 4 miles there is scarcely enough air for breathing.

Refraction of Light by the Atmosphere.

—In figure 153 C is the centre of the Earth and A the station of an observer on its surface. S is a star. If there were no atmosphere the observer would see the star along the line AS. But the atmosphere acts like a lens and bends (refracts) the light from the star along the curved line e, d, c, b, a, and the light from the star comes to the observer along the line AS'. He sees the star projected on the celestial sphere at S', therefore, and not in its true place S. The star is (apparently) thrown nearer to his zenith by refraction. It will rise sooner and set later, therefore, on this account.

At the zenith the refraction is 0, at 45° zenith distance the refraction is 1', and at 90° it is 34' 30". The rays of light traverse greater thicknesses of air at large zenith distances and are more refracted therefore. Stars at the zenith distances of 45° and 90° appear elevated above their true places by 1' and 34½' respectively. If the sun has just risen—that is, if its lower edge is just in apparent contact with the horizon—it is in fact entirely below the true horizon, for the refraction (35′) has elevated its centre by more than its whole apparent diameter (32′).

The moon is full when it is exactly opposite the sun, and therefore, were there no atmosphere, moon-rise of a full moon and sunset would be simultaneous. In fact, both bodies being elevated by refraction, we see the full moon risen before the sun has set.

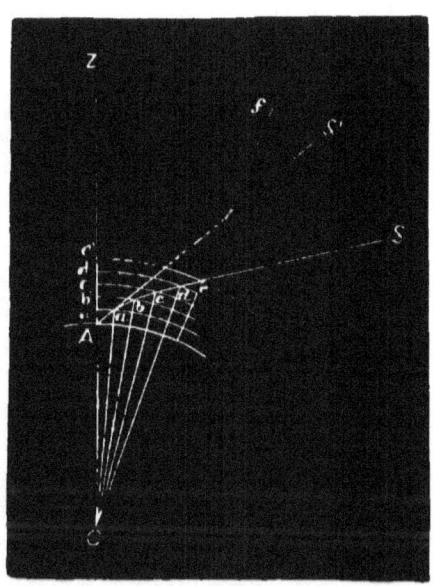

FIG. 153.—REFRACTION OF THE LIGHT OF A STAR BY THE EARTH'S ATMOSPHERE.

Twilight.—It is plain that one effect of refraction is to lengthen the duration of daylight by causing the Sun to appear above the horizon before the time of his geometrical rising and after the time of true sunset.

Daylight is also prolonged by the *reflection* of the Sun's rays (after sunset and before sunrise) from the small particles of matter suspended in the atmosphere. This produces a general though faint illumination of the atmos phere, just as the light scattered from the floating particles of dust illuminated by a sunbeam let in through a crack in a shutter may brighten the whole of a darkened room.

The Sun's *direct* rays do not reach an observer on the Earth after the instant of sunset, since the solid body of the Earth intercepts them. But the Sun's direct rays illuminate the clouds of the upper air, and are reflected downwards so as to produce a general illumination of the atmosphere, which is called twilight.

In the figure let *ABCD* be the Earth and *A* an observer on its surface, to whom the Sun *S* is just setting. *Aa* is

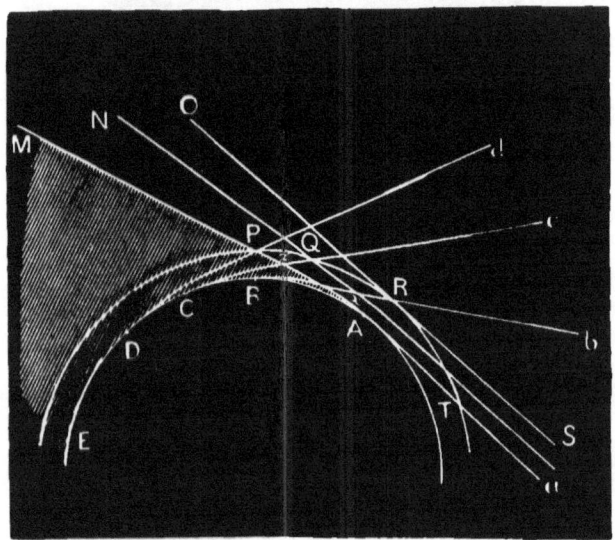

FIG. 154.—THE PHENOMENA OF TWILIGHT.

the horizon of *A*; *Bb* of *B*; *Cc* of *C*; *Dd* of *D*. Let the circle *PQR* represent the upper layer of the atmosphere. Between *ABCD* and *PQR* the air is filled with suspended particles that reflect light. The lowest ray of the Sun, *SAM*, just grazes the Earth at *A*; the higher rays *SN* and *SO* strike the atmosphere above *A* and leave it at the points *Q* and *R*.

Each of the lines *SAPM*, *SQN* is bent from a straight course by refraction, but *SRO* is not bent since it just touches the upper limits of the atmosphere. The space *MABCDE* is the Earth's shadow. An observer at *A* receives the (last) direct rays from the Sun, and also has his sky illuminated by the reflection from all the particles lying in the space *PQRT* which is all above his horizon *Aa.*

An observer at *B* receives no direct rays from the Sun. It is after his sunset. Nor does he receive any light from that portion of the atmosphere below *APM*; but the portion *PRx*, which lies above his horizon *Bb* is lighted by the Sun's rays, and reflects some light to *B.* The *twilight* is strongest at *R*, and fades away gradually towards *P.* The altitude of the twilight at *B* is *bd.*

To an observer at *C* the twilight is derived from the illumination of the portion *PQz* which lies above his horizon *Cc.* The altitude of the twilight at *C* is *cd.*

To an observer at *D* it is night. All of the illuminated atmosphere is below his horizon *Dd.*

The twilight arch is more marked in summer than in winter; in high latitudes than in low ones. There is no true night in Scotland at midsummer, for example, the morning twilight beginning before the evening twilight has ended; and in the torrid zone there is no perceptible twilight. Twilight ends when the Sun reaches a point about 20° below the horizon. The student should observe the phenomena of twilight for himself. It is best seen in the country, shortly after sunset, as far away from city lights as may be.

Astronomical Measures of Time to the Inhabitants of the Earth.—The simplest unit of time is the *sidereal day*, that is the interval of time required for the Earth to turn once on its axis. It is measured by the interval between two successive transits of the same star over the observer's meridian; and it is divided into 24 sidereal hours.

The most obvious unit of time is the (apparent) *solar day*, that is the interval of time between two successive transits of the true Sun over the observer's meridian. As apparent solar days are not equal in length, a more convenient unit has been devised, that is the *mean solar day*, which is the interval of time between two successive transits of the mean Sun (see page 90) over the observer's meridian. The relation between the sidereal and mean solar day has been previously given (page 95) and is as below:

$$366.24222 \text{ sidereal days} = 365.24222 \text{ mean solar days,}$$
$$1 \text{ sidereal day} = 0.997 \text{ mean solar day,}$$
$$24 \text{ sidereal hours} = 23^h\ 56^m\ 4^s.091 \text{ mean solar time,}$$
$$1 \text{ mean solar day} = 1.03 \text{ sidereal days,}$$
$$24 \text{ mean solar hours} = 24^h\ 3^m\ 56^s.555 \text{ sidereal time.}$$

The quantity to be added to (or subtracted from) apparent solar time to obtain mean solar time is calculated beforehand and printed in the Nautical Almanac under the heading " Equation of Time." (See page 151.)

The *months* now or heretofore in use among the peoples of the globe may for the most part be divided into two classes:

(1) The lunar month pure and simple, or the mean interval between successive new Moons.

(2) An approximation to the twelfth part of a year, without respect to the motion of the Moon.

The mean interval between consecutive new Moons being nearly 29½ days, it was common in the use of the pure lunar month to have months of 29 and 30 days alternately.

The interval between two successive returns of the Sun to the same star is called the *sidereal year*. Its length is found by observation to be

365 (mean solar) days 6 hours 9 minutes 9 seconds $= 365^d.25636$.

The interval between two successive returns of the Sun to the same equinox is called the *equinoctial year*. Its length is found by observation to be

365 (mean solar) days 5 hours 48 minutes 46 seconds $= 365^d.24220$.

The sidereal year measures the time of the revolution of the Earth in her orbit. The equinoctial year governs the recurrence of the seasons, because the seasons depend on the Sun's declination (see page 175) and the declination changes from south to north at the vernal equinox—at the passage of the Sun across the celestial equator.

The solar year of 365¼ days has been a unit of time-reckoning from very early times. Four such years are equal to 1461 days. The cycle of four years, three of them of 365 days and the fourth of 366, which we use, was adopted in China in the remotest historic times.

The Julian Calendar.—The civil calendar now in use throughout Christendom had its origin among the Romans, and its foundation was laid by JULIUS CÆSAR. Before his time, Rome can hardly be said to have had a chronological system. The length of the year was not prescribed by any invariable rule, and it was changed from time to time to suit the caprice or to compass the ends of the rulers.

Instances of this tampering disposition are familiar to the historical student. It is said, for instance, that the Gauls having to pay a certain monthly tribute to the Romans, one of the governors ordered the year to be divided into 14 months, in order that the pay-days might recur more rapidly. CÆSAR fixed the year at 365 days, with the addition of one day to every fourth year. The old Roman months were afterwards adjusted to the Julian year in such a way as to give rise to the somewhat irregular arrangement of months which we now have. The names of our days are partly from Roman, partly from Scandinavian mythology. The student should consult a dictionary for the derivations of their names.

Old and New Styles.—The mean length of the Julian year is about 11¼ minutes greater than that of the equinoctial year, which measures the recurrence of the seasons. This difference is of little practical importance, as it only amounts to a week in a thousand years, and a change of this amount in that period can cause no inconvenience. But, in order to have the year as correct as possible, two changes were introduced into the calendar by Pope GREGORY XIII. with this object. It was decreed that

(1) The day following October 4, 1582, was to be called the 15th instead of the 5th, thus advancing the count 10 days.

(2) The closing year of each century, 1600, 1700, etc., instead of being always a leap-year, as in the Julian calendar, was to be such only when the number of the century is divisible by 4. Thus while 1600 remained a leap-year, as before, 1700, 1800, and 1900 were to be common years.

This change in the calendar was speedily adopted by all Catholic countries, and more slowly by Protestant ones, England holding out until 1752. In Russia, the Julian calendar is still continued without change. The Russian reckoning is therefore 12 days behind ours, the ten days dropped in 1582 being increased by the days dropped from the years 1700 and 1800 in the new reckoning.* The modified calendar is called the *Gregorian Calendar*, or *New Style*, while the old system is called the *Julian Calendar*, or *Old Style*.

It is to be remarked that the practice of commencing the year on January 1st was not universal until comparatively recent times. The most common times of commencing were, perhaps, March 1st and March 22d, the latter being the time of the vernal equinox. But January 1st gradually made its way, and became universal after its adoption by England in 1752.

Precession of the Equinoxes.—It has just been said that observation proves the sidereal year to have a length of 365.25636 mean solar days, and the equinoctial year to have a length of 365.24220 days. The Sun in his annual circuit of the heavens moves from a star to the same star again in the sidereal year, from an equinox to the same equinox again in the equinoctial year.

As the stars are fixed, the Sun's revolution around the ecliptic from star back to the same star again must be a revolution through exactly 360° 0′ 0″ of right-ascension. As the equinoctial year is shorter than the sidereal year, the Sun's revolution from equinox to equinox must be a revolution through an angle slightly less than 360°.

$$\left\{ \begin{array}{c} 365^d.25636 \\ \text{sidereal year} \end{array} \right\} : \left\{ \begin{array}{c} 365^d.24220 \\ \text{equinoctial year} \end{array} \right\} = 360^\circ : 359^\circ\ 59'\ 10'',\ \text{approx.}$$

The equinox must therefore be moving in space so that

* Russia will adopt the New Style in A.D. 1901

when it is met a second time the Sun has made one revolution *less* 50″.   The Sun's annual circuit is performed
among the stars from west to east.   The equinox therefore
moves (to meet the Sun) westward in right-ascension at the
rate of about 50″ per year.

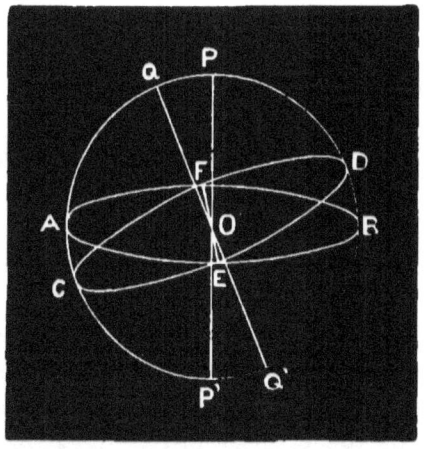

Fig. 155.—The Celestial Equator (*AB*) and the Ecliptic
(*CD*) ; *E*, is the Vernal Equinox.

The equinox (*E* in the figure) is nothing but the point
where the ecliptic (*CD*) intersects the celestial equator
(*AB*).   If their point of intersection changes it must be
because one or both of these circles is moving.   If the plane
of the celestial equator is moving the declinations of all the
stars will change from year to year.   Observation shows
that the declinations do change slightly from year to year.*
If the plane of the ecliptic is fixed the celestial latitudes of
all the stars (their angular distances from the ecliptic) will
not change from year to year.   Observation shows that

* The right-ascensions also change slightly because the equinox,
which is the origin of R A., is moving.   The effect of annual precession on the places of stars is given in the fourth and sixth columns
of Table V at the end of this book.

while the declinations of all the stars do change annually by small amounts their celestial latitudes do not change. Hence the plane of the ecliptic is fixed; and hence the westward motion of the equinox is entirely due to a motion of the plane of the celestial equator.

If the plane of a circle of the celestial sphere is fixed the place of the pole of that circle on the celestial sphere is stationary. The ecliptic (*CD*) is fixed (see the figure), and hence the place of its pole (*Q*) among the stars is stationary. If the pole of the ecliptic is 10° from a star in 1800 it will be 10° from that star in 1900. On the other hand, if the plane of the celestial equator (*AB*) is moving, as it is, the place of its pole (*P*) among the stars must be moving. The north pole of the heavens is now near to *Polaris*, but it will in time move away from it. At the time when the pyramids were built, about B.C. 2700, *Polaris* was not the "north-star," but the star *Alpha Draconis* (see star-map No. VI).

The pole of the ecliptic (*Q*) is fixed; the pole of the celestial equator (*P*) is moving. The angle between the plane of the ecliptic and the plane of the celestial equator ($POQ = 23\frac{1}{2}°$) does not change. Therefore the pole *P* must revolve about the fixed pole *Q* in a circle. The inclination of the two planes *CD* and *AB* will not be changed by such a revolution, but their line of intersection (*EF*) will move slowly round the celestial sphere. Their line of intersection is the line joining the two equinoxes. The *annual* motion of the equinox is, as we have seen, 50″ of arc, so that in about 25,920 years the equinox (*E*) will move completely around the circle of the ecliptic and will return to its starting-point. In the same period the pole of the celestial equator (*P*) will move in a circle completely around the pole of the ecliptic (*Q*).

$$25,920 \times 50'' = 1,296,000'' = 360°.$$

The student can trace the path of the north pole of the heavens among the stars on Star-map No. IV, following. Turning this map upside-down let him find the constellations *Draco, Ursa minor, Cepheus, Cygnus,* and *Lyra.*

About 3000 years ago the pole was near α in *Draco,*

At the present time the pole is near α in *Ursa minor,*

About 2000 years hence the pole will be very near to α in *Ursa minor,*

    "   4000   "   "   "   "   "   " " near γ in *Cepheus,*

    "   7500   "   "   "   "   "   " " α in   "

    " 11500   "   "   "   "   "   " " δ in *Cygnus,*

    " 14000   "   "   "   "   "   " " α in *Lyra.*

If he has a celestial globe at hand he will find the path of the north pole of the heavens about the north pole of the ecliptic marked down among the stars.

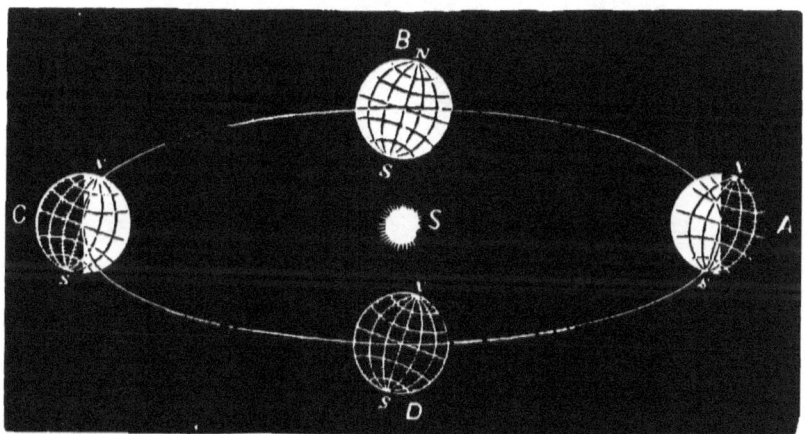

FIG. 156.—THE SEASONS ON THE EARTH.

The effects of the motion of the pole of the heavens on our seasons may be studied in the figure. The figure represents the Earth in four positions during its annual revolution. Its axis inclines to the right in each of these positions. In Chapter VIII it was said that the Earth's axis always remained parallel to itself. The phenomena of precession show that this is not absolutely true, but that, in reality, the direction of the axis is changing with extreme slowness. After the lapse of some 6400 years, the north pole of the Earth, as represented in the figure, will not incline to the right, but towards the reader, the amount of the inclination remaining nearly the same. The result will evidently be a shifting of the seasons. At *D* we shall have the winter solstice, because the north pole will be inclined towards the reader and therefore from the Sun, while at *A* we shall have the vernal equinox instead of the winter solstice, and so on.

In 6400 years more the north pole will be inclined towards the left, and the seasons will be reversed. Another interval of the same length, and the north pole will be inclined from the reader, the seasons being shifted through another quadrant. Finally, at the end of about 25,900 years, the axis will have resumed its original direction.

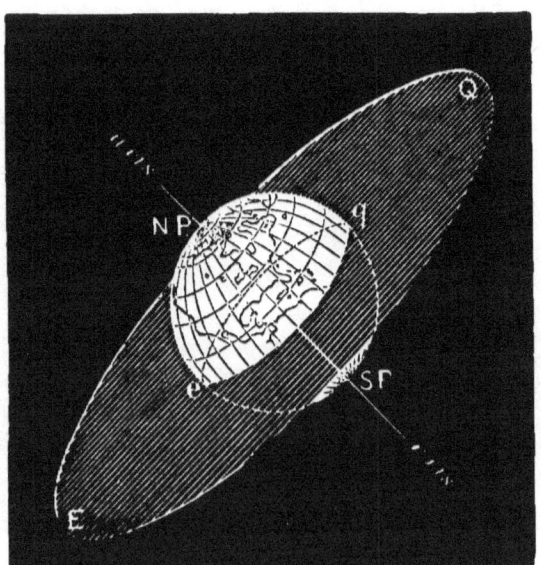

FIG. 157.—THE EARTH'S AXIS AND EQUATOR.

The north pole of the heavens is the point where the celestial sphere is met by the axis of the Earth prolonged. The celestial equator is the plane of the terrestrial equator produced. The axis of the Earth does not move relatively to the Earth's crust. The Earth's equator always passes through the same countries—Ecuador, Brazil, Africa,

Sumatra. The latitudes of places on the Earth do not change. Precession is not due to a motion of the Earth's axis simply, but to a motion of the whole Earth that carries the axis with it.

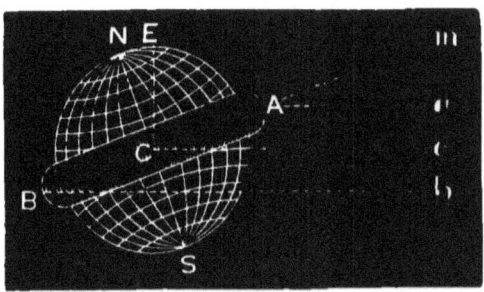

Fig. 158.—Diagram to Illustrate the Cause of Precession.

THE CAUSE OF PRECESSION.

The cause of precession, etc., is illustrated in the figure, which shows a spherical Earth surrounded by a ring of matter at the equator. If the Earth were really spherical there would be no precession. It is, however, ellipsoidal with a protuberance at the equator. The effect of this protuberance is to be examined. Consider the action between the Sun and Earth alone. If the ring of matter were absent, the Earth would revolve about the Sun as is shown in Fig. 156 (Seasons).

The Sun's North Polar Distance is 90° at the equinoxes, and $66\frac{1}{2}$° and $113\frac{1}{2}$° at the solstices. At the equinoxes the Sun is in the direction Cm; that is, NCm is 90°. At the winter solstice the Sun is in the direction Cc; $NCc = 113\frac{1}{2}$°. It is clear that in the latter case the effect of the Sun on the ring of matter will be to pull the Earth downwards so that the direction Cm tends to become the direction Cc. An opposite effect will be produced by the Sun when its polar distance is $66\frac{1}{2}$°.

The Moon also revolves round the Earth in an orbit inclined to the equator, and in every position of the Moon it has a different action on the ring of matter. The Earth is all the time rotating on its axis, and these varying attractions of Sun and Moon are equalized and distributed since different parts of the Earth are successively presented to the attracting body. The result of all the complex motions we have described is a conical motion of the Earth's axis *NC* about the line *CE*.

The Earth's shape is of course not that given in the figure, but an ellipsoid of revolution. The ring of matter is not confined to the equator, but extends away from it in both directions. The effects of the forces acting on the Earth as it is are, however, similar to the effects just described. The motion of precession is not uniform, but is subject to several small inequalities which are called *nutation*.

The fact of precession was discovered by HIPPARCHUS more than 2000 years ago. He observed: (1) That the Sun made a revolution from equinox to equinox in a shorter time than that required for its revolution from star to star. (2) As the stars were fixed the equinox must be moving. (3) The equinox is the intersection of the ecliptic and the celestial equator, and hence one or both of these planes must be moving. (4) The ecliptic was not moving because the celestial latitudes of stars did not change. (5) The celestial equator was in motion because the declinations of all the stars (and their right-ascensions also) did change. This was a mighty discovery, and it required a genius of the first order to make it.

COPERNICUS, in 1543, declared that precession was due to a conical motion of the Earth's axis of rotation about the line joining the Earth's centre with the pole of the ecliptic.

NEWTON, in 1687, worked out the complete explanation. This could not possibly have been done until the theory of gravitation was thoroughly understood nor until the science of mathematics had been developed (by NEWTON'S own researches) to a high point. Three of the greatest names of science are associated in this discovery.

The Progressive Motion of Light.—GALILEO made experiments to determine whether light required *time* to pass from one place to another. His methods were not sufficiently refined to decide the question, but the subject was not lost sight of. In the year 1675, OLAUS ROMER, a

Danish astronomer (to whom we owe the invention of the transit instrument, among other things), was engaged in making tables of the times of the eclipses of the satellites of *Jupiter*.

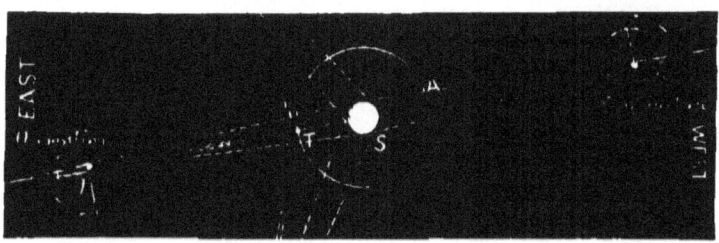

F IG. 159.—T HE E CLIPSES OF J UPITER'S S ATELLITES AND THE P ROGRESSIVE M OTION OF L IGHT.

S, is the Sun : *T*, is the Earth in its orbit : *J*, is *Jupiter* in opposition with the Sun : *J'''* is *Jupiter* in conjunction with the Sun.

The figure shows the Earth at *T*. When *Jupiter* is at *J* it is nearest to the Earth; when *Jupiter* is at *J '''* (and the Earth at *T*) the two bodies are as far apart as possible. *TJ'''* is larger than *TJ* by the diameter of the Earth's orbit; by about 186,000,000 miles therefore. *Jupiter* casts a long shadow (see the cut) and one of its satellites (its orbit is the small circle about *J* and about *J'''*) is eclipsed at every revolution. R OMER calculated the times at which an observer on the Earth would see such eclipses. He found that his tables could be reconciled with observation only by supposing that the light from the satellite required *time* to pass from *Jupiter* to the Earth. When *Jupiter* is at *J* its light has to pass over the line *J T* to reach the Earth. When *Jupiter* is at *J'''* its light has to pass over the longer line *J''' T*. Accurate observations show that eclipses of the satellites are seen 16 minutes 38 seconds earlier when the planet is at *J* than when it is at *J'''*. Light requires 16^m 38^s to pass over the diameter of the Earth's orbit, therefore, or 8^m 19^s to pass over the radius of the orbit.

In 499ˢ light travels 92,900,000 miles, or at the rate of
186,200 miles in one second of time.* The sunlight is
499 seconds old when it reaches the Earth. As the velocity
of light is uniform it follows that (approximately):

Sunlight is   3ᵐ old when it reaches *Mercury,*
    "   "   6ᵐ "   "   "   "   *Venus,*
    "   "   8ᵐ "   "   "   "   *Earth,*
    "   "   13ᵐ "   "   "   "   *Mars,*
    "   "   43ᵐ "   "   "   "   *Jupiter,*
    "   "1ʰ 19ᵐ "   "   "   "   *Saturn,*
    "   "2ʰ 38ᵐ "   "   "   "   *Uranus,*
    "   "4ʰ 8ᵐ "   "   "   "   *Neptune.*

The time required for the light of a planet to reach the Earth is
called the planet's aberration-time. For instance, the aberration-t.me
of *Neptune* is about 4ʰ 8ᵐ. This means that the light by which
we see *Neptune* now—this instant—is 4ʰ 8ᵐ old when it reaches us.
Neptune may have vanished 4ʰ 7ᵐ ago for all we know. We can only
find out by waiting. The stars are very much further away than
Neptune. We shall see, later on, that the light of even the nearest
star is more than 4 years on its passage to the Earth. The light from
Polaris takes more than 40 years to reach us. *Polaris* may have
vanished 40 years ago for all we know—now ; we can only find out
by waiting. Only a very few of the stars are so near as this. Most
of them are immensely further away.

The theory of ROMER was not fully accepted by his contemporaries.
The velocity of light was so much greater than any known terrestrial velocity that it seemed difficult to accept it. Even the motion
of the Earth in its orbit was only 18½ miles per second. The velocity
of light was 10,000 times as large. In the year 1729 JAMES BRADLEY,
afterwards Astronomer Royal of England, observed a phenomenon of
a different character that entirely confirmed ROMER'S conclusions.
BRADLEY discovered that the stars are not seen in their true places,
but that each star is displaced by a small angle (never more than
21″). This displacement occurs because the Earth is moving among
the stars with a velocity that is comparable with the velocity of light.

In the figure suppose *AB* to be the axis of a telescope, *S* a
star, and *SAB′* a ray of light which emanates from the star. The

* The most accurate determinations give 186,330 miles.

student may imagine AB to be a rod which an observer at B seeks to point at the star S. It is evident that he must point this rod in such a way that the ray of light shall run accurately along its length. If the observer (and the Earth) were at rest at B he will point the rod along the line SB.

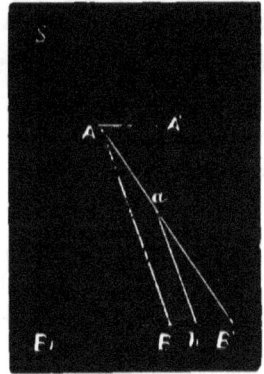

Suppose now that the observer (and the Earth) are moving from B toward B' with such a velocity that he moves from B to B' during the time required for a ray of light to move from A to B'. Suppose, also, that the ray of light from S (SA) reaches A at the same time that the end of his rod does. Then it is clear that while the rod is moving from the position AB to the position $A'B'$, the ray of light will

FIG. 156.

move from A to B, and will therefore run accurately along the length of the rod.

For instance, if b is one third of the way from B to B', then the light, at the instant when the rod takes the position ba, will be one third of the way from A to B', and will therefore be accurately on the rod. Consequently, to the observer, the rod will appear to be pointed at the star. In reality, however, the pointing will not be in the true direction of the star, but will deviate from it by a certain angle depending upon the *ratio* of the velocity with which the observer is carried along to the velocity of light.

If the Earth stood still there would be no aberration. If the velocity of light were 10,000 times greater than it is the aberration would be vanishingly small.

Effects of Aberration.—The velocities of light and of the Earth being what they are, the apparent displacement of a star's position, due to aberration is always less than 21″.

Aberration phenomena can be observed on the Earth on any rainy day with no wind. (See fig. 157.) The rain-drops descend vertically. If the observer stands still he must hold his umbrella straight above his head. Now let him walk briskly towards the south. He will find that he must incline his umbrella southwards (in the direction of *his* motion) to protect himself. If he walks towards the west he must incline his umbrella westwards (in the direction of *his* motion). If instead of walking he runs, the same effects are produced, only he will find that he must incline his umbrella still more. All this while each rain-drop is falling vertically; yet every change of *his* direction of motion and of *his* velocity (relative to the velocity of the falling drops of rain) requires him to alter the inclination of his protecting umbrella. The experiment is so easy that the student should not fail to try it.

— What is the Earth's distance from the Sun? (Answer, about 93,000,000 miles.) Do the seasons depend on the Earth's proximity to the Sun? What is the shape of the Earth? How is the figure of the Earth determined? Define the mass, the density, the volume of a body. Define the weight of a body. Does a body—say a cubic inch of copper—weigh the same in Brazil and in Iceland? If you could take it 10,000 miles above the Earth would it weigh less or more than in New York? How is the density of specimens of rocks determined? How is the density of the whole Earth, considered as one mass, determined? Is the temperature of the Earth greater 10 miles below the surface than 5 miles deep? Does the Earth receive all the Sun's heat? What is the refraction of light by the Earth's atmosphere? Does refraction increase or diminish the apparent zenith distance of the Sun? Describe the phenomena of twilight? Did you ever see it yourself? Define the different kinds of *day.* What is a month? Define the sidereal and the equinoctial year. Which is the longer? What does that prove? Will *Polaris* always be our pole-star? What is the cause of precession? What three great names are connected with the discoveries regarding precession? and at what dates? How was it first proved that light required time to pass from place to place? About how long does it take sunlight to reach the Earth? to reach *Neptune?* About how long does it require for the light of the *nearest* star to reach the Earth? (Answer, 4 years.)

CHAPTER XIV.

CELESTIAL MEASUREMENTS OF MASS AND DISTANCE.

29. The Celestial Scale of Measurement.—The units of length and mass employed in Astronomy are necessarily different from those used in daily life. The distances and magnitudes of the heavenly bodies are never reckoned in miles or other terrestrial measures for astronomical purposes; when so expressed it is only for the purpose of making the subject clearer to the general reader. The mass of a body may be expressed in terms of that of the Sun or of the Earth, but never in kilogrammes or tons, unless in popular language.

There are two reasons for this course. One is that in most cases celestial distances have first to be determined in terms of some celestial unit—the Earth's distance from the Sun, for instance—and it is more convenient to retain this unit than to adopt a new one. The other is that the values of celestial distances in terms of ordinary terrestrial units are more or less uncertain, while the corresponding values in astronomical units are known with great accuracy.

An example of this practice is afforded when we determine the dimensions of the solar system. By a series of observations of their positions on different dates, investigated by means of KEPLER'S laws and the theory of gravitation, it is possible to determine the forms of the planetary orbits, the positions of their planes, and their relative dimensions, with great precision.

KEPLER'S third law enables us to determine the mean distance of a planet from the Sun when we know its

260

period of revolution (see page 200). All the major planets, as far out as *Saturn*, have been observed through so many revolutions that their *periodic times* can be determined with great exactness—in fact within a fraction of a millionth part of their whole amount. The more recently discovered planets, *Uranus* and *Neptune*, will, in the course of time, have their periods determined with equal precision. Then, if we square the periods expressed in years and decimals of a year, and extract the cube root of this square, we have the *mean distance* of the planet with the same order of precision.

Again, the *eccentricities* of the orbits are exactly determined by careful observations of the positions of the planets during successive revolutions. Thus we can draw a map of the planetary orbits so exact that its errors will entirely elude the most careful scrutiny, though the map itself might be many yards in extent.

On such a map we can lay down the magnitudes of the planets as accurately as our micrometers can measure their angular diameters. Thus we know that the mean diameter of the Sun, as seen from the earth, subtends an angle of 32'. We can therefore, on such a map of the solar system, lay down the Sun in its true size, on the scale of the map. This can be done in the same way for each of the planets, the Earth and Moon excepted. There is no immediate and direct way of finding how large the Earth or Moon would look from the Sun or from a planet; whence the exception.

But without further research we shall know nothing about the *scale* of our map. That is, we shall have no means of knowing how many miles in space correspond to an inch on the map. If we can learn either the distance or magnitude of any one of the planets laid down on the map, in miles or in semidiameters of the Earth, we shall be able at once to find the scale.

The general custom of astronomers is not to attempt to use a scale *of miles* at all, but to employ the mean distance of the Sun from the Earth as the unit in celestial measurements. Thus, in astronomical language, we say that the distance of *Mercury* from the Sun is 0.387, that of *Venus* 0.723, that of *Mars* 1.523, that of *Saturn* 9.539, and so on in terms of the Earth's distance = 1.000. But this gives us no information respecting the distances in terms of terrestrial measures.

The distance of the Earth in miles is not the only unknown quantity on our map. We know nothing respecting the distance of the Moon from the Earth, because KEPLER's laws apply directly to bodies moving around the Sun. We must therefore determine the distance of the Moon as well as that of the Sun. When these two things are done a map of the solar system can be made in which every measurement can be expressed in miles.

THE SOLAR AND LUNAR PARALLAX.

The problem of distances in the solar system is thus reduced to measuring the distances of the Sun and Moon in miles or in terms of the Earth's radius (= 4000 miles). The most direct methods of doing this are as follows:

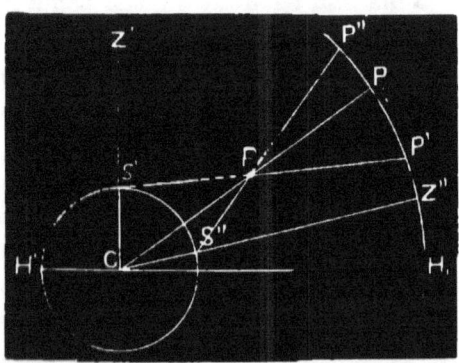

FIG. 158.—DETERMINATION OF THE DISTANCE OF THE MOON.

Distance of the Moon.—In the figure C is the centre of the Earth, and S' and S'' are the positions of two observers on its surface. P is the Moon in space and PC is the distance to be determined (in miles). The observer at S'' sees the Moon on the celestial sphere at P'', and he measures its zenith distance $Z''P''$. At the same instant the observer at S' sees the Moon on the celestial sphere at P' and he measures its zenith distance $Z'P'$. (The student must imagine the circle $Z''P''$ to be completed, and Z' a point in the circle.) $Z''P''$ and $Z'P'$ are then known arcs and $Z''S''P''$ and $Z'S'P'$ are known angles, since they are measured by known arcs. The angle $PS''C$ is known; it is $180° - PS''Z''$. The angle $PS'C$ is known; it is $180° - PS'Z'$. As the two observers are at stations whose latitudes are known, the angle $S'CS''$ is known. It is the difference of their latitudes (for if $H'H_1$ is the plane of the Earth's equator, $S''CH_1$ is the latitude of S'' and $S'CH_1$ is the latitude of S' and therefore $S'CS''$ is known).

In the quadrilateral $S'CS''P$ the three angles whose vertices are at C, at S', and at S'' are known, and therefore the fourth angle whose vertex is at P is known. In this quadrilateral two of the sides are known because they are radii of the Earth. Hence the distances $S'P$ and $S''P$ are known. From either of the triangles $S'CP$ or $S''CP$ the distance of the Moon, CP, can be calculated.

This is one method of determining the distance of the Moon. Knowing the actual dimensions of the Earth in miles, observations of the Moon made at stations widely separated in latitude, as Paris and the Cape of Good Hope, can be combined so as to give the Moon's distance in miles. On precisely the same principles the distances of *Venus* or *Mars* have been determined in miles.

The Distance of the Sun from Transits of Venus.—When *Venus* is at inferior conjunction she is between the Sun and the Earth. If her orbit lay in the ecliptic, she would be projected on the Sun's disk at every inferior conjunction. The inclination of her orbit is, in fact, about $3\frac{1}{2}°$, and thus *transits* of *Venus* occur only when she is near the node of her orbit at the time of inferior conjunction. In Fig. 159 let E, V, S be the Earth, *Venus*, and the Sun. *DC* is a part of *Venus'* orbit. An observer at B will see *Venus* impinge on the Sun's disk at I, be just internally tangent at II, move across the disk to III, and off at IV.

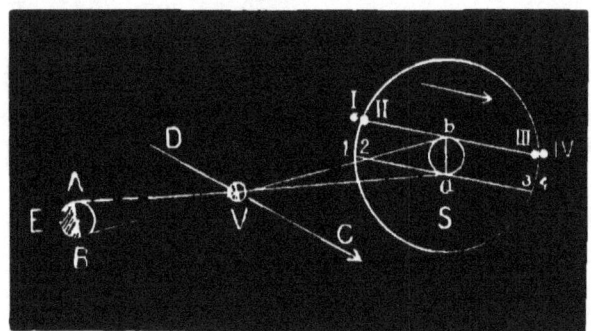

FIG. 159.—DETERMINATION OF THE DISTANCE OF THE SUN.

Similar phenomena will occur for A at 1, 2, 3, 4. When A sees *Venus* at a, B will see her at b. $ab : AB :: Va : VA$; but $VA : Va$ as $1 : 2\frac{1}{2}$ nearly. ab therefore occupies on the Sun's disk a space $2\frac{1}{2}$ times as large as the Earth's diameter. If we *measure* the angular dimension ab in any

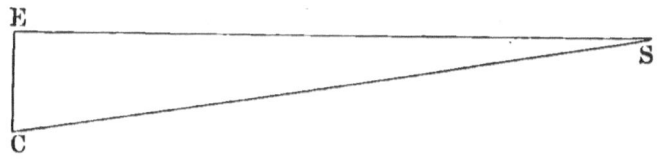

FIG. 160.

way, and divide the resulting angle by $2\frac{1}{2}$, we shall have the angle subtended at the Sun by the Earth's *diameter;* or if we divide it by 5, the angle subtended at the Sun by the Earth's *radius.* (Fig. 160.) Having this angle we can calculate the Earth's distance from the Sun in miles from the right triangle *SEC*, where *S* is the Sun, *C* the Earth's centre, and *E* the end of the Earth's radius.

The angular space *ab* can be calculated at a transit of *Venus*, when we know the length of the chords *II*, *III*, and 2, 3. The length of each chord is known by observing the interval of time elapsed from phase *II* to phase *III*.

Other Methods of Determining Solar Parallax.—The most accurate method of measuring the Sun's distance depends upon a knowledge of the velocity of light. The time required for light to pass from the Sun to the Earth is known with considerable exactness, being very nearly 498 seconds.* If we can determine experimentally how many miles light moves in a second, we shall at once have the distance of the Sun in miles by multiplying that quantity by 498. The velocity of light is about 186,330 miles per second. Multiplying this by 498, we obtain 92,800,000 miles for the distance of the Sun. The time required for light to pass from the Sun to the Earth is still somewhat uncertain, but this value of the Sun's distance is probably the best yet obtained.

RELATIVE MASSES OF THE SUN AND PLANETS.

In estimating the masses as well as the distances of celestial bodies it is necessary to use what we may call celestial units; that is, to take the mass of some celestial body as a unit, instead of any multiple of the pound or kilogram. The reason of this is that the *ratios* between the masses of the planetary system, or, what is the same thing, the mass of each body in terms of that of some one body as the unit, can be determined without knowing the mass of any one of them in pounds or tons. To express a mass in kilograms or other terrestrial units, it is first necessary to find the mass of the Earth in such units, as already explained. This, however, is entirely unnecessary for astronomical purposes. In estimating the masses of

* See page 256.

the individual planets, that of the Sun is generally taken as a unit. The planetary masses are then all very small fractions.

The mass of the Sun being 1.00, the mass of *Mercury* is $\frac{1}{10580000}$;

"   "   "   "   "   *Venus*   is $\frac{1}{405000}$;

"   "   "   "   "   *Earth*   is $\frac{1}{354470}$;

"   "   "   "   "   *Mars*   is $\frac{1}{3093500}$;

"   "   "   "   "   *Jupiter* is $\frac{1}{1048}$;

"   "   "   "   "   *Saturn*   is $\frac{1}{3509}$;

"   "   "   "   "   *Uranus*   is $\frac{1}{22600}$;

"   "   "   "   "   *Neptune* is $\frac{1}{19380}$.

The mass of the Earth being 1, the mass of the Moon is $\frac{1}{81}$.

The masses of the planets that have satellites are determined by measuring the attraction that is exerted by the planet on the satellite. If the distance of the planet from the Sun (M) is R and its periodic time is T, and if the planet whose mass is m has a satellite revolving in a circular orbit whose radius is r in a time t, it is proved in Mechanics that

$$M : m = \frac{R^3}{T^2} : \frac{r^3}{t^2},$$

by which expression we can determine m, the mass of the planet, in fractions of the Sun's mass M, because R, T, r, t are known. In this way the masses of all the planets that are attended by satellites are calculated, after making suitable allowances for the fact that the orbits of the satellites are ellipses and not circles.

Mercury and *Venus* have no satellites, and their masses are calculated by determining the perturbations that they cause in the motions of other planets (and of comets) in their vicinity.

The *angular diameters* of the planets are measured with a micrometer attached to a telescope. The result is expressed in seconds of arc. Knowing the distance of the planet in miles, the diameter can also be expressed in miles. (See page 144.)

The *surface* of a planet is proportional to the *square*, and its *volume* to the *cube* of its diameter. The *mass* of a planet is deduced as above described. Its *density* is obtained by dividing its mass by its volume.

In what has gone before the methods of determining the mass, the distance, the diameter, the orbit, etc., of each planet have been described with more or less fullness. The fundamental principles of the methods are all that can be given here. The details of the processes of observation are explained in works on Practical Astronomy. The mathematical forms involved are treated in works on Celestial Mechanics. It will at least be obvious to the student that the masses, the distances, and the orbits of the planets *can* be determined in the ways that have been explained, though he will not know the details of the processes actually employed.

The results that have been obtained are given in two tables printed in Chapter XV. These two tables contain data sufficient to enable us to construct the map of the solar system that was spoken of on page 261. With the numbers there set down a plan of the solar system can be made with great exactness. The orbit of each planet can be drawn in its true shape and situation. The place of each planet at any past or future time can be assigned. The diameter of each planet can be marked on the map to the proper scale. The mass, the force of gravity at the surface, the volume, the density of each planet is known. The problems that were attacked by PTOLEMY, COPERNICUS, KEPLER, and NEWTON are solved. The solar system considered as a collection of heavy bodies revolving in space under the law of gravitation is explained.

In order to complete the description of the solar system something more is necessary. We desire to know the topography, the meteorology, the physical condition of each planet just as we know the topography, the climates, the physics of our own Earth. We wish to know the geology and the chemistry of the stars just as we know the geology and the chemistry of the Earth. The science that treats of the physical condition of the Sun, Moon, planets, stars, and other celestial bodies is called Astronomical Physics or Astro-physics. The methods of this science are the methods of terrestrial physics extended so as to deal with all celestial bodies. A description of the physical condition of the heavenly bodies is called Descriptive Astronomy. The second part of this book is chiefly devoted to such a description, which it is necessary to give in a very abbreviated form. The student can supplement what is printed here by consulting articles on the Sun, Moon, and planets, etc., in any good encyclopedia, or by reading some of the excellent books on Popular Astronomy written by Sir ROBERT BALL, FLAMMARION, PROCTOR, and others.

— What is the most convenient *unit of length* in the description of the solar system? How is the *periodic-time* of a planet determined? Knowing the periodic-time, how do you obtain its *mean-distance*? How is the *angular diameter* of a planet found? Explain the principle by which the *distance of the Moon* from the Earth may be determined. Explain how the *distance of the Sun* from the Earth is found from Transits of Venus over the Sun's disk. Explain how the Sun's distance can be found when we know the velocity of light. What is the most convenient *unit of mass* in the description of the solar system? On what principle are the masses of *Mars, Jupiter*, etc., determined?—the masses of *Mercury* and *Venus*? When the mass and the *volume* of a planet is known, how is its density obtained?

PART II.

THE SOLAR SYSTEM.

CHAPTER XV.

THE SOLAR SYSTEM.

30. The solar system consists of the sun as a central body, around which revolve the major and minor planets, with their satellites, a few periodic comets, and a number of meteor swarms. These are permanent members of the system. Other comets appear from time to time and make part of a revolution around the sun, and then depart into space again, thus visiting the system without being permanent members of it.

The bodies of the system may be classified as follows:

I. The central body—the Sun.

II. The four inner planets—*Mercury, Venus,* the *Earth, Mars.*

III. A group of small planets, called *Asteroids,* revolving outside of the orbit of *Mars.*

IV. A group of four outer planets—*Jupiter, Saturn, Uranus,* and *Neptune.*

V. The satellites, or secondary bodies, revolving about the planets, their primaries.

VI. A number of comets and meteor swarms revolving in very eccentric orbits about the Sun.

The eight planets of Groups II and IV are classed

together as the *major planets*, to distinguish them from the
five hundred or more *minor planets* of Group III. *Mercury*
and *Venus* are *inferior planets ;* the other major planets
are called *superior* planets.

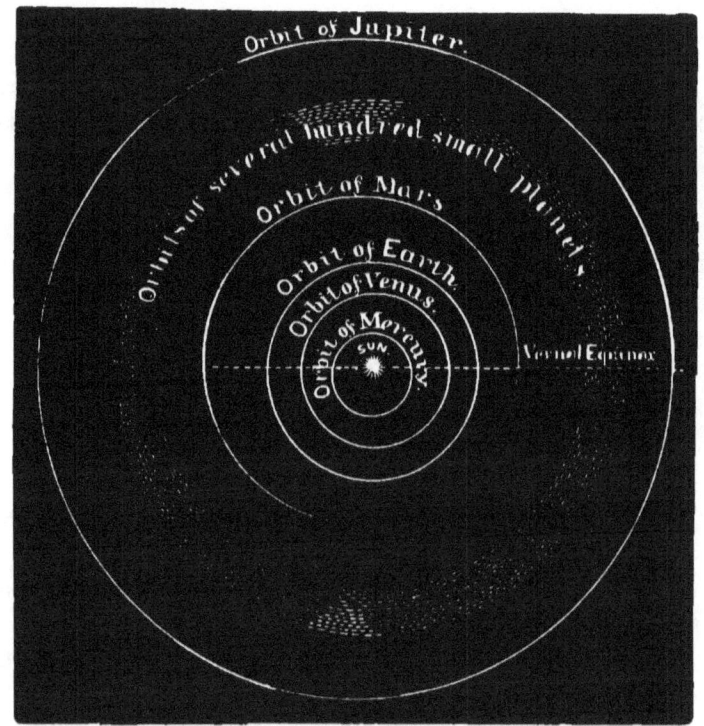

Fig 161.—Plan of the Solar System.

Dimensions of the Solar System.—The figure gives a plan
of part of the solar system as it would appear to a spectator
immediately above or below the plane of the ecliptic. It is
drawn approximately to scale, the mean distance of the
Earth (= 1) being half an inch. On this scale the mean
distance of *Saturn* would be 4.77 inches, of *Uranus* 9.59
inches, of *Neptune* 15.03 inches. On the same scale the

distance of the *nearest* fixed star would be over one and one half miles. The student should remember that the immense spaces between the planets and between the stars are empty except for a few comets and for swarms of meteors. The striking fact is how few are the bodies that circulate in these immense regions of space.

The arrangement of the planets and satellites is, then—

The Inner Group.	Asteroids.	The Outer Group.
Mercury.		Jupiter and 5 satellites.
Venus.	500 minor planets, and probably many more.	Saturn and 9 satellites.
Earth and Moon.		Uranus and 4 satellites.
Mars and 2 satellites.		Neptune and 1 satellite.

The different planets are at very different distances from the Sun. To the nearest planets, *Mercury* and *Venus*, the Sun appears as a very large disk. To the earth the Sun appears as a disk about half a degree in diameter. The amount of light and heat received from the Sun by any planet varies as $\frac{1}{r^2}$ where r is the planets' distance. The surface of the circles in figure 162 also vary as $\frac{1}{r^2}$ and hence the surfaces show the relative amounts of light and heat received by the planets (*Flora* and *Mnemosyne* are two of the asteroids). The distance of *Neptune* from the Sun is eighty times that of *Mercury* and it receives only $\frac{1}{6400}$ part as much light and heat.

To avoid repetitions, the elements of the major planets and other data are collected into the following tables, to which the student should constantly refer in his reading. The units in terms of which the various quantities are given are those familiar to us, as miles, days, etc., yet some of the distances, etc., are so immensely greater than any known to our daily experience that we must have recourse to illustrations to obtain any idea of them at all.

For example, the distance of the sun is said to be about **93** *million* miles.   It is of importance that some idea should be had of this distance, as it is the unit, in terms of which not only the distances in the solar system are expressed, but also distances in the stellar

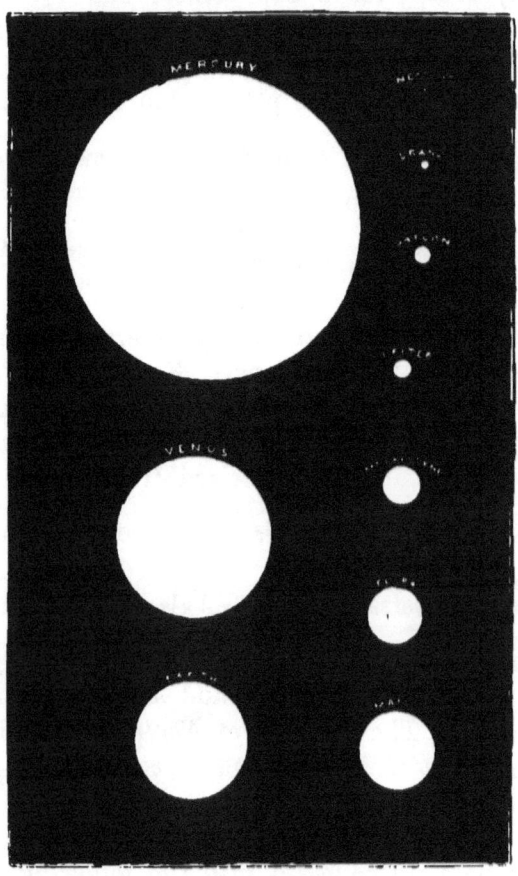

Fig. 162.—The Apparent Size of the Sun as Viewed from the Different Planets.

universe.   Thus when we say that the distance of the *nearest* star is over 200,000 times the mean distance of the sun, it becomes necessary to see if some conception can be obtained of one factor in this.

Of the abstract number, 93,000,000, we have no idea.   It is far too

great for us to have counted. We have never taken in at one view
even a million similar discrete objects. The largest tree has less
than 500,000 leaves. To count from 1 to 200 requires, with very
rapid counting, 60 seconds. Suppose this kept up for a day without
intermission ; at the end we should have counted 288,000, which is
about $\frac{1}{313}$ of 93,000,000. Hence over 10 months' uninterrupted
counting by night and day would be required simply to enumerate
the *number*, and long before the expiration of the task all *idea* of it
would have vanished.

We may take other and perhaps more striking examples. We
know, for instance, that the time of the fastest express-trains between
New York and Chicago, which average 40 miles per hour, is about a
day. Suppose such a train to start for the sun and to continue running at this rapid rate. It would take 363 years for the journey.
Three hundred and sixty-three years ago there was not a European
settlement in America.

A cannon-ball moving continuously across the intervening space
at its highest speed would require about eight years to reach the sun.
In a little less than a day it would go once round the earth if its
course was properly curved. To reach the sun it would have to
travel for eight years at this velocity. The report of the cannon, if
it could be conveyed to the sun with the velocity of sound in air,
would arrive there four years after the projectile. Such a distance
is entirely inconceivable, and yet it is only a small fraction of those
with which astronomy has to deal, even in our own system. The
distance of *Neptune* is 30 times as great.

If we examine the dimensions of the various orbs, we meet almost
equally inconceivable numbers. The diameter of the sun is 866,400
miles ; its radius is but 433,200, and yet this is nearly twice the
mean distance of the moon from the earth. Try to conceive, in
looking at the moon in a clear sky, that if the centre of the sun could
be placed at the centre of the earth, the moon would be far within
the sun's surface.

Or again, conceive of the force of gravity at the surface of the
various bodies of the system. At the sun it is nearly 28 times that
known to us. A pendulum beating seconds here would, if transported
to the sun, vibrate with a motion more rapid than that of a watch-
balance. The muscles of the strongest man would not support him
erect on the surface of a planet of the mass of the sun : even lying
down he would be crushed to death under his own weight of more
than two tons. At the moon's surface the weight of a man would be
about one-sixth of his weight on the earth (since the Moon's mass is

about one-sixth of the Earth's), and his muscular force, on such a planet, would enable him to bound along with leaps of 30 feet or more. There are, of course, no human beings on the sun or on the moon. One of these bodies is too hot, the other too cold, to support human life. We may by these illustrations get some rough idea of the meaning of the numbers in these tables, and of the incapability of our limited powers to comprehend the true dimensions of even the solar system. When we come to a description of the stellar universe we shall meet with distances and dimensions almost infinitely larger.

It is important that the student should *realize*, so far as he can, the data given in these tables; and there is no better way to do this than to make drawings to scale from the numbers there set down. For instance, let the student draw lines to represent the apparent angular diameters of the different planets as seen from the Earth (Table II) on a scale of one inch = 30", and then draw the circles corresponding to these diameters. None of the circles for the planets will be more than two and a half inches in diameter; but if he wishes to draw a circle to represent the apparent disk of the Sun on this scale it will have to be over five feet in diameter. If a diagram of this sort is actually constructed it will impress the student's mind far more than a mere reading of the figures of the table. If he makes a drawing, to scale, of the system of *Jupiter's* satellites putting in the data of Table III and whatever else he can find in Chapter XVIII, a definite idea of the arrangement and sizes of these satellites will be acquired and it will not soon be forgotten. The distances of the periodic comets given in Table IV should be platted to scale along with the major axes of the Earth, *Mars*, *Jupiter*, *Saturn*, *Uranus*, and *Neptune*.

Similar diagrams of the inclinations of the planetary orbits, of their periodic times, volumes, masses, densities, etc., will serve to impress the mind with the resemblances and with the differences in the different bodies of the system.

The mass of the sun is far greater than that of any single planet in the system, or indeed than the combined mass of all of them. If the mass of the earth is represented by a single grain of wheat the mass of the Sun will be represented by about four bushels of such grains. It is a remarkable fact that the mass of any given planet exceeds the sum of the masses of all the planets of less mass than itself.

The total mass of the asteroids, like their number, is unknown, but it is probably less than one-thousandth that of our Earth. The Sun's mass is over 700 times greater than that of all the other bodies, and the fact of its central position in the solar system is thus explained. In fact, the *centre of gravity* of the whole solar system is very little out-side the body of the Sun, and will be inside of it when *Jupiter* and *Saturn* are in opposite directions from it (when their celestial longi-tudes differ by 180°).

There are very few persons who realize in any vivid way the distances and dimensions of the planets of the solar system. No very keen realization is to be had by merely reading the figures of the tables. If it is practicable the student should, once in his life, make a plan of the solar system in the following way. If a whole class can make the experiment in company it will be an advantage.

From the Tables I and II it should first be proved that if the Sun were two feet in diameter instead of 866,400 miles the different planets would be fairly well represented in bulk as follows :

Mercury by a grain of mustard-seed, *Venus* by a very small green pea, The *Earth* by a common-sized green pea, *Mars* by the head of a rather large pin, *Jupiter* by a ball of the size of an orange, *Saturn* by a golf-ball, *Uranus* by a common marble, *Neptune* by a rather larger marble.

The scale of the plan of the solar system is to be two feet = 870,-000 miles. To make the plan a level road about 2¼ miles long is needed. A stake should be driven into the ground to represent the place of the Sun, and if the length of the stake above ground is two feet the Sun's diameter will be represented by it.

The distances of the planets must be laid off on the same scale of two feet = 870,000 miles. Steps of two feet long will serve to measure the distances. The student should first verify the following from the numbers given in Table I. On the adopted scale the dis-tance from the Sun to *Mercury* is 82 steps ; from *Mercury* to *Venus* is 60 steps ; from *Venus* to the *Earth* is 73 steps ; from the *Earth* to

Mars is 108 steps ; from *Mars* to *Jupiter* is 785 steps ; from *Jupiter* to *Saturn* is 934 steps ; *Saturn* to *Uranus* is 2,086 steps ; and from *Uranus* to *Neptune* is 2,322 steps.

With these distances let the student set out from the stake that represents the Sun and deposit the models of the different planets at their proper distances—*Mercury* at 82 steps from the stake, *Venus* at 142 steps, and so on to *Neptune*, which will be 6,450 steps away— nearly 2¼ miles.

A marble 2¼ miles away from a globe 2 feet in diameter represents the relation in distance and in size between *Neptune* and the *Sun*. A few other globes, all very small, at large intervals, represent the *major* planets. A few grains of sand represent the asteroids. The spaces of the solar system between the planets are empty except for a few comets and meteor-swarms.

On the scale of the model the distance of the *nearest* fixed star from the stake that represents the Sun is 8,000 miles. A globe about three or four feet in diameter at Peking might stand for this star if the model of the solar system were made in New York. A morning spent in actually making such a model of the solar system will not be wasted. There is no better way of *realizing* the dimensions of the bodies of the solar system and the immense extent of empty space between them.

TABLE I.

(APPROXIMATE) ELEMENTS OF THE ORBITS OF THE EIGHT MAJOR PLANETS.

NAME.	Mean Distance from Sun.		Eccentricity of Orbit.	Longitude of Perihelion.	Inclination to Ecliptic.		Longitude of the Node.	Mean Longitude of Planet, 1850.	Time Required for Sunlight to reach the Planet.	
	Astronom- ical Units.	Mil- lions of Miles.								
Mercury..	0.387099	36.0	0.21	75°	7°	0′	47°	323°	0ʰ	3ᵐ
Venus....	0.723332	67.2	0.01	129	3	24	75	244	0	6]
Earth ...	1.000000	92.9	0.02	100	0	0	0	100	0	8
Mars. ...	1.523691	141	0.09	333	1	51	48	83	0	13
Jupiter ..	5.202800	483	0.05	12	1	19	99	160	0	43
Saturn..	9.538861	886	0.06	90	2	29	112	15	1	19
Uranus ..	19.18329	1782	0.05	171	0	46	73	29	2	38
Neptune..	30.05508	2791	0.01	46	1	47	130	335	4	8

TABLE II.

Dimensions, etc., of the Bodies of the Solar System.

Name.	Masses.	Apparent Angular Diameters seen from the Earth. Polar.	Albedo.*	Mean Diameter in Miles.	Density. Water = 1.	Density. Earth = 1.	Axial Rotation.	Gravity at Surface ⊕ = 1.	Periodic Time.	Orbital Velocity in Miles per Second.
Sun......	Unity.	....	......	866400	1.4	0.3	25 7m 48s	27.7	Days.	......
Mercury...	1/10138000	32' 04" mean	0.13	3030	3.1	0.6	Unknown.	0.2	87.97	23 to 35
Venus ...	1/408000	5" to 13"	0.50	7700	4.9	0.9	Unknown.	0.8	224.70	21.9
Earth	1/354470	11" to 67"	0.20?	7918	5.6	1.0	23h 56m 4s.09	1.0	365.26	18.5
Mars.....	1/3090000	....	0.26	4230	4.0	0.7	24h 37m 22s.7	0.4	686.98	15.0
Jupiter....	1/1048	32" to 50"	0.62	86500	1.3	0.2	9h 55m	2.7	Years. 11.86	8.1
Saturn ...	1/3502	14" to 20"	0.52	73000	0.7	0.1	10h 14m 23s.8	1.2	29.46	6.0
Uranus ...	1/24600	3".8 to 4".1	0.64	31900	1.2	0.2	Unknown.	0.9	84.02	4.2
Neptune..	1/19380	2".7 to 2".9	0.46	34800	1.1	0.2	Unknown.	0.9	164.78	3.4

* The *albedo* of any substance is its power of reflecting the rays of light that fall upon it. If it reflects all such rays its albedo is 1.00.

TABLE III.
The Satellites of the Solar System.

Name	Discovered by	Mean Distance from its Planet.	Sidereal Period of Revolution. (d h m s)	Inclination of Orbit to the Ecliptic. (° ' ")	Diameter in Miles.	Remarks.
The moon........	....	miles. 238840	27 7 43 11.5	5 8 40	2162	Density = 8.44; Albedo = 0.17 }{ Its mass is $\frac{1}{81}$ of the Earth's mass.
} Phobos........	Hall 1877	5850	− 7 39 15.1	25 17 12	about 7	} Satellites of Mars.
} Deimos........	" 1877	14650	1 6 17 54.0	25 47 12	" 5	
V = ?............	Barnard 1892	112000	0 11 57 22.7	......	" 100	
I = Io............	Galileo 1610	261000	1 18 27 33.5	2 8 3	" 2500	Satellite III has a mass $\frac{1}{11600}$ of Jupiter's mass; the mass of I is $\frac{1}{25000}$ the mass of Jupiter. Satellites of Jupiter.
II = Europa......	" 1610	415000	3 13 13 42.1	1 38 57	" 2100	
III = Ganymede...	" 1610	664000	7 3 42 33.4	1 59 53	" 3550	
IV = Callisto.....	" 1610	1167000	16 16 32 11.2	1 57 0	" 2960	
1 = Mimas........	W.Herschel 1789	117000	− 22 37 5.7	28 10 10	about 600	Satellites of Saturn. The orbits of 1, 2, 3, 4 and 5 are in or very near to the plane of the ring. The mass of Titan is $\frac{1}{4700}$ of that of Saturn.
2 = Enceladus....	" 1789	157000	1 8 53 6.9	28 10 10	" 900	
3 = Tethys.......	Cassini 1684	186000	1 21 18 25.6	28 10 10	" 1100	
4 = Dione........	" 1684	238000	2 17 41 9.3	28 10 10	" 1200	
5 = Rhea.........	" 1672	332000	4 12 25 11.6	28 10 10	" 1500	
6 = Titan........	Huyghens 1655	771000	15 22 41 23.2	27 38 49	" 3500	
7 = Hyperion.....	Bond 1848	934000	21 6 39 27.0	27 4 48	" 500	
8 = Iapetus......	Cassini 1671	2225000	79 7 54 17.1	18 31 30	" 2000	
9 = ...	Pickering 1898	?	9	......	......	
1 = Ariel........	Lassell 1851	120000	2 12 29 21.1	97 51	" 500	Satellites of Uranus. Their motion in their orbits is retrograde.
2 = Umbriel......	" 1851	167000	4 3 27 37.2	97 51	" 400	
3 = Titania......	W.Herschel 1787	273000	8 16 56 29.5	97 51	" 1000	
4 = Oberon.......	" 1787	365000	13 11 7 6.4	97 51	" 500	
1 = Nameless.....	Lassell 1846	225000	5 21 2 44.2	145 12	" 2000	Satellite of Neptune. Its motion in its orbit is retrograde.

TABLE IV.

THE COMETS OF THE SOLAR SYSTEM (PERIODIC COMETS).

No.	Name.	Time of Perihelion Passage.	Period in Years.	Perihelion Distance (approx.)	Aphelion Distance (approx.)	Inclination of Orbit (approx.)
1	Encke............	1895 Feb. 4	3.30	0.34	4.10	13°
2	Tempel	1894 April 23	5.22	1.35	4.67	13°
3	Brorsen	1890 Feb. 24	5.46	0.59	5.61	29°
4	Tempel-Swift	1891 Nov. 14	5.53	1.09	5.17	5°
5	Winnecke	1892 June 30	5.82	0.89	5.58	15°
6	Da Vico-Swift.....	1894 Oct. 12	5.86	1.39	5.11	3°
7	Tempel...........	1885 Sept. 25	6.51	2.07	4.90	11°
8	Biela............	1852 Sept. —	6.6–	0.86	6.2–	13°
9	Finlay...........	1893 July 12	6.62	0.99	6.06	3°
10	D'Arrest.........	1890 Sept. 17	6.69	1.32	5.78	16°
11	Wolf	1891 Sept. 3	6.82	1.59	5.60	25°
12	Brooks	1896 Nov. 4	7.10	1.96	5.43	6°
13	Faye.............	1881 Jan. 22	7.57	1.74	5.97	12°
14	Tuttle...........	1885 Sept. 11	13.76	1.02	10.46	55°
15	Pons-Brooks......	1884 Jan. 25	71.48	0.76	33.67	74°
16	Olbers....	1887 Oct. 8	72.63	1.20	33.62	45°
17	Halley...........	1835 Nov. 15	76.37	0.59	35.41	162°

CHAPTER XVI.

THE SUN.

31. The Sun is a huge globe 866,400 miles in diameter. Its mass is 333,470 times that of the Earth, its volume is 1,310,000 times the Earth's volume, its density one fourth of the Earth's density. The force of gravity on its surface is nearly 28 times the force of gravity on the Earth. On the Earth a heavy body falls 16 feet during the first second of its descent; at the Sun it would fall 444 feet. Some idea of its enormous size can be had by remembering that the Earth and Moon are but 238,000 miles apart while the Sun's *radius* is 433,200 miles. If the Sun were hollow and the Earth was at its centre the Moon would revolve far within the outer shell of the Sun's surface. The motions of all the planets are controlled by its attraction.

The Sun is a *star*. It is a sphere of incandescent gases and metallic vapors. It shines by its own light and gives out enormous quantities of heat unceasingly. Only the smallest fraction of the Sun's heat reaches the Earth. Yet that small fraction (about $\frac{1}{2000000000}$ part) supports all the life on the Earth, both of animals and plants. It maintains the circulation of winds, of ocean currents, the flow of glaciers and of rivers; it is the cause of the rains, the clouds, the dews that support vegetation; it controls the seasons and the climates of all the regions of our globe and of all the planets in the solar system. In the strictest sense all the life, energy, and activity on the Earth are maintained by the Sun and principally and chiefly by the Sun's

280

heat. If the Sun's heat were cut off all life on the Earth would quickly cease.

While it is true that the Sun is as different as possible from the Earth in its present state, it is to be especially noted that the difference is chiefly due to a difference of temperature. The spectroscope detects the presence of (the vapors of) metals and earths in the Sun and it is likely that there is no " element " on the Earth that is not found on the Sun. Calcium, carbon, copper, hydrogen, iron, magnesium, nickel, silver, sodium, zinc, among others, have been detected, some of them in great abundance. There is every reason to believe that if the Earth were to be suddenly raised to the temperature of the Sun it would become at once, and in virtue of temperature alone, a *Sun* —that is a *star*.

Photosphere.—The visible shining *surface* of the Sun is called the *photosphere*, to distinguish it from the body of the Sun as a whole. The apparently flat surface presented by a view of the photosphere is called the Sun's *disk*.

Spots.—When the photosphere is examined with a telescope, dark patches of varied and irregular outline are frequently found upon it. These are called the *solar spots*.

Rotation.—When the spots are observed from day to day, they are found to move over the Sun's disk from east to west in such a way as to show that the Sun rotates on its axis in a period of 25 or 26 days. The Sun, therefore, has *axis*, *poles*, and *equator*, like the Earth, the axis being the line around which it rotates. It turns on its axis from west to east in 25 days, 7 hours, 48 minutes.

Faculæ.—Groups of minute specks brighter than the general surface of the Sun are often seen in the neighborhood of spots or elsewhere. They are clouds of the vapors of metals and are called *faculæ*.

Chromosphere.—Just above the solar photosphere there is a layer of glowing vapors and gases from 5000 to 10,000 miles in depth. At the bottom of it lie the vapors of many metals, magnesium, sodium, iron, etc., volatilized by the intense heat, while the upper portions are composed principally of hydrogen gas. The vaporous atmosphere is called the *chromosphere.* It is entirely invisible to direct vision, whether with the telescope or naked eye, except for a few seconds about the beginning or end of a total eclipse, but it may be seen on any clear day through the spectroscope.

Prominences, Protuberances, or Red Flames.—The gases of the chromosphere are frequently thrown up in irregular masses to vast heights above the photosphere, it may be 50,000, 100,000, or even 200,000 kilometres (120,000 miles). These masses can never be directly viewed except when the sunlight is cut off by the intervention of the Moon during a total eclipse. They are then seen as rose-colored flames, or piles of bright red clouds of irregular and fantastic shapes rising from the edge of the Sun. The spectroscope shows that they are chiefly composed of incandescent calcium, helium, and hydrogen.

Corona.—During total eclipses the Sun is seen to be

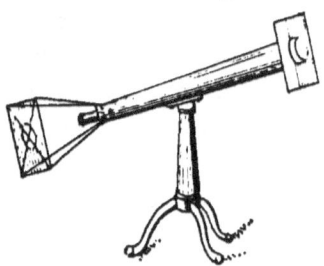

enveloped by a mass of soft white light, much fainter than the chromosphere, and extending out on all sides far beyond the highest prominences. It is brightest around the edge of the Sun, and fades off toward its outer boundary by insensible gradations. This halo of light is called the

FIG. 163.—A METHOD OF OBSERVING THE SUN WITH A TELESCOPE.

corona, and is a very striking object during a total eclipse. (Fig. 163.)

Methods of Observing the Sun.—The light and heat of the Sun concentrated at the focus of a telescope are very intense. An experiment with a burning-glass will illustrate this obvious fact. Special

eye-pieces are made so that the Sun can be looked at directly with
the telescope, but the method of projecting the Sun's image on a
sheet of cardboard (as in the figure) is very convenient, especially
because several observers can examine the image at the same time.
A sheet of white cardboard is fastened to the telescope (accurately
perpendicular to its axis) by a light wooden or metal frame.   The
image of the Sun is projected on the cardboard and must be made
as sharp and neatly defined as possible by moving the eye piece to
and fro till the right focus is found.   It is desirable to fasten another
sheet of cardboard over the tube of the telescope to shut off a part
of the daylight, as in the figure.

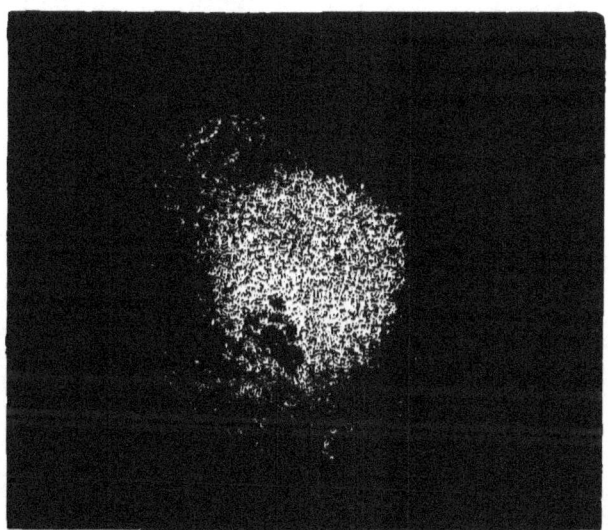

FIG. 164.—COPY OF A PHOTOGRAPH OF THE SUN SHOWING THE
CENTRE OF THE DISK TO BE BRIGHTER THAN THE EDGES.

One of the best ways to study the Sun is to photograph it with a
camera of long focus—the longer the better.   The exposures must
be very short indeed—a few thousandths of a second in most cases.
The surroundings of the Sun—its red flames, its corona—can be seen
with the naked eye at a total solar eclipse, and they can then be
photographed.   The spectroscope is used for the study of the Sun's
surroundings and of its surface, as explained in the Appendix on
Spectrum Analysis.   If the student is not already familiar with the
subject through his study of physics, he should interrupt his reading of this chapter and master the principles explained in the Appendix, as they are necessary to an understanding of what follows.

The Photosphere.—The disk of the Sun is circular in
shape, no matter what side of the Sun's globe is turned
towards the Earth, whence it follows that the Sun is a
sphere.   The disk of the Sun is not equally bright over all
the circle of the surface.   The centre of the disk is most
brilliant and the edges are shaded off so as to appear much
less brilliant, as in Fig. 164.   The deficiency of brightness
at the edges is due to the fact that the rays that reach us
from the centre of the disk traverse a smaller depth of the
Sun's atmosphere than those from the edges and are less
absorbed by the Sun's atmosphere therefore.

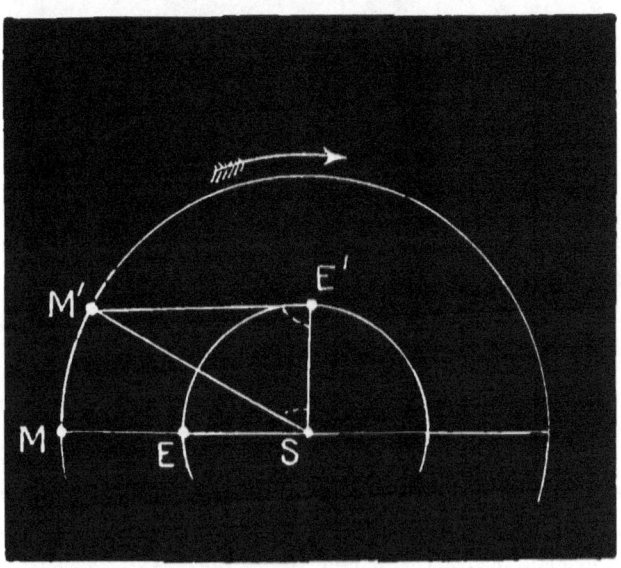

Fig 165.—The Absorption of the Sun's Rays is Greater at
the Edges of the Disk than at the Centre.

In figure 165 let *SE* be the Sun's radius and *SM* the radius of his
atmosphere.   A person stationed beyond *M* (to the left hand of the
figure) looking at the Sun along the lines *ME* and *M'E'* would see
the centre of the disk by rays that had traversed the distance *ME*
only; while the edge of the disk would be seen by rays that had
traversed the much greater distance *M'E'*.

The ray which leaves the centre of the Sun's disk in passing to the Earth traverses the smallest possible thickness of the solar atmosphere, while the rays from points of the Sun's body which appear to us near the limbs pass, on the contrary, through the maximum thickness of atmosphere, and are thus longest subjected to its absorptive action.

The Solar Spots.—When the Sun's disk is examined with the telescope several *Sun-spots* can usually be seen. The smallest are mere black dots in the shining surface 500 miles or so in diameter. The largest solar spots are thousands of miles in diameter (100,000 miles or more).

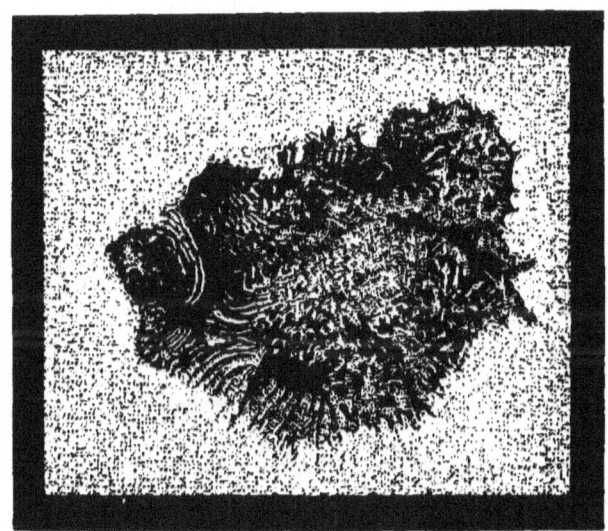

Fig. 166.—A Large Sun-spot seen in the Telescope.

Solar spots generally have a black central *nucleus* or *umbra*, surrounded by a border or *penumbra*, intermediate in shade between the central blackness and the bright photosphere.

The first printed account of solar spots was given by Fabritius in 1611, and Galileo in the same year (May, 1611) also described them. Galileo's observations showed them to belong to the Sun itself, and to move uniformly across the solar disk from east to west. A spot just visible at the east limb of the Sun on any one day travelled slowly across the disk for 12 or 13 days, when it reached the west limb, behind which it disappeared. After about the same period, it reappeared at the eastern limb.

The spots are not permanent in their nature, but disappear after a few days, weeks, or months somewhat as cyclonic storms in the Earth's atmosphere persist for hours or days and then are dissipated. But so long as the spots last they move regularly from east to west on the Sun's apparent disk, making one complete rotation in about 25 days. This period of 25 days is therefore approximately the rotation period of the Sun itself.

Spotted Region.—It is found that the spots are chiefly confined to two zones, one in each hemisphere, extending from about 10° to 35° or 40° of heliographic latitude. In the polar regions spots are scarcely ever seen, and on the solar equator they are much more rare than in latitudes 10° north or south. Connected with the spots, but lying on or above the solar surface, are *faculæ*, mottlings of light brighter than the general surface of the Sun. Many of the *faculæ* are clouds of incandescent calcium.

Solar Axis and Equator.—The spots revolve with the surface of the Sun about his axis, and the directions of their motions must be approximately parallel to his equator. Fig. 167 shows the appearances as actually observed, the dotted lines representing the apparent paths of the spots across the Sun's disk at different times of the year.

In June and December these paths, to an observer on the Earth, seem to be right lines, and hence at these times the observer must be in the plane of the solar equator. At other times the paths are ellipses, and in March and September the planes of these ellipses are most oblique, showing the spectator to be then furthest from the plane of the solar equator. The inclination of the solar equator to the plane of the ecliptic is about 7° 9', and the axis of rotation is, of course, perpendicular to it.

Form of the Solar Spots.—The Sun-spots are probably depressions in the photosphere. When a spot is first seen at the edge of the disk it appears as a notch, and is elliptical in shape. As the Sun's rotation carries it further on to the disk it becomes more and more circular. At the centre it is often circular, and as it passes off the disk the shape again becomes elliptical. The appearances are shown in fig. 168, and are due to perspective.

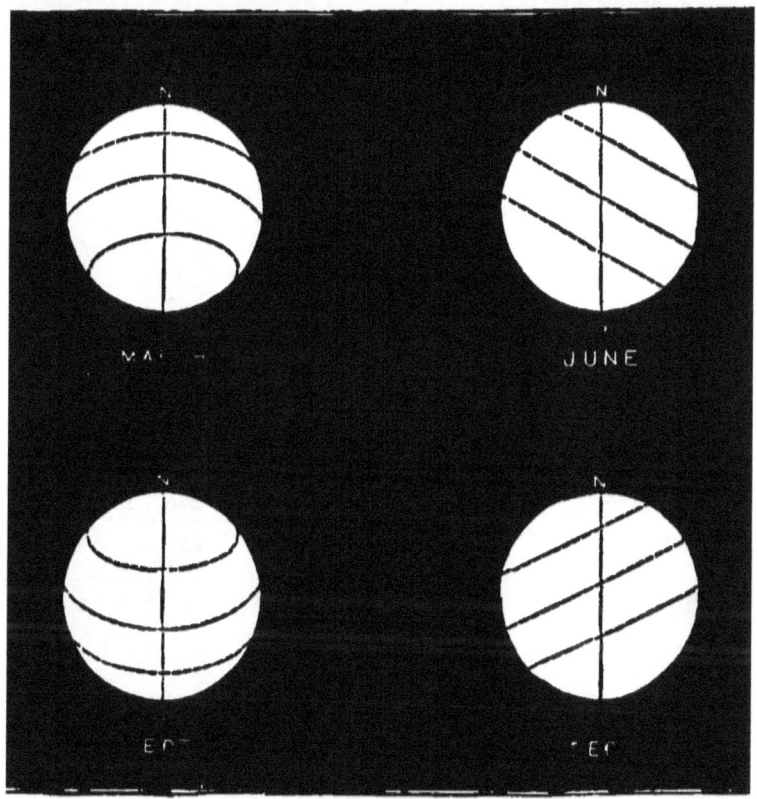

FIG. 167.—APPARENT PATHS OF THE SOLAR SPOTS TO AN OBSERVER ON THE EARTH AT DIFFERENT SEASONS OF THE YEAR.

The Number of Solar Spots varies Periodically.—The number of solar spots that are visible varies from year to year. Although at first sight this might seem to be what we call a purely accidental circumstance, like the occurrence of cloudy and clear years on the Earth, observations of sun-spots establish the fact that this number varies *periodically.*

That the solar spots vary periodically will appear from the following summary :

From 1828 to 1831 the Sun was without spots on only   1 day.
In 1833   "   "   "   *139 days.*
From 1836 to 1840   "   "   "   3   "
In 1843   "   "   "   *147* "
From 1847 to 1851   "   "   "   2   "
In 1856   "   "   "   *193* "
From 1858 to 1861   "   "   "   no day.
In 1867   "   "   "   *195 days.*

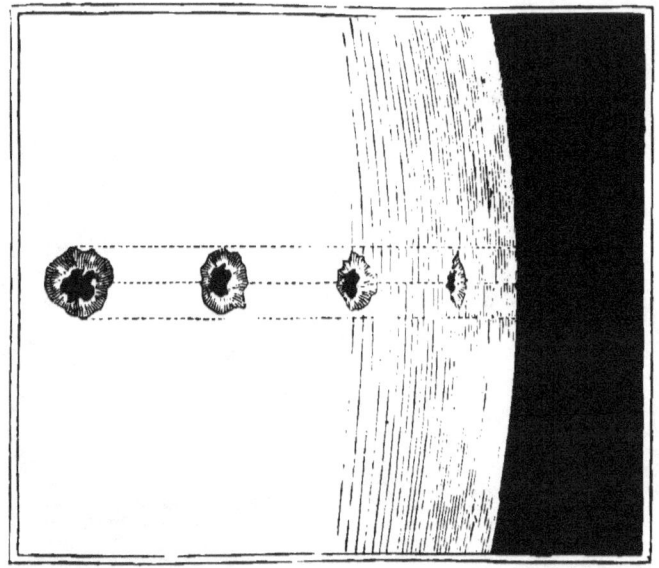

Fig. 168.—Appearance of the Same Solar Spot near the
Centre of the Sun and near the Edge.

Every eleven years there is a minimum number of spots, and about
five years after each minimum there is a maximum.   There was a
maximum of spots in 1893 ; the minimum occurred in 1899.   If, instead of merely counting the number of spots, measurements are
made on solar photographs of the extent of *spotted area*, the period
comes out with greater distinctness.

The cause of this periodicity is as yet unknown.   It probably lies
within the Sun itself, and is similar to the cause of the periodic action of a geyser.

The sudden outbreak of a spot on the Sun is often accompanied by
violent disturbances in the magnetic needle ; and there is a complete

concordance between certain changes in the magnetic declination and the changes in the Sun's spotted area.

The agreement is so close that it is now possible to say what the changes in the magnetic needle have been so soon as we know what the variations in the Sun's spotted area are.

There is a direct action between the Sun and the Earth that we call their mutual gravitation; and the foregoing facts show that they influence each other in yet another way. These actions take place across the space of 93,000,000 miles which separates the Sun and Earth. No doubt a similar effect is felt on every planet of the solar system.

The Sun's Chromosphere and Corona. Phenomena of Total Eclipses.

When a total solar eclipse is observed with the naked eye its beginning is marked simply by the small black notch made in the luminous disk of the Sun by the advancing edge or limb of the Moon. This always occurs on the western half of the Sun, because the Moon moves from west to east in its orbit. An hour or more elapses before the Moon has advanced sufficiently far in its orbit to cover the Sun's disk. During this time the disk of the Sun is gradually hidden until it becomes a thin crescent.

The actual amount of the Sun's light may be diminished to two thirds or three fourths of its ordinary amount without its being strikingly perceptible to the eye. What is first noticed is

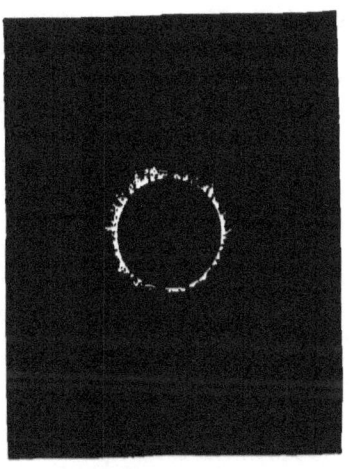

FIG. 169.—THE SOLAR CORONA AT THE TOTAL SOLAR ECLIPSE OF JANUARY, 1889, FROM PHOTOGRAPHS.

the change which takes place in the color of the surrounding landscape, which begins to wear a ruddy aspect. This grows more and more pronounced, and gives to the adjacent country that weird effect which lends so much to the impressiveness of a total eclipse.

The reason for the change of color is simple. The Sun's atmosphere absorbs a large proportion of the bluer rays, and as this absorption is dependent on the thickness of the solar atmosphere through which the rays must pass, it is plain that just before the Sun is totally covered, the rays by which we see it will be redder than ordinary sunlight, as they are those which come from points near the Sun's limb, where they have to pass through the greatest thickness of the Sun's atmosphere.

The color of the light becomes more and more lurid up to the moment of total eclipse. If the spectator is upon the top of a high mountain, he can then begin to see the Moon's shadow rushing toward him at the rate of a kilometre in about a second. Just as the shadow reaches him there is a sudden increase of darkness ; the brighter stars begin to shine in the dark lurid sky, the thin crescent of the Sun breaks up into small points or dots of light, which suddenly disappear, and the Moon itself, an intensely black ball, appears to hang isolated in the heavens.

An instant afterward the corona is seen surrounding the black disk of the Moon with a soft effulgence quite different from any other light known to us. Near the Moon's edge it is intensely bright, and to the naked eye uniform in structure ; 5' or 10' from the limb this inner corona has a boundary more or less defined, and from this extend streamers and wings of fainter and more nebulous light. They are of various shapes, sizes, and brilliancy. No two solar eclipses yet observed have been alike in this respect.

Superposed upon these wings may be seen (sometimes with the naked eye) the red flames or protuberances which were first discovered during a solar eclipse. They need not be more closely described here, as they can now be studied at any time by aid of the spectroscope.

The total phase lasts for a few minutes, and during this time, as the eye becomes more and more accustomed to the faint light, the outer corona becomes visible further and further away from the Sun's limb. At the eclipse of 1878, July 29th, it was seen to extend more than 6° (about 9,000,000 miles) from the Sun's limb. Photographs of the corona show even a greater extension. Just before the end of the total phase there is a sudden increase of the brightness of the sky, due to the increased illumination of the Earth's atmosphere near the observer, and in a moment more the Sun's rays are again visible, seemingly as bright as ever. From the end of totality till the last contact the phenomena of the first half of the eclipse are repeated in inverse order.*

Telescopic Aspect of the Corona.—Such are the appearances to the

---

* The Total Solar Eclipse of May 28, 1900, will be visible in the United States. Its track will pass from New Orleans to Norfolk in Virginia. The duration of the total phase will be about 1m. 19s. in Louisiana and 1m. 49s. in North Carolina. The totality occurs about 7.30 A.M. (local time) at New Orleans, and about 9 A.M. at Norfolk. The width of the shadow track is about 55 miles.

naked eye. The corona, as seen through a telescope, is, however, of a very complicated structure. It is best studied on photographs, several of which can be taken during the total phase, to be subsequently examined at leisure.

The corona and red prominences are solar appendages. It was formerly doubtful whether the corona was an atmosphere belonging to the Sun or to the Moon. At the eclipse of 1860 it was proved by measurements that the red prominences belonged to the Sun and not to the Moon, since the Moon gradually covered them by its motion, they remaining attached to the Sun. The corona is also a solar appendage.

Gaseous Nature of the Prominences.—The eclipse of 1868 was total in India, and was observed by many skilled astronomers. A discovery of M. JANSSEN'S will make this eclipse forever memorable. He was provided with a spectroscope, and by it observed the prominences. One prominence in particular was of vast size, and when the spectroscope was turned upon it, its spectrum was discontinuous, showing the bright lines of hydrogen gas.

The brightness of the spectrum was so marked that JANSSEN determined to keep his spectroscope fixed upon it even after the reappearance of sunlight, to see how long it could be followed. It was found that its spectrum could be seen perfectly well after the return of complete sunlight ; and that the prominences could be observed at any time by taking suitable precautions.

One great difficulty was conquered in an instant. The red flames which formerly were only to be seen for a few moments during total eclipses, and whose observation demanded long and expensive journeys to distant parts of the world, could now be regularly observed with all the facilities offered by a fixed observatory.

This great step in advance was independently made by Sir NORMAN LOCKYER, and his discovery was derived from pure theory, unaided by observations of the eclipse itself. The prominences are now carefully mapped day by day all around the Sun, and it has been proved that around this body there is a vast atmosphere of hydrogen gas—the *chromosphere.* From this the prominences are projected sometimes to heights of 100,000 miles or more.

Spectrum of the Corona.—The spectrum of the corona was first observed by two American astronomers—Professors YOUNG and HARKNESS—at the total solar eclipse of 1869. Since that time it has been regularly observed at every total eclipse and often photographed. Expeditions are sent to observe all total eclipses, no matter in what parts of the Earth they occur, as up to the present time there is no other way of investigating the corona and its spectrum.

The spectrum of the corona consists of several bright lines superposed on a faint continuous band. The continuous spectrum is
probably due to sunlight reflected from the particles (like fog or dust
particles) present in the corona. The bright lines prove that the
corona is chiefly made up of self-luminous gases and vapors.

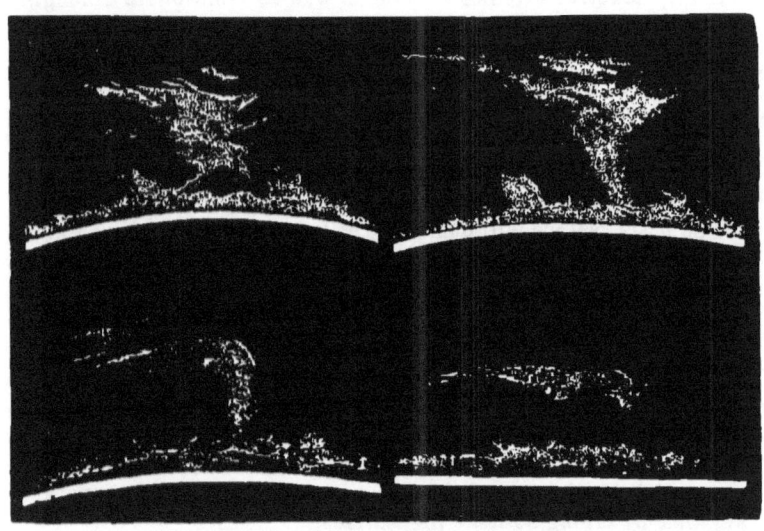

Fig. 170.—Forms of the Solar Prominences as seen with
the Spectroscope.

The corona is a mass of inconceivably rarefied matter
enveloping the Sun and extending far out into space. It
is excessively rarefied, as is proved by the fact that comets
moving round the Sun close to it (and thus passing through
the corona) are not appreciably retarded in their motions.
The gas of which it is chiefly made up has, so far, not been
discovered on the Earth.

The Sun's Light and Heat.—The light of the Sun
received at the Earth can be compared with our gas-jets or
electric lights. Our ordinary gas-burners or electric lights
have from ten to twenty "candle-power." The quantity
of sunlight is 1,575,000,000,000,000,000,000,000,000 times
as great as the light of a standard candle. The Sun sends

us 618,000 times as much light as the full Moon, and about 7,000,000,000 times as much light as the brightest star—*Sirius.*

Amount of Heat Emitted by the Sun.—Owing to the absorption of the solar atmosphere, we receive only a portion—perhaps a very small portion—of the rays emitted by the Sun's photosphere.

If the Sun had no absorptive atmosphere, it would seem to us hotter, brighter, and more blue in color, since the blue end of the spectrum is absorbed proportionally more than the red end.

The amount of this absorption is a practical question to us on the Earth. So long as the central body of the Sun continues to emit the same quantity of rays, it is plain that the thickness of the solar atmosphere determines the number of such rays reaching the Earth. If in former times this atmosphere was much thicker, as it may have been, less heat would have reached the Earth. Glacial epochs *may*, perhaps, be explained in this way. If the Sun has had different emissive powers at different times, as it may have had, this again would have produced variations in the temperature of the Earth in past times.

Amount of Heat Radiated.—There is at present no way of determining accurately either the absolute amount of heat emitted from the central body or the amount of this heat stopped by the solar atmosphere itself. All that can be done is to measure the amount of heat actually received by the Earth.

Experiments upon this question lead to the conclusion that if our own atmosphere were removed, the solar rays would have energy enough to melt a layer of ice 170 feet thick over the whole Earth each year.

This action is constantly at work over the whole of the Sun's surface. To produce a similar effect by the combustion of coal at the Sun would require that a layer of coal nearly 20 feet thick spread all over the Sun's surface should be consumed every *hour.* If the Sun were of solid coal and produced its own heat by combustion alone it would burn out in 5000 years.

Of the total amount of heat radiated by the Sun the Earth receives but an insignificant share. The Sun is capable of heating the entire surface of a sphere whose radius is the Earth's mean distance, to the same degree that the Earth is now heated. The surface of such a sphere is 2,170,000,000 times greater than the angular dimensions of the Earth as seen from the Sun, and hence the Earth receives less than one two-billionth part of the solar radiation.

We have expressed the energy of the Sun's heat in terms of the ice it would melt daily on the Earth. If we compute how much coal it would require to melt the same amount, and then further calculate how much work this coal would do if it were used to drive a steam-engine for instance, we shall find that the Sun sends to the Earth an amount of heat which is equivalent to one horse-power continuously acting day and night for every 25 square feet of the Earth's surface. Most of this heat is expended in maintaining the Earth's temperature ; but a small portion, about $\frac{1}{1000}$, is stored away by animals and vegetables.

Solar Temperature.—From the amount of heat actually radiated by the Sun, attempts have been made to determine the actual temperature of the solar surface. The estimates reached by various authorities differ widely, as the laws that govern the absorption within the solar envelope are almost unknown. Some law of absorption has to be assumed in any such investigation, and the estimates have differed widely according to the adopted law.

Professor YOUNG states this temperature at about 18,000° Fahr. According to all sound philosophy, the temperature of the Sun must far exceed any terrestrial temperature. There can be no doubt that if the temperature of the Earth's surface were suddenly raised to that of the Sun, no single chemical element would remain in its present condition. The most refractory materials would be at once volatilized.

We may concentrate the heat received upon several square feet (the surface of a huge burning-lens or mirror, for instance), examine its effects at the focus, and, making allowance for the condensation by the lens, see what is the minimum possible temperature of the Sun. The temperature at the focus of the lens cannot be higher than that of the source of heat in the Sun ; we can only concentrate the heat received on the surface of the lens to one point and examine its effects. No heat is created by the lens.

If a lens three feet in diameter be used, the most refractory materials, as fire-clay, platinum, the diamond, are at once melted or volatilized. The effect of the lens is plainly the same as if the Earth were brought closer to the Sun, in the ratio of the diameter of the focal image to that of the lens. In the case of the lens of three feet, allowing for the absorption, etc., this distance is yet greater than that of the Moon from the Earth, so that it appears that any comet or planet so close as 240,000 miles to the Sun must be vaporized if composed of materials similar to those in the Earth.

How is the Sun's Heat Maintained?—It is certain that the Sun's heat is not kept up by combustion. If the Sun were entirely composed of pure coal its combustion would not serve to maintain the Sun's supply of heat for more than 5000 years. We know that the Earth has been inhabited by people of high civilization (in Egypt for example) for a much longer time than this. Moreover the Sun cannot be a huge mass once very hot and now cooling because there has certainly been no *great* diminution of terrestrial temperatures in the past 3000 years, as is shown by what is known of the history of the vine, the fig, etc. A body freely cooling in space would lose its heat rapidly.

There are two explanations that deserve mention. The first is that the Sun's heat is maintained by the constant falling of meteors on its surface. It is well known that great amounts of heat and light are produced by the collision of two rapidly moving heavy bodies, or even by the passage of a heavy body like a meteorite through the atmosphere of the Earth. In fact, if we had a certain mass available with which to produce heat by burning, it can be shown that, by burning it at the surface of the Sun, we should produce less heat than if we simply allowed it to fall into the Sun. If it fell from the Earth's distance, it would give 6000 times more heat by its fall than by its burning.

The *least* velocity with which a body from space can fall upon the Sun's surface is about 280 miles in a second of time, and the velocity may be as great as 350 miles.

No doubt immense numbers of meteorites do fall into the Sun daily and hourly, and to each one of them a certain considerable portion of heat is due. It is found that to account for the present amount of radiation meteorites equal in mass to the whole Earth would have to fall into the Sun every century. It is in the highest degree improbable that a mass so large as this is added to the Sun in this way per century, because the Earth itself and every other planet would receive far more than its present share of meteorites, and would become quite hot from this cause alone.

The meteoric theory deserves a mention, but it is probably not a sufficient explanation.

There is still another way of accounting for the Sun's constant supply of energy, and this has the advantage of appealing to no cause outside of the Sun itself in the explanation. It is by supposing the heat, light, etc., to be generated by a constant and gradual contraction of the dimensions of the solar sphere. As the globe cools by radiation into space, it must shrink. As it shrinks, heat is produced and given out.

When a particle of the Sun moves towards the Sun's centre the same amount of heat is produced if its motion is caused by a slow shrinking as would be developed by its sudden fall through the same distance.

This theory is in complete agreement with the known laws of force. It also admits of precise comparison with facts, since the laws of heat enable us, from the known amount of heat radiated, to infer the exact amount of contraction in inches which the linear dimensions of the Sun must undergo in order that this supply of heat may be kept unchanged, as it is practically found to be.

With the present size of the Sun, it is found that it is only necessary to suppose that its diameter is diminishing at the rate of about 250 feet per year, or 4 miles per century, in order that the supply of heat radiated shall be constant. Such a change as this may be taking place, since we possess no instruments sufficiently delicate to have detected a change of even ten times this amount since the invention of the telescope.

It may seem a paradoxical conclusion that the cooling of a body may cause it to give out heat. This indeed is not true when we suppose the body to be solid or liquid. It is, however, proved that this law holds for gaseous masses—but only so long as they are gaseous.

We cannot say whether the Sun has yet begun to liquefy in his interior parts, and hence it is impossible to predict at present the duration of his constant radiation. It can be shown that after about 5,000,000 years, if the Sun radiates heat as at present, and still remains gaseous, his present volume will be reduced to one half. If the volume is reduced to one half the density will be then two times greater (since the mass will remain the same). ($D = M \div V$, see page 237.) It seems probable that somewhere about this time the solidification will have begun, and it is roughly estimated, from this line of argument, that the present conditions of heat radiation cannot last greatly over 10,000,000 years.

The future of the Sun (and hence of the Earth) cannot, as we see, be traced with great exactitude. The past can be more closely followed if we assume (which is tolerably safe) that the Sun up to the present has been a gaseous and not a solid or liquid mass. Four hundred years ago, then, the Sun was about 16 miles greater in diameter than now ; and if we suppose the process of contraction to have regularly gone on at the same rate (a very uncertain supposition), we can fix a date when the Sun filled any given space, out even to the orbit of *Neptune ;* that is, to the time when the solar system consisted of but one body, and that a gaseous or nebulous one.

It is not to be taken for granted, however, that the amount of heat to be derived from the contraction of the Sun's dimensions is infinite, no matter how large the primitive dimensions may have been. A body falling from any distance to the Sun can only have a certain finite velocity depending on this distance and upon the mass of the Sun itself, which, even if the fall be from an infinite distance, cannot exceed, for the Sun, 350 miles per second. In the same way the amount of heat generated by the contraction of the Sun's volume from any size to any other is finite and not infinite.

It has been shown that if the Sun has always been radiating heat at its present rate, and if it had originally filled all space, it has required some 18,000,000 years to contract to its present volume. In other words, assuming the present rate of radiation, and taking the most favorable case, the age of the Sun does not exceed 18,000,000 years. The Earth is, of course, less aged.

The supposition lying at the base of this estimate is that the radiation of the Sun has been constant throughout the whole period. This is quite unlikely, and any changes in this datum will affect the final number of years to be assigned. While this *number* may be greatly in error, yet the method of obtaining it seems to be satisfactory, and the main conclusion remains that the past of the Sun is finite, and that in all probability its future is a limited one.

The exact number of centuries that it is to last are of

no especial moment even were the data at hand to obtain them: the essential point is that, so far as we can see, the Sun, and incidentally the solar system, has a finite past and a limited future, and that, like other natural objects, it passes through its regular stages of birth, vigor, decay, and death, in one order of progress.

CHAPTER XVII.

THE PLANETS MERCURY, VENUS, MARS.

32. Mercury—Venus—Mars.—*Mercury* is the nearest planet to the Sun. Its mean *distance* is 36,000,000 miles, about $\frac{39}{100}$ of the Earth's distance. Its orbit is quite eccentric, so that its maximum distance from the Sun is 43,500,000 miles, and its minimum only 28,500,000. At its mean distance (0.39) it would receive about $6\frac{6}{10}$ times as much light and heat from the Sun as the Earth, because

$$(1.00)^2 : (0.39)^2 = 6.6 : 1.0.$$

Its *sidereal year* is 88 days. Its time of *rotation* on its axis is not certainly known, but the observations of SCHIAPARELLI and others make it likely that it revolves once on its axis in the same time that it makes one revolution about the Sun, just as our own Moon revolves once on its axis during one of its revolutions about the Earth. The apparent angular diameter of *Mercury* can be measured with the micrometer (see page 144). Knowing the angle that the diameter of the planet subtends and knowing the planet's distance (in miles) the diameter of the planet in miles can be calculated. The *diameter* of *Mercury* is about 3000 miles. Its *surface* is $\frac{1}{7}$ of the Earth's surface and its *volume* about $\frac{1}{18}$. The *mass* of the planet is determined by calculating how much matter it must contain to affect the motions of comets as it is observed to do. In this way it results that its mass is about $\frac{1}{30}$ of the Earth's mass. Its *density* is about $\frac{6}{10}$ of the Earth's density.

Venus' mean *distance* is 67,200,000 miles. Its *sidereal year* is 225 days. It is not yet certain that its period of rotation may not be about 24 hours—one day, but the observations of SCHIAPARELLI and others make it likely that its *rotation* on its axis is performed in 225 days also. If this be so *Mercury* and *Venus* will always turn the same face to the Sun, just as our Moon always turns the same face to the Earth. The *diameter* of *Venus* is 7700 miles, only a little less than the diameter of the Earth (7918) and it has therefore about the same *volume*. The mass of *Venus* is determined by calculating how much matter the planet must contain in order to affect the motion of the Earth as it is observed to do. Its *mass* is about $\frac{8}{10}$ of the Earth's mass and its *density* about $\frac{9}{10}$ that of the Earth.

Very little is certainly known about the geography of *Mercury* and of *Venus*. *Mercury* is never seen far distant from the Sun and observations of the planet in the daytime are unsatisfactory because the heated atmosphere of the Earth is usually in constant motion and produces an effect on telescopic images like the twinkling of stars to the naked eye. *Venus* shows only faint markings on her surface.

It is likely that *Mercury* has little or no atmosphere; and it is certain that *Venus* has an atmosphere of some kind which is, in all probability, extensive. If the surface of *Venus* which we see with the telescope is nothing but the outer rim of its envelope of clouds we know nothing of the real surface of the planet. Nothing whatever is known as to whether either of these planets is inhabited; and very little as to whether either of them is habitable.

Apparent Diameters of Mercury and Venus.—In Fig. 171 *S* is the Sun, *E* the Earth in its orbit and *LIMC* the orbit of an inferior planet. If the Earth is at *E* and the planet at *I*, the planet is at inferior conjunction (nearest the Earth); if at *C*, at superior conjunction; if at *L* or *M*, at elongation. The Sun will be seen from *E* along the line *EC*. It is plain that the planet can never appear at a greater angle from the Sun than *SEM* or *SEL*. It is clear from the figure that the apparent angular diameter of the inferior planet will vary greatly. It will be greatest when the planet is nearest the Earth (inferior conjunction) and least when the planet is most distant.

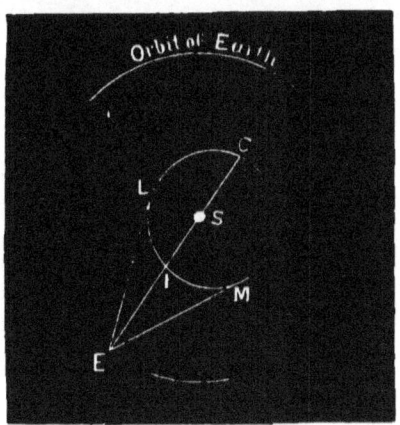

FIG. 171 —THE MOTION OF AN INFERIOR PLANET WITH REFER-
ENCE TO THE EARTH.

In representing the apparent angular magnitude of these planets, in Figs. 172 and 173 we suppose their whole disks to be visible, as they would be if they shone by their own light. But since they can be seen only by the reflected light of the Sun, those portions of the disk are alone seen which are at the same time visible from the Sun and from the Earth. A very little consideration will show that the proportion of the disk which can be seen by us constantly diminishes as the planet approaches the Earth, and that the planet's diameter subtends a larger angle.

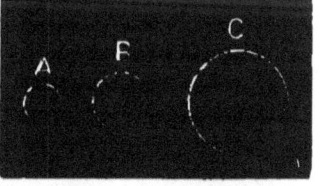

FIG. 172. — APPARENT DI-
AMETER OF MERCURY; A,
AT GREATEST DISTANCE;
B, AT MEAN DISTANCE;
C, AT LEAST DISTANCE.

Phases of Mercury and Venus.
When the planet is at its greatest distance, or in superior conjunction (C, Fig. 171), its whole illuminated hemisphere can be seen from the Earth. As it moves around and approaches the Earth, the illuminated hemisphere is gradually turned from us. At the point of greatest elongation, M or L, one half the hemi-

sphere is visible, and the planet has the form of the Moon at first or second quarter. As it approaches inferior conjunction, the apparent visible disk assumes the form of a crescent, which becomes thinner and thinner as the planet approaches the Sun. (See Fig. 174.)

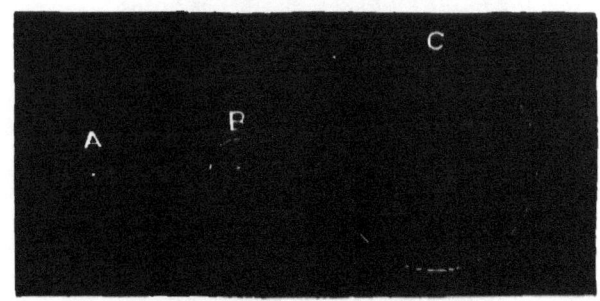

FIG. 173.—APPARENT DIAMETER OF VENUS; *A*, AT GREATEST; *B*, AT MEAN; *C*, AT LEAST DISTANCE.

The phases of an inferior planet were first observed by GALILEO in 1610. They are not visible to the naked eye and hence their discovery dates from the invention of the

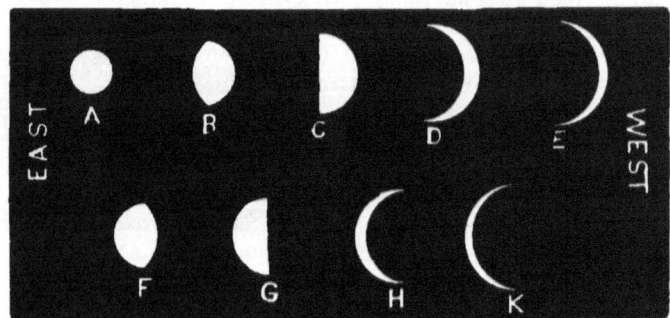

FIG. 174.—PHASES PRESENTED BY AN INFERIOR PLANET AT DIFFERENT POINTS OF ITS ORBIT; *K*, NEAR INFERIOR—*A*, NEAR SUPERIOR CONJUNCTION.

telescope. If the student will turn to the plan of the Ptolemaic system (Fig. 124) he will see that PTOLEMY supposed both *Mercury* and *Venus* to revolve about the

Earth and to be nearer to the Earth than the Sun. There was no time, according to PTOLEMY's system, when the whole disk of *Mercury* or *Venus* could be seen illuminated. But GALILEO's telescope showed the disk as a full circle at every superior conjunction. The inference that the Ptolemaic system was not true was irresistible. The failure of PTOLEMY's theory cleared the way for the adoption of the heliocentric theory of COPERNICUS.

Transits of Mercury and Venus.—When *Mercury* or *Venus* passes between the Earth and Sun, so as to appear projected on the Sun's disk as a dark circle the phenomenon is called a *transit*. If these planets moved around the Sun exactly in the plane of the ecliptic, it is evident that there would be a transit at every inferior conjunction, but their orbits are inclined to the ecliptic by angles of 7° and 3° respectively.

The longitude of the descending node of *Mercury* at the present time is 227°, and therefore that of the ascending node 47°. The Earth has these longitudes on May 7th and November 9th. Since a transit can occur only within a few degrees of a node, *Mercury* can transit only within a few days of these epochs.

The longitude of the descending node of *Venus* is now about 256° and therefore that of the ascending node is 76°. The Earth has these longitudes on June 6th and December 7th of each year. Transits of *Venus* can therefore occur only within two or three days of these times. (See page 264.)

Transits of *Mercury* will occur in 1907, 1914 etc., and of *Venus* in 2004 and 2012.

Mars is the fourth planet in order going outwards from the Sun. Its mean distance is 141,500,000 miles, about 1½ times the Earth's distance. Its orbit is quite eccentric so that its distance from the Sun at different times may be as large as 153,000,000 or as small as 128,000,000 miles. Its *distances* from the Earth *at opposition* will vary in the same way. When its distance from the Sun is the largest the distance from the Earth will be about 60,000,000 miles (= 153,000,000 − 93,000,000). When its distance from the Sun is the smallest the distance from the Earth will be about 35,000,000 miles (= 128,000,000 − 93,000,000).

When *Mars* is in conjunction with the Sun its average distance is about 234,000,000 miles (= 141,000,000 + 93,000,000). Its greatest distance at conjunction is about 246,000,000 miles.

The apparent angular diameter of the planet varies directly as the distance and is sometimes as small as 3″.6, sometimes seven times larger (246 ÷ 35 = 7). The amount of light received by *Mars* from the Sun varies as $\frac{1}{R^2}$ (where $R = Mars'$ radius vector), so that the amount of light received by the Earth from *Mars* varies as $\frac{1}{R^2 r^2}$ (where r is the distance of *Mars* from the Earth). The amount of light received by us from the planet varies enormously at different times, therefore.

The *periodic time* of Mars is 687 days. Its *diameter* is 4200 miles—a little more than half that of the Earth. Its *surface* is about ¼ and its *volume* is ⅐ of the Earth's. Its *mass* is determined (by calculating the effect of the planet on the orbits of its satellites) to be about ⅛ of the Earth's mass. Its *density* is accurately $\frac{12}{100}$ of the Earth's density, and the force of gravity at its surface is about $\frac{4}{10}$ of the Earth's. A body weighing 100 pounds on the Earth would weigh a little less than 40 pounds on *Mars*.

Mars necessarily exhibits phases, but they are not so well marked as in the case of *Venus*, because the hemisphere which it presents to the observer on the Earth is always more than half illuminated. The greatest phase occurs when its direction is 90° from that of the Sun, and even then six sevenths of its disk is illuminated, like that of the Moon, three days before or after full moon. The phases of *Mars* were observed by GALILEO in 1610.

Mars has little or no Atmosphere.—The Moon reflects $\frac{17}{100}$ of the light falling upon it—about as much as sandstone rocks. *Mercury* reflects $\frac{14}{100}$. These bodies have little or no atmosphere. *Venus* reflects (from the outer surface of its envelope of clouds) $\frac{50}{100}$ of the incident light. *Jupiter* ($\frac{62}{100}$), *Saturn* ($\frac{52}{100}$), *Uranus* ($\frac{64}{100}$), *Neptune* ($\frac{46}{100}$), are all bodies surrounded by extensive atmospheres and all of them have high reflecting powers. The corresponding number for *Mars* ($\frac{24}{100}$) is so small as to indicate that this planet has little atmosphere, if any.

The planet's surface has been under careful scrutiny for many years and observers are all but unanimous in their report that no clouds are visible over the surface.

The centres of the disks of bodies with extensive atmospheres (the Sun, *Jupiter*, *Saturn*, etc.) are always brighter than the edges (see page 283). The centre of the Moon, which has no atmosphere, is not so bright as the edge. *Mars* is like the Moon in this respect and not like *Jupiter*. Finally the only satisfactory spectroscopic observations of the planet (made independently at the Lick Observatory by CAMPBELL and at the Allegheny Observatory by KEELER) show no evidence whatever of an atmosphere to *Mars* and no sign of water-vapor about the planet. If there is any atmosphere at all it can hardly be more dense than the Earth's atmosphere at the high summits of the Himalaya mountains—not enough to support human life therefore. As there is no evidence of the presence of water-vapor and of clouds, etc., it follows that there is little or no water on the planet's surface. The spectrum of *Mars* and the spectrum of the Moon are identical in every respect. This could not be true if *Mars* had any considerable atmosphere.

It is proper to say that a number of astronomers hold different views and that popular writers on astronomy, with few exceptions, proclaim the existence of water, air, vegetation and intelligent human beings on the planet. It is an announcement that finds thousands of interested listeners who are only too glad to welcome so momentous a conclusion. The popular writings referred to have little weight in themselves, but they have undoubtedly spread a general belief among intelligent people that *Mars* is a planet much like the Earth (which it certainly is not), fit for human habitation, and very likely inhabited by beings like ourselves. The questions involved are inexpressibly important in themselves and they relate to matters in which every human being is interested. The duty of Science is to investigate them by every possible means (and this has been and will be done), but Science can only be discredited by premature and incorrect announcements made without a proper sense of responsibility.

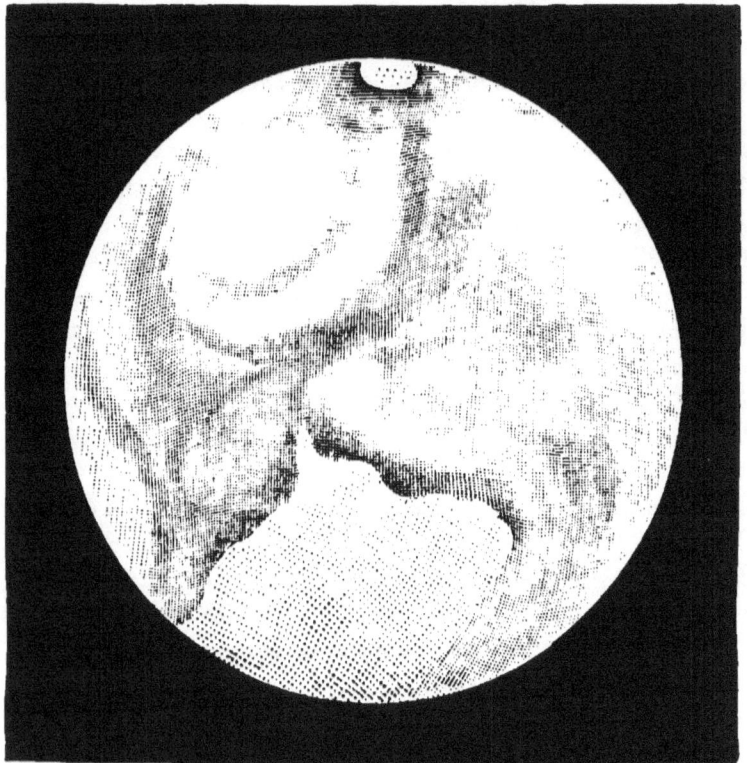

FIG. 175.—TELESCOPIC VIEW OF THE SURFACE OF MARS SHOW-
ING A SMALL "POLAR CAP."

The important and long-continued observations of SCHIAPARELLI on *Mars* led him to announce that the planet was provided with an elaborate system of water-courses ("oceans, seas, lakes, canals, etc."), and the authority of this distinguished observer is the chief support of those who maintain that this planet is fit for human habitation, etc. Complete explanations of all the phenomena presented by the

planet cannot be given in the light of our present knowledge.
This is not to be wondered at in spite of the industry and ability
of the observers who have spent years in studying the planet. The
case is much the same for the planets *Mercury, Venus, Jupiter, Saturn,
Uranus, Neptune.* We know very little of the real conditions that
prevail on their surfaces. We know comparatively little of the interior of the Earth on which we live and next to nothing about the
interior of other planets. There is every reason to believe that

FIG. 176.—DRAWING OF MARS MADE AT THE LICK OBSERVATORY
MAY 21, 1890.

complete explanations will be forthcoming in time. It is, at any rate,
certain that the conclusions of SCHIAPARELLI, named above, cannot
be accepted without serious modification, as will be shown in this
Chapter.

Appearance of the Disk of Mars in the Telescope.—The
appearance of *Mars* in large telescopes is shown in Figs.
175 and 176. The main body of the planet is reddish
(shown white in the cuts). The portions shown dark in

the pictures are bluish, greenish, or grayish in the telescope. The "cap" in Fig. 175 is a brilliant white. Most
of the markings on *Mars* are permanent. They are seen
in the same places year after year. Observations on these
permanent markings prove that the planet revolves on its
axis once in 24^h 37^m 22^s.7. Its equator is inclined to the
ecliptic about 26°.

When Sir WILLIAM HERSCHEL was examining *Mars* in
the XVIII century he called the red areas of *Mars* "land"
and the greenish and bluish areas "water." It was a
general opinion in his day that all the planets were created
to be useful to man. Astronomers of the XVIII century
set out with this belief very much as the philosophers of
PTOLEMY's time set out with the fundamental theorem that
the Earth was the centre of the motions of the planets.
For example, HERSCHEL maintained that the Sun was cool
and habitable underneath its envelope of fire. He says
(1795) " The Sun appears to be nothing else than a very
eminent, large and lucid planet . . . most probably also
inhabited by beings whose organs are adapted to the
peculiar circumstances of that vast globe." It is certain
that the Sun is not inhabited by any beings with organs.
This conclusion is now as obvious as that no beings
inhabit the carbons of an electric street-lamp. HERSCHEL'S
guess that the red areas on *Mars* were "land" and the
blue areas " water " had no more foundation than his guess
that the Sun might be inhabited.

The next careful studies of *Mars* were made by MAEDLER
about 1840. He also called the red areas of the disk
"land" and the dark areas "water." In this he followed
HERSCHEL. There was no reason why he should not have
called the red areas " water " and the dark areas " land."
He had no evidence on the point. The same is true of
later observers down to the first observations of SCHIA-
PARELLI about 1877.

SCHIAPARELLI gave reasons for these names, though his reasons are not convincing. He pointed out that the narrow dark streaks ("canals") generally ended in large dark areas ("oceans") or in smaller dark areas ("lakes"). The narrow dark streaks (very seldom less than 60 miles wide) are quite straight. They cannot be "rivers" then. *If* they are water at all the name "canal" is not inappropriate though 60 or 100 miles is a very wide canal. *If* they are water, then the large dark areas must be "seas." The narrow dark streaks are not water, however, because it was discovered by Dr. SCHAEBERLE at the Lick Observatory that the so-called "seas" sometimes had so-called "canals" crossing them. A "sea" traversed by a "canal" is an absurdity. If it could be imagined it would prove the "inhabitants" and the "engineers" of *Mars* to be the exact reverse of "intelligent." It is maintained by some recent observers of *Mars* that some of the dark areas are water and some are not so. The bluish-green color of the dark spots is said to "suggest vegetation." But who can know what colors the vegetation on *Mars* may have?

The foregoing very brief abstract proves that the dark areas on *Mars* are not "water." The red areas are not known to be "land." The spectroscopic and other evidence proves that *Mars* has little or no atmosphere—little or no water-vapor—no clouds. It is not yet known what the real nature of the red areas and of the dark areas is. It is one of the many unsolved problems of Astronomy to discover the answer to this fundamental question. There is no doubt the red areas and the large dark areas have a real existence, since some of the markings on *Mars* have been seen for more than two centuries.

It is not certain that all the "canals" that have been mapped really exist. Some of them are probably mere optical illusions. If they were real streaks on the planet's surface (like wide fissures, broad watercourses, etc.) they would *always* appear broadest when they were at the centre of the disk and would always be narrower when they were at the edges. The laws of perspective demand this. It is found by observation that the reverse is frequently true.

SCHIAPARELLI was the first to observe that many of the "canals" oftentimes appear to be doubled. That is, a canal running in a certain direction which generally appeared single, thus,

───────────────

at certain times was no longer single but attended by a companion, thus:

───────────────

Marvels of ingenious speculation have been printed to explain why "intelligent inhabitants" having one "canal" not sufficient for "commerce," did not widen it, but preferred to dig another parallel to it, and why this second "canal" sometimes vanished altogether in "a few hours." Recent experiments have proved that these companion canals are optical illusions produced by fatigue of the eye and by bad focusing. Some, at least, of the single narrow dark streaks ("canals") have a real existence. It is probable that many of those laid down and named on the maps of SCHIAPARELLI, LOWELL and others are mere illusions. It is likely that all the double canals were so.

Temperature of Mars.—The distance of *Mars* from the Sun is $1\frac{1}{2}$ times the Earth's distance. The heat received by the Earth from the Sun *is to* the heat received by *Mars* as $(1.5)^2 = 2.25$ *to* 1. *Mars* receives less than one half as much Sun heat as the Earth. If the Earth had no more atmosphere than the Moon the Earth's temperature would be like that of the Moon. If the Earth had no denser atmosphere than that on the summits of the Himalayas the temperature of the Earth would always be below zero. Human life could not exist here. The case is the same with *Mars*. The temperature of the whole surface of the planet must be extremely low—even in its equatorial regions. The temperature at the poles of *Mars* must be several hundred degrees (Fahrenheit) below zero when the pole is turned away from the Sun and below zero even when the pole is turned towards the Sun.

Before going further it is worth while to consider the circumstances under which *Mars* is seen by an observer on the Earth. The mean distance of the Moon from the Earth is 240,000 miles. If it is viewed through a field-glass magnifying 4 times, it is virtually brought within 60,000 miles of the observer (240,000 ÷ 4 = 60,000). The nearest approach of *Mars* to the Earth is 35,000,000 miles. The planet can very seldom be viewed to advantage with a magnifying power so high as 500. If such a power is employed when *Mars* is nearest, the planet is virtually brought within 70,000 miles (35,000,000 ÷ 500 = 70,000). It follows therefore that *we never see Mars so advantageously even with the largest telescopes as we may see the Moon in a common field-glass.* If the student will examine the Moon with a field-glass magnifying 4 times he will have a realizing sense of the *best* conditions under which it is possible to see *Mars*, and he will be surprised that so much is known of the planet. The industry and fidelity of observers can only be appreciated after such an experiment.

The Polar Caps of Mars.—We have now to present another result of observation which must be interpreted in the light of the foregoing facts—namely, that *Mars* has little or no water-vapor and that its temperature is appallingly low. The main facts of observation are as follows. Cassini, the royal astronomer of France, discovered in 1666 that *Mars* sometimes had dazzling white circular patches near his poles (see Fig. 175). In 1783 Sir William Herschel observed these patches to wax and wane and he called them "snow" caps, thus begging the question as to their real nature. Herschel's observations and those of all later observers show that these caps wax and wane with the Martian seasons. In the Martian polar summer they are smallest, or they even vanish. In the Martian polar winter they are largest. As HERSCHEL started out with the conviction that all planets were analogous to the Earth and were meant to be inhabited, his conclusion was that the polar winter condensed water-vapor into snow and that the polar summer melted this snow—and so on. A more scientific conclusion would have been that *some* vapor was condensed and subsequently dissipated by the solar heat. It is practically certain that the phenomena of the waxing and waning of the caps depend on solar heat.

If the caps are " snow " condensed from water-vapor the layer of snow must be exceedingly thin, because when these caps are " melted " no clouds appear. When snow melts on the Earth clouds are formed and our atmosphere is charged with the vapor of water. No clouds are seen on *Mars* and no water-vapor is to be found above its surface by any spectroscopic test.

The polar-caps may be formed by the vapor of some other substance than water. It is worth while to inquire whether they may not be carbon-dioxyd in a solid state. This substance is a heavy gas (carbonic-acid gas) at ordinary temperatures. It would lie at the bottom of valleys and fill cañons or ravines. At a temperature of about one hundred Fahrenheit below zero it is a colorless liquid. At temperatures such as must obtain at the pole of *Mars* turned away from the Sun it becomes a snow-like solid. Caps of carbon-dioxyd would wax and wane at the poles of *Mars* under variations of solar heat such as obtain at these poles, very much as caps of snow and ice wax and wane in our Arctic regions which, under all circumstances, are at a far higher temperature than the poles of *Mars*.

There is so far no observational proof that the polar-caps of *Mars* are formed of carbon-dioxyd. There is convincing proof that they are *not* formed of water. The question as to the nature of the polar-caps is still an open one. There is little doubt that it will, one day, be settled. The scientific attitude of mind is to wait for proofs of matters still unsolved; to accept such proofs as exist; and to eschew unfounded speculations. All that is now known goes to show that *Mars* has little or no atmosphere, little or no water-vapor, no "oceans," no "lakes,"no "canals," no clouds. Its general surface is rather flat, although a few mountain chains exist. It is not a planet like the Earth. It is much more like the Moon. It cannot possibly be "inhabited by beings like ourselves."

Satellites of Mars.—Until the year 1877 *Mars* was supposed to have no satellites. But in August of that year Professor HALL, of the Naval Observatory, instituted a systematic search with the great equatorial, which resulted in the discovery of two such objects.

These satellites are by far the smallest celestial bodies known. It is of course impossible to measure their diameters, as they appear in the telescope only as points of light. The outer satellite is probably about six miles and the inner one about seven miles in diameter. The outer one was seen with the telescope at a distance from the Earth of 7,000,000 times this diameter. The proportion wo·ld be that of a ball two inches in diameter viewed at a distance equal to that between the cities of Boston and New York. Such a feat of telescopic seeing is well fitted to give an idea of the power of modern optical instruments in detecting faint points of light like stars or satellites.

The outer satellite, called *Deimos*, revolves around the planet in 30ʰ 18ᵐ, and the inner one, called *Phobos*, in 7ʰ 39ᵐ. The latter is only 5800 miles from the centre of *Mars*, and less than 4000 miles from its surface. It would therefore be almost possible to see an object the size of a large animal on the satellite if one of our telescopes could be used at the surface of *Mars*.

The short distance and rapid revolution make the inner satellite of *Mars* one of the most interesting bodies with which we are acquainted. It performs a revolution in its orbit from west to east in less than half the time that *Mars* revolves on its axis. *In consequence, to the inhabitants of Mars it would seem to rise in the west and set in the east.*

Let the student prove this statement for himself by drawing a figure somewhat like Fig. 31.   Suppose *N* to be *Mars*, *a* the spectator, *ZH* the celestial equator, *Z* to be *Phobos* on the meridian.   In

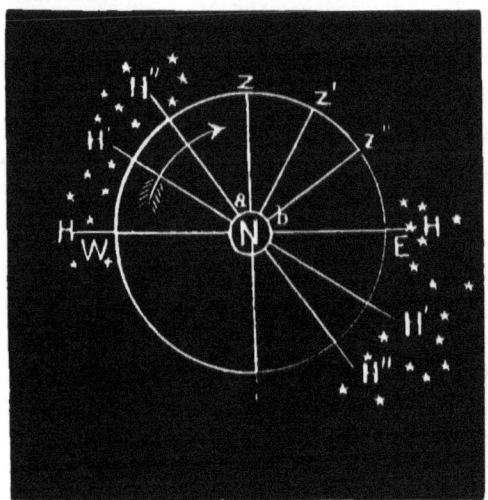

Fig. 31 *bis.*

1ʰ the spectator will have moved to ——; and *Phobos* to ——; in 2ʰ, etc. etc.

The light of *Phobos* is about $\frac{1}{80}$ of the light of our Moon; of *Deimos* about $\frac{1}{1800}$.

CHAPTER XVIII.

THE MOON—THE MINOR PLANETS.

33. The Moon.—The Moon—the satellite of the Earth—revolves about its primary in a *periodic-time* of 27^d.32116 at a *mean distance* of 238,840 miles. Its daily motion among the stars is $\frac{360°}{27.32116}$ = about 13° 11′. The apparent angular diameter of the Moon is about half a degree, so that the Moon moves daily among the stars about 26 of its own diameters. The interval from new moon to new moon is about 29 days and the Moon comes to the meridian of an observer about 51 minutes later each day (on the average). The orbit of the Moon is inclined to the plane of the ecliptic by a little more than 5°.

The *velocity* of the Moon *in* her *orbit* is about 3350 feet *per* second. Her *diameter* is 2163 miles, her *surface* $\frac{1}{100}$ of the Earth's, her *volume* $\frac{1}{49}$, and her *mass* $\frac{1}{80}$ of the Earth's. The *density* of the Moon is about 3.4 times the density of water. The heaviest lavas of the Earth's crust are about 3.3 in density, so that the conclusion that the Earth and Moon once formed one body is not contradicted by these facts. *Gravity* on the Moon's surface is $\frac{1}{6}$ as great as at the Earth's. Hence an explosion of subterranean steam would form a much more extensive crater on the Moon than on the Earth, and mountains would stand at a much steeper average angle on the Moon. As there is no air and no water on the Moon's surface there is no frost constantly working to overthrow cliffs and sharp peaks as

315

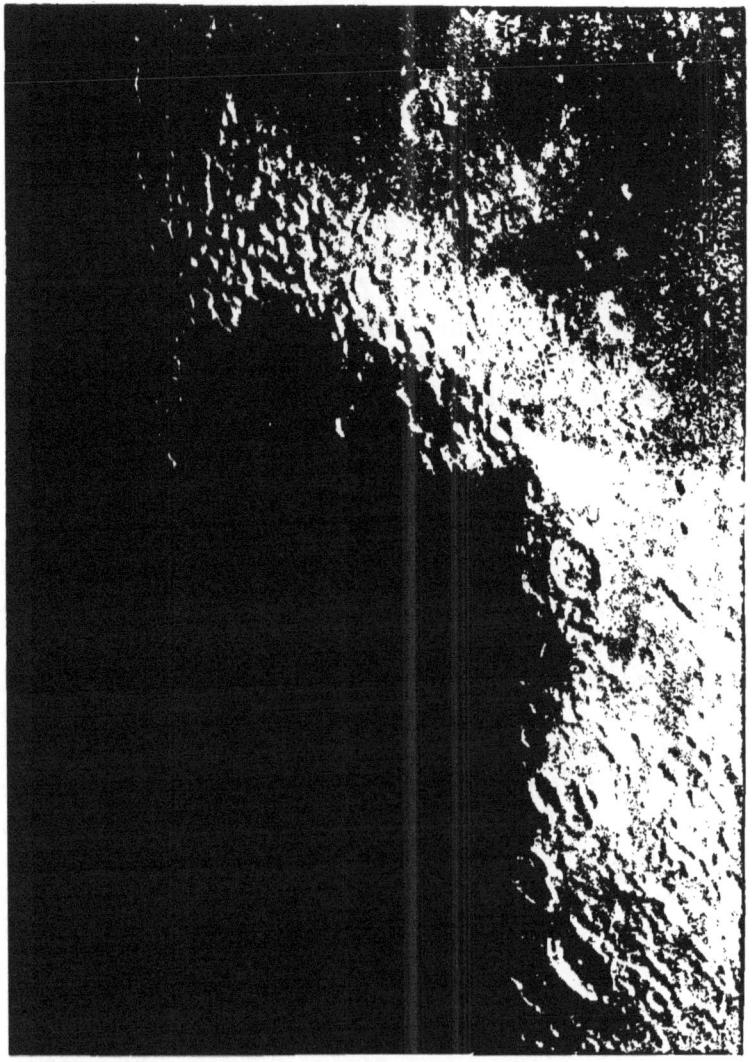

Fig. 177.—Lunar Landscape (*Mare Crisium*) from Photographs
Taken at the Lick Observatory.

in the case of the Earth. The *albedo* of the Moon is $\frac{17}{100}$; about that of weathered sandstone rocks.* The angle of slope of the lunar volcanoes is about the same as the angle of terrestrial lavas. These and many other facts support the conclusion that the Earth and Moon are made of like materials.

The Moon has extremely little if any atmosphere because the *occultation* of a star by the lunar disk takes place instantaneously. If the Moon had an atmosphere, the star's rays would be refracted by it and there would be a change of the star's color and a gradual disappearance. The *spectrum* of the Moon is nothing but a fainter solar spectrum. This proves that moonlight is reflected sunlight; and that the Moon has no absorbing atmosphere of its own. No doubt the Moon, in remote past times had an atmosphere. Its constituents have probably been absorbed by the rocks of the lunar crust as they cooled. The water on the Moon has probably been absorbed in the same way.

The quantity of light received by the Earth from the full Moon is $\frac{1}{618000}$ of the light received from the Sun. The *temperature* of the Moon's surface is probably always below freezing-point, even in the full sunshine of a long lunar "day." If the Earth's atmosphere were to be removed the temperature of our summers would be extremely low—much lower than it now is at the summits of our highest mountains. The lunar "night" is 14 terrestrial days long. The temperature of a part of the Moon after being deprived of the Sun's light (and heat) for 14 days must be extremely low—several hundred degrees Fahr. below zero.†

The Moon only Shows one Face to the Earth.—The Moon rotates on her axis from west to east, and the time required for one rotation is the

* The *albedo* of any substance is its power of reflecting rays of light that fall upon it. If it reflects all such rays its albedo is 100.

† These are the conditions that prevail on airless bodies like the Moon and *Mars*.

same as that required for one revolution in her orbit, viz., 27 days. If a line be drawn from the Earth to the Moon at any time whatever this line will always touch the same hemisphere of the Moon: and the Moon does not rotate at all with reference to this line. If a line be drawn through the *Sun* parallel to the Moon's axis, the Moon some-times turns one face and sometimes another to this line. An observer on the Earth sees but one hemisphere of the moon. An observer on the Sun would successively see all regions of the Moon (see Fig. 133).

When it became clearly understood after the invention of the telescope that the ancient notion of an impassable gulf between the character of " bodies celestial and bodies terres-trial " was unfounded, the question whether the Moon was like the Earth became one of great importance. The point of most especial interest was whether the Moon could, like the Earth, be peopled by intelligent inhabitants. Accord-ingly, when the telescope was invented by GALILEO, one of the first objects examined was the Moon. With every im-provement of the instrument the examination became more thorough, so that at present the topography of the Moon is very well known. Photographic maps of the Moon show the details of its surface in an admirable way.

With every improvement in the means of research, it has become more and more evident that circumstances at the surface of the Moon are totally unlike those on the Earth. There are no oceans, seas, rivers, air, clouds, or vapors. We can hardly suppose that animal or vegetable life exists under such circumstances. We might almost as well suppose a piece of granite or lava to be the abode of life as the surface of the Moon.

The length of one mile on the Moon would, as seen from the Earth, subtend an angle of about 1″ of arc. In order that an object may be plainly visible to the naked eye, it must subtend an angle of nearly 60.″ Consequently a magnifying power of 60 is required to render a round object one mile in diameter on the surface of the Moon plainly visible.

The following table shows the diameters of the smallest objects

N. B.—The Quadrants are marked I, II, III, IV on the borders of the Map.

I. FIRST QUADRANT.

1. Pallas
2. Gambart
3. Stadius
4. Copernicus
5. Reinhold
6. Kepler
7. Hevelius
8. Eratosthenes
9. Marius
10. Archimedes
11. Timocharis
12. Euler
13. Aristarchus
14. Herodotus
15. Laplace
16. Heraclides
17. Blanchini
18. Sharp
19. Mairan
20. Plato
21. Condamine
22. Harpalus

II. SECOND QUADRANT.

51. Moretus
52. Cysatus
53. Blancanus
54. Scheiner
55. Clavius
56. Maginus
57. Longomontanus
58. Schiller
59. Phocylides
60. Wargentin
61. Saussure
62. Pictet
63. Tycho
64. Heinsius
65. Hainzel
66. Schickard
67. Hell
68. Gauricus
69. Wurzelbauer
70. Pitatus
71. Hesiodus
72. Cichus
73. Capuanus
74. Ramsden
75. Vitello
76. Regiomontanus
77. Purbach
78. Thebit
79. Mercator
80. Campanus
81. Bullialdus
82. Doppelmayer
83. Fourier
84. Vieta
85. Mersenius
86. Arzachel
87. Alphonsus
88. Alpetragius
89. Davy
90. Guericke
91. Lubiniezky
92. Gassendi
93. Billy
94. Hansteen
95. Sirsalis
96. Ptolemæus
97. Herschel
98. Moesting
99. Lalande
100. Damoiseau

* The names are those
of scientific men, usually
of astronomers.

N. B.—From new moon (0days)
to full moon (15d) the *west* limb of
the moon is fully lighted. The
position of the terminator for
each intermediate day is marked
by the upper set of numbers
along the moon's equator; 2, 3,
4 . . . 15. From full moon to the
following new moon the *east*

SOUT

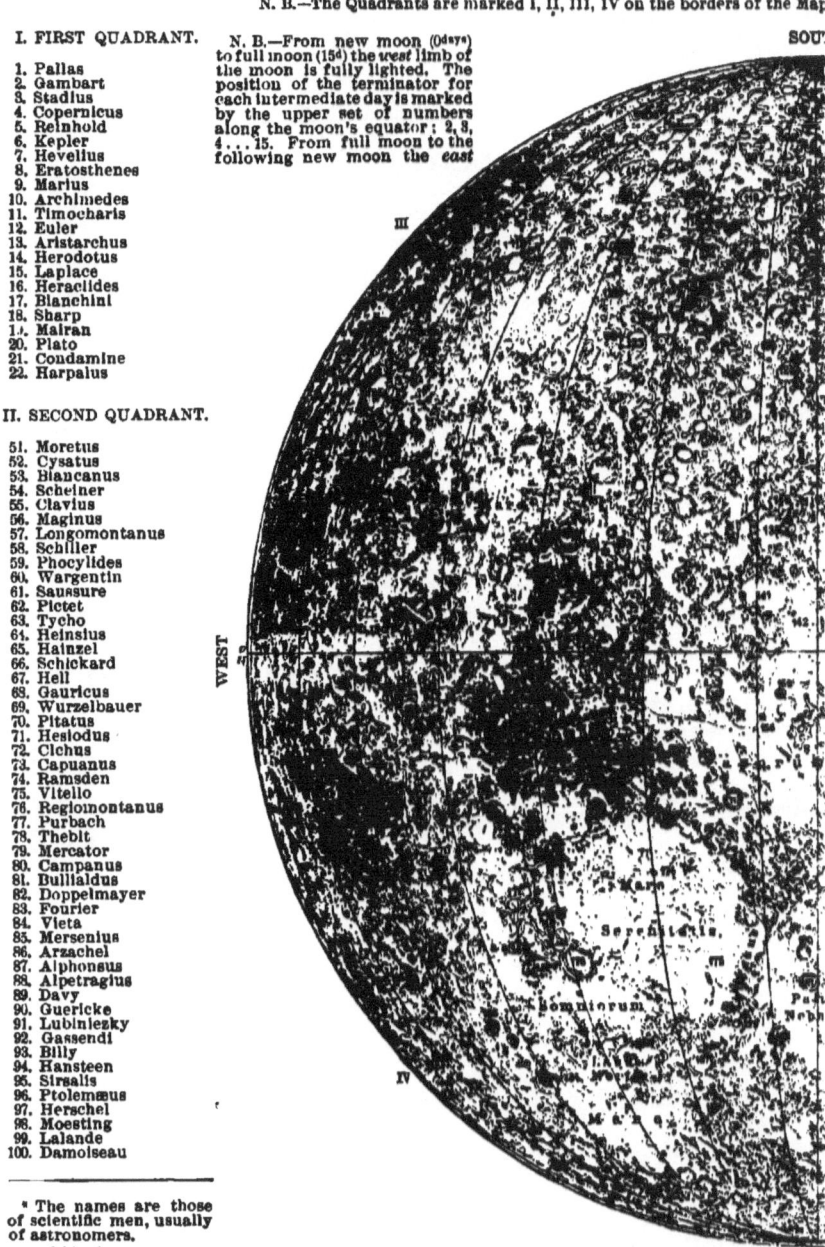

NOR

FIG. 178.—THE MOON AS

see the numbers plainly, a common hand-glass should be used.

limb is fully lighted, and the position of the terminator for each intermediate day is marked by the lower set of numbers; 17, 19...28, 30. These numbers give the moon's *age*, in days, when the terminator passes through their positions on the map.

III. THIRD QUADRANT.

101. Manzinus
102. Mutus
103. Bousingault
104. Boguslawsky
105. Curtius
106. Zach
107. Jacobi
108. Lilius
109. Baco
110. Pitiscus
111. Hommel
112. Fabricius
113. Metius
114. Rheita
115. Nicolai
116. Barocius
117. Maurolycus
118. Clairaut
119. Cuvier
120. Stoeffler
121. Funerius
122. Riccius
123. Zagut
124. Lindenau
125. Aliacensus
126. Werner
127. Aplanus
128. Sacrobosco
129. Santbach
130. Fracastor
131. Petavius
132. Vendelinus
133. Langrenus
134. Goclenius
135. Guttenberg
136. Theophilus
137. Cyrilius
138. Catherina
139. Albategnius
140. Parrot
141. Hipparchus
142. Réaumur
143. Delambre

IV. FOURTH QUADRANT.

151. Taruntius
152. Sabine
153. Ritter
154. Arago
155. Ariadæus
156. Godin
157. Agrippa
158. Hyginus
159. Triesnecker
160. Condorcet
161. Azout
162. Picard
163. Vitruvius
164. Plinius
165. Acherusia
166. Menelaus
167. Manilius
168. Einmart
169. Cleomedes
170. Macrobius
171. Roemer
172. Le Monnier
173. Linnæus
174. Bessel
175. Gauss
176. Messala
177. Geminus
178. Posidonius
179. Calippus
180. Aristillus
181. Autolycus
182. Cassini
183. Atlas
184. Hercules
185. Franklin
186. Bürg
187. Eudoxus
188. Aristotle
189. Endymion

AWN BY LOHRMANN.

that can be seen with different magnifying powers, at the Moon's distance.

Power   60 ; diameter of object 1 mile.
Power   150 ; diameter 2000 feet.
Power   500 ; diameter 600 feet.
Power 1000 ; diameter 300 feet.

If telescopic power could be increased indefinitely, there would be no limit to the minuteness of an object that could be seen on the Moon's surface. But the imperfections of all telescopes are such that only in exceptional cases can anything be gained by increasing the magnifying power beyond 1000. The influence of warm and cold currents in our atmosphere will forever prevent the advantageous use of very high magnifying powers.

Character of the Moon's Surface.—The most striking point of difference between the Earth and Moon is seen in the total absence from the latter of anything that looks like the water-worn surfaces of terrestrial plains, prairies, and hills. Valleys and mountain-chains exist on the Moon, but they are abrupt and rugged, not in the least like our formations of the same name. The lowest surface of the Moon which can be seen with the telescope appears to be nearly smooth and flat, or, to speak more exactly, spherical (because the Moon is a sphere). This surface has different shades of color in different regions. Some portions are of a bright silvery tint, while others have a dark gray appearance. These differences of tint seem to arise chiefly from differences of material.

Upon this surface as a foundation are built numerous formations of various sizes, usually of a very simple character. Their general form can be made out by the aid of Fig. 179, and their dimensions by remembering that one.inch on the figure is about 30 miles. The largest and most prominent features are known as craters. They have a typical form consisting of a round or oval rugged wall rising from the plain in the manner of a circular fortification. These walls are frequently 10,000 feet or more in height, very rough and broken. In their interior we see the plane surface of the Moon already described. It is, however, generally strewn with fragments or broken up by chasms.

In the centre of the craters we frequently find a conical formation rising up to a considerable height. The craters resemble the volcanic formations upon the Earth, the principal difference being that some of them are very much larger than anything known here. The diameter of the larger ones ranges from 50 to 100 miles, while the smallest are a half-mile or less, in diameter—mere crater-pits.

Heights of the Lunar Mountains.—When the Moon is only a few days old, the Sun's rays strike very obliquely upon the lunar mountains, and they cast long shadows. From the known position of the Sun, Moon, and Earth, and from the measured length of the shadows, the heights of the mountains can be calculated. It is thus found that some of the mountains near the south pole rise to a height of 8000 or 9000 metres (from 25,000 or 30,000 feet) above the general surface of the Moon. Heights of from 3000 to 7000 metres are very common over almost the whole lunar surface.

Is there any Change on the Surface of the Moon?—When the surface of the Moon was first found to be covered by craters like the volcanoes of the Earth, it was very naturally thought that the lunar volcanoes might be still in activity, and exhibit themselves to our telescopes by their flames. Not the slightest evidence of any eruption at the Moon's surface has been found.

Several instances of supposed changes of shape of features on the Moon's surface have been described in recent times, however.

Photographs of the Moon.—To make a complete map of the Moon requires a lifetime. The map of the Moon (six feet in diameter) made by Dr. SCHMIDT, Director of the Observatory of Athens, occupied the greater part of his time during the years 1845–1865.

A photograph of the full moon can now be taken in a fraction of a second that shows most features far better than SCHMIDT'S map; and a series of such photographs exhibits substantially every lunar feature better than any map can do. The first photographs of the Moon were made in America. The best lunar photographs are those of the observatories of Mt Hamilton (Lick Observatory) and of Paris.

Key-chart of the Moon.—The accompanying chart of the Moon will be found of use to the student who has a small telescope or even an opera-glass at his command. After acquiring a general acquaintance with the lunar topography by observations continued throughout a lunation, he should begin to study the craters in detail, making drawings of them as accurately as he can. Such drawings may not be of value to science, but they will be invaluable to the student himself; for they will train him to see what is to be seen, and to register it accurately. The changes in the appearance of lunar craters during a lunation are very marked, and to seek the explanation of each particular change is a valuable discipline.

GALILEO supposed some of the plains of the Moon to be seas, and named them *Mare Tranquilitatis* (the tranquil sea), etc. The principal mountain-chains on the Moon are named *Apennines, Alps, Cau-*

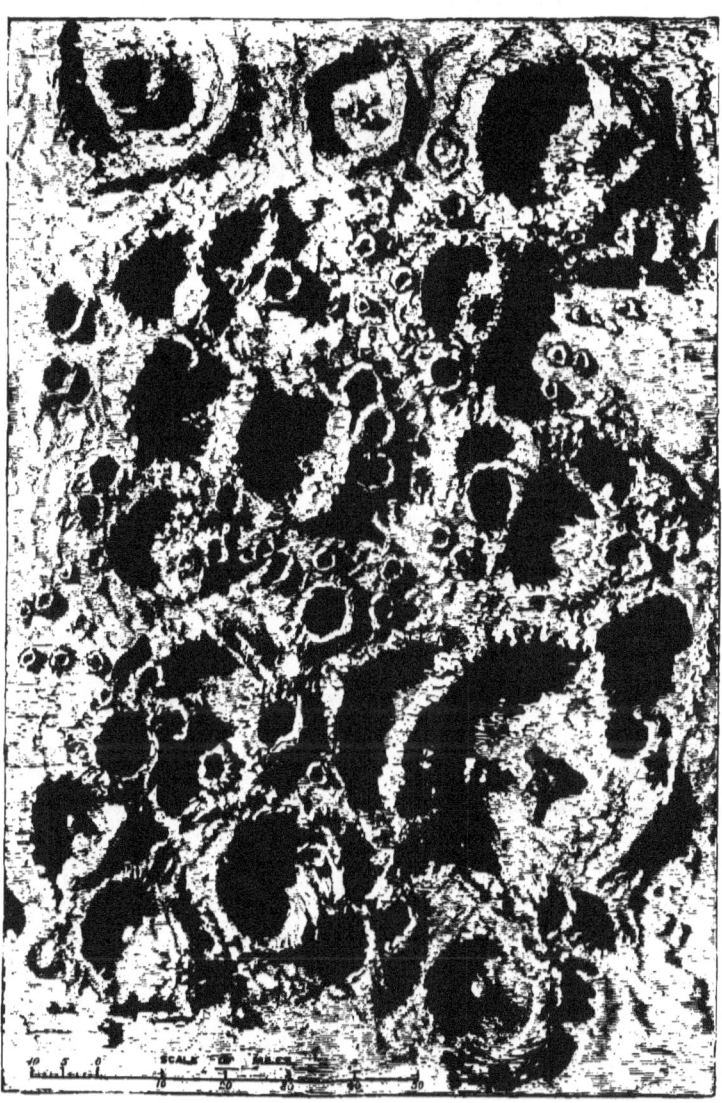

FIG. 179.—A DRAWING OF THE LUNAR SURFACE.

casus, etc.   The craters are usually named after noted astronomers, *Kepler, Copernicus, Tycho.*

34. The Minor Planets.—We have next to consider the group of *minor planets*, also called *asteroids* (because they resemble stars in appearance) or *planetoids* (because they are planets).   None of them was known until the beginning of the nineteenth century.

First of all, a curious relation between the distances of the planets, known as Bode's law, must be mentioned.   If to the numbers

0, 3, 6, 12, 24, 48, 96, 192, 384,

each of which (the second excepted) is twice the preceding, we add 4, we obtain the series

4. 7, 10, 16, 28, 52, 100, 196, 388,

These last numbers represent approximately the distances of the planets from the Sun (except for *Neptune*, which was not discovered when the law was announced) by Bode in 1772.

This is shown in the following table :

PLANETS.	Actual Distance.	BODE'S LAW.
Mercury.......... ·	3.9	4 0
Venus..............................	7.2	7.0
Earth...............................	10.0	10.0
Mars....	15.2	16.0
[Ceres] (one of the asteroids)........ ...	27.7	28.0
Jupiter...................	52.0	52.0
Saturn...	95.4	100.0
Uranus.............	191.8	196.0
Neptune	300.4	388.0

Although the so-called law was purely arbitrary, the agreement between the distances predicted by the law and the actual distances was sufficiently close to draw attention to the fact that a gap existed in the succession of the planets between *Mars* and *Jupiter*.

It was therefore supposed by the astronomers of the seventeenth and eighteenth centuries that a new major planet might be found in the region between *Mars* and

Jupiter. A search for this object was instituted, but before it had made much progress a minor planet in the place of the one so long expected was found by PIAZZI, of Palermo. The discovery was made on the first day of the present century, 1801, January 1. It was named *Ceres.*

In the course of the following seven years the astronomical world was surprised by the discovery of three other planets, all in the same region, though not revolving in the same orbit. Seeing four small planets where one large one ought to be, OLBERS suggested that these bodies might be fragments of a large planet that had been broken to pieces by the action of some unknown force.

A generation of astronomers now passed away without the discovery of more than these four. It was not until 1845 that a fifth planet of the group was found. In 1847 three more were discovered, and many discoveries have since been made. The number is now nearly 500, and the discovery of additional ones is going on as fast as ever. The frequent announcements of the discovery of planets which appear in the public prints all refer to bodies of this group. Seventy-seven of them have been discovered by American astronomers.

The minor planets are distinguished from the major ones by many characteristics. Among these we may mention their small size; their positions, all but one being situated between the orbits of *Mars* and *Jupiter;* the great eccentricities and inclinations of their orbits. The inclination of the orbit of *Pallas* to the ecliptic is 35°, for example.

Number of Small Planets.—It would be interesting to know how many of these planets there are in the group, but it is as yet impossible even to guess at the number. As already stated, about 500 are now known, and new ones are found every year.

A minor planet presents no sensible disk, and therefore looks exactly like a small star. It can be detected only by its motion among the surrounding stars, which is so slow that some hours must elapse before it can be noticed. Nowadays they are found by photographing a region of the sky with two or three hours' exposure and noticing whether any of the objects on the plate show a motion in that time. A fixed star will show no motion. An asteroid will make a *trail* on the plate.

Magnitudes.—It is impossible to make any precise measurement of the diameters of the minor planets. The diameters in miles that are sometimes quoted are subject to very large errors. The amount of light which the planet reflects is a better guide than measures made with ordinary micrometers. Supposing the proportion of light reflected to be the same as in the case of the larger planets, the diameters of the three or four largest range between 300 and 600 kilometres, while the smallest are from 20 to 50 kilometres in diameter. The average diameter is perhaps less than 150 kilometres (say 90 miles) ; that is, scarcely more than one hundredth that of the Earth. The volumes of solid bodies vary as the cubes of their diameters ; it might therefore take a million of these planets to make one of the size of the Earth.

Mass and Density of the Asteroids.—Nothing is known of the mass of any single asteroid. If their density is the same as that of the Earth the mass of the larger asteroids will be about $\frac{1}{50000}$ of the Earth's mass. The force of gravity on the surface of such a body would be about $\frac{1}{50}$ of the force of gravity on the Earth. A bullet shot from a rifle would fly quite away from the planet and would circulate about the Sun. It is not probable that any of them has an extensive atmosphere.

CHAPTER XIX.

THE PLANETS JUPITER, SATURN, URANUS, AND NEPTUNE.

35. Jupiter.—*Jupiter* is much the largest planet in the system. His mean *distance* is 483,300,000 miles. His mean *diameter* is 86,500 miles, the polar diameter being 83,000, the equatorial 88,200 miles. His linear diameter is about $\frac{1}{10}$, his surface is $\frac{1}{100}$, and his volume $\frac{1}{1000}$ that of the Sun. His *mass* is $\frac{1}{1048}$. His *density* is nearly the same as the Sun's density, that is $1\frac{3}{10}$ times the density of water. The densities of *Venus*, the Earth, the Moon, and of *Mars* are all more than three times the density of water. A cubic foot of the materials of each of these bodies weighs *at least* 200 lbs. A cubic foot of the stuff out of which *Jupiter* is made weighs, on the average, no more than 83 lbs. *Jupiter* is, in this respect, like the Sun and not like the inner planets.

He is attended by five satellites, four of which were discovered by GALILEO on January 7, 1610. He named them, in honor of the MEDICIS, the *Medicean stars*. They are now known as Satellites I, II, III, and IV, I being the nearest. They are large bodies, from 2100 to 3500 miles in diameter, comparable in size to the Moon or to *Mercury*. The fifth satellite was discovered by BARNARD with the great telescope of the Lick Observatory in 1892. It is a very small object, about 100 miles in diameter, revolving very close to the surface of *Jupiter*. Observations show that the larger satellites revolve about *Jupiter*, always turn-

ing the same face to the planet just as our own Moon turns
always the same face to the Earth.

The *rotation-time* of the planet is not the same in all latitudes ;
nor, in the same latitude, at all depths below the outer surface of its
clouds. The average time of rotation is about 9ʰ 55ᵐ, which is notice-
ably shorter than the rotation-times of *Mars* and the Earth. The

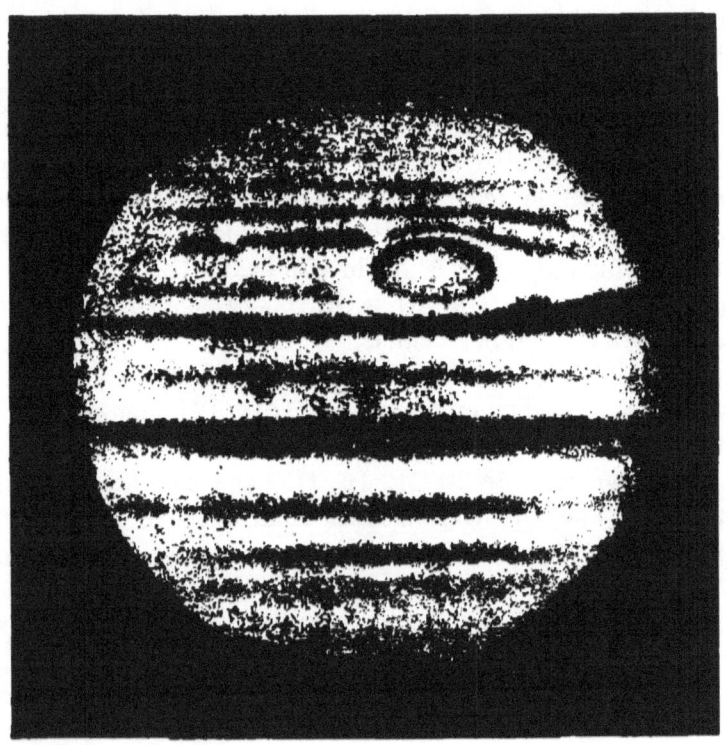

FIG. 180.—DRAWING OF JUPITER MADE AT THE LICK OBSERVA-
TORY, AUGUST 28, 1890.

figure of the planet is markedly spheroidal ; its disk is easily seen to
be elliptical in shape. The *phases* of *Jupiter* are slight—scarcely
noticeable. The reflecting-power (*albedo*) of the planet is $\frac{62}{100}$, not
very much less than that of newly fallen snow ($\frac{78}{100}$). In this respect
Jupiter and all the outer planets differ very materially from *Mars*
and all the inner planets (except *Venus*). The *periodic-time* of *Jupiter*

is 11.86 years, about the period in which the solar spots vary from maximum to maximum again. Figure 180 shows in the upper third of the disk an oval spot that has remained on the planet for the past 30 years (*The Great Red Spot*). Its surface is red and it probably lies at a deeper level than many of the whitish clouds in the same latitudes. It is remarkable that the red spot has endured for so long a time on the surface of the planet where all other features are so changeable. The red spot is not fixed in position, but is slowly drifting to the east. It is as if Australia were slowly moving eastwardly on the earth. The rotation time of the red spot was 9^h 55^m $34^s.5$ in 1869 ; $34^s.1$ in 1879 ; $39^s.0$ in 1884 ; $40^s.4$ in 1889 ; $41^s.0$ in 1894 ; $41^s.9$ in 1898. It is as if an island of slag were drifting on the surface of a lake of liquid lava.

The *temperature* of *Jupiter* is, in all probability, very high. The planet may even be incandescent. The rapid changes observed in the surface of *Jupiter* prove that the visible surface is gaseous—an atmospheric envelope. These changes are due to heat. As the solar heat at *Jupiter* is only $\frac{1}{27}$ of the solar heat at the Earth, it is likely that the changes are due to the internal heat of the planet itself. The solar heat at *Saturn* is only $\frac{1}{90}$ of the solar heat at the Earth, and as it is also surrounded by a gaseous envelope, there is good reason for supposing *Saturn*, also, to be a hot body.

The surface of *Jupiter* has been carefully studied with the telescope, particularly within the past thirty years. Although further from us than *Mars*, many of the details on his disk are much more plainly marked. The most characteristic features are shown in the drawings appended. These features are, *first*, the dark bands of his equatorial regions, and, *secondly*, the cloud-like forms spread over nearly the whole surface. Near the edges of the disk all these details become indistinct, and finally vanish, thus indicating a highly absorptive atmosphere like that of the Sun. The light from the centre of the disk is twice as bright as that from the poles. The bands can be seen with instruments no more powerful than those used by GALILEO, yet he makes no mention of them.

The general color of the bands is reddish. Their position varies slightly in latitude, but in the main they remain as permanent features of the region to which they belong.

FIG. 181 —VIEW OF JUPITER AND HIS SATELLITES IN A SMALL TELESCOPE.

HERSCHEL, in the year 1793, attributed the aspects of the bands to zones of the planet's atmosphere more tranquil and less filled with clouds than the remaining portions, so as to permit the true surface of the planet to be seen through these zones, while the clouds prevailing in the other regions give a brighter tint to the latter. It is not likely that we see the true surface of the planet, in the belts, but rather the outer surfaces of the inner layers of the planet's atmosphere.

The clouds themselves can easily be seen at times, and they have every variety of shape. In general they are similar in form to a series of white *cumulus* clouds such as are frequently seen piled up near the horizon, and the spaces between them have the deep salmon color of the spaces between cumulus clouds before a summer storm. This color is due to the absorption of the dense atmosphere of the planet, probably. The bands themselves and the red

spot seem frequently to be veiled over with something like
the thin *cirrus* clouds of our atmosphere.

Such clouds can be tolerably accurately observed, and
may be used to determine the rotation-time of the planet.
The observations show that the clouds often have a proper
motion of their own.

Fig. 182.—View of Jupiter in a Large Telescope, with a
Satellite and its Shadow seen on the Disk.

Motions of the Satellites.—The satellites move about *Jupiter* from
west to east in nearly circular orbits. When one of these satellites
passes between the Sun and *Jupiter*, it casts a shadow upon *Jupiter's*
disk (see Fig. 182) precisely as the shadow of our Moon is thrown upon
the Earth in a solar eclipse. If the satellite passes through *Jupiter's*
own shadow in its revolution, an eclipse of the satellite takes place.
If it passes between the Earth and *Jupiter*, it is projected upon *Jupiter's* disk, and we have a transit of the satellite (see Fig. 182); if *Ju-*

piter is between the Earth and the satellite, an occultation of the latter occurs. All these phenomena can be seen with a common telescope, and the times are predicted in the *Nautical Almanac.* These shadows are seen black upon *Jupiter's* surface by contrast, because *Jupiter* is very much brighter than the satellites.

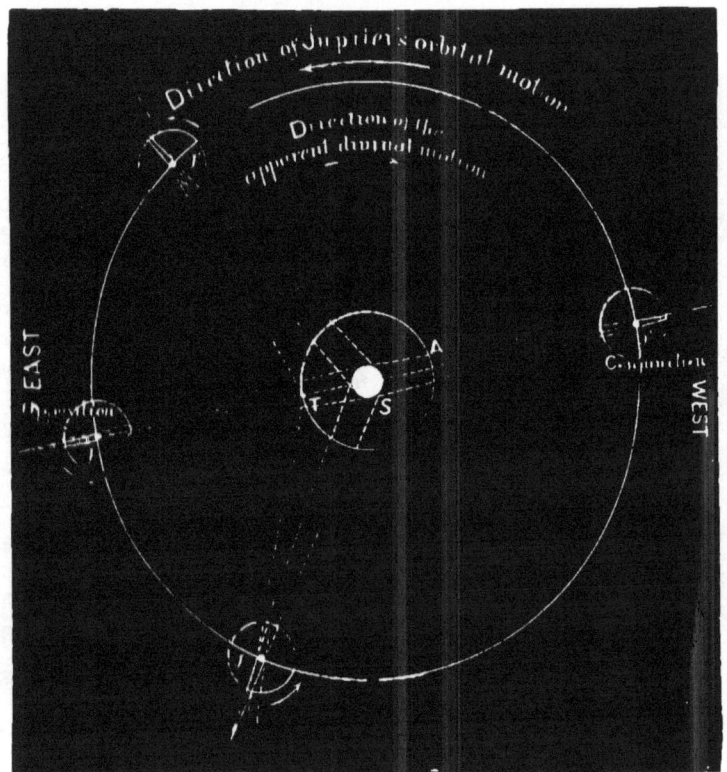

FIG. 183 —THE ECLIPSES OF JUPITER'S SATELLITES.

S is the Sun, *T* the Earth, *J*, *J'*. *J''*, *J'''* are different positions of *Jupiter.*

Telescopic Appearance of the Satellites. —Under ordinary circumstances, the satellites of *Jupiter* are seen to have disks ; under very favorable conditions, markings have been seen on these disks.

The satellites completely disappear from telescopic view when they enter the shadow of the planet. This shows that neither planet nor satellite is self-luminous to any marked degree. If the satellite were

self-luminous, it would be seen by its own light; and if the planet
were luminous, the satellite might be seen by the reflected light of
the planet.

The Progressive Motion of Light.—The discovery that light requires
time to travel was first made by the observations of the satellites of
Jupiter, as has been said. (See page 255.) *Jupiter* casts a shadow
just as our Earth does, and its inner satellite passes through this
shadow and is eclipsed at every revolution.

The eclipses can be observed from the Earth, the satellite vanishing
from view as it enters the shadow, and reappearing when it leaves it.
The astronomers of the seventeenth century made tables by which
the times of the eclipses could be predicted. It was found by ROMER
that these times *depended on the distance of Jupiter from the Earth.*

When the Earth was nearest *Jupiter*, the eclipses were seen *earlier*
than the predicted time. *Jupiter* and the Earth were near each other.
When the Earth was farthest from *Jupiter* the eclipses were seen
later than the predicted time. *Jupiter* and the Earth were far apart.

The light from the satellite required *time* to cross the intervening
spaces. The velocity with which light travels is 186,330 miles per
second. At that rate it traverses the distance from the Sun to the
Earth in 499 seconds. The sunlight is 8ᵐ 19ˢ old when it reaches us.

Longitudes by Observation of the Satellites of Jupiter.—The difference of longitude of two places on the Earth is the difference of their
simultaneous local times. If we know beforehand (by calculation) the
Greenwich time of an eclipse of one of the satellites—and if we observe
the eclipse by a clock keeping our own local time, the difference of
the two times (observed and calculated) is our longitude from Greenwich. GALILEO suggested that a method like this might be useful
in determining terrestrial longitudes and the method has often been
tested. The difficulty of observing the eclipses with accuracy, and
the fact that the aperture of the telescope employed has an important
effect on the appearances seen, have so far kept this method from a
wide utility, which it at first seemed to promise.

36. Saturn and its System.—*Saturn* is the most distant
of the major planets known to the ancients. It revolves
around the Sun in 29½ years, at a *mean distance* of about
886,000,000 miles. The equatorial *diameter* of the ball of
the planet is about 75,000 miles and the polar diameter
about 68,000 miles. It revolves on its axis in 10ʰ 14ᵐ 24ˢ,
or less than half a day, which accounts, as in the case of

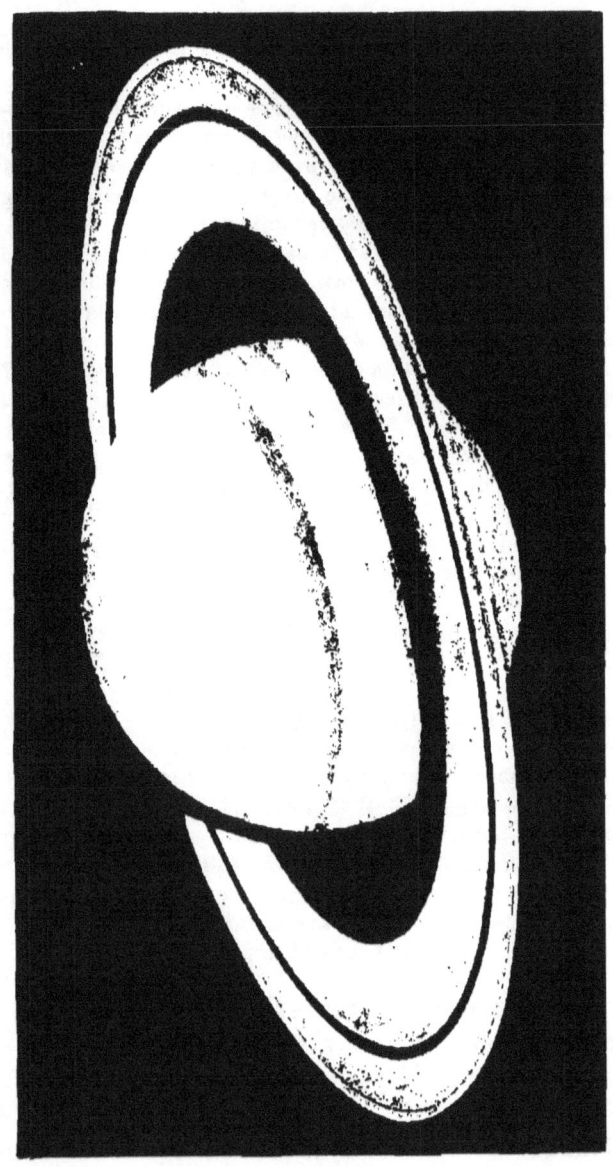

FIG. 184.—DRAWING OF SATURN MADE AT THE LICK OBSERVA-
TORY, JANUARY 7, 1888.

Jupiter, for the ellipticity of the disk. The *mass* of the planet is only 95 times the mass of the Earth, though its *volume* is 760 times greater. The force of *gravity* at its surface is only a little greater than that of the Earth. It is remarkable for its small *density*, which is less than that of any other heavenly body, and even less than that of water. No doubt the planet is in great part, if not entirely, gaseous. The edges of the planet are fainter than the centre, as in the case of *Jupiter*, and for the same reason.

FIG. 185.—VIEW OF THE SATURNIAN SYSTEM IN A SMALL TELE-SCOPE.

Saturn is the centre of a system of its own, in appearance quite unlike anything else in the heavens. Its most noteworthy feature is a pair of rings which surround it at a considerable distance from the planet itself. Outside of these rings revolve no less than nine satellites. The planet, rings, and satellites are altogether called the *Saturnian system.* The general appearance of this system, as seen in a small telescope, is shown in Fig. 185. Fig. 184 was drawn with the great telescope of the Lick Observatory.

The Rings of Saturn.—The rings are the most remarkable and characteristic feature of the Saturnian system. Fig. 186 gives two views of the ball and rings. The upper one shows one of their aspects as actually presented in the telescope, and the lower one shows what the appearance would be if the planet were viewed from a direction at right angles to the plane of the ring (which it never can be from the Earth). The shadow of the ball of the planet on the rings should be noticed in both views. The *periodic-time* of the planet is a little less than 29½ years.

The first telescopic observers of *Saturn* were unable to see the rings in their true form, and were greatly perplexed to account for the appearance which the planet presented. GALILEO described the planet as "tri-corporate," the two ends of the ring having, in his imperfect telescope, the appearance of a pair of small planets attached to the central one. "On each side of old *Saturn* were servitors who aided him on his way." This discovery was announced to his friend KEPLER in this logogriph :

"smaismrmilmepoetalevmibunenugttaviras," which, being transposed, becomes—

"Altissimum planetam tergeminum observavi " (I have observed the most distant planet to be tri-form).

The phenomenon constantly remained a mystery to its first observer. In 1610 he had seen the planet accompanied, as he supposed, by two lateral stars ; in 1612 the latter had vanished and the central body alone remained. GALILEO inquired "whether *Saturn* had devoured his children, according to the legend."

It was not until 1655 (after seven years of observation) that the celebrated HUYGHENS discovered the true explanation of the remarkable and recurring series of phenomena present by the tri corporate planet.

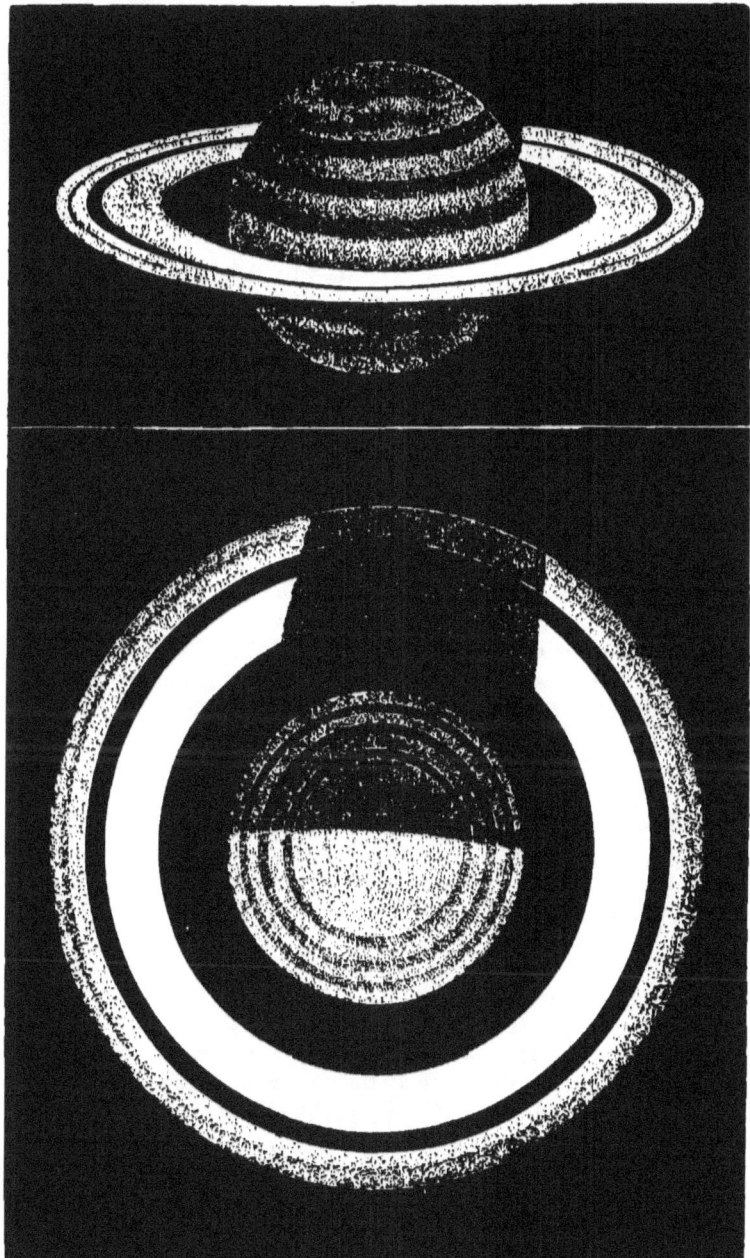

FIG. 186.—THE PLANET SATURN.

1° as it sometimes appears to an observer on the Earth; 2° as it would
appear to an observer over the polar region of the planet.

He announced his conclusions in the following logogriph :

" aaaaaa ccccc d eeeee g h iiiiiii llll mm nnnnnnnnn oooo pp q rr s ttttt uuuuu," which, when arranged, read—

" Annulo cingitur, tenui, plano, nusquam coherente, ad eclipticam inclinato" (it is girdled by a thin plane ring, nowhere touching, inclined to the ecliptic).

This description is complete and accurate, as to the appearance in a small telescope.

In 1675 it was found by CASSINI that what HUYGHENS had seen as a single ring was really two. A division extended all the way around near the outer edge. The division is shown in the figures. This division is permanent. Others are sometimes seen at different places and this fact of observation suggests that the rings cannot be permanent solids, nor liquids.

In 1850 the Messrs. BOND, of Harvard College Observatory, found that there was a third ring, of a dusky and nebulous aspect, attached to the inner edge of the inner ring. It is known as *Bond's dusky ring*. It is a difficult object to see in a small telescope. It is not separated from the bright ring, but attached to it. The latter shades off toward its inner edge, and merges gradually into the dusky ring, Fig. 184.

Aspect of the Rings.—As *Saturn* revolves around the Sun, the plane of the rings remains parallel to itself. That is, if we consider a straight line passing through the centre of the planet, perpendicular to the plane of the ring, as the axis of the latter, this axis will always point in the same direction in space—among the stars. In this respect the motion is similar to that of the Earth around the Sun. The ring of *Saturn* is inclined about 27° to the plane of its orbit. Consequently, as the planet revolves around the sun, there is a change in the direction in which the Sun shines upon it similar to that which produces the change of seasons upon the Earth, as shown in Fig. 110.

The corresponding changes for *Saturn* are shown in Fig. 187. During each revolution of *Saturn* (29¼ years) the plane of the ring passes through the Sun twice. This occurred in the years 1878 and 1891, at two opposite points of the orbit, as shown in the figure, and will occur in 1907. At two other points, midway between these, the Sun shines upon the plane of the ring at its greatest inclination, about 27°. Since the Earth (shown in the picture) is little more than one-tenth as far from the Sun as *Saturn* is, an observer sees *Saturn* nearly, but not quite, as if he were upon the Sun. Hence at certain times the rings of *Saturn* are seen edgeways ; while at other times they are at an inclination of 27°, the aspect depending upon the position of *Saturn* in its orbit. The following are the times of some of the phases :

1878 and 1907.—The edge of the ring is turned toward the Sun. It is seen only as a thin line of light.

1885.—The planet having moved forward 90°, the south side of the rings is seen at an inclination of 27°.

1891.—The planet having moved 90° further, the edge of the ring is again turned toward the Sun.

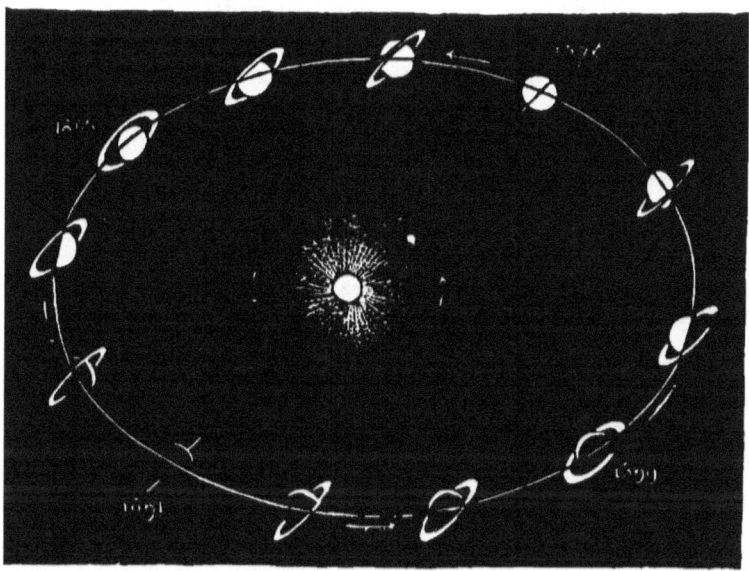

Fig. 187.—Different Aspects of the Ring of Saturn as seen from the Earth in Different Years.

1899.—The north side of the ring is inclined toward the sun, and is seen at its greatest inclination.

The rings are extremely thin in proportion to their extent. Consequently, when their edges are turned toward the Earth, they appear as a mere line of light, which can be seen only with powerful telesc pes.

Constitution of the Rings of Saturn.—The nature of these objects has been a subject both of wonder and of investigation by mathematicians and astronomers ever since

they were discovered. They were at first supposed to be
solid bodies; indeed, from their appearance it was difficult
to conceive of them as anything else. The question then
arose: What keeps them from falling on the planet? It
was shown mathematically by La Place that a homogeneous and solid ring surrounding the planet could not
remain in a state of equilibrium, but must be precipitated
upon the central ball by the smallest disturbing force.

It is now established both by mathematical processes and
by spectroscopic observation that the rings do not form a
continuous mass, but are really a countless multitude of
small separate particles or satellites, each of which revolves
in its own orbit. These satellites are individually far too
small to be seen in any telescope, but so numerous that
when viewed from the distance of the Earth they appear as
a continuous mass, like particles of dust floating in a sunbeam.

The thickness of the rings is not above 100 miles. The outer diameter of the outer ring (ring *A*) is 173,000 miles. It is 11,500 miles
wide. The Cassini division separating *A* from *B* is 2400 miles wide.
The outer diameter of ring *B* is 145,000 miles, and it is 17,500 miles
wide. The outer diameter of ring *C* (the dusky ring) is 100,000, and
its inner diameter is 90,000 miles. Dr. Keeler has proved, spectroscopically, that different parts of the rings revolve about the planet
at different rates, so that the rings must necessarily be composed
of discrete particles. The rotation time of the ball of *Saturn* is 10^h
14^m; the periodic-time of the innermost particle of the dusky ring is
5^h 50^m. Inside of this particle the space is empty.

Satellites of Saturn.—Outside of the rings of *Saturn* revolve its nine
satellites, the order and discovery of which are shown in the table on
page 339.

The distances are given in radii of the planet. The satellites *Mimas*
and *Hyperion* and satellite No. 9 are visible only in the most powerful telescopes. The brightest of all is *Titan*, which can be seen in a
telescope of ordinary size. The mass of *Titan* is $\frac{1}{4800}$ of *Saturn's* mass,
and it is some 3000 miles in diameter. *Japetus* is nearly as bright as
Titan when west of the planet, and is so faint as to be visible only in
large telescopes when on the other side. Like our moon, it always

presents the same face to the planet, and one side of it is dark and the other side light. When west of the planet, the bright side is turned toward the Earth and the satellite is visible. On the other side of the planet, the dark side is turned toward us, and it is nearly invisible. Satellites 3, 4, 5, 6, and 8 can be seen with telescopes of moderate power.

No.	NAME.	Distance from Planet.	Discoverer.	Date of Discovery.	Periodic-time.
1	*Mimas*	3.3	Herschel	1789	About 0ᵈ 23ʰ
2	*Enceladus*	4.3	Herschel	1789	" 1ᵈ 9ʰ
3	*Tethys*	5.3	Cassini	1684	" 1ᵈ 21ʰ
4	*Dione*	6.8	Cassini	1684	" 2ᵈ 18ʰ
5	*Rhea*	9.5	Cassini	1672	" 4ᵈ 13ʰ
6	*Titan*	20 7	Huyghens	1655	" 15ᵈ 23ʰ
7	*Hyperion*	26.8	Bond	1848	" 21ᵈ 7ʰ
8	*Japetus*	64.4	Cassini	1671	" 79ᵈ 8ʰ
9	?	225.4	Pickering	1899	" 510 days.

37. The Planet Uranus.—*Uranus* was discovered on March 13, 1781, by Sir WILLIAM HERSCHEL (then an amateur observer) with a ten-foot reflector made by himself. He was examining a portion of the sky when one of the stars in the field of view attracted his notice by its peculiar appearance. On further scrutiny, it proved to be a planet. We can scarcely comprehend now the enthusiasm with which this discovery was received. No new body (save comets) had been added to the solar system since the discovery of the third satellite of *Saturn* in 1684, and all the major planets of the heavens had been known for thousands of years.

Uranus revolves about the Sun in 84 years. Its apparent diameter as seen from the Earth varies little, being about 3″.9. Its true diameter is about 31,000 miles, and its figure is spheroidal.

In physical appearance it is a small greenish disk without markings. The centre of the disk is slightly brighter than the edges. At its nearest approach to the Earth, it shines as a star of the sixth magnitude, and is just visible to an acute eye when the attention is directed to its place. In small telescopes with low powers, its appearance is not markedly different from that of stars of about its own brilliancy.

Sir WILLIAM HERSCHEL discovered two satellites to *Uranus.* Two additional ones were discovered by LASSELL in 1847.

			Days.
I. *Ariel* (LASSELL)	Period =		2.520383
II. *Umbriel* "	"	=	4.144181
III. *Titania* (HERSCHEL)	"	=	8.705897
IV. *Oberon* "	"	=	13.463269

Ariel varies in brightness on different sides of the planet, and the same phenomenon has also been suspected for *Titania.* This indicates that these satellites always present the same face to the planet.

The most remarkable feature of the satellites of *Uranus* is that their orbits are nearly perpendicular to the ecliptic instead of having a small inclination to that plane, like those of all the orbits of both planets and satellites previously known.

The four satellites move in the same plane. This fact renders it highly probable that the planet *Uranus* revolves on its axis in the same plane with the orbits of the satellites, and is therefore an oblate spheroid like the Earth. If the planes of the satellites' orbits were not kept together by some cause, they would gradually deviate from each other owing to the attractive force of the Sun upon the planet. The different satellites would deviate by different amounts, and it would be extremely improbable that all the orbits would be found in the same plane at any particular epoch. Since we now see them in the same plane, we conclude that some force keeps them there, and the oblateness of the planet is the efficient cause of such a force.

The Planet Neptune.—After the planet *Uranus* had been observed for some thirty years, tables of its motion were prepared by BOUVARD—a French astronomer. He had not only all the observations since the date of its discovery in 1781, but also observations extending back as far as 1695, when the planet was observed and supposed to be a fixed star. It was expected that the ancient observations would materially aid in obtaining exact accordance between the theory and observation. But it was found that, after allowing for all perturbations produced by the known planets, the ancient and modern observations, though undoubtedly referring to the same object, were yet not to be reconciled with each other, but differed systematically. BOUVARD was forced to found his theory upon the modern observations alone. By so doing, he obtained a good agreement between theory and the observations of the few years immediately succeeding 1820.

BOUVARD made the suggestion that a possible cause for the discrepancies noted might be the existence of an unknown planet, exterior to *Uranus.*

In the year 1830 it was found that BOUVARD's tables, which represented the motion of the planet well during the years 1820–25, were 20″ in error. In 1840 the error was 90″, and in 1845 it was over 120.″

These progressive changes attracted the attention of astronomers to the subject of the theory of the motion of *Uranus.* The actual discrepancy (120″) in 1845 was not a quantity large in itself. Two stars of the magnitude of *Uranus*, and separated by only 120″, would be seen as one to the unaided eye. It was on account of its systematic and progressive increase that suspicion was excited.

Several astronomers attacked the problem in various ways. The elder STRUVE, at Pulkova in Russia, searched for a new planet with the large telescope of the Imperial Observatory. BESSEL, at Koenigsberg, set a student of his own, FLEMING, to make a new comparison of observation with theory, in order to furnish data for a new determination. ARAGO, then Director of the Observatory at Paris, suggested this subject in 1845 as an interesting field of mathematical research to LE VERRIER. Mr. J. C. ADAMS, a student in Cambridge University, England, had become aware of the problems presented by the anomalies in the motion of *Uranus*, and had attacked this question as early as 1843.

In October, 1845, ADAMS communicated to the Astronomer Royal of England elements of a new planet so situated as to produce the perturbations of the motion of *Uranus* which had actually been observed. Such a prediction from an entirely unknown student, as ADAMS then was, did not carry entire conviction with it. A series of accidents prevented the unknown planet being looked for by one of the largest telescopes in England, and so the matter apparently dropped. It may be noted, however, that we now know ADAMS' elements of the new planet to have been so near the truth that if it had been really looked for by the powerful telescope which afterward discovered its satellite, it could scarcely have failed of detection.

BESSEL'S pupil FLEMING died before his work was done, and BESSEL'S researches were temporarily brought to an end. STRUVE'S search was unsuccessful. LE VERRIER, however, continued his investigations, and in the most thorough manner. He first computed anew the perturbations of *Uranus* produced by the action of *Jupiter* and *Saturn*. Then he examined the nature of the irregularities observed. These showed that if they were caused by an unknown planet, it could not be between *Saturn* and *Uranus*, because *Saturn* would have been more affected than was the case.

If the new planet existed at all it was outside of *Uranus*. In the summer of 1846, LE VERRIER obtained complete elements of a new planet, which would account for the observed irregularities in the motion of *Uranus*, and these were published in France. They were very similar to those of ADAMS, and this striking fact renewed the interest in ADAMS' work. It was determined to search in the heavens for the planet foretold by theory.

Professor CHALLIS, the Director of the Observatory of Cambridge, England, began a search for such an object, and as no star-maps were at hand for this region of the sky, he commenced by mapping the surrounding stars. In so doing the new planet was actually observed, both on August 4 and 12, 1846, but the observations remained unreduced, and the planetary nature of the object was not recognized till afterwards.

In September of the same year LE VERRIER wrote to Dr. GALLE, then Assistant at the Observatory of Berlin, asking him to search for the new planet, and directing him to the place where it should be found. By the aid of an excellent star-chart of this region, which had just been completed, the new planet was found September 23, 1846.

The strict rights of discovery lay with LE VERRIER, but ADAMS deserves an equal share in the honor attached to this most brilliant achievement. Indeed, it was only by the most unfortunate succession of accidents that the discovery did not attach to Adams' researches. One thing must in fairness be said, and that is that the results of LE VERRIER were reached after a most thorough investigation of the whole ground, and were announced with an entire confidence which, perhaps, was lacking in the other case.

This brilliant discovery created even more enthusiasm than the discovery of *Uranus*, as it was by an exercise of far higher intellectual qualities that it was achieved. It was nothing short of marvellous that a mathematician could say to an observer that if he would point his telescope to a

certain small area, he would find within it a major planet
hitherto unknown. Yet so it was. By somewhat similar
processes previously unknown companions to the bright
stars *Sirius* and *Procyon* have been predicted, and these
companions have subsequently been discovered with the
telescope.

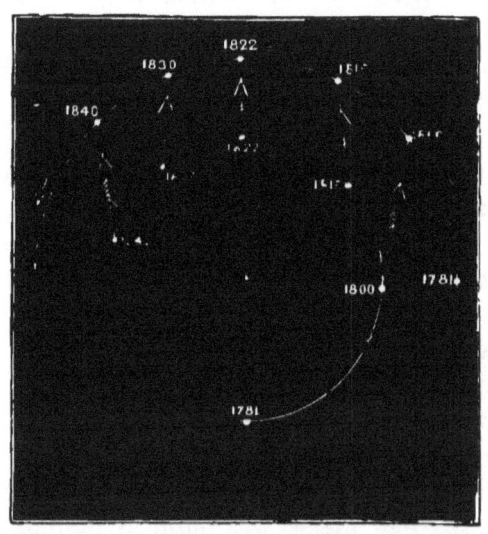

Fig. 188.—Perturbations of *Uranus* by a Planet Exterior
to it—*Neptune.*

The general nature of the disturbing force which revealed the new
planet may be seen by Fig. 188, which shows the orbits of the two
planets, and their respective motions between 1781 and 1840. The
inner orbit is that of *Uranus*, the outer one that of *Neptune.* The
arrows show the directions of the attractive force of *Neptune.*

Our knowledge regarding *Neptune* is mostly confined to
a few numbers representing the elements of its motion.
Its mean distance is more than 2,775,000,000 miles; its
periodic time is 164.78 years; its apparent diameter is 2.6
seconds, corresponding to a true diameter of about 34,000
miles. Gravity at its surface is about nine tenths of the

corresponding terrestrial surface gravity. Of its rotation and physical condition nothing is known. Its color is a pale greenish blue. It is attended by one satellite, which was discovered by Mr. LASSELL, of England, in 1847. The satellite requires a telescope of twelve inches' aperture or upward to be well seen. It is not unlikely that the planet may have a second very faint satellite.

38. The Physical Constitution of the Planets.—The solar system is composed of three groups of planets differing widely in their characteristics. The first group consists of *Mercury, Venus, the Earth, Mars*; the second group is the asteroids; the third consists of *Jupiter, Saturn, Uranus,* and *Neptune.* The *diameters* of the first group vary from 3000 to 8000 miles, their *periodic-times* are less than two years, their *masses* are never greater than $\frac{1}{500000}$ of the Sun's mass, their densities are from 3 to $5\frac{1}{4}$ times the density of water. The Moon, the satellite of the Earth, belongs in this group. Its density is 3.4 times the density of water. Two planets of this group—*Venus* and the Earth—are certainly surrounded by atmospheres. The others probably have little or no atmosphere. The planets of this group were named by ALEXANDER VON HUMBOLDT *terrestrial planets.* They are in some respects like the Earth. At any rate, all of them are much more like the Earth than like the giant planets beyond *Mars.*

The *asteroids* are quite unique among the planets. *Jupiter, Saturn, Uranus, Neptune* present many striking resemblances. They are of giant size. Their *diameters* vary from 30,000 to 90,000 miles. Their *masses* are relatively large ($\frac{1}{38000}$ to $\frac{1}{1000}$ of the Sun's mass), their densities are all small (none greater than $1\frac{1}{4}$ times the density of water). At least two of them have a very short period of *rotation*, and all of them have a high reflecting power. Their surfaces are covered with clouds and there is good reason to believe that one of them—*Jupiter*—is still a very hot body. Very likely all of them consist of masses of molten matter surrounded by envelopes of vapor. This view is further strengthened by their very small specific gravity, which can be accounted for by supposing that the liquid interior is nothing more than a comparatively small central core, and that the greater part of the bulk of each planet is composed of vapor of small density. Some of the satellites of this group are about as large as *Mars* or *Mercury.*

Finally the central body of the whole system—the Sun—is immensely larger than all the planets taken together; it is very hot; it is almost or entirely gaseous ; its density is less than $1\frac{4}{10}$ the density of water—and this in spite of the immense pressure on its interior parts. *Mercury, Mars*, the Moon, are airless, cold, dense, small. We know little of *Venus* except that she is covered with clouds. *Venus may* be more like the Earth than any other planet. The asteroids are mere fragments, probably all airless and cold. The giant planets are (probably) all hot, with a solid or liquid nucleus and a deep atmosphere. And at the end of the series comes the Sun, hot, gaseous, immensely larger than the planets.

The differences between these different bodies are chiefly due to temperature. If any one of them were to be suddenly raised to the Sun's temperature it would probably be a miniature Sun. Each of these bodies is cooling by the radiation of its heat into space. None of the heat radiated returns to the body, so far as is known. The Sun in cooling will probably become a body somewhat like *Jupiter*. *Jupiter* in cooling will probably become a body somewhat like the Earth. The Earth in cooling will probably become a body somewhat like the Moon. The Moon has already reached its permanent state. Its heat has gone; it has no atmosphere; and its temperature on the side turned away from the Sun is the temperature of space hundreds of degrees below zero Fahrenheit.

The temperature of any planet in the system thus depends, in an important degree, on its age. It depends also on a thousand other circumstances—on the kind of matter of which it is made up, on its size, etc. When we come to consider the Nebular Hypothesis of KANT and LAPLACE, which is an attempt to explain the evolution of the solar system, these facts (and others not here explicitly set down) will be found to be highly significant.

CHAPTER XX.

METEORS.

39. Phenomena of Meteors and Shooting-stars.—Any one who watches the heavens at night for a few hours will see *shooting-stars* or *meteors*. They suddenly appear as bright points of light, move along an arc in the sky and then disappear. Large meteors—*aerolites*—are often as bright as *Venus* or even very much brighter; they are usually followed by brilliant trains; they frequently explode in the air, like rockets, and leave clouds of meteoric dust behind them. Sometimes their bursting or their passage through the atmosphere is accompanied by an audible noise. Occasionally fragments of the *aerolite* fall to the Earth. Large collections of such fragments are preserved in our museums, and some of the specimens weigh hundreds of pounds. Usually, however, they are much smaller.

Most of the specimens of aerolites are stones; some of them are nearly pure iron alloyed with nickel, etc.

When we consider that the aerolites come from regions beyond the Earth and that they never had any direct connection with it before their fall on its surface, it is a highly significant fact that they contain no chemical elements not found on the Earth. It indicates that all the bodies of the solar system are similar in constitution. Moreover, of the seventy or more elements known to us more than twenty have been found in meteoric masses. The *minerals* formed by the combination of the elements are often somewhat different in the aerolites from the corresponding minerals found in the Earth's crust, which seems to show that they

347

FIG. 189.—THE GREAT CALIFORNIA METEOR OF 1894.

were combined under quite different conditions of heat, pressure, etc. An aerolite is a little planet out of the celestial spaces, evident to our sight, it may be to our touch.

Path of a Meteor.—The positions of a meteor can be observed by referring it to neighboring stars—we can draw its path on a star-map, and note the time of its appearance or bursting. If such observations are made by observers at different stations on the Earth, the orbit of the meteor can be calculated. It is found that most *aerolites*, or large meteors, were moving in elliptic orbits about the Sun before they fell into the sphere of the Earth's attraction. The Earth, of course, alters such an orbit, and draws the body downwards into the atmosphere with a high velocity. In most cases it is consumed—burned up completely—in our atmosphere. Occasionally pieces of it fall to the ground, as has been said.

Cause of the Light and Heat of Meteors.—Why do meteors burn with so great an evolution of light on reaching our atmosphere? To answer this question we must have recourse to the mechanical theory of heat. Heat is a vibratory motion in the particles of solid bodies and a progressive motion in those of gases. The more rapid the motion the warmer the body. By simply blowing air against any combustible body with high velocity it can be set on fire, and, if the body is incombustible, it can be made red-hot and finally melted.

Experiments show that a velocity of about 50 metres (about 164 feet) per second corresponds to a rise of temperature of one degree Centigrade. From this the temperature due to *any* velocity can be calculated on the principle that the increase of temperature is proportional to the "energy" of the particles, which again is proportional to the square of the velocity. A velocity of 500 metres (about 1640 feet) per second corresponds to a rise of 100° C. above the actual temperature of the air, so that if the latter was at the freezing-point the body would be raised to the temperature of boiling water. A velocity of 1500 metres (4921 feet, about twice the velocity of a cannon-ball) per second would produce a red heat.

The Earth moves around the Sun with a velocity of about 30,000 metres (18½ miles) per second; consequently if it met a body at rest the concussion between the latter and the atmosphere would correspond to a temperature of more than 300,000°. This would instantly change any known substance from a solid to a gaseous form.

It must be remembered that these enormous temperatures are *potential,* not *actual,* temperatures. The body is not actually raised to a temperature of 300,000°, but the air acts upon it as if it were suddenly plunged into a furnace heated to this temperature. It is rapidly destroyed just as if it were in such a furnace.

The potential temperature is independent of the density of the medium, being the same in the rarest as in the densest atmosphere. But the actual effect on the body is not so great in a rare as in a dense atmosphere. Every one knows that he can hold his hand for some time in air at the temperature of boiling water. The rarer the air the higher the temperature the hand would bear without injury. In an atmosphere as rare as ours at the height of 50 miles, it is probable that the hand could be held for an indefinite period, though its temperature should be that of red-hot iron; hence the meteor is not consumed so rapidly as if it struck a dense atmosphere with a like velocity. In the latter case it would probably disappear like a flash of lightning.

The amount of heat evolved is measured not by that which would result from the combustion of the body, but by the *vis viva* (energy of motion) which the body loses in the atmosphere. The student of physics knows that motion, when lost, is changed into a definite amount of heat.

The amount of heat which is equivalent to the energy of motion of a pebble having a velocity of 20 miles a second is sufficient to raise about 1300 times the pebble's weight of water from the freezing to the boiling point. This is many times as much heat as could result from burning pure carbon.

Meteoric Phenomena.—Meteoric phenomena depend upon the substance out of which the meteors are made and the velocity with which they move in the atmosphere. With very rare exceptions, they are so small and fusible as to be entirely dissipated in the upper regions of the air. On rare occasions the body is so hard and massive as to reach the Earth without being entirely consumed. The potential heat produced by its passage through the atmosphere is expended in melting and destroying its outer layers, the inner nucleus remaining unchanged. When a meteor first strikes the denser portion of the atmosphere, the resistance becomes so great that the body is generally broken to pieces. A single large aerolite may produce a shower of small meteoric stones.

Heights of Meteors.—Many observations have been made to determine the height at which meteors are seen. This is effected by two observers stationing themselves several miles apart and mapping out the courses of such meteors as they can observe.

Meteors and shooting-stars commonly commence to be visible at a height of about 70 statute miles. The separate results vary widely, but this is a rough average. They are generally dissipated at about half this height, and therefore above the highest atmosphere which reflects the rays of the Sun. The Earth's atmosphere must, then, extend at least as high as 70 miles.

While there are few *aerolites* or large meteors, there are millions of the smaller sort—*shooting-stars*. A single observer will see, on the average, from four to eight every hour. If the whole sky is watched at any one place on the Earth from 30 to 60 are visible every hour. They fill space like particles of dust, only these particles of the dust of space are, on the average, about 200 miles apart. The Earth sweeps along in its orbit at the rate of $18\frac{1}{2}$ miles per second and in its daily journey of some 1,600,000 miles it meets, or is overtaken by millions of these bodies. From 10 to 15 *millions* of meteors fall into the Earth's atmosphere every day. The *mass* of the single meteors is extremely small—several thousands of them being required to make up a pound's weight. If each meteor has a mass of one grain the Earth is growing heavier daily by about a ton. Theoretically the Earth is daily receiving heat by the fall of meteorites, also; but calculation shows that the Sun sends us ten times as much heat in a second as is received from meteors in a year; so that there is no noteworthy effect from this cause.

Meteoric Showers.—Shooting-stars may be seen by a careful observer on almost any clear night. In general, not more than half-a-dozen will be seen in an hour, and these are usually so minute as hardly to attract notice. But they sometimes fall in great numbers as a meteoric shower. On rare occasions the shower has been so striking as to fill the beholders with terror. Ancient and mediæval records contain many accounts of such phenomena.

One shower of this class occurs at an interval of about a third of a century. It was observed by HUMBOLDT, on the

Andes, on the night of November 12, 1799, for instance, and often before that time. A great shower was seen in this country in 1833. On the night of November 13, 1866, a remarkable shower was seen in Europe, while on the corresponding night of the year following it was again seen in this country, and, in fact, was repeated for two or three years, gradually dying away, as it were. This great shower will appear in 1899, once more.

The occurrence of a *shower* of meteors evidently shows that the Earth encounters a *swarm* of such bodies moving together in space. The recurrence at the same time of the year (when the Earth is in the same point of its orbit) shows that the Earth meets the swarm at the same point in space in successive years. All the meteors of the swarm must be moving in the *same direction in space* or else they would soon be widely scattered.

Radiant Point.—Suppose that, during a meteoric shower, we mark the path of each meteor on a star-map, as in figure 190. If we continue the observed paths backward in a straight line, we shall find that they all meet near one and the same point of the celestial sphere; that is, they move as if they all radiated from this point. The latter is, therefore, called the *radiant point.* In the figure the lines do not all pass accurately through the same point owing to the unavoidable errors made in marking out the path.

It is found that the radiant point is always in the same position among the stars, wherever the observer may be situated, and that, *as the stars apparently move toward the west, the radiant point moves with them.*

The existence of a radiant point proves that the meteors that strike the Earth during a shower are all moving in the same direction. Their motions will all be parallel ; hence when the bodies strike our atmosphere the paths described by them in their passage will all be parallel straight lines. A straight line in space seen by an observer is projected as a great circle of the celestial sphere, with the observer at its centre. If we draw a line from the observer parallel to the paths of the meteors, the direction of that line intersects the celestial sphere in a point through which all the meteor-paths will seem to pass.

Orbits of Showers of Meteors.—The position of the radiant point indicates the *direction* in which the meteors move relatively to the

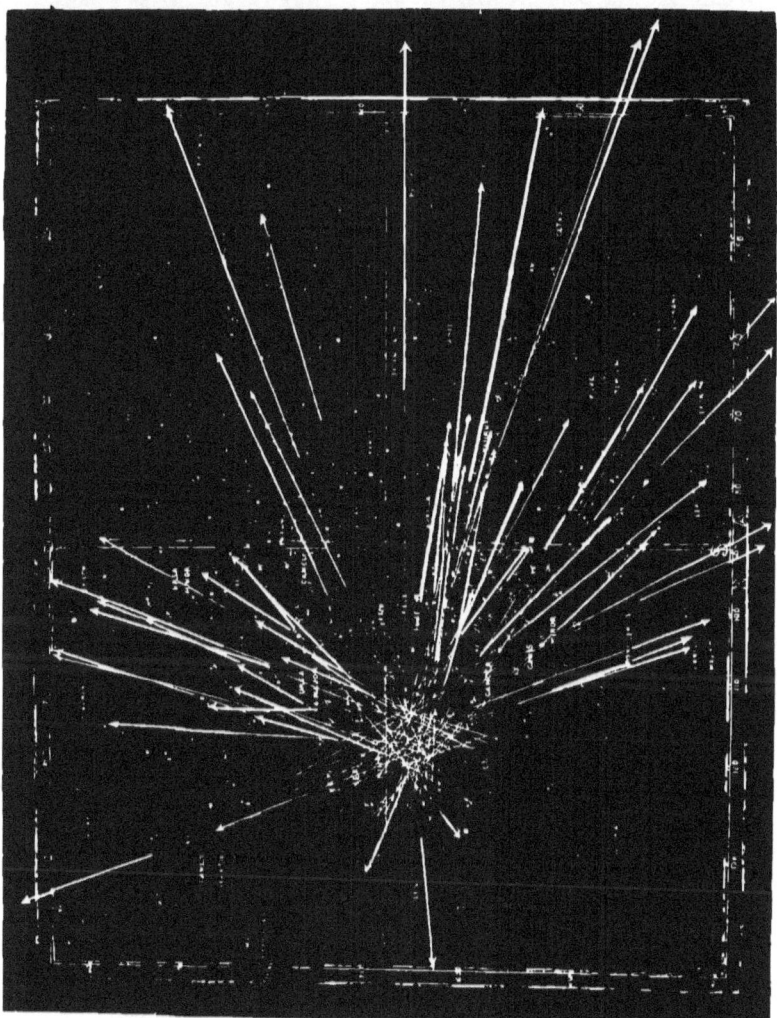

Fig. 190.—The RADIANT POINT of a Meteoric Shower.

Earth. If we also knew the *velocity* with which they are really moving in space, we could make allowance for the motion of the Earth,

and thus determine the direction of their actual motion in space, and determine the orbit of the swarm around the Sun.

The radiant point of the shower of August 10 (*Perseids*) is R.A. 3ʰ 4ᵐ Decl. + 57° ; of the shower of November 13 (*Leonids*) R.A. 10ʰ 0ᵐ, Decl. + 23° ; of the shower of November 26 (*Andromedes*) R.A. 1ʰ 41ᵐ, Decl. + 43°. The student should observe these showers.

Relations of Meteors and Comets.—The *velocity* of the meteors in space does not admit of being determined from observation of the meteors themselves. It is necessary to determine their velocity in the orbit from the periodic-time of the swarm about the Sun. The orbit of the swarm giving the 33-year shower was calculated shortly after the great shower of 1866 with the results that follow:

Period of revolution.......... 33.25 years
Eccentricity of orbit.......... 0.9044
Least distance from the sun.... 0.9890
Inclination of orbit.......... 165° 19′
Longitude of the node.......... 51° 18′
Position of the perihelion...... (near the node)

The orbit of the meteor-swarm presents an extraordinary likeness to the orbit of a periodic comet discovered by TEMPEL. The elements of the comet's orbit are:

Period of revolution............... 33.18 years.
Eccentricity of orbit.............. 0.9054
Least distance from the sun........ 0.9765
Inclination of orbit............... 162° 42′
Longitude of the node.............. 51° 26′
Longitude of the perihelion........ 42° 24′

If the two orbits are compared, the result is evident. *The swarm of meteors which causes the November showers moves in the same orbit with* TEMPEL'S *comet.*

The *comet* passed its perihelion in January, 1866. The *shower* was not visible until the following November.

Therefore, the swarm which produced the showers followed after TEMPEL'S comet, moving in the same orbit with it. The recurrence of the phenomenon every 33 years was traced backward in historical records and it was shown that for centuries this swarm had been revolving about the Sun. The swarm is stretched out in a long mass and the Earth crosses the orbit in November of every year. The Earth finds the swarm in its path every 33 years. The radiant point of the November shower is in the constellation *Leo* and hence these meteors are called *Leonids*. The August meteors radiate from *Perseus* and are called *Perseids*. The relation between comets and meteors suggested the question whether a similar connection might not be found between other comets and other meteoric showers.

Other Showers of Meteors.—Although the November showers (which occur about November 14) are the only ones so brilliant as to strike the ordinary eye, it has long been known that there are other nights of the year (notably August 10) in which more shooting-stars than usual are seen, and in which the large majority radiate from one point of the heavens. They also arise from swarms of meteoroids moving together around the Sun.

The honor of the discovery of this remarkable and unexpected relation between meteors and comets is shared between several astronomers. Professors OLMSTED and TWINING of Yale College were the first to show that meteors were extra-terrestrial bodies revolving in swarms about the Sun. Professors ERMAN of Germany, LE VERRIER of France, ADAMS of England, SCHIAPARELLI of Italy and particularly Professor NEWTON of Yale College developed the whole subject.

Many meteor-swarms revolve in the same orbits with comets. In some cases the swarms follow the comet in a more or less compact mass. In others the meteors are scattered all around the orbit. If a comet, originally, is nothing but a close cluster of meteors it will partially break up into its parts under the influence of planetary attractions (perturbations) and especially at every one of its perihelion passages. The longer a comet has been in the solar system the more the meteors will be spread out along its orbit. But it is by no means certain that comets are, in the first place, only aggregations of meteors, so that it can only be said that there is, certainly, a very close connection between meteors and comets, and that it is likely that certain meteor-swarms are no more than the *débris* of comets. Beside the meteors known to be connected with comets there are millions upon millions of others scattered through space.

The Zodiacal Light.—If we observe the western sky during the winter or spring months, about the end of the evening twilight, we shall see a stream of faint light, a little like the Milky Way, rising obliquely from the west, and directed along the ecliptic toward a point southwest from the zenith. This is called the *Zodiacal Light.* It may also be seen in the east before daylight in the morning during the autumn months, and can be traced all the way across the heavens. A brighter mass opposite to the Sun's place is called the *Gegenschein.* The Zodiacal Light is probably due to solar light reflected from an extremely thin cloud either of meteors or of semi-gaseous matter like that composing the tail of a comet, spread all around the Sun inside the Earth's orbit. Its spectrum is probably that of reflected sunlight, a result which gives color to the theory that it arises from a cloud of meteors revolving round the Sun. The student should trace out the Zodiacal Light in the sky.

CHAPTER XXI.

COMETS.

40. Aspect of Comets.—Comets are distinguished from the planets both by their aspects and their motions. Only a few comets belong permanently to the solar system (see Table IV, p. 279). Most of them are mere visitors. They enter the system, go round the Sun once, and then leave it forever.

The *nucleus* of a comet is, to the naked eye, a point of light resembling a star or planet. Viewed in a telescope, it generally has a small disk, but shades off so gradually that it is difficult to estimate its magnitude. In large comets it is sometimes several hundred miles in diameter.

The nucleus is always surrounded by a mass of foggy light, which is called the *coma*. To the naked eye the nucleus and coma together look like a star seen through a mass of thin fog, which surrounds it with a sort of halo. The nucleus and coma together are generally called the *head* of the comet. The head of the great comet of 1858 was 250,000 miles in diameter.

The *tail* of the comet is a continuation of the coma, extending out to a great distance, and usually directed away from the Sun. It has the appearance of a stream of milky light, which grows fainter and broader as it recedes from the head. The length of the tail varies from 2° or 3° to 90° or more. The tail of the great comet of 1858 was 45,000,000 miles in length and 10,000,000 miles in breadth. All that area was filled with matter sufficiently condensed to send light to the Earth and to appear as a continuous

357

Fig. 191.—The Great Comet of 1858.

sheet. The *mass* of comets is extremely small, so small
that no comet has yet been observed to produce perturbations in the motion of any planet. It is to be remembered
that we do not see the tail of a comet in its true shape, but
only its projection on the celestial sphere, and it is further-
more to be noted that the tail is not the *débris* of the comet
left behind the comet in its motion. The tail of a comet
is behind the nucleus as the comet approaches the Sun, but
it precedes the nucleus as the comet moves away from the
Sun. The vapors that arise from the nucleus, owing chiefly
to the Sun's heat, are repelled by the Sun—driven away
from him probably by electric repulsion. The nucleus itself is always attracted and performs its revolution about
the Sun in obedience to the attraction of gravitation.

FIG. 192.—TELESCOPIC COMET
WITHOUT A NUCLEUS AND
WITHOUT A TAIL.

FIG. 193.—TELESCOPIC COMET
WITH A NUCLEUS, BUT WITH-
OUT A TAIL.

When large comets are studied with a telescope, it is
found that they are subject to extraordinary changes. To
understand these changes, we must begin by saying that
comets do not, like the planets, revolve around the Sun in
nearly circular orbits, but in orbits always so elongated that
the comet is visible in only a very small part of its course
(see Figs. 195, 196, 197)—namely, in that part of its orbit
near the Sun (and Earth).

The Vaporous Envelopes.—If a comet is very small, it may undergo no changes of aspect during its entire course. If it is an unusually bright one, a bow surrounding the nucleus on the side toward the Sun will develop as the comet approaches the Sun. (*a*, Fig. 194.) This bow will gradually rise and spread out on all sides, finally assuming the form of a semicircle having the nucleus in its centre, or, to speak with more precision, the form of a parabola having the nucleus near its focus. The two ends of this parabola will extend out further and further so as to form a part of the tail, and finally be joined to it. Other bows will successively form around the nucleus, all slowly rising from it like clouds of vapor (Fig. 194).

FIG. 194.—FORMATION OF ENVELOPES.

These distinct vaporous masses are called the *envelopes :* they shade off gradually into the coma so as to be with difficulty distinguished from it. The appearances are apparently caused by masses of vapor streaming up from that side of the nucleus nearest the Sun (and therefore hottest) and gradually spreading around the comet on each side as if repelled by the Sun. The form of the bow is, of course, not the real form of the envelopes, but only the apparent one in which we see them projected against the background of the sky.

Perhaps their forms can be best imagined by supposing the Sun to be directly above the comet (see Fig. 194) and a fountain, throwing a vapor horizontally on all sides, to be built upon that part of the comet which is uppermost. Such a fountain would throw its vapor in the form of a sheet, falling on all sides of the cometic nucleus, but not touching it. Two or three vapor surfaces of this kind are sometimes seen around the comet, the outer one enclosing each of the inner ones, but no two touching each other.

The tail also develops rapidly as the comet draws near to the Sun, and sometimes several tails are developed. The principal tail is directed away from the Sun, as if under electric repulsion.

The Constitution of Comets.—To tell exactly what a comet is, we should be able to show how all the phenomena it presents would follow from the properties of matter, as we learn them at the surface of the Earth. This, however, no one has been able to do, many of the phenomena being such as we should not expect from the known constitution of matter. All we can do, therefore, is to present the principal characteristics of comets, as shown by observation, and to explain what is wanting to reconcile these characteristics with the known properties of matter.

In the first place, all comets which have been examined with the spectroscope show a spectrum which indicates that the comets are principally made up of gases mostly compounds of carbon and hydrogen. Sodium and several other substances are often found. Part of the comet's light is undoubtedly reflected sunlight.

It is, at first sight, difficult to comprehend how a mass of gas of extreme tenuity can move in a fixed orbit just as if it were a solid planetary mass. The difficulty vanishes when we remember that the spaces in which comets move are practically empty—as empty as the vacuum of an air-pump. In such a vacuum a feather falls as freely and as rapidly as a block of metal.

The Orbits of Comets.—Previous to the time of NEWTON only bright comets had been observed and nothing was known of their actual motions, except that no one of them moved around the Sun in an ellipse as the planets moved. NEWTON found that a body moving under the attraction of the Sun might move in any one of the three "conic sections," the ellipse, parabola, or hyperbola. Bodies moving in an ellipse, as the planets, complete their orbits at regular intervals of time over and over again. A body moving in a parabola or an hyperbola never returns to the Sun after once passing it, but moves away from it forever. Most comets move in parabolic orbits, and therefore a. proach the Sun but once during their whole existence (Fig. 195).

A few comets revolve around the Sun in elliptic orbits, which differ from those of the planets only in being much more eccentric. (See p. 279.) But nearly all comets move about the Sun in orbits which we are unable to distinguish from parabolas, though it is possible that some of them may be extremely elongated ellipses. It is noteworthy that the orbits of comets are inclined at all angles to the ecliptic and that their directions of motion are often retrograde. In these respects they differ widely from the planets.

In the last chapter it was shown that swarms of minute particles, small meteors, accompany certain comets in their orbits. This is probably true of all comets. We can only regard such meteors as fragments or *débris* of the comet. On this theory a telescopic comet which has no nucleus is simply a cloud of these minute bodies. Perhaps each one of the minute particles has a little envelope of gases about it. The nucleus of the brighter comets may either be a more condensed mass of such bodies or it may be a solid or liquid body itself.

If the student has difficulty in reconciling this theory of detached particles with the view already presented, that the envelopes from which the tail of the comet is formed consists of layers of vapor, he must remember that vaporous masses, such as clouds, fog, and

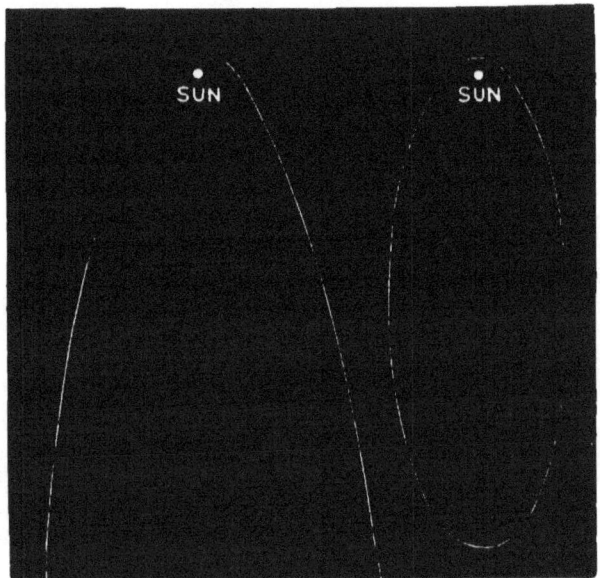

Fig. 195.—Elliptic and Parabolic Orbits.

smoke, are in fact composed of minute and separate particles of water, carbon and so forth.

The gases shut up in the cavities of meteoric stones have been spectroscopically examined, and they show the characteristic comet spectrum. This gives a new proof of the connection between comets and meteors.

Formation of the Comet's Tail.—The tail of the comet is not a permanent appendage, but is composed of masses of vapor which ascend from the nucleus, and afterwards move away from the Sun. The tail which we see on one evening is not absolutely the same we saw the evening before. A portion of the latter has been dissipated, while new matter has taken its place, as with the stream of smoke from a steamship. It is an observed fact that the vapor which rises from the nucleus of a comet is repelled by the Sun instead of being attracted toward it, as larger masses of matter are ; as indeed the nucleus itself is.

No adequate explanation of this repulsive force has yet been given. It is probably electrical.

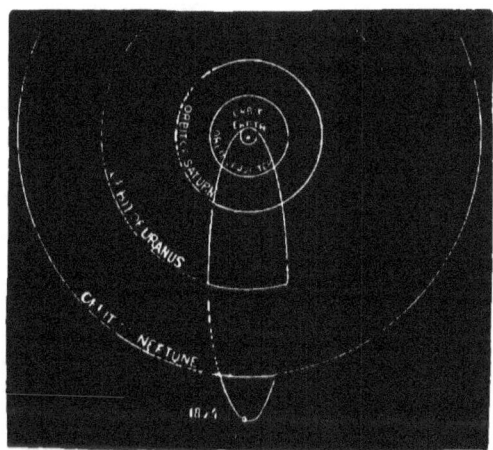

Fig. 196.—Orbit of Halley's Comet.

Periodic Comets.—The first discovery of the periodicity of a comet was made by Halley in connection with the great comet of 1682. This comet moves in an immense elliptic orbit with a periodic time of 76 years. Halley predicted that it would return in 1758. Clairaut, a French astronomer, worked out its orbit by Newton's methods, and the comet returned, obedient to law, on Christmas day, 1758. (See Fig. 196.)

Gravitation was thus, for the first time, shown to rule the erratic motions of comets as well as the orderly revolutions of the planets.

The figure shows the very eccentric orbit of Halley's comet and the nearly circular orbits of the four outer planets. It attained its greatest distance from the Sun, far beyond the orbit of *Neptune,* about the year 1873, and then commenced its return journey. The figure also shows the position of the comet in 1874. It will return to perihelion again in the year 1910.

Orbit of a Parabolic Comet.—Figure 197 shows the orbit of a comet discovered by PERRINE at the Lick Observatory on November 17, 1895. The places of the comet in its parabolic orbit are marked for November 20 and subsequent dates. The places of the Earth in its orbit are marked for the same dates. Lines joining the correspond-

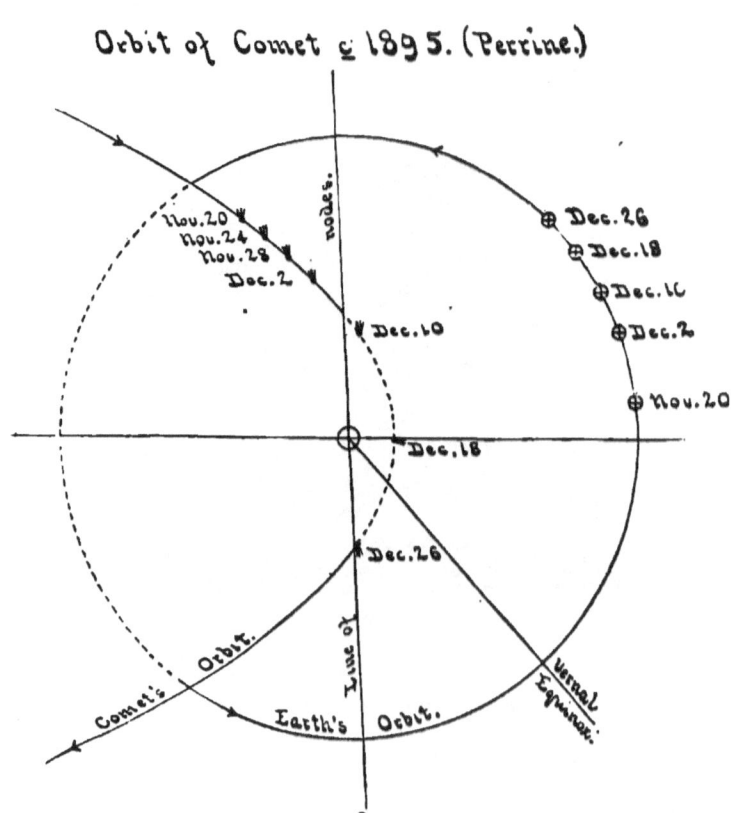

FIG. 197.—THE ORBIT OF COMET *C.* 1895, AND THE ORBIT OF THE EARTH, DRAWN TO SCALE. THE SUN IS AT THE CENTRE OF THE DIAGRAM.

ing dates in the two orbits will show the direction in which the comet was seen from the Earth. A line shows the direction of the Vernal Equinox. The plane of the paper is the plane of the Ecliptic. All that part of the comet's orbit which is drawn *full* is north of the Ecliptic; the dotted portion is south of it. The line of nodes of the comet's orbit is marked on the diagram. The comet was nearest to the Sun (at perihelion) on December 18, when its distance was 0.19 (the Earth's distance = 1.00). The positions of the comet were

		R. A.	Decl.
Nov.	20	208°	− 0°
	24	211°	− 3°
	28	214°	− 5°
Dec.	2	219°	− 10°
	10	236°	− 22°
	18	274°	− 31°
	26	287°	− 23°

Remarkable Comets.—In former years bright comets were objects of great dread. They were supposed to

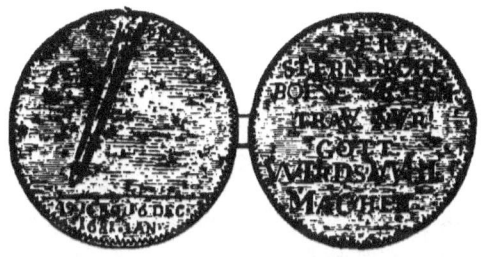

Fig. 198.—Medal of the Great Comet of 1680–81.

presage the fall of empires, the death of monarchs, the approach of earthquakes, wars, pestilence, and every other calamity that could afflict mankind. In showing the entire groundlessness of such fears, science has rendered one of its greatest benefits to mankind.

The number of comets visible to the naked eye, so far as recorded, has generally ranged from twenty to forty in a century. Only a few of these, however, have been so bright as to excite universal notice.

In 1456 the comet, afterwards known as HALLEY'S, appeared when the Turks were making war on Christendom, and caused such terror that Pope CALIXTUS III ordered prayers to be offered in the churches for protection against it. This is the origin of the popular fable that the Pope once excommunicated a comet.

Comet of 1680.—One of the most remarkable of the brilliant comets is that of 1680. It inspired such terror that a medal was struck to quiet popular apprehension. A free translation of the inscription is: "The star threatens evil things; trust only! God will turn them to good."* This comet is especially remarkable in the history of Astronomy because NEWTON calculated its orbit, and showed that it moved around the Sun obedient to the law of gravitation.

Great Comet of 1811.—It has a period of over 3000 years, and its aphelion distance is about 40,000,000,000 miles.

Great Comet of 1843.—It was visible in full daylight close to the Sun. At perihelion it passed nearer the Sun than any other body has ever been known to pass, the least distance being only about one fifth of the Sun's semidiameter. With a very slight change of its original motion, it would have actually fallen into the Sun, and become a part of it.

Great Comet of 1858.—It is frequently called DONATI'S comet from the name of its discoverer. It was visible for about nine months and was thoroughly studied by many astronomers, particularly by BOND at Harvard College. At its greatest brilliancy its tail was 40° in length and 10° in bread that its outer end, about 45,000,000 and 10,000,000 miles in real (no perspective) dimensions. Its period is 1950 years. (See Fig. 191.)

Great Comet of 1882.—It was visible in full daylight at its brightest, and it was seen with the telescope until it actually appeared to touch the Sun's disk. It passed across the face of the Sun (half a degree) in less than fifteen minutes, with the enormous velocity of more than 300 miles per second. Its least distance from the surface of the Sun was less than 300,000 miles, so that it passed through the denser portions of the Sun's Corona.

The orbit of this comet has been calculated from observations taken *before* its perihelion passage, and also from observations taken *after* it. If the Corona had had any effect on the comet's motion these two orbits would have differed; but they do not differ; they

---

*The student should notice the care which the author of the inscription has taken to make it consolatory, to make it rhyme, and to give implicitly the year of the comet by writing certain Roman numerals larger than the other letters.

agree exactly. This shows of how rare substances the Corona is made up.

The periodic-time of this comet is about 840 years and its orbit is the same curve in space as the orbits of the comets of 1668, 1843 and 1880 and 1887. But the comets themselves are different bodies. The comet of 1882 and that of 1880 cannot possibly be the same. body. They travel in the same path, however, and belong to the same *family of comets.*

Observations of comets made at the Lick Observatory and elsewhere have shown that comets sometimes break up into fragments which thereafter travel in similar paths one behind the other. Photographs of comets sometimes actually show the formation of companion comets left behind or rejected by the main comet. From these photographs it appears that the head of a comet sends out enormous quantities of matter to form the tail, so that the material that forms it on one day may not be and probably is not the same material that formed the tail of a few days previous. The observations and photographs referred to have opened a new field for investigation, and it is likely that very many important questions as to the constitution of comets will be settled when the next bright comet appears.

Encke's Comet and the Resisting Medium.—The period of this comet is between three and four years. Viewed with a telescope, it appears simply as a mass of foggy light. Under the most favorable circumstances, it is just visible to the naked eye. The circumstance that has lent most interest to this comet is that observations extended over many years indicate that it is gradually approaching the Sun.

ENCKE attributed this change in its orbit to the existence in space of a resisting medium, so rare as to have no appreciable effect upon the motion of the planets, and felt only by bodies of extreme tenuity, like the telescopic comets. The approach of the comet to the Sun is shown by a gradual diminution of the period of revolution.

If the change in the period of this comet were actually due to the causes which ENCKE supposed, then other faint comets of the same kind ought to be subject to a similar influence. But the investigations which have been made in recent times on these bodies show no deviations of the kind. It might, therefore, be concluded that the change in the period of ENCKE's comet must be due to some other cause. There is, however, one circumstance which leaves us in doubt.

ENCKE's comet passes nearer the Sun than any other comet of

short period which has been observed with sufficient care to decide the question. It may, therefore, be supposed that the resisting medium, whatever it may be, is densest near the Sun, and does not extend out far enough for the other comets to meet it. The question is one very difficult to settle. The fact is that all comets exhibit slight anomalies in their motions which prevent us from deducing conclusions from them with the same certainty that we should from those of solid bodies like the planets. One of the chief difficulties in investigating the orbits of comets with all rigor is due to the difficulty of obtaining accurate positions of the centre of so ill-defined an object as the nucleus.

PART III.

THE UNIVERSE AT LARGE.

CHAPTER XXII.

INTRODUCTION.

41. Although the solar system comprises the bodies which are most important to us who live on the Earth, yet they form only an insignificant part of creation. Besides the Earth, only seven of the bodies of the solar system are plainly visible to the naked eye, whereas some 2000 or more stars can be seen on any clear night. Our Sun is simply one of these stars, and does not, so far as we know, differ from its fellows in any essential characteristic. It is rather less bright than the average of the nearer stars, and overpowers them by its brilliancy only because it is so much nearer to us.

The distance of the stars from each other, and therefore from the Sun, is immensely greater than any of the distances in the solar system. In fact, the nearest known star is about seven thousand times as far from us as the planet *Neptune.* If we suppose the orbit of this planet to be represented by a child's hoop, the nearest star would be three or four miles away. We have no reason to suppose that contiguous stars are, on the average, any nearer together than this, except in special cases where they are collected together in clusters.

The total number of the stars is estimated by millions, and they are separated one from another by these wide intervals. It follows that, in going from the Sun to the nearest star, we are simply taking a single step in the universe. The most distant stars are probably a thousand times more distant than the nearest one, and we do not know what may lie beyond the distant stars.

The planets, though millions of miles away, are comparatively near us, and form a little family by themselves. The planets are, so far as we can see, worlds not exceedingly different from the Earth on which we live, while the stars are suns, generally larger and brighter than our own Sun. Each star may, for aught we know, have planets revolving around it, but their distance is so immense that even the largest planets will forever remain invisible with the most powerful telescopes man can construct.

We shall see in what follows that only a few stars are so near to us that their light can reach the Earth in 10, 20, or even 50 years. The vast majority are so distant that the light which we *now* see left them a century ago, or more. If one of these were suddenly destroyed it would continue to shine for years afterwards. The aspect of the sky at any moment does not then represent the present state of the stellar universe, but rather its past history. The Sun's light is already eight minutes old when it reaches us; that of *Neptune* left the planet about four hours before; the nearest fixed stars appear as they were no less than four years ago ; while the Milky Way shines with a light which may have been centuries on its journey.

The difference between the Earth and the Sun is almost entirely due to a difference in their temperature. Nearly every element in the Earth is present in the Sun. If the Earth were to be suddenly raised to the Sun's temperature it would become a miniature Sun; that is, a miniature star. Some of the elements present in the Sun are found to be plentiful in other stars, in nebulæ, and even in comets and meteors. All the bodies of the solar system appear to be, in the main, of like constitution; and their wonderfully different physical conditions to be due, in the main, to differences of temperature. The stars, likewise, are made up of elements often the same as the elements we know on the Earth. The extraordinary diversity exhibited by the bodies of the visible universe thus appears to be largely due to differences in their temperature. The past and the future of the Sun, the Earth, and the Moon can, therefore, be investigated by inquiring what temperatures these bodies have had in past times and what temperatures they are likely to have in the future.

General Aspect of the Heavens.—Constellations.—When we view the heavens with the unassisted eye, the stars appear to be scattered nearly at random over the surface of the celestial vault. The only deviation from an entirely random distribution which can be noticed is a certain apparent grouping of the brighter ones into constellations. A few stars are comparatively much brighter than the rest, and there is every gradation of brilliancy, from that of the brightest to those which are barely visible. We also notice at a glance that the fainter stars far outnumber the bright ones; so that if we divide the stars into classes according to their brilliancy, the fainter classes will contain the most stars.

There are in the whole celestial sphere about 6000 stars visible to the naked eye. Of these, however, we can never see more than a part at any one time, because one half of the sphere is always below the horizon. If we could see a star in the horizon as easily as in the zenith, one half of the whole number, or 3000, would be visible on any clear night. But stars near the horizon are seen through so great a thickness of atmosphere as greatly to obscure their light; consequently only the brightest ones can there be

seen. It is not likely that more than 2000 stars can ever
be taken in at a single view by any ordinary eye. About
2000 other stars are so near the south pole that they never
rise in our latitudes. Hence out of the 6000 visible, only
4000 ever come within the range of our vision, unless we
make a journey toward the equator. .

The Galaxy.—The *Galaxy*, or *Milky Way*, is a magnifi-
cent stream or belt of white milky light 10° or 15° in
breadth, extending obliquely around the celestial sphere.
During the spring months it nearly coincides with our
horizon in the early evening, but it can be seen at all other
times of the year spanning the heavens like an arch. For
a portion of its length it is split longitudinally into two
parts, which remain separate through many degrees, and
are finally united again. The student will obtain a better
idea of it by actual examination than from any description.
He will see that its irregularities of form and lustre are
such that in some places it looks like a mass of brilliant
clouds (see Fig. 199).

When GALILEO first directed his telescope to the heavens,
about the year 1610, he perceived that the Milky Way was
composed of stars too faint to be individually seen by the
unaided eye. HUYGHENS in 1656 resolved a large portion
of the Galaxy into stars, and concluded that it was composed entirely of them. KEPLER considered it to be a vast
ring of stars surrounding the solar system, and remarked
that the Sun must be situated near the centre of the ring.
This view agrees very well with the one now received,
except that the stars which form the Milky Way, instead
of lying near to the solar system, as KEPLER supposed, are
at distances so vast as to elude all our powers of imagination.

The most recent researches have shown that the Milky
Way is a vast cluster of stars intermixed with nebulæ, and
that these stars and nebulæ are, in all probability, physi-

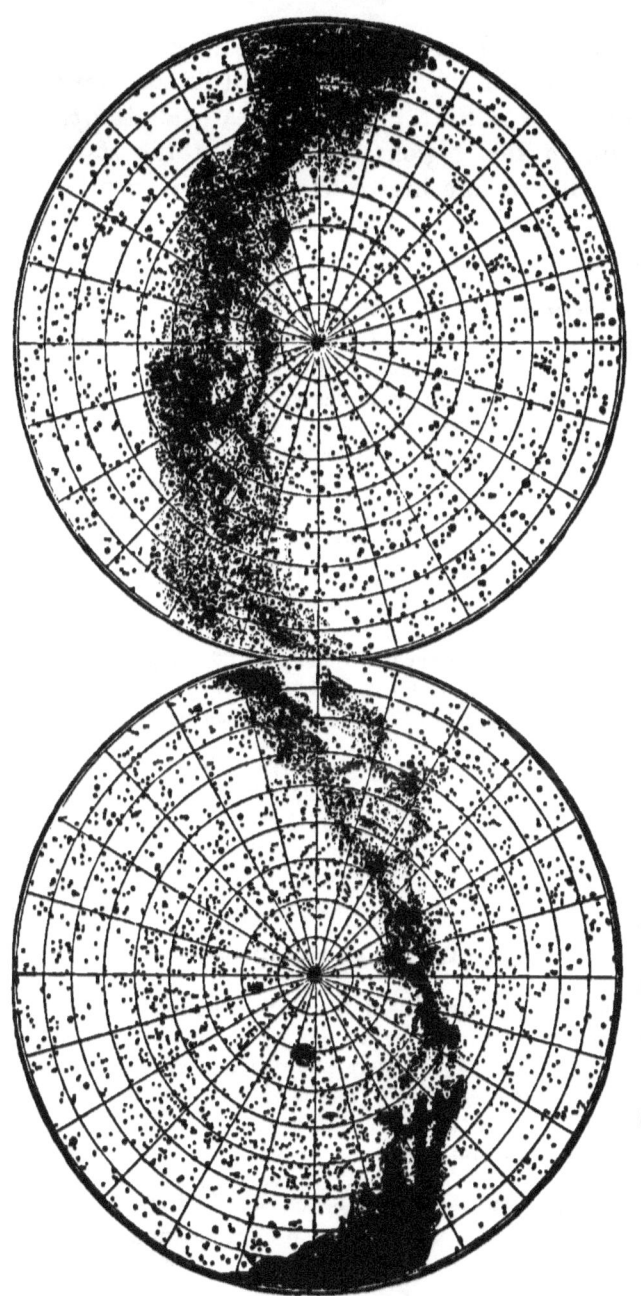

FIG. 199.—THE STARS TO SIXTH MAGNITUDE INCLUSIVE WITH THE MILKY WAY.

cally connected and not merely perspectively projected in
the same part of the sky. A majority of its stars are of the
same spectral type (like *Sirius*). Nearly all the *gaseous*
nebulæ are in this region; and most of the stars with
bright-line spectra are here. We must then consider the
Milky Way as mainly a physical system, and only partly as
a geometrical appearance.

Lucid and Telescopic Stars.—When we view the heavens with a
telescope, we find that there are innumerable stars too small to be
seen by the naked eye. We may therefore divide the stars, with respect to brightness, into two great classes.

Lucid Stars are those which are visible without a telescope.

Telescopic Stars are those which are not so visible.

Magnitudes of the Stars.—The stars were classified by PTOLEMY
into six orders of magnitude. The fourteen brightest visible in our
latitudes were designated as of the first magnitude, while those barely
visible to the naked eye were said to be of the sixth magnitude. This
classification is entirely arbitrary, since there are no two stars of absolutely the same brightness. If all the stars were arranged in the
order of their actual brilliancy, we should find a regular gradation
from the brightest to the faintest, no two being precisely the same.
Between the north pole and 35° south declination there are:

14 stars of the first magnitude.
48   "   "   second   "
152 "   "   third   "
313 "   "   fourth   "
854 "   "   fifth   "
3974 "   "   sixth   "
——————
5355 of the first six magnitudes.

Of these, however, nearly 2000 of the sixth magnitude are so faint
that they can be seen only by an eye of extraordinary keenness.
Measures of the light of the stars show that a star of the second
magnitude is four tenths as bright as one of the first; one of the third
is four tenths as bright as one of the second, and so on. The ratio
$\frac{4}{10}$ is called the *light-ratio*.

The Constellations and Names of the Stars. — The
ancients divided the stars into constellations, and gave

special names to these groups and to many of the more conspicuous stars also.

Considerably more than 3000 years before the commencement of the Christian chronology the star *Sirius*, the brightest in the heavens, was known to the Egyptians under the name of *Sothis*. The seven stars of the *Great Bear*, so conspicuous in our northern sky, were known under that name to HOMER (800 B.C.), as well as the group of the *Pleiades*, or Seven Stars, and the constellation of *Orion*. All the earlier civilized nations, Egyptians, Chinese, Greeks, and Hindoos, had some arbitrary division of the surface of the heavens into irregular and often fantastic shapes, which were distinguished by names. The area within which the Sun and planets move—the Zodiac—was probably divided and named before the year 2000 B.C., and the 48 constellations given by PTOLEMY were probably formed at least as early as this time.

In early times the names of heroes and animals were given to the constellations. Each figure was supposed to be painted on the surface of the heavens, and the stars were designated by their position upon some portion of the figure. The ancient and mediæval astronomers spoke of "the bright star in the left foot of *Orion*," "the eye of the *Bull*," "the heart of the *Lion*," "the head of *Perseus*," etc. These figures are still retained upon some star-charts, and are useful where it is desired to compare the older descriptions of the constellations with our modern maps. Otherwise they have ceased to serve any really useful purpose, and are often omitted from maps designed for purely astronomical uses.

The Arabians gave special names to a large number of the brighter stars. Some of these names are in common use at the present time, as *Aldebaran*, *Fomalhaut*, etc.

In 1654 BAYER, of Germany, mapped the constellations and designated the brighter stars of each constellation by the letters of the Greek alphabet. When this alphabet was exhausted he introduced the letters of the Roman alphabet. In general, the brightest star was designated by the first letter of the alphabet, α, the next by the following letter, β, etc.

On this system, a star is designated by a certain Greek letter, followed by the genitive of the Latin name of the constellation to which it belongs. For example α *Canis Majoris*, or, in English, α of the Great Dog, is the designation of *Sirius*, the brightest star in the heavens. The brightest stars of the *Great Bear* are called α *Ursæ Majoris*, β *Ursæ Majoris*, etc. *Arcturus* is α *Boötis*. The student will here see a resemblance to our way of designating individuals by a Christian name followed by the family name. The Greek letters furnish the Christian names of the separate stars, while the name of the constellation is that of the family. As there are only fifty letters in the two alphabets used by BAYER, only the fifty brightest stars in each constellation could possibly be designated by this method.

After the telescope had fixed the position of many additional stars, some other method of denoting them became necessary. FLAMSTEED, about the year 1700, prepared an extensive catalogue of stars, in which those of each constellation were designated by numbers in the order of right-ascension. These numbers were entirely independent of the designations of BAYER—that is, he did not omit the BAYER stars from his system of numbers, but numbered them as if they had no Greek letter. Hence those stars to which BAYER applied letters have two designations, the number and the letter. The fainter stars are designated nowadays either by their R.A. and Decl., or by their numbers in some well-known catalogue of stars.

Numbering and Cataloguing the Stars.—As telescopic power is increased, we still find fainter and fainter stars. But the number cannot go on increasing forever in the same ratio as the brighter magnitudes, because, if it did, the whole night sky would be a blaze of starlight, instead of a dark sphere dotted with brilliant points.

If telescopes with powers far exceeding our present ones are made, they will, no doubt, show very many new stars. But it is highly probable that the *number* of such successive orders of stars would not increase in the same ratio as is observed in the 8th, 9th, and 10th magnitudes, for example.

In special regions of the sky, which have been searchingly examined by various telescopes of successively increasing apertures, the number of new stars found is by no means in proportion to the increased instrumental power. If this is found to be true elsewhere, the conclusion may be that, after all, the stellar system can be experimentally shown to be of finite extent, or to contain only a finite number of stars, rather.

We have already stated that in the whole sky an eye of average power will see about 6000 stars. With a telescope this number is greatly increased, and the most powerful telescopes of modern times will probably show more than 100,000,000 stars.

In ARGELANDER's *Durchmusterung* of the stars of the northern heavens there are recorded as belonging to the northern hemisphere 314,926 stars from the first to the 9.5 magnitude, so that there are about 600,000 in the whole heavens.

We can readily compute the amount of light received by the Earth on a clear but moonless night from these stars. The brightness of an average star of the first magnitude is 0.5 of that of α *Lyræ*. A star of the 2d magnitude will shine with a light expressed by $0.5 \times 0.4 = 0.20$, and so on. (See p. 374.)

The total brightness of					
The total brightness of	10	1st magnitude stars is			5.0
" "	37	2d	"	"	7.4
" "	128	3d	"	"	10 2
" "	310	4th	"	"	9.9
" "	1,016	5th	"	"	13.0
" "	4,328	6th	"	"	22 1
" "	13,593	7th	"	"	27 8
" "	57,960	8th	"	"	47.4

Sum = 142.8

It thus appears that from the stars to the 8th magnitude, inclusive, we receive 143 times as much light as from α *Lyræ*. α *Lyræ* has been determined by ZÖLLNER to be about 44,000,000,000 times fainter than the Sun, so that the proportion of starlight to sunlight can be computed. It also appears that the stars too faint to be individually visible to the naked eye are yet so numerous as to affect the general brightness of the sky more than the so-called lucid stars (1st to 6th magnitude). The sum of the last two numbers of the table is greater than the sum of all the others.

The Star Maps printed in this book furnish a means by which the constellations and principal stars can be identified by the student.

Maps of the stars down to the 14th or 15th magnitude are now made by photography, using special telescopes and long exposures (two or three hours). Such complete maps as this will throw a flood of light on the distribution and arrangement of the constituent stars of the Stellar Universe.

The Stars are Suns.—Spectroscopic observations prove that nearly all of the stars are suns, very like our own Sun. They are self-luminous and intensely hot. They have extensive atmospheres of incandescent gases and metallic vapors. The light from a whole class of stars is, so far as can be determined, precisely like sunlight in quality. We may say in general that *stars are suns.*

The light *received* from even the brightest star is a very small quantity because even the nearest star is very distant. From *Sirius,* the brightest star in the sky, we receive $\dfrac{1}{7,000,000,000}$ of the light received from the Sun. Let l be the light received from a star at a distance D from us and L the light we should receive from this star if it were at the Sun's distance from us $(= 1)$. Then

$$L : l = 1 : \frac{1}{D^2} \text{ or } L = l \cdot D^2.$$

In the case of *Sirius,* $l = \dfrac{1}{7,000,000,000}$ as above, and $D =$ about 542,000 times the Sun's distance. Hence $L = \dfrac{(524,000)^2}{7,000,000,000} = 42.$ That is, *Sirius* emits forty-two times as much light (and presumably about forty-two times as much heat) as the Sun. The Sun is a small star, compared to *Sirius.* The pole-star, *Polaris,* emits about two hundred times as much light as the Sun, while the light received from it is insignificant compared to sunlight.

If we compare stars with the Sun in this way we shall see that some of them emit several thousand times more light, while some emit perhaps $\frac{1}{1000}$ part as much light. These are great differences, but they are not enormous.

The *masses* of a few stars are known. It is found that some of these stars have masses perhaps a hundred times greater, while others have masses very much smaller, than the Sun's mass. Here again there are great differences, but the differences are not enormous. Our Sun is an average star, we may say.

CHAPTER XXIII.

MOTIONS AND DISTANCES OF THE STARS.

42. Proper Motions.—To the unaided vision, the fixed stars appear to preserve the same relative position in the heavens through many centuries, so that if the ancient astronomers could again see them, they could detect only the slight changes in their arrangement. But the accurate measurements of modern times show that there are slow changes in the positions of the brighter stars. Many of them have small motions on the celestial sphere. Their right-ascensions and declinations change (slightly) from year to year, apparently with uniform velocity. The changes are called *proper motions,* since they are real motions peculiar to the star itself.

In general, the proper motions even of the brightest stars are only a fraction of a second of arc in a year, so that thousands of years would be required for them to change their place in any striking degree, and hundreds of thousands to make a complete revolution around the celestial sphere. The circumference of a sphere contains 1,296,000″.

Proper Motion of the Sun.—It is *a priori* evident that stars, in general, must have proper motions, when once we admit the *universality* of gravitation. That any fixed star should be entirely at rest would require that the attractions on all sides of it should be exactly balanced. Any—the slightest—change in the position of this star would break up this balance, and thus, in general, it follows that stars must be in motion, since each of them cannot occupy such a critical position as has to be assumed.

If but one fixed star is in motion, all the rest are affected, and we cannot doubt that every single star, our Sun included, is in motion by amounts which vary from small to great. If the Sun alone has a motion, and all the other stars are at rest, the consequence would be that all the fixed stars would appear to be retreating *en masse* from that point in the sky toward which we were moving. Those nearest us would move more rapidly, those more distant less so. And in the same way, the stars from which the solar system was receding would seem to be approaching each other.

If the stars, instead of being quite at rest, as just supposed, have motions proper to themselves, as they do, then we shall have a double complexity. They would still appear to an observer in the solar system to have motions. One part of these motions would be truly proper to the stars, and one part would be due to the advance of the Sun itself in space.

Observations of the positions of stars—of their right-ascensions and declinations—can show only the *resultant* of these two motions. It is for reasoning to separate this resultant into its two components. The first question is to determine whether the results of observation indicate any solar motion at all. If there is none, the proper motions of stars will be directed along all possible lines. If the Sun does truly move in space along some line, then there will be a general agreement in the resultant motions of the stars near the ends of the line along which it moves, while those at the sides, so to speak, will show comparatively less systematic effect. It is as if one were riding in the rear of a railway train and watching the rails over which it has just passed. As we recede from any point, the rails at that point seem to come nearer and nearer together.

If we were passing through a forest, we should see the trunks of the trees from which we were going apparently come nearer and nearer together, while those on the sides of us would remain at their constant distance, and those in front would grow further and further apart.

These phenomena, that occur in a case where we are sensible of our own motion, serve to show how we may deduce a motion, otherwise unknown, from the appearances which are presented by the stars in space.

In this way, acting upon suggestions which had been thrown out previously to his own time, Sir WILLIAM HERSCHEL demonstrated that the Sun, together with all its system, was moving through space in an unknown and majestic orbit of its own. The centre round which this motion is directed cannot yet be assigned. We can only determine the point in the heavens toward which our course is directed—"the apex of solar motion."

A number of astronomers have since investigated this motion with a view of determining the exact point in the heavens toward which the Sun is moving. Their results differ slightly, but the points toward which the Sun is moving all fall in or near the constellation *Hercules* not far from the bright star *Alpha Lyræ* (Vega). The amount of the motion is such that if the Sun were viewed at right angles to the direction of motion from an average star of the first magnitude, it would appear to move *about* one third of a second per year.

Spectroscopic observations will give the direction and the amount of the solar motion in another and an independent way (see Chapter XVII).

Distances of the Fixed Stars.—The ancient astronomers supposed all the fixed stars to be situated at a short distance outside of the orbit of the planet *Saturn*, then the outermost known planet. The idea was prevalent that Nature would not waste space by leaving a great region beyond *Saturn* entirely empty.

When COPERNICUS announced the theory that the Sun

was at rest and the Earth in motion around it, the problem of the distance of the stars acquired a new interest. It was evident that if the Earth described an annual orbit, then the stars would appear in the course of a year to oscillate back and forth in corresponding orbits, *unless* they were so immensely distant that these oscillations were too small to be seen.

The apparent oscillation of *Mars* produced in this way was described p. 188 *et seq.* These oscillations were, in fact, those which the ancients represented by the motion of the planet around a small epicycle (see Fig. 124). But

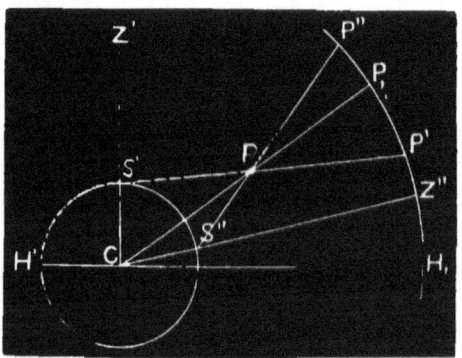

FIG. 200.—THE THEORY OF PARALLAX.

no such oscillation was detected in a fixed star until the year 1837; and this fact seemed to the astronomers of GALILEO's time to present an almost insuperable difficulty in the reception of the Copernican system. As the instruments of observation were from time to time improved, this apparent annual oscillation of the stars was ardently sought for.

The parallax of a planet (*P* in the figure) is the angle at the planet subtended by the Earth's radius (*CS′* = 4000 miles). The *annual* parallax of a star (*P*) is the angle at the star subtended by the radius of the Earth's orbit ($CS' = 93,000,000$ miles). See page 109. The *annual* parallax of *Saturn* is about 6° and of *Neptune* it is about 2°, and these are angles easily detected with the astronomical instruments of the ancients. It was very evident, without telescopic observation, that the stars could not have a parallax of one half a degree. A change of place of one half a degree could be readily detected by the naked eye. They must therefore be at least twelve times as far as *Saturn* if the Copernican system were true.

When the telescope was applied to measurement, a continually increasing accuracy was gained by the improvement of the instruments. Yet the parallax of the fixed stars eluded measurement. Early in the present century it became certain that even the brighter stars had not, in general, an annual parallax so great as $1''$, and thus it became certain that they must lie at a greater distance than 200,000 times that which separates the Earth from the Sun (see page 23). $R = 206,264''$.

Success in actually measuring the parallax of the stars was at length obtained almost simultaneously by two astronomers, BESSEL of Königsberg and STRUVE of Dorpat. BESSEL selected 61 *Cygni* for observation, in August, 1837. The result of two or three years of observation was that this star had a parallax of about one third of a second. This would make its distance from the Sun nearly 600,000 astronomical units. The reality of this parallax has been well established by subsequent investigators, only it has been shown to be a little larger, and therefore the star a little nearer than BESSEL supposed. The most probable parallax is now found to be $0''.45$, corresponding to a distance of about 400,000 radii of the Earth's orbit.

The distances of the stars are frequently expressed by the time required for light to pass from them to our system. The velocity of light is, it will be remembered, about

300,000 kilometres per second, or such as to pass from the Sun to the Earth in 8 minutes 18 seconds.

The cut shows the arrangement of some of the nearer stars in space. They are shown on a plane, and not in solid space. The dot in the centre of the figure is the solar system. The circles of the figure stand for spheres,

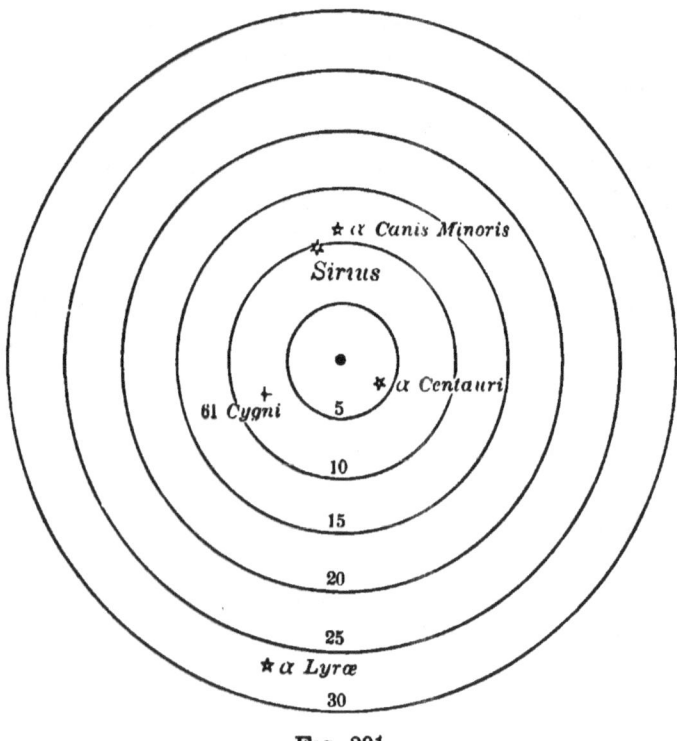

Fɪɢ 201.

whose radii are 5, 10, 15, 20, 25, 30 light-years; that is, for spheres whose radii are of such lengths that light, which moves 186,000 miles *in a second* requires 5, 10, etc., *years* to traverse these radii.

The time required for light to reach the Earth from a

few of the stars, whose parallax has been measured, is as
follows:

STAR.	Years.	STAR.	Years.
α Centauri	4½	*Vega* (α Lyræ)...........	27
61 *Cygni*............. ...	7	*Aldebaran* (α Tauri).....	32
Sirius (α Canis majoris)....	8	*Polaris* (α Ursæ minoris).	47
Procyon (α Canis minoris) ..	12	*Arcturus* (α Boötis).......	160

If the star *Polaris* were to be suddenly destroyed—now
—this instant—its light would continue to shine for nearly
half a century more.

CHAPTER XXIV.

VARIABLE AND TEMPORARY STARS.

43. Stars Regularly Variable.—Since the end of the sixteenth century, it has been known that all stars do not shine with a constant light. The *period* of a variable star is the interval of time during which it goes through all its changes, and returns to its original brilliancy.

The most noted variable stars are *Mira Ceti* (*o Ceti*) (star-map VI, in the southeast) and *Algol* (*β Persei*) (star-map I, near the zenith). *Mira* is usually a ninth-magnitude star and is therefore invisible to the naked eye. Every eleven months it increases to its greatest brightness (sometimes as high as the 2d magnitude, sometimes not above the 4th), remaining at this maximum for some time, then gradually decreases until it again becomes invisible to the naked eye, and so remains for about five or six months. The average period, from minimum to minimum, is about 333 days, but the period varies greatly. It has been known as a variable since 1596.

Algol has been known as a variable star since 1667. This star is commonly of the 2d magnitude; after remaining so about 2½ days, it falls to 4th magnitude in the short time of 4½ hours, and remains of 4th magnitude for 20 minutes. It then increases in brilliancy, and in another 3½ hours it is again of the 2d magnitude, at which point it remains for the rest of its period, about $2^d 12^h$.

These examples of two classes of variable stars give an idea of the extraordinary nature of the phenomena they present.

386

Several hundred stars are known to be variable. A short list of variables is given in Table VII.

The color of more than three fourths of the variable stars is red or orange. It is a very remarkable fact that certain star-clusters contain large numbers of variable stars.

Temporary or "New" Stars.—There are a few cases known of stars that have suddenly appeared, attained more or less brightness, and slowly decreased in magnitude, either disappearing totally, or finally remaining as comparatively faint objects. A new star that appeared in 134 B.C. led HIPPARCHUS to form his catalogue of stars.

The most famous new star appeared in 1572, and attained a brightness greater than that of *Jupiter*. It was even visible to the eye in daylight. TYCHO BRAHE first observed this star in November, 1572, and watched its gradual increase in light until its maximum in December. It then began to diminish in brightness, and in January, 1573, it was fainter than *Jupiter*. In February it was of the 1st magnitude, in April of the 2d, in July of the 3d, and in October of the 4th. It continued to diminish until March, 1574, when it became invisible to the naked eye.

The history of temporary stars is, in general, similar to that of the star of 1572, except that none have attained so great a degree of brilliancy. As more than a score of such objects are *known* to have appeared, many of them before the making of accurate observations, it is probable that many others have appeared without recognition. Among telescopic stars there is but a small chance of detecting a new or temporary star.

Theories to Account for Variable Stars.—Two main classes of variable stars exist and two theories must be mentioned here.

I. Stars in general, like the Sun, are subject to eruptions of glowing gas from their interior, and to the formation of dark spots on their surfaces. These eruptions and formations have in most cases a greater or less tendency to a regular period, like the period of a gigantic geyser.

In the case of our Sun, the period is 11 years, but in the case of many of the stars it is much shorter. Ordinarily, as in the case of the Sun and of a large majority of the stars, the variations are too slight to affect the total quantity of light to any noteworthy extent.

In the case of the variable stars this spot-producing power and the liability to eruptions are very much greater, and we have changes of light sufficiently marked to be perceived by the eye.

This theory explains why so large a proportion of the variable stars are red. It is well known that glowing bodies emit a larger proportion of red rays, and a smaller proportion of blue ones, the cooler they become. It is therefore probable that the red stars have the least heat. This being the case, spots are more easily produced on their surfaces just as cooling iron is covered with a crust. If their outside surface is so cool as to become solid in certain regions, the glowing gases from the interior will burst through with more violence than if the surrounding shell were liquid or gaseous. The cause of the *periodic* nature of these eruptions is probably *similar* to the cause of the periodic outbursts of geysers.

II. There is, however, another class of variable stars whose variations are due to an entirely different cause; *Algol* is the best representative of the class. The extreme regularity with which the light of this object fades away and disappears suggests the possibility that a dark body may be revolving around it, partially eclipsing it at every revolution. The law of variation of its light is so different from that of the light of most other variable stars as to suggest a different cause. Most others are near their maximum for only a small part of their period, while *Algol* is at its maximum for nine tenths of it. Others are subject to nearly continuous changes, while the light of *Algol* remains constant during nine tenths of its period. Spectroscopic observations show that *Algol* (a bright body) is accompanied by a dark satellite that revolves about it in an orbit which is presented to us nearly edgewise. The satellite is about as large in diameter as *Algol* and is about 3,000,000 miles distant from it. When the dark satellite is in front of *Algol* some of its light is cut off. When it is to one side, *Algol* shines with its full brightness, and we do not see the satellite because it is not self-luminous. Probably both *Algol* and its dark companion revolve about a third dark star. The diameter of *Algol* is about 1,000,000 miles. The diameter of the dark satellite is about 800,000 miles. Each of these stars is about the size of our Sun. The *mass* of both combined is about ⅔ of the Sun's mass. Their *density* is therefore much less than that of water. They are like heavy spherical clouds.

Dark Stars.—The existence of "dark stars" is proved in several ways. *Algol* and other stars of its class are accompanied by non-luminous satellites, as is shown by the phenomena of their variability. *Sirius* and *Procyon* are also so accompanied, as is demonstrated by periodic irregularities of their motion. There is no reason why there may not be "as many dark stars as bright ones." A bright star is one that is (comparatively) young. Its heat is still so ardent as to make it self-luminous. A dark star is one that has lost its heat in the lapse of centuries—probably thousands of centuries. In our own solar system *Jupiter* was probably a self-luminous planet not so very many centuries ago. The Earth and other planets are dark, but still have some of their native heat. The moon is dark (*i. e.*, not self-luminous) and it is also cold.

We must figure the stellar universe to ourselves as containing not only the stars that we see, but also as containing perhaps as many more that we shall never see, because they have lost the light and heat that they (probably) once possessed. Most of the dark stars will forever remain unknown to us, but occasionally we meet with cases like those of *Algol* or of *Sirius*, which make it certain that dark stars exist. Their is reason to believe that their number is very large.

CHAPTER XXV.

DOUBLE, MULTIPLE, AND BINARY STARS.

44. Double and Multiple Stars.—When we examine the heavens with telescopes, we find many cases in which two or more stars are extremely close together, so as to form a pair, a triplet, or a group. It is evident that there are two ways to account for this appearance.

1. We may suppose that the stars happen to lie nearly in the same straight line from the Earth, but have no connection with each other. It is evident that in this case a pair of stars might appear double, although one was hundreds or thousands of times farther off than the other. It is, moreover, impossible, from mere inspection, to determine which is the farther off. (See Fig. 3, t, t, t).

2. We may suppose that the stars are really near together, as they appear, and do, in fact, form a connected pair or group.

A couple of stars in the first case is said to be *optically double*.

Stars that are really physically connected are said to be *physically double*. Their physical connection can only be proved by observations which show that the two stars are revolving about their common centre of gravity. There are tens of thousands of stars in the sky that appear to be double and hundreds that have already been proved to be physically connected.

There are several cases of stars which appear double to the naked eye. ε *Lyræ* is such a star and is an interesting object in a small telescope, from the fact that each of the two stars which compose it is itself double. This minute pair of points, capable of being distinguished as double only by the most perfect eye (without the telescope), is really composed of two pairs of stars wide apart, with a group of smaller stars between and around them. The figure shows the appearance in a telescope of considerable power.

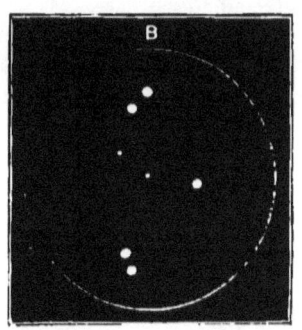

Revolutions of Double Stars—Binary Systems.—It is evident that if stars physically double are subject to the force of gravitation, they must be revolving around each other, as the Earth and planets revolve around the Sun, else they would be drawn together as a single star.

FIG. 202.—THE QUADRUPLE STAR ε LYRÆ.

The method of determining the period of revolution of a pair of stars, A and B, is illustrated by the figure, which is supposed to represent the field of view of an inverting telescope pointed toward the south. The arrow shows the direction of the apparent diurnal motion. The telescope is pointed so that the brighter star is in the centre of the field. The angle of position of the smaller star (NAB) is measured by means of a divided circle, and their distance apart (AB) is measured with the micrometer (see page 141) at the same time.

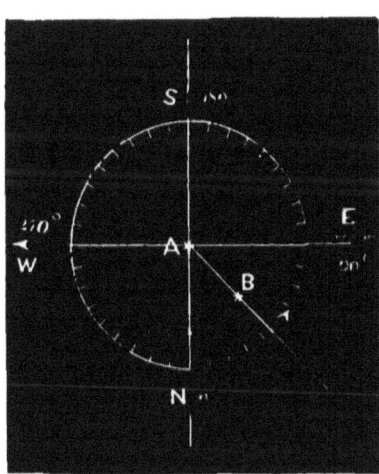

FIG. 203.—POSITION-ANGLE OF A DOUBLE STAR.

If, by measures of this sort, extending through a series of years, the distance or position-angle of a pair of stars is found to change *periodically*, it shows that one star is revolving around the other. Such a pair is called a *binary star* or *binary system*. The only distinction that we can make between binary systems and ordinary double stars is founded on the presence or absence of this observed motion. It is probable that nearly all the very close double stars are really binary systems, but that many hundreds of years are required to perform a revolution in some instances, so that their motion has not yet been detected.

Certain pairs of binary stars whose components are entirely too close to be separable by the telescope have been discovered by the spectroscope. If two stars, *A* and *B*, are binary, and therefore revolving in orbits, they will sometimes be in this position to an observer on the Earth, thus :

If they are too close to be separated by the telescope, still the spectrum of the pair will show the lines of both stars. That is, certain of the spectrum lines will appear double. At other times one star will be behind the other, as seen from the Earth, thus :

and the spectrum lines will be seen single. If changes like these occur periodically, as they do, then the orbit of one star about the other can be calculated. In this way a number of " spectroscopic binary stars" has been found. The star *Zeta Ursæ Majoris* (*Mizar*) (see Fig. 95) is a binary of this class, whose period is about 52 days. The mass of this system is about 40 times the Sun's mass.

The existence of binary systems shows that the law of gravitation includes the stars as well as the solar system in its scope, and thus that it is truly universal.

When the parallax of a binary star is known, as well as the orbit, it is possible to compute the mass of the binary system in terms of the Sun's mass. It is an important fact that the stars of such binary systems as have been investigated do not differ very greatly in mass from our Sun.

CHAPTER XXVI.

NEBULÆ AND CLUSTERS.

45. Nebulæ.—In the star-catalogues of PTOLEMY and the earlier writers, there was included a class of nebulous or cloudy stars, which were in reality star-clusters. They were visible to the naked eye as masses of soft diffused light like parts of the Milky Way. The telescope shows that most of these objects are clusters of stars.

As the telescope was improved, great numbers of such patches of light were found, some of which could be resolved into stars, while others could not. The latter were called *nebulæ* and the former *star-clusters*.

About 1656 HUYGHENS described the great nebula of *Orion*, one of the most remarkable and brilliant of these objects. It is just visible to the naked eye as a cloudiness about the middle star of the sword of *Orion* (a line from the *r* of *Orion* in Fig. 204 to the *r* of *Eridanus* passes through the nebula). The student should look for this nebula with the eye on a clear winter's night. An opera-glass will show the nebulosity distinctly; but a telescope is needed to show it well. Sir WILLIAM HERSCHEL with his great telescopes first gave proof of the enormous number of these masses. In 1786 he published a catalogue of one thousand new nebulæ and clusters. This was followed in 1789 by a catalogue of a second thousand, and in 1802 by a third catalogue of five hundred new objects of this class. Sir JOHN HERSCHEL added about two thousand more nebulæ. About nine thousand nebulæ, mostly very faint, are now known.

Classification of Nebulæ and Clusters.—In studying these objects, the first question we meet is this: Are all these bodies clusters of stars

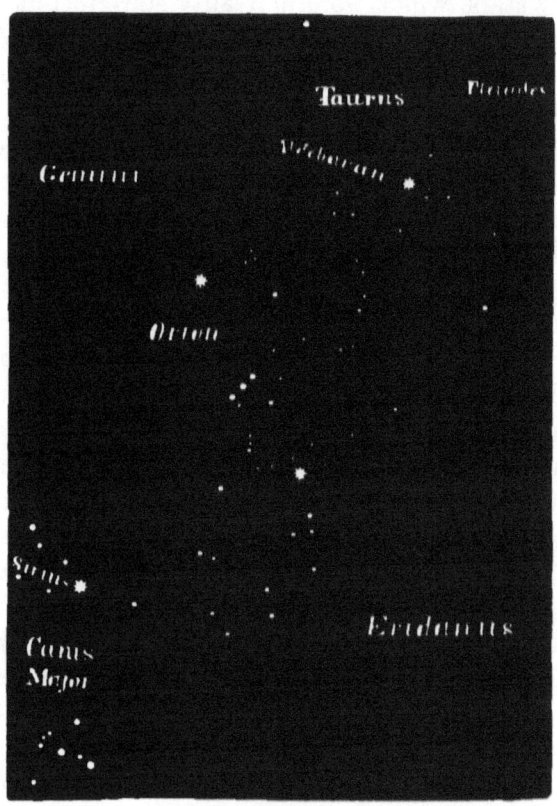

Fig. 204 —THE CONSTELLATION ORION AS SEEN WITH THE NAKED EYE.

which look diffused only because they are so distant that our telescopes cannot distinguish the separate stars? or are some of them in reality what they seem to be; namely, diffused masses of matter?

In his early memoirs, Sir WILLIAM HERSCHEL took the first view. He considered the Milky Way as nothing but a congeries of stars, and all nebulæ seemed to be but stellar clusters, so distant as to cause the individual stars to disappear in a general milkiness or nebulosity.

In 1791, however, he discovered a *nebulous star* (properly so called) —that is, a star which was undoubtedly similar to the surrounding stars, and which was encompassed by a halo of nebulous light. His reasoning on this discovery is instructive.

He says: "Supposing the nucleus and halo to be connected, we may, first, suppose the whole to be of stars, in which case either the nucleus is enormously larger than other stars of its stellar magnitude,

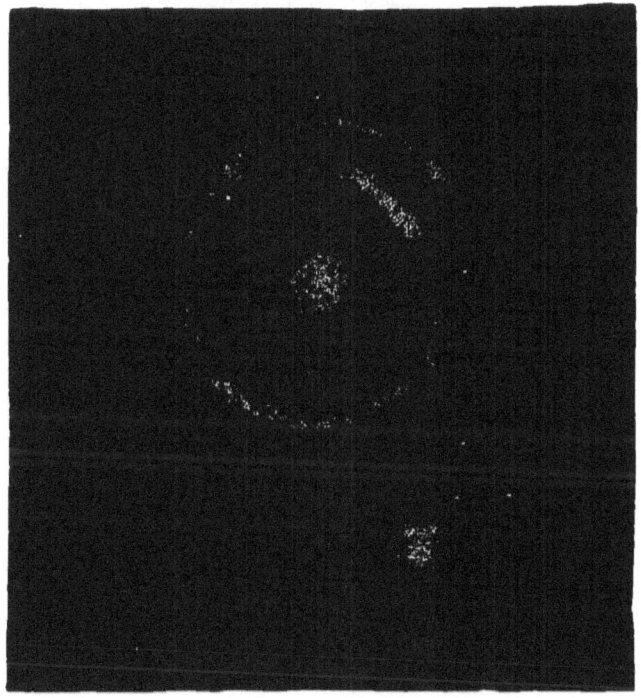

FIG. 205.— SPIRAL NEBULA.

or the envelope is composed of stars indefinitely small; or, second, we must admit that the star is *involved in a shining fluid of a nature totally unknown to us.*

"The shining fluid might exist independently of stars. The light of this fluid is no kind of reflection from the star in the centre. If this matter is self-luminous, it seems more fit to produce a star by its condensation than to depend on the star for its existence."

This was the first exact statement of the idea that, beside stars and

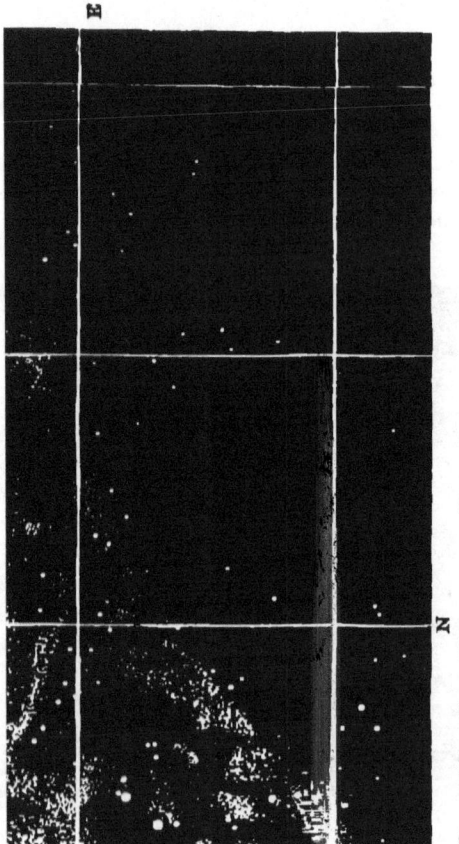

FIG. 206.—THE HORSESHOE NEBULA.

star-clusters, we have in the universe a totally distinct series of objects, probably much more simple in their constitution. Observations on the spectra of these bodies have entirely confirmed the conclusions of HERSCHEL. The spectroscope shows that the true nebulæ are gaseous.

Nebulæ and clusters are divided into classes. A *planetary nebula* is circular or elliptic in shape, with a definite outline like a planet. *Spiral nebulæ* are those whose convolutions have a spiral shape. This class is quite numerous.

The different kinds of nebulæ and clusters will be better understood from the cuts and descriptions which follow than by formal

FIG. 207.—THE MOON PASSING NEAR THE PLEIADES.

definitions. It must be remembered that there is an almost infinite variety of such shapes. The real shape of the nebula in space appears to us much changed by perspective.

Vast areas of the sky are covered with faint nebulosity.

Star-clusters.—The most noted of all the clusters is the *Pleiades*, which may be seen during the winter months to the northwest of the constellation *Taurus* The average naked eye can easily distinguish six stars within it, but under favorable conditions ten, eleven, twelve, or more stars can be counted. With the telescope, several hundred stars are seen.

The clusters represented in Figs. 208 and 209 are good examples of their classes. The first is globular and contains several thousand small stars. The second is a cluster of about 200 stars, of magnitudes varying from the ninth to the thirteenth and fourteenth, in which the brighter stars are scattered.

Clusters are probably subject to central powers or forces. This was seen by Sir WILLIAM HERSCHEL in 1789. He says :

" Not only were *round* nebulæ and clusters formed by central powers, but likewise every cluster of stars or nebula that shows a gradual condensation or increasing brightness toward a centre.

" Spherical clusters are probably not more different in size among themselves than different individuals of plants of the same species. As it has been shown that the spherical figure of a cluster of stars is owing to central powers, it follows that those clusters which, *cæteris paribus*, are the most complete in this figure must have been the longest exposed to the action of these causes.

FIG. 208.—GLOBULAR CLUSTER.

" The maturity of a sidereal system may thus be judged from the disposition of the component parts.

" Though we cannot see any individual nebula pass through all its stages of life, we can select particular ones in each peculiar stage," and thus obtain a single view of their entire course of development.

Spectra of Nebulæ and Clusters.—In 1864, five years after the invention of the spectroscope, the examination of the spectra of the nebulæ by Sir WILLIAM HUGGINS led to the discovery that while the spectra of stars were invariably continuous and crossed with dark lines similar to those of the solar spectrum, those of many nebulæ were *discontinuous*, showing these bodies to be composed of glowing gas. The nebulæ have proper motions just as do the stars. The great nebula of *Orion* is moving away from the Sun eleven miles every second.

The spectrum of most clusters is continuous, indicating that the individual stars are truly stellar in their nature. In a few cases,

FIG 209.—COMPRESSED CLUSTER.

however, clusters are composed of a mixture of nebulosity (usually near their centre) and of stars, and the spectrum in such cases is compound in its nature, so as to indicate radiation from both gaseous and solid matter.

CHAPTER XXVII.

SPECTRA OF FIXED STARS.*

46. Stellar spectra are found to be, in the main, similar to the solar spectrum; *i.e.*, composed of a continuous band of the prismatic colors, across which dark lines or bands are laid, the latter being fixed in position. These results show the fixed stars to resemble our own Sun in general constitution, and to be composed of an incandescent nucleus surrounded by a gaseous and absorptive atmosphere of lower temperature containing the vapors of metals, etc.—iron, magnesium, hydrogen, etc. The atmosphere of many stars is quite different in constitution from that of the Sun, as is shown by the different position and intensity of the various dark lines that are due to the absorptive action of the atmospheres of the stars.

Different Types of Stars.—In a general way the spectra of all stars are similar. All of them are bodies of the same general kind as the Sun. Yet there are characteristic differences between star and star, and certain large groups into which stars can be classified—certain types of stellar spectra. It is probable that these different types represent different phases in the life-history of a star. Of two stars of the same size and general constitution the whitest is probably the hottest and the youngest ; the reddest is probably the coolest and oldest. The hottest stars have the simplest spectra ; the red stars have complicated spectra and are often variable. The bright stars of the constellation of *Orion* have spectra of the simplest type—their atmospheres are mainly made up of helium and hydrogen gases. Stars like *Sirius* have little helium in their atmospheres, but much

* See Appendix.

400

hydrogen and a little calcium. Stars like *Procyon* have hydrogen and calcium and magnesium in marked quantities, besides other metallic lines. Stars like *Arcturus* are characterized by many metallic lines in their spectra, such as those of iron. Our Sun belongs to this class. Stars with considerably less extensive hydrogen atmospheres and with considerably more metallic vapors surrounding them form the next class (like *Alpha Orionis, Alpha Herculis* and the variable star *Mira Cetis*). The red stars, none of which are very bright, and most of which are variable, form the last type.

It appears that the stars can be arranged in classes corresponding to diminishing temperatures. The hottest stars have extensive hydrogen atmospheres, simple in constitution. They are analogous to nebulæ in many respects and probably are condensed from nebulous masses. As a star grows older and cooler its spectrum grows more unlike a nebulous spectrum, more complex, more individual, so to speak. After passing through a stage like that of our Sun it reaches the stage of pronounced variability, like the red stars, and finally becomes a "dark star" like the companion to *Algol*, for example.

Stellar Evolution: An irregular and widely extended nebula subject to gravitating forces tends to become a spherical mass ; spherical masses of nebulosity subject to central powers tend to become more condensed and to form nuclei at their centres. It appears to be likely that such nebulæ may condense still further into stars. Stars very hot and white go through a cycle of changes, and after losing all their light and heat become "dark stars." This is, in general, the final stage. If, however, two stellar systems moving through space should collide, all the bodies of both systems would be quickly raised to very high temperatures, and in this way a "dark star" might be re-created and begin a new cycle of existence. If a dark star like the Earth, for example, were to be suddenly raised to a very high temperature it would become a gaseous body—a miniature Sun, for example. It is probable that the phenomena of some of the "new stars" are to be explained in this way.

Motion of Stars in the Line of Sight.—Spectroscopic observations of stars not only give information in regard to their chemical and physical constitution, but have been applied so as to determine approximately the velocity in miles per second with which the stars are approaching to or receding from the Earth along the line joining Earth and star (the line of sight). The theory of such a determination is briefly as follows:

In the solar spectrum we find a group of dark lines, as a, b, c, which always maintain their relative position. From laboratory experiments, we can show that the three bright lines of incandescent hydrogen (for example) have always the same relative position as the solar dark lines a, b, c. From this it is inferred that the solar dark lines are due to the presence of hydrogen in the absorptive atmosphere of the Sun.

Now, suppose that in a stellar spectrum we find three dark lines, a', b', c', whose relative position is exactly the same as that of the solar lines a, b, c. Not only is their relative position the same, but the characters of the lines themselves, so far as the fainter spectrum of the star will allow us to determine them, are also similar ; that is, a' and a, b' and b, c' and c are alike as to thickness, blackness, nebulosity of edges, etc., etc. From this it is inferred that the star contains in its atmosphere the substance whose existence has been shown in the Sun—hydrogen, for example.

If we contrive an apparatus by which the stellar spectrum is seen in the lower half, say, of the eyepiece of the spectroscope, while the spectrum of hydrogen is seen just above it, we find in some cases this remarkable phenomenon. The three dark stellar lines, a', b', c', instead of being exactly coincident with the three hydrogen lines a, b, c, are seen to be all thrown to one side or the other by a like amount ; that is, the whole group a', b', c', while preserving its relative distances the same as those of the comparison group a, b, c, is shifted toward either the violet or red end of the spectrum by a small yet measurable amount. Repeated experiments by different instruments and observers always show a shifting in the same direction, and of like amount. The figure shows a shifting of the F line in the spectrum of *Sirius*, compared with one fixed line of hydrogen. The bright line of hydrogen is nearer to one side of the dark line in the stellar spectrum than to the other.

This displacement of the spectral lines is accounted for by a motion of the star toward or from the Earth. It is shown in Physics that if the source of the light which gives the spectrum a', b', c' is moving away from the Earth, this group will be shifted toward the red end of the spectrum ; if toward the Earth, then the whole group will be shifted toward the blue end. The amount of this shifting depends upon the velocity of recession or approach, and this velocity in miles per second can be calculated from the measured displacement. This has already been done for many stars.

The principle upon which the calculation is made can be understood by an analogy drawn from the phenomena of sound. Every one who has ridden in a railway train has noticed that the bell of a passing engine does not always give out the same note. As the two trains approach the sound of the bell is pitched higher, and as they separate after passing the sound of the bell is lower. It is certain that the driver of the passing engine always hears his bell give out one and the same note. The explanation of this phenomenon is as follows: the bell of the passing engine gives out the note

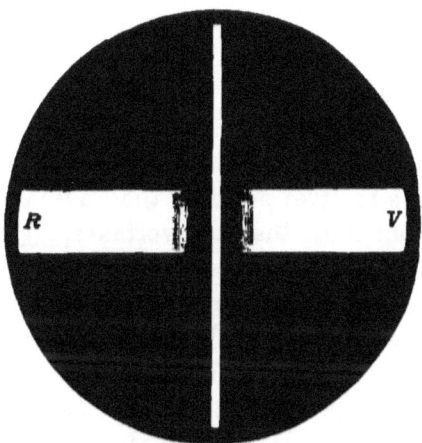

Fig. 210.—*F* Line of Hydrogen Superposed on the Spectrum of Sirius (*VR*).

C (the middle *C* of the pianoforte) let us say. That is it gives out 512 vibrations, sound-waves, in every second. Any sonorous body giving out 512 waves per second makes the note *C*. If more than 512 sound-waves reach the ear in a second the note is higher—*C♯* for example. If fewer than 512 waves reach the ear in a second the note is lower —*C♭* for example. The engineer hears 512 vibrations every second. The note of his bell is *C♮*. All the air around him is filled with sound-waves of this frequency.

The traveller *approaching* the bell hears the 512 vibrations given out by the bell every second, and also other vibrations that his swiftly moving train meets—the note of the bell to him is $C\sharp$ let us say, because his ear collects more than 512 vibrations every second. The traveller *receding* from the bell hears fewer than 512 vibrations per second. Not all of the waves given out by the bell can overtake him as he moves swiftly away—the note of the bell is to him $C\flat$—let us say.

The case is the same for light-waves. The F line of hydrogen gives out in the laboratory a certain number of waves per second. If a star is at rest with respect to the Earth just as many waves reach the observer's eye from the F line *of the star* as reach it from the F line of a comparison-spectrum of hydrogen. Both sources of light are at rest with respect to him. If he is moving swiftly towards the star his eye receives not only the waves sent out by the star, but also all those that he overtakes. If he is moving swiftly away from the star his eye receives fewer waves than the star sends out because not all of them can overtake him. (It is as if the $F\natural$ of the star became $F\sharp$ in one case, $F\flat$ in the other.) A shifting of the star-line towards the violet end of the spectrum indicates an approach of the Earth to the star; a shifting towards the red end indicates a recession. The velocity of the motion of approach or recession is proportional to the amount of the shifting. It is by a principle of this kind that we can calculate from the observed shifting of lines in the stellar spectrum the velocity with which the Earth is approaching a star, or receding from it.

Motion of the Solar System in Space.—If observation shows that the Earth is approaching a star at the rate of 40 miles per second, we know that the Sun and all the planets must be moving towards that star, since the Earth moves in her orbit only 18 miles per second. By making

allowance for the Earth's motion, the exact velocity of the
Sun towards the star can be calculated. The Sun carries
all his family—all the planets—with him as he moves
through space. Astronomers are now engaged in solving,
by spectroscopic means, the problem of how fast the solar
system is moving in space, and in what direction it is
moving.

The method employed is somewhat as follows : A large
number of stars is spectroscopically observed and the velocity with which the Sun is approaching each separate
star is accurately determined.

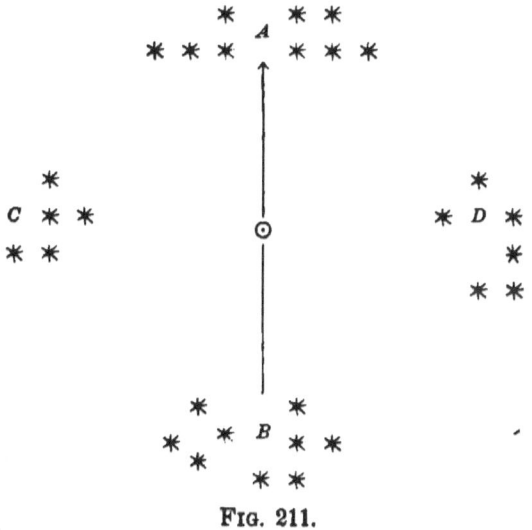

Fig. 211.

Suppose the observations to show that the Sun (⊙) is *approaching* the group of stars *A* with an average velocity of
12 miles per second; that it is *receding* from the group of
stars *B* (180° away from *A*—opposite to *A* in the celestial
sphere) at the same velocity; then it follows that the Sun
with the whole solar system is moving through space towards *A* with a velocity of 12 miles per second.

Some of the stars of group *A* may be moving towards the Sun; some of them may be moving away from the Sun; if a great many stars are contained in the group their average motion with respect to the Sun will be zero: there is no reason to suppose that stars in general have any tendency to move towards our Sun or away from it. Groups of stars at *C* and *D* and all around the celestial sphere are observed in the same way, and the final result is made to depend on all the observed velocities. Researches like this are in progress at Potsdam, Paris, at the Lick Observatory, and elsewhere. Final conclusions have not yet been reached. All that can now be said is that the solar system is moving towards a point *near* to the bright star *Alpha Lyræ* with a velocity of *about* 12 miles per second. It will require some years yet to reach final values. So far as we know the solar motion is uniform and in a straight line.

CHAPTER XXVIII

COSMOGONY.

47. A theory of the operations by which the physical universe received its present form and arrangement is called *Cosmogony*. This subject does not treat of the origin of matter, but only of its transformations.

Three systems of Cosmogony have prevailed at different times:

(1) That the universe had no beginning, but existed from eternity in the form in which we now see it. This was the view of the ancients.

(2) That it was created in its present shape in six days. This view is based on the literal sense of the words of the Old Testament. Theological commentators have assumed that it was created "out of nothing," but the Scripture does not say so.

(3) That it came into its present form through an arrangement of previously existing materials which were before "without form and void." This may be called the evolution theory. No attempt is made to explain the origin of the primitive matter. The theory simply deals with its arrangement and changes.

The scientific discoveries of modern times show conclusively that the universe could not always have existed in its present form; that there was a time when the materials composing it were masses of glowing vapor, and that there will be a time when the present state of things will cease. Geology proves beyond a doubt, that the arrangement of the primitive matter to form a habitable Earth has required millions of years, and Anthropology proves also beyond a doubt, that the Earth has been inhabited by men for many thousands. It was not until the latter half of the XVIII century that such opinions could be held without fear of persecution, for the lesson " that a scientific fact is as sacred as a moral principle " has only been fully learned within the last half century.

An explanation of the processes through which the Earth and all the planets came into their present forms was first propounded by the philosophers SWEDENBORG, KANT, and LAPLACE, and, although since greatly modified in detail, their fundamental views are, in the main, received. The nebular hypotheses proposed by these philosophers all start with the statement that the Earth and Planets, as well as the Sun, were once a fiery mass.

It is certain that the Earth has not received any great supply of heat from outside since the early geological ages, because such an accession of heat at the Earth's surface would have destroyed all life, and even melted all the rocks. Therefore, whatever heat there is in the *interior* of the Earth must have been there from before the commencement of life on the globe, and remained through all geological ages.

The interior of the Earth is very much hotter than its surface, and hotter than the celestial spaces around it. It is continually losing heat, and there is no way in which the losses are made up. We know by the most familiar observation that if any object is hot inside, the heat will work its way through to the surface. Therefore, since the Earth is a great deal hotter at the depth of 50 miles than it is at the surface, and much hotter at 500 miles than at 50, heat must be continually coming to the surface. On reaching the surface, it must be radiated off into space, else the surface would have long ago become as hot as the interior.

Moreover, this loss of heat must have been going on since the beginning, or at least since a time when the surface was as hot as the interior. Thus, if we reckon backward in time, we find that there must have been more and more heat in the Earth the further back we go, so that we reach a time when the Earth was so hot as to be molten, and finally reach a time when it was so hot as to be a mass of fiery vapor.

The Sun is cooling off like the Earth, only at an incomparably more rapid rate. The Sun is constantly radiating heat into space, and, so far as we know, receiving none back again. A very small portion of this heat reaches the Earth, and on this portion depends the existence of life and motion on the Earth's surface. If our supply of solar heat were to be taken away, all life on the Earth would cease. The quantity of heat which strikes the Earth is only about $\frac{1}{2000000000}$ of that which the Sun radiates. This fraction expresses the ratio of the apparent surface of the Earth, as seen from the Sun, to that of the whole celestial sphere.

Since the Sun is constantly losing heat, it must have had more heat yesterday than it has to-day ; more two days ago than it had yesterday; and so on. The further we go back in time, the hotter the Sun must have been. Since we know that heat expands all bodies, it follows that the Sun must have been larger in past ages than it is now, and we can calculate the size of the Sun at any past time.

Thus we are led to the conclusion that there must have been a time when the Sun filled up the whole of the space now occupied by the planets. It must then have been a very rare mass of glowing vapor. The planets could not then have existed separately, but must have formed a part of this mass of vapor. The glowing vapor—"a fiery mist"—was the material out of which the solar system was formed.

The same process may be continued into the future. Since the Sun by its radiation is constantly losing heat, it must grow cooler and cooler as ages advance, and must finally radiate so little heat that life and motion can no longer exist on our globe.

It is a noteworthy confirmation of this hypothesis that the revolutions of all the planets around the Sun take place in the same direction and in nearly the same plane. This similarity among the different bodies of the solar system must have had an adequate cause. The Sun and planets were once a great mass of vapor, larger than the present solar system, that revolved on its axis in the same plane in which the planets now revolve.

The spectroscope shows the nebulæ to be masses of glowing vapor. We thus actually see matter in the celestial spaces under the very form in which the nebular hypothesis supposes the matter of our solar system to have once existed. Some of these nebulæ now have the very form that the nebular hypothesis assigns to the solar nebula in past ages. (See the frontispiece.) The nebulæ are gradually cooling. The process of cooling must at length reach a point when they will cease to be vaporous and will condense into objects like stars and planets. All the stars must, like the Sun, be radiating heat into space.

The telescopic examination of the planets *Jupiter* and *Saturn* shows that changes on their surfaces are constantly going on with a rapidity and violence to which nothing on the surface of our Earth can compare. Such operations can be kept up only through the agency of heat or some equivalent form of energy. At the distance of *Jupiter* and *Saturn*, the rays of the Sun are entirely insufficient to produce such changes. *Jupiter* and *Saturn* must be hot bodies, and must therefore be cooling off like the Sun, stars, and Earth.

These and many other allied facts lead to the conclusion that most bodies of the universe are hot, and are cooling off by radiating their heat into space.

There is no way known to us in which the heat radiated by the Sun and stars might be collected and returned to them. It is a fundamental principle of the laws of heat that " heat can never pass from a cooler to a warmer body "—that a body can never grow warmer in a space that is cooler than the body itself.

All differences of temperature tend to equalize themselves, and the only state of things to which the universe can tend, under its present laws, is one in which all space and all the bodies contained in space will be at a uniform temperature, and then all motion and change of temperature, and hence the conditions of vitality, must cease. And then all such life as ours must cease also unless sustained by entirely new methods.

The general result drawn from all these laws and facts is, that there was once a time when all the bodies of the universe formed either a single mass or a number of masses of fiery vapor, having slight motions in various parts, and different degrees of density in different regions. A gradual condensation around the centres of greatest density then took place in consequence of the cooling and the mutual attraction of the parts, and thus arose a number of separate nebulous masses. One of these masses formed the material out of which the Sun and planets are supposed to have been formed. It was probably at first nearly globular, of nearly equal density throughout, and endowed with a very slow rotation in the direction in which the planets now move. As it cooled off, it grew smaller and smaller, and its velocity of rotation increased in rapidity.

The rotating mass we have described had an axis around which it rotated, and an equator everywhere 90° from this axis. As the velocity of rotation increased, the centrifugal force also increased. This force varies as the radius of the circle described by any particle multiplied by the square of its angular velocity. Hence when the masses, being reduced to half the radius, rotated four times as fast, the centrifugal force at the equator would be increased $\frac{1}{2} \times 4^2$, or eight times. The gravitation of the mass at the surface, being inversely as the square of the distance from the centre, or of the radius, would be increased only four times. Therefore, as the masses continued to contract, the centrifugal force increased more rapidly than the central attraction. A time would therefore come when they would balance each other at the equator of the mass.

The mass would then cease to contract at the equator, but at the poles there would be no centrifugal force, and the gravitation of the mass would grow stronger and stronger in this neighborhood.

In consequence the mass would at length assume the form of a lens or disk very thin in proportion to its extent. The denser portions of this lens would gradually be drawn toward the centre, and there more or less solidified by cooling. At length, solid particles would begin to be formed throughout the whole disk. These would gradually condense around each other and form a single planet, or break up into small masses and form a group of planets. As the motion of rotation would not be altered by these processes of condensation, these planets would all rotate around the central part of the mass, which condensed to form our Sun.

These planetary masses, being very hot, were composed of a central mass of those substances which condensed at a very high temperature, surrounded by the vapors of other substances which were more volatile. We know, for instance, that it takes a much higher temperature to reduce lime and platinum to vapor than it does to reduce iron, zinc, or magnesium. Therefore, in the original planets, the limes and earths would condense first, while many other metals would still remain in a state of vapor.

Each of the planetary masses would rotate more rapidly as it grew smaller, and would at length form a mass of melted metals and vapors in the same way as the larger mass out of which the Sun and planets were formed. These separate masses would then condense into a planet, with satellites revolving around it, just as the original mass condensed into Sun and planets.

At first the planets would be in a molten condition, each shining like the Sun. They would, however, slowly cool by the radiation of heat from their surfaces. So long as they remained liquid, the surface, as fast as it grew cool, would sink into the interior on account of its greater specific gravity, and its place would be taken by hotter material rising from the interior to the surface, there to cool off in its turn.

There would, in fact, be a motion something like that which occurs when a pot of cold water is set upon the fire to boil. Whenever a mass of water at the bottom of the pot is heated, it rises to the surface, and the cool water moves down to take its place. Thus, on the whole, so long as the planet remained liquid, it would cool off equally throughout its whole mass, owing to the constant motion from the centre to the circumference and back again.

A time would at length arrive when many of the earths and metals would begin to solidify. At first the solid particles would be carried up and down with the liquid. A time would finally arrive when they would become so large and numerous, and the liquid part of the general mass so viscid, that their motion would be obstructed. The planet would then begin to solidify. Two views have been entertained respecting the process of solidification.

According to one view, the whole surface of the planet would solidify into a continuous crust, as ice forms over a pond in cold weather, while the interior was still in a molten state. The interior liquid could then no longer come to the surface to cool off, and could lose no heat except what was conducted through this crust. Hence the subsequent cooling would be much slower, and the globe would long remain a mass of lava, covered over by a comparatively thin solid crust like that on which we live.

The other view is that, when the cooling attained a certain stage, the central portion of the globe would be solidified by the enormous pressure of the superincumbent portions, while the exterior was still fluid, and that thus the solidification would take place from the centre outward.

It is still an unsettled question whether the Earth is now solid to its centre, or whether it is a great globe of molten matter with a comparatively thin crust. Astronomers and physicists incline to the former view ; some geologists to the latter one. Whichever view may be correct, it appears certain that there are lakes of lava immediately beneath the active volcanoes.

It must be understood that the nebular hypothesis is not a perfectly established scientific theory, but only a philosophical conclusion founded on the widest study of nature, and supported by many otherwise disconnected facts. The widest generalization associated with it is that, so far as can now be known, the universe is not self-sustaining, but is a kind of organism which, like all other organisms known to us, must come to an end in consequence of those very laws of action which keep it going. It must have had a beginning within a certain number of years that cannot yet be calculated with certainty, but which cannot in any event much exceed 20,000,000, and it must end in a system of cold, dead globes at a calculable time in the future, when the Sun and stars shall have radiated away all their heat, unless it is re-created by the action of forces at present unknown to science.

It must be carefully noted that these conclusions, which are correct in the main, relate entirely to the *transformations* of matter in the past and future time, and say nothing as to its *origin*. The original nebula must have contained all the matter now in the universe, and it must have possessed, potentially, all the energy now operative as light, heat, etc., besides the vast stores of energy that have been expended in past ages. The process by which the *physical* universe was transformed from one condition to a later one is the subject of the nebular hypothesis. The field of physical science is a limited one, although within that field it deals with profound problems. Astronomy has nothing to say on the question of the origin of matter nor on the vastly more important questions as to the origin of life, intelligence, wisdom, affection.

CHAPTER XXIX.

PRACTICAL HINTS ON OBSERVING.

48. A few Practical Hints on Making Observations.— Lists of a few Interesting Celestial Objects.—Stars, Double Stars, Variable Stars, Nabulæ, Clusters.—Maps of the Stars. —In the paragraphs that follow a few hints are given for the benefit of the student who wishes to begin to make simple observations for himself. Long and detailed instructions might be set down which would perhaps save many mistakes. But it is by mistakes made and corrected that one learns. A genius is a person who never makes the same mistake twice. The rest of mankind must educate themselves by slow and patient correction of the errors they commit. Therefore only enough is here set down to start the student on his way. It will depend on himself and his opportunities how far he goes.

Observations of the Planets.—The accurate places of the planets are printed in the *Nautical Almanac* (address Nautical Almanac office, Navy Department, Washington, D. C.); and many other almanacs give their approximate positions. The *Publications of the Astronomical Society of the Pacific* (address 819 Market Street, San Francisco), and the journal *Popular Astronomy* (address Northfield, Minnesota), contain such information, in a form useful to amateurs. Lists of the eclipses of each year, and of morning and evening stars, are printed in most diaries, as well as the phases of the Moon, and the hours of sunrise and moonrise, etc. The daily newspapers frequently print articles naming the planets and stars that are in a favorable position for observation.

Mercury is often to be seen, if one knows just where to look. Its greatest elongation from the Sun is about 29°, so that it is seldom visible in our latitudes more than two hours after sunset, or before sun rise. The student will do well to know its place (from some almanac) before looking for it, so that no time may be lost in discovering this planet over again. The greatest elongation of *Venus* from the Sun is about 45°, so that this planet is usually not visible more than about three hours after sunset, or before sunrise. In a clear sky, however, *Venus* may be seen in the daytime, if the position is known. *Mars* is easy to distinguish from the other planets by his ruddy color. *Jupiter* is the planet next in brightness to *Venus*, and both *Jupiter* and *Venus* are brighter than the most brilliant fixed star—*Sirius*. The place of *Sirius* in the sky can be found on any one of the star-maps, and hence *Sirius* can always be distinguished from the planets. *Saturn* looks like a rather dull (not sparkling) fixed star. These are the planets easily visible to the naked eye. If the student finds a bright object in the sky, he can decide from the star-maps whether it is a fixed star. If it is not a star, it will not be difficult for him to determine which of the planets he has found. *Uranus* is occasionally (just) visible to the naked eye, but *Neptune* always is invisible, except in a telescope. At least one of the asteroids (*Vesta*) is sometimes visible to the naked eye.

The motions of the planets may be studied with the unaided eye, but nothing can be known of their disks or of their phases without a telescope. An opera-glass (which usually magnifies about 2 or 3 times) or, better, a field-glass, will be of much use in viewing the Moon, and if nothing better is available it should be used to view the planets. But even a small telescope is much more satisfactory.

The student must not expect to see the planetary disks as they are shown in the drawings of this book. These drawings have usually been made with large telescopes. Even under very favorable conditions such observations are more or less disappointing to observers who are not practised.

Observations of Stars, Nebulæ, Comets, etc.—The brighter stars can be identified in the sky from the star-maps in this book. Some of the variable stars and clusters are marked in Fig. 213. Tables V to VIII (pages 417 to 421) give the places of some of the principal fixed stars, double-stars, etc. These objects (if they are bright enough) should first be identified with the naked eye and then studied with the best telescope available. An opera-glass is better than nothing; a good field-glass or a spy-glass is better yet (it represents GALILEO'S equipment), but a telescope of several inches aperture with a magnifying power of 50 diameters or more, on a firm stand, should be used if it is possible to obtain it.

Photography in observation.—If the student understands photography let him try his camera on the heavens. If he directs it to the north pole and gives an exposure of a couple of hours he will obtain the *trails* of the brighter circumpolar stars (see Fig. 29). An exposure of a few minutes on a bright group of stars near the zenith or in the south (the *Pleiades* or *Orion*, for example) will give trails of a different kind (see Fig. 30). In both these observations the camera must remain fixed, undisturbed by wind or jars of any kind.

If he can strap his camera to the tube of a telescope (like that shown in Fig. 79) he can follow a group of stars in their motion from rising to setting by using the telescope as a finder in the following way: I. Select the group to be photographed. It should be visible in the camera and some bright star of the group should be visible in the telescope at the same time. The eyepiece of the telescope should be provided with a pair of cross wires, thus +, which the observer can easily insert, if necessary. II. The image of one of the group of stars must be kept on the cross-wires (by gently and constantly moving the telescope from east towards west—from rising toward setting) so long as the exposure is going on. In this way fairly long exposures can be made. If the image of the guiding-star is put slightly out of focus the guiding is sometimes easier. This method is also available for photographing a bright comet; only the student must remember to use the comet itself as a guiding-star (in the telescope), because the comet has a motion among the stars. Photographs of the Moon (and Sun) can be made with small cameras, but unless the camera has a long focus they are disappointingly small in size. Let the student try to make them, however. For the Moon, use the quickest plates. For the Sun, use the slowest plates, the smallest stop and the quickest exposure. In these, as in all observations, the important matter to the student is to *make* them and to find out what is wrong; and then to make them over again, correcting mistakes; and so on until a satisfactory result is obtained.

It is desirable that the school should own apparatus to be used by the students under the direction of the master. A short list follows: A celestial globe; a cheap watch regulated to sidereal time; a straightedge some three feet long; a plumb-line; a field-glass; a small telescope; a star-atlas (UPTON'S, McCLURE'S edition of KLEIN'S, PROCTOR'S, are good); books on practical Astronomy (begin with SERVISS' Astronomy with an Opera-Glass, PROCTOR'S Half Hours with the Stars, J. WESTWOOD OLIVER'S Astronomy for Amateurs, WEBB'S Celestial Objects for Common Telescopes, and add to these as needs arise); books on descriptive Astronomy (begin with the works of Sir ROBERT BULL, Miss CLERKE'S History of Astronomy in the XIX Century, FLAMMARION'S Popular Astronomy, etc., and add to these as opportunity offers); text-books of Astronomy (begin with YOUNG's General Astronomy).

TABLE V.

MEAN RIGHT ASCENSION AND DECLINATION OF A FEW BRIGHT STARS, VISIBLE AT WASHINGTON, FOR JANUARY 1, 1899.

NAME OF STAR.	Mag.	Right Ascension.			Annual Varia-tion.	Declination.			Annual Varia-tion.
		h.	m.	s.	s.	°	′	″	″
α Andromedæ..................	2	0	3	9.9	+ 3.06	+ 28	31	58	+ 20.1
α Cassiopeiæ............*Var.*	2½	0	34	46.3	+ 3.37	+ 55	59	0	+ 19.8
β Ceti	2	0	38	31.2	+ 3.00	− 18	32	28	+ 19.8
α Ursæ Minoris (*Pole Star*)...	2	1	22	8.0	−24.99	+ 88	46	8	+ 18.8
β Arietis	3	1	49	3.5	+ 3.30	+ 20	18	52	+ 17.8
α Arietis....................	2	2	1	28.7	+ 3.36	+ 22	59	6	+ 17.3
α Ceti......................	2½	2	56	59.9	+ 3.13	+ 3	41	36	+ 14.4
α Persei....................	2	3	17	6.5	+ 4.26	+ 49	30	6	+ 13.1
η Tauri	3	3	41	28.7	+ 3.56	+ 23	47	34	+ 11.4
γ¹ Eridani................	3	3	53	18.9	+ 2.79	− 13	47	45	+ 10.5
α Tauri (*Aldebaran*)........	1	4	30	7.4	+ 3.43	+ 16	18	23	+ 7.7
ι Aurigæ	2½	4	50	24.9	+ 3.90	+ 33	0	23	+ 6.0
α Aurigæ (*Capella*)	1	5	9	13.5	+ 4.42	+ 45	53	43	+ 4.4
β Orionis (*Rigel*)....	1	5	9	41.0	+ 2.88	− 8	19	5	+ 4.4
β Tauri...	2	5	19	54.4	+ 3.79	+ 28	31	20	+ 3.5
δ Orionis................	2½	5	26	50.7	+ 3.06	− 0	22	26	+ 2.9
α Leporis	2½	5	28	16.5	+ 2.65	− 17	53	41	+ 2.8
ε Orionis.................	2	5	31	5.3	+ 3 04	− 1	15	59	+ 2.5
α Columbæ	2½	5	35	59.5	+ 2.17	− 34	7	40	+ 2.1
α Orionis	1	5	49	42.2	+ 3.25	+ 7	23	18	+ 0.9
γ Geminorum	2	6	31	52.6	+ 3.46	+ 16	29	8	− 2.8
α Canis Majoris (*Sirius*)......	1	6	40	41.9	+ 2.68	− 16	34	41.	− 3.5
ε Canis Majoris	1½	6	54	39.3	+ 2.36	− 28	50	4	− 4.7
α² Geminorum (*Castor*)	2	7	28	9.4	+ 3.85	+ 32	6	36	− 7.5
α Canis Minoris (*Procyon*)....	1	7	34	1.0	+ 3.19	+ 5	29	3	− 8.0
β Geminorum (*Pollux*)........	1	7	39	8.2	+ 3.73	+ 28	16	12	− 8.4
15 Argûs	3	8	3	14.5	+ 2.56	− 24	0	48	− 10.3
ι Ursæ Majoris..............	3	8	52	17.7	+ 4.17	+ 48	26	18	− 13.7
α Hydræ	2	9	22	37.4	+ 2.95	− 8	13	15	− 15.5
θ Ursæ Majoris...........	3	9	26	6.3	+ 4.14	+ 52	8	15	− 15.7
α Leonis (*Regulus*)......	1	10	2	59.6	+ 3.22	+ 12	27	39	− 17.5
γ¹ Leonis	2½	10	14	24.3	+ 3.39	+ 20	21	9	− 18.0
α Ursæ Majoris...........	2	10	57	29.8	+ 3.76	+ 62	17	46	− 19.3
β Leonis	2	11	43	54.5	+ 3.10	+ 15	8	12	− 20.0
γ Ursæ Majoris...........	2½	11	48	31.2	+ 3.17	+ 54	15	23	− 20.0
ε Corvi....................	3	12	4	55.7	+ 3.08	− 22	3	30	− 20.0
β Corvi....................	3	12	29	4.8	+ 3.14	− 22	50	18	− 19.9
α Canum Venaticorum.	3	12	51	18.2	+ 2.83	+ 38	51	50	− 19.6
α Virginis (*Spica*).........	1	13	19	52.2	+ 3.16	− 10	38	3	− 18.8
η Ursæ Majoris............	2	13	43	33.7	+ 2.38	+ 49	49	2	− 18.0
α Boötis (*Arcturus*).........	1	14	11	3.2	+ 2.81	+ 19	42	30	− 16.9
α Libræ	3	14	45	17.3	+ 3.32	− 15	37	20	− 15.1
β Ursæ Minoris............	2	14	50	59.7	− 0.21	+ 74	34	6	− 14.7
β Libræ	2½	15	11	34.2	+ 3.23	− 9	0	38	− 13.4
α Coronæ Borealis...	2½	15	30	24.6	+ 2.53	+ 27	3	16	− 12.2
α Serpentis ..... .,........	2½	15	33	17.5	+ 2.94	+ 6	44	36	− 11.6
β¹ Scorpii..................	3	15	59	33.7	+ 3.48	− 19	31	45	− 10.1
η Draconis.................	3	16	22	37.4	+ 0.81	+ 61	44	34	− 8.3
α Scorpii (*Antares*)...........	1	16	23	12.7	+ 3.67	− 26	12	28	− 8.2
α¹ Herculis...	3½	17	10	2.5	+ 2.74	+ 14	30	19	− 4.3
β Draconis	3	17	28	9.0	+ 1.36	+ 52	22	34	− 2.8

TABLE V.—*Continued.*

Name of Star.	Mag.	Right Ascension.			Annual Variation.	Declination.			Annual Variation.
		h.	m.	s.	s.	°	′	″	″
α Ophiuchi	2	17	30	14.7	+ 2.78	+ 12	38	0	− 2.6
α Lyræ (*Vega*)	1	18	33	31.1	+ 2.01	+ 38	41	22	+ 2.9
β¹ Lyræ (*var.*)	3½–4½	18	46	21.0	+ 2.21	+ 33	14	43	+ 4.0
α Aquilæ (*Altair*)	1	19	45	51.3	+ 2.89	+ 8	36	5	+ 8.9
α Cygni	1½	20	37	59.3	+ 2.04	+ 44	55	9	+ 12.8
α Cephei	2½	21	16	10.1	+ 1.41	+ 62	9	27	+ 15.1
β Aquarii	3	21	26	14.5	+ 3.16	− 6	0	56	+ 15.7
α Aquarii	3	22	0	35.7	+ 3.06	− 0	46	38	+ 17.4
α PiscisAustralis(*Fomalhaut*)	1½	22	52	4.1	+ 3.30	− 30	9	27	+ 19.3
α Pegasi (*Markab*)	2½	22	59	43.7	+ 2.98	+ 14	39	42	+ 19.4
ω Piscium	4	23	54	7.4	+ 3.07	+ 6	18	15	+ 20.0

N.B.—The Mean Right Ascension and Declination for any other year than 1899 may be found from this table by multiplying the annual variation by the number of years elapsed, and applying the result to the quantities given in this table. If the required date be *earlier* than 1899, the *signs* of the annual variations must be changed. In applying such corrections to the Declinations the corrections must be added *algebraically.* For example, the mean place of *Aldebaran* for July 1, 1901 (= 1901.5) is R. A. 4ʰ 30ᵐ 16ˢ.0 Decl. + 16° 18′ 42″.

N.B.—The *Nautical Almanac* gives the *apparent* R.A.'s of these and other stars at intervals of ten days.

N.B.—When any one of these stars is on the observer's meridian at any date, his local sidereal time is equal to that star's apparent right ascension on that date.

The foregoing table will serve to set the observer's watch to sidereal time within a few minutes so soon as he knows his meridian (see page 151). A watch set approximately to sidereal time is, of course, necessary in identifying objects in the sky.

TABLE VI.

LIST OF A FEW DOUBLE STARS, MOST OF WHICH ARE OBSERVABLE IN SMALL TELESCOPES.

Name.	R. A.	Declination	Magnitudes.	Position Angle.	Distance.	Remarks.
35 *Piscium*	0ʰ 9ᵐ	+ 8° 9′	6 and 6	150°	12″	An 8 mag. star also.
38 "	0 11	+ 8 12	7½ " 7½	240	4	
η *Cassiopeiæ*	0 42	+ 57 11	4 " 7½	147	6	The colors are yellow and blue.
Polaris	1 15	+ 88 40	2 " 9½	212	19	
γ *Arietis*	1 47	+ 18 42	4 " 4	0	8	
α *Piscium*	1 56	+ 2 11	5 " 6	325	3½	
ε *Trianguli*	2 5	+ 29 44	5 " 7	74	3½	
P. * 2 *Cassiopeiæ*	2 9	+ 66 52	5 " 8	108	8	The 8th mag. star is a double, distance 2″.
γ *Ceti*	2 37	+ 2 44	3½ " 7	290	3	
7 *Camelopardalis*	4 48	+ 53 33	4 " 11	239	27	The principal star is a close double, 4 and 8 mags., distance 1″.
δ *Orionis*	5 26	− 0 23	2 " 7	0	53	
11 *Monocerotis*	6 23	− 6 57	5 " 6½	131	7	Triple star.
α *Geminorum (Castor)*	7 27	+ 32 9	3 " 3½	124	9½	A beautiful object for small telescopes.
ε *Hydræ*	8 40	+ 6 51	3 " 8	230	5½	Binary, period 60 years, maximum distance = 3″.
35 *Sextantis*	10 37	+ 5 23	7 " 8	240	3	Colors, orange and lilac.
ζ *Ursæ Majoris*	11 12	+ 32 12	7 " 8	......	20	The middle star of the handle of the Great Dipper. Another star (*Alcor*) near by.
24 *Comæ Berenices*	12 29	+ 19 12	5½ " 7	271	......	A very interesting group.
ξ *Ursæ Majoris*	13 19	+ 55 33	3 " 5	147	14	Binary star.
44 *Boötis*	15 0	+ 48 7	5 " 6	240	5	Fine colors.
α *Herculis*	17 9	+ 14 32	3½ " 5½	119	4½	The naked eye can just see this star as two stars A and B about 3′ apart. Both A and B are double, distance about 3″.
ε *Lyræ*	18 40	+ 39 33			3	Beautiful colors.
β *Cygni*	19 26	+ 27 42	3 " 7	56	34	
γ *Delphini*	20 41	+ 15 42	4 " 5	273	12	
ζ *Aquarii*	22 23	− 0 38	4 " 4	326	3	
σ *Cassiopeiæ*	23 53	+ 55 6	5½ " 7½	324	3	

N.B.—A few of these objects are difficult in small telescopes, but most of them are easy. All are interesting on one account or another.

TABLE VII.

A LIST OF A FEW VARIABLE STARS.

STAR.	R. A.		Decl.		Period.	Magnitude.		Remarks.
						Max.	Min.	
	h	m	°	′	Days.			
Mira Ceti......	2	14	− 3	26	331	1.7	9.5 }	It is best seen about October.
Algol (β Persei).	3	2	+ 40	34	2⅞	2.3	3.5 }	Observe it in October & November.
ε *Aurigæ*	4	55	+ 43	41	?	3	4.5 }	Irregular. Of the Algol type.
ζ *Geminorum*	6	58	+ 20	43	10	3.7	4.5	
R *Leonis*	9	42	+ 11	54	313	5.2	10	
R *Ursæ Majoris*..	10	38	+ 69	18	305	6	13	
R *Hydræ*	13	24	− 22	46	497	3.5	9.7	
α *Herculis*.........	17	10	+ 14	30	90?	3.1	3.9	Irregular period.
X *Sagittarii.*	17	41	− 27	48	7	4	6	Observe it in June.
β *Lyræ*	18	46	+ 33	15	12.9	3.4	4.5 }	Observe it at mid-summer.
δ *Cephei*	22	25	+ 57	54	5⅜	3.7	4.9 }	Observe it in Aug. and September.
R *Cassiopeiæ*... ..	23	53	+ 50	50	429	5	12	

TABLE VIII.

LIST OF A FEW OF THE BRIGHTER NEBULÆ AND CLUSTERS OF STARS.

No. in New General Catalogue	Position 1890. R.A. (H. M.)	Position 1890. Declination	Brief Description of the Object.
224	0 36.7	+40 32	Great nebula in Andromeda. Visible to the naked eye.
288	0 47.3	-27 11	Globular cluster. Stars 12-16 mag.
598	1 27.6	+30 5	Bright and exceedingly large. West of α Trianguli.
650	1 35.4	+51 1	Very bright, double nebula. Near θ Andromedæ.
869	2 9.9	+56 33	Very large cluster. Stars 7 to 14 mag. }
884	2 13.3	+56 31	Large cluster.
1952	5 27.9	+21 56	The "Crab" nebula near ζ Tauri. Resolvable into stars, with large telescopes.
1976	5 29.9	-5 28	Great nebula surrounding θ Orionis.
2168	8 45.9	+34 3	Bright and large Elliptical.
3031	9 46.5	+69 35	Exceedingly bright and large. }
3034	9 46.7	+70 13	A bright ray.
3242	10 18.5	-17 59	Very bright planetary nebula. 45" diameter. Blue.
3587	10 19.5	-18 5	Bright. Planetary nebula. 45" diameter. Blue.
3627	11 8.4	+55 37	Fine planetary nebula. Near β Ursæ Majoris. Diameter 3'. "The owl nebula."
4254	12 14.5	+13 36	Large elliptical nebula near β Leonis.
4321	12 13.3	+15 2	Very fine spiral nebula with 3 branches.
4472	12 17.4	+16 26	Very fine spiral nebula with 2 branches.
4486	12 24.2	+8 37	Bright, round nebula. Resolvable into stars.
4565	12 25.6	+12 58	Very bright and large. much brighter in centre.
4590	12 30.9	+28 36	A ray of bright nebulosity.
5194	12 33.7	-26 9	Compressed globular cluster. Stars 12th magnitude.
5236	13 25.2	+47 46	Spiral nebula. Double. Near η Ursæ Majoris.
5272	13 30.8	+29 18	Large and bright, spiral nebula. With 3 branches.
5904	13 37.1	+28 56	Globular cluster, visible to naked eye. 7' diameter.
5907	15 18.0	+2 29	Globular cluster, visible to naked eye. 5' diameter.
	15 13.0	+56 44	Large elliptical nebula. Another nebula near by.

TABLE VIII.—*Continued.*

No. in New General Catalogue.	Position 1890.		Brief Description of the Object.
	R.A.	Declination	
	H. M.	° '	
6093	16 10.5	−22 42	Globular cluster. Stars 14th magnitude.
6205	16 37.7	+36 40	Fine globular cluster, visible to naked eye. 6' diameter. The cluster in *Hercules.*
6218	16 41.5	− 1 45	Cluster of stars, 10th magnitude, and fainter. 4' diameter.
6333	17 12.8	−18 24	Compressed globular cluster of stars. 4' diameter.
6341	17 13.8	+43 15	Fine globular cluster, 14th magnitude stars.
6402	17 31.8	− 3 11	Fine globular cluster, 15th magnitude stars. 4' diameter.
6514	17 55.7	−23 1	Bright large trifid nebula.
6543	17 58.6	+66 38	Bright, pretty small planetary nebula.
6618	18 14.4	−16 13	Bright, and extremely large. The Horseshoe nebula.
6656	18 29.7	−24 0	Globular cluster of stars, 11–15th magnitude.
6705	18 44.0	− 6 25	Very bright large cluster of stars.
6720	18 49.5	+32 54	The bright ring nebula in *Lyra* between β and γ.
6779	19 12.5	+30 0	Bright globular cluster of stars.
6853	19 54.9	+22 25	The "Dumb-bell" nebula.
6960	20 41.1	+30 19	Bright, large and irregular. The star χ Cygni is involved in the nebula.
7009	20 57.1	−11 53	Very bright elliptical planetary nebula.
7078	21 24.7	+11 41	Globular cluster of small stars. 5' diameter.
7099	21 27.8	− 1 19	Globular cluster of small stars. 5' diameter.
7099	21 31.1	−23 46	Globular cluster. 12–16th magnitude stars. 3' diameter.
7660	23 20.6	+41 54	Small. Very bright. Planetary or ring nebula.

N.B.—Most of these objects can be well seen with a 3-inch telescope in a dark sky (no moonlight and no haze). To find them, put on that eyepiece of the telescope which has the lowest magnifying power and the largest field of view and point the telescope to the proper R.A. and Decl. sweeping it gently to and fro. After the object is found increase the magnifying power till it is seen most satisfactorily. Some of the objects in this list can be seen to advantage with a good field-glass.

To see a nebula with advantage it is sometimes advisable to set the telescope a very little west of it so that the nebula may enter the field of view by its diurnal motion and pass slowly across it. This can be repeated as often as desired. Nearly all of these objects are so faint

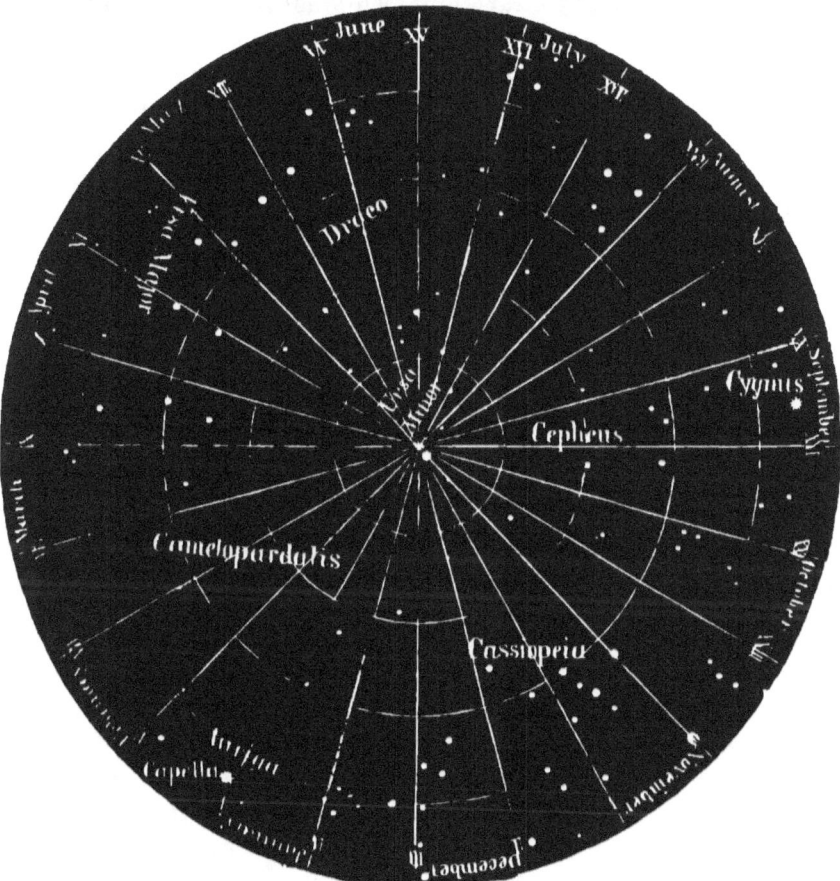

FIG. 212.—MAP OF THE STARS (TO FOURTH MAGNITUDE INCLU-SIVE) NEAR THE NORTH CELESTIAL POLE.

The *names* of these stars can be found in figures 214 to 219 following.

that no artificial lights should be near the observer's place. The word "bright" in the descriptions is a relative term. A bright nebula is faint compared to a planet.

MAPS OF THE STARS.

The Northern Stars.—The constellations near the pole can be seen on any clear night, while most of the southern ones can only be seen during certain seasons, or at certain hours of the night.   Fig. 212 shows all the stars down to the fourth magnitude, inclusive, within 50° of the pole.

The Roman numerals around the margin show the meridians of right ascension, one for every hour.   In order to have the map represent the northern constellations as they are, it must be held so that the hour of *sidereal* time at which the observer is looking at the heavens shall be at the top of the map.   The names of the months around the margin of the map show the regions near the zenith during those months.   Suppose the observer to look at nine o'clock (*mean solar time*) in the evening, to face the north, and to hold the map with the month upward, he will have the northern heavens as they appear, except that the stars near the bottom of the map may be cut off by his horizon.

The Equatorial Stars.—The folded map, Figure 213, shows the equatorial stars lying between 30° north and 30° south declination.   The outlines of the constellations are indicated by dotted lines.   The figures of men and animals with which the ancients covered the sky are omitted. The Latin name within each boundary is the name of the constellation.   The Greek letters serve to name the brightest stars.   The parallels of declination (for every 15°) and the hour-circles (every hour) are laid down.

The magnitudes of the stars are indicated by the sizes of the dots.   To use this map it must be remembered that as you face the south *greater* right ascensions are on your left hand, *less* on your right.   The right ascensions of the stars immediately to the south between 6 and 7 P.M. are:

For January	1,	1 hour;	For July	1, 13 hours;
" February	1,	3 hours;	" August	1, 15 "
" March	1,	5 "	" September	1, 17 "
" April	1,	7 "	" October	1, 19 "
" May	1,	9 "	" November	1, 21 "
" June	1,	11 "	" December	1, 23 "

This map and the map preceding it will be found useful in various ways. The six star-maps that follow are more convenient for ordinary use, however.

Six Star-maps showing the Brighter Stars visible in the Northern Hemisphere.[*]—The star-maps in this series were originally adapted to a north latitude of about 52°, so that, for the latitudes of the United States, they will be slightly in error, but not so much as to cause inconvenience. Under each map will be found the date and time at which the sky will be as represented in the accompanying map; *e. g.*, Map No. 1 shows the sky as it appears on November 22d at midnight, December 5th at 11 o'clock, December 21st at 10 o'clock, January 5th at 9 o'clock, and January 20th at 8 o'clock.

The maps are intended for use between the hours of 8 o'clock in the evening and midnight, and the titles are given with reference to such a use.

It should be borne in mind, however, that the same map represents the aspect of the constellations on other dates than those given, but at a *different hour* of the night. Map No. I, for example, shows the aspect of the sky on October 23d at 2 A. M., September 23d at 4 A. M., and also on February 20th at 6 P. M., as well as on the dates and at the hours given in the map. For any date *between* those given, the map will represent the sky at a time *between* the hours given; for instance, on November 26th, Map No. I will represent the sky at 11:45 o'clock, on November 30th at 11:30 o'clock, and on December 2d at 11:15 o'clock.

If the maps are held with the centre overhead and the *top* pointing to the north, the lower part of the map will be

[*] From the publications of the Astronomical Society of the Pacific, 1898.

to the south, the right-hand portion will be to the west, and
the left-hand to the east, and the circle bounding the map
will represent the horizon.   Each map is intended to show
the whole of the sky visible at these times.

The names of the *constellations* are inserted in capitals,
while the names of *stars* and other data are in small letters.

Constellations on the meridian about midnight:

January:	*Camelopardus, Lynx, Gemini, Monoceros, Orion, Canis major.*
February:	*Ursa major, Lynx, Cancer, Hydra.*
March:	*Ursa major, Leo, Hydra.*
April:	*Boötes, Libra.*
May:	*Hercules, Ophiuchus, Scorpio.*
June:	*Lyra, Hercules, Sagittarius.*
July:	*Cygnus, Aquila, Sagittarius.*
August:	*Cepheus, Cygnus, Capricornus.*
September:	*Cepheus, Pegasus, Aquarius.*
October:	*Cassiopeia, Andromeda, Pisces.*
November:	*Perseus, Aries, Cetus.*
December:	*Camelopardus, Taurus, Orion*

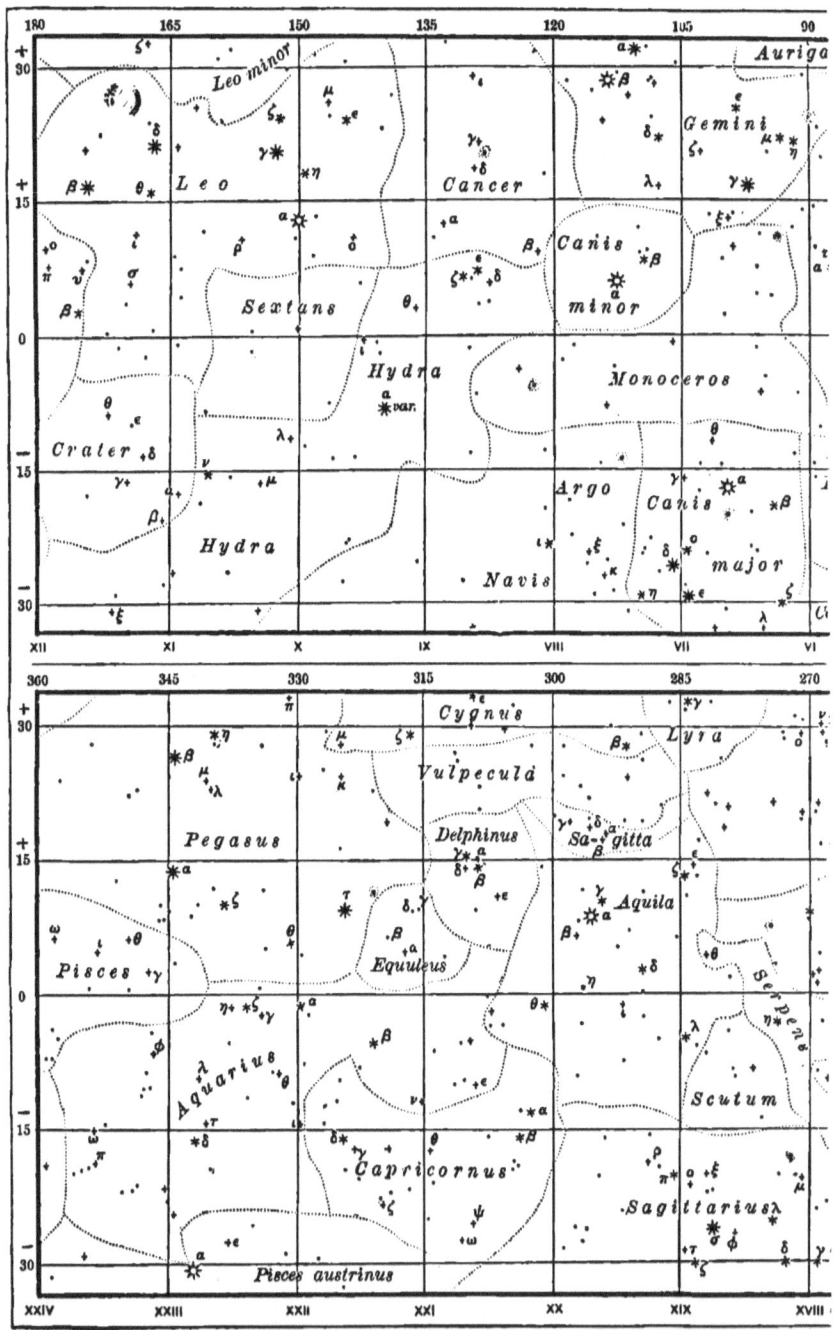

Fig. 213.—Map of Stars between 3

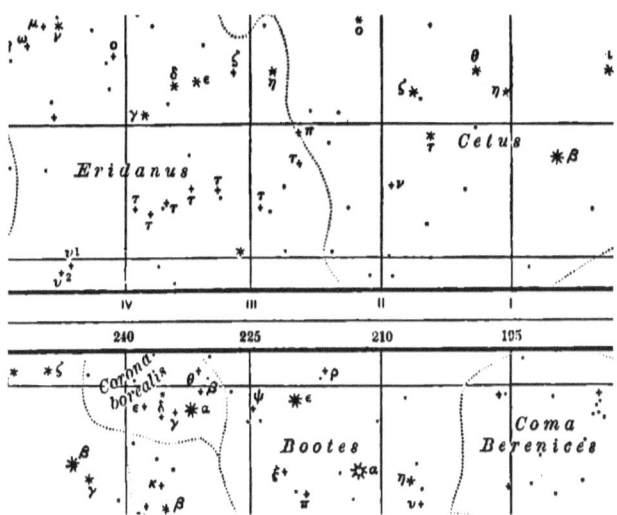

IV   III   II   I

240   225   210   195

MAP I.
North.

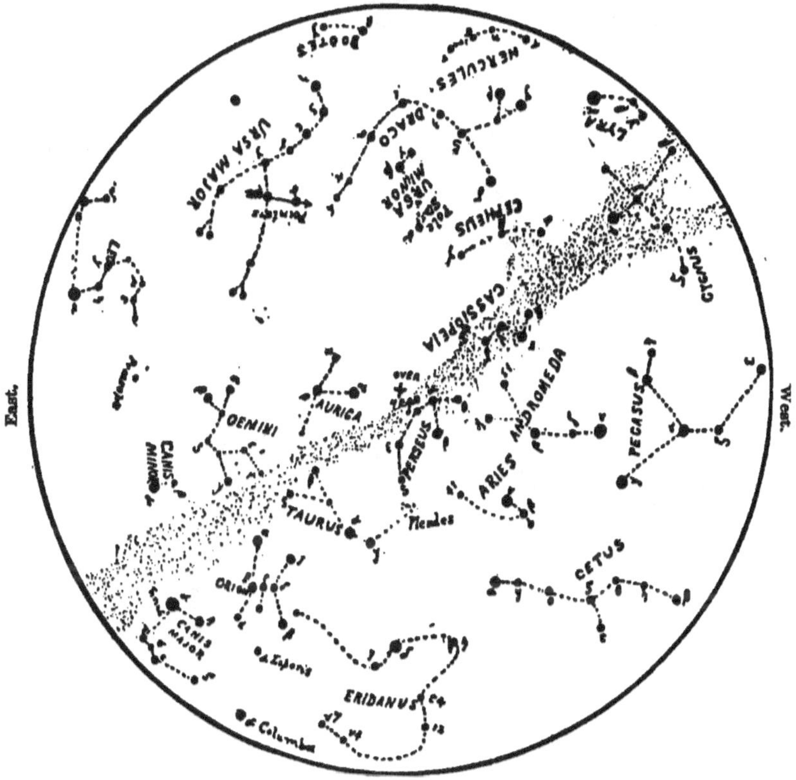

South.

FIG. 214.

The sky on November 22, at 12 o'clock P.M.
December   6, at 11 o'clock P.M.
December 21, at 10 o'clock P.M.
January   5, at 9 o'clock P.M.
January   20, at 8 o'clock P.M.

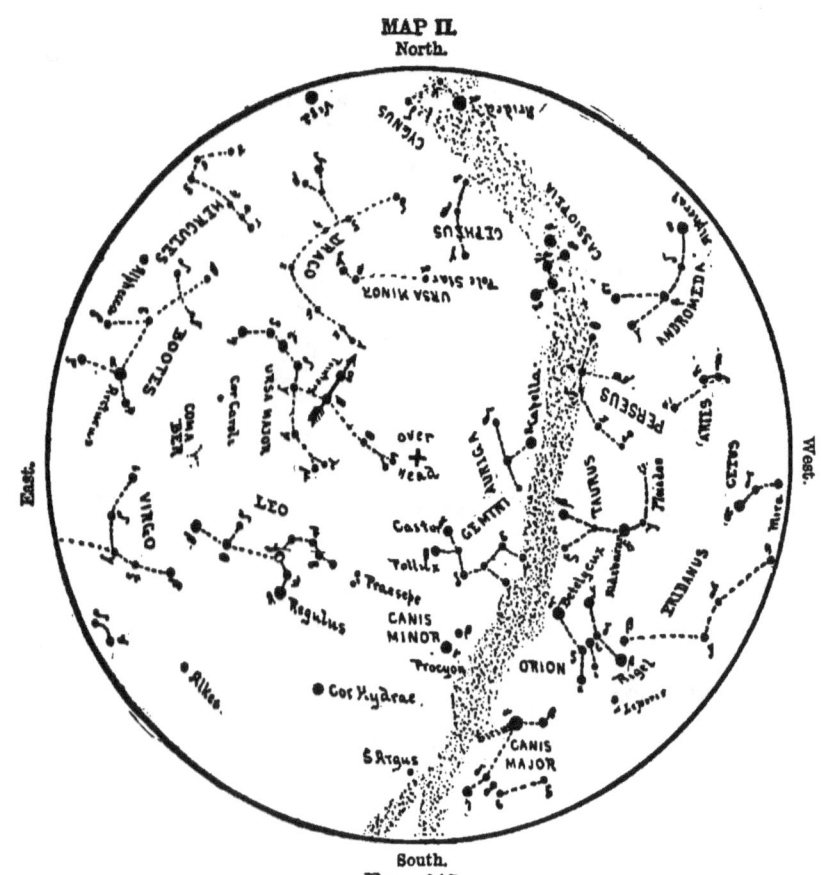

MAP II.
North.

South.

FIG. 215.

The sky on January 20, at 12 o'clock P.M.
February 4, at 11 o'clock P.M.
February 19, at 10 o'clock P.M.
March   6, at 9 o'clock P.M.
March   21, at 8 o'clock P.M.

MAP III.
North,

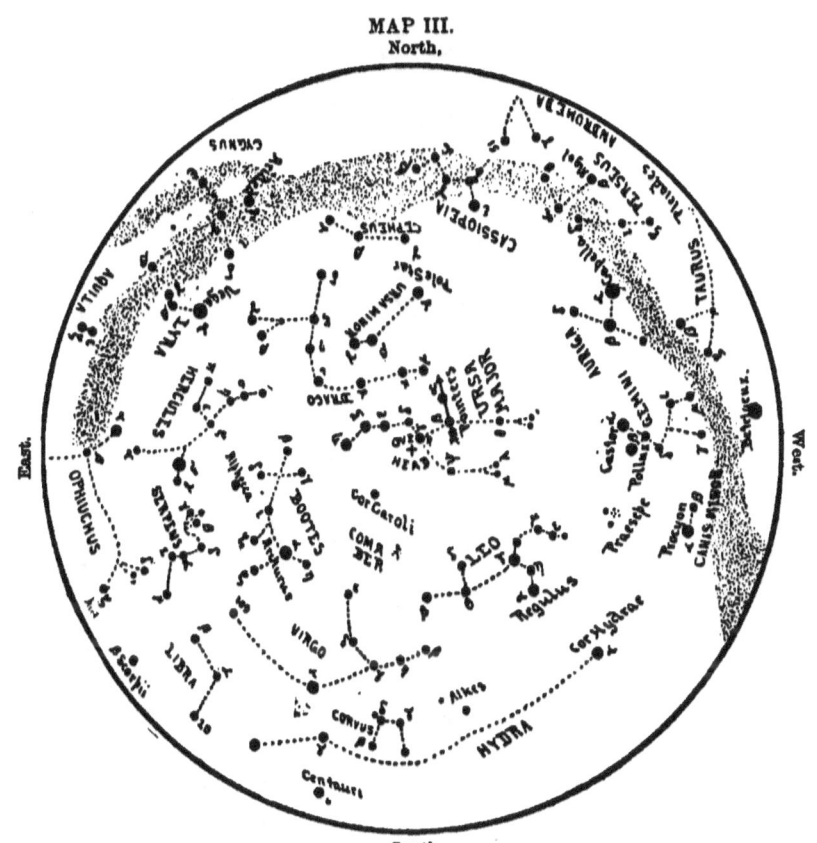

South.

FIG. 216.

The sky on March 21, at 12 o'clock P.M.
April   5, at 11 o'clock P.M.
April 20, at 10 o'clock P.M.
May   5, at 9 o'clock P.M.
May   21, at 8 o'clock P.M.

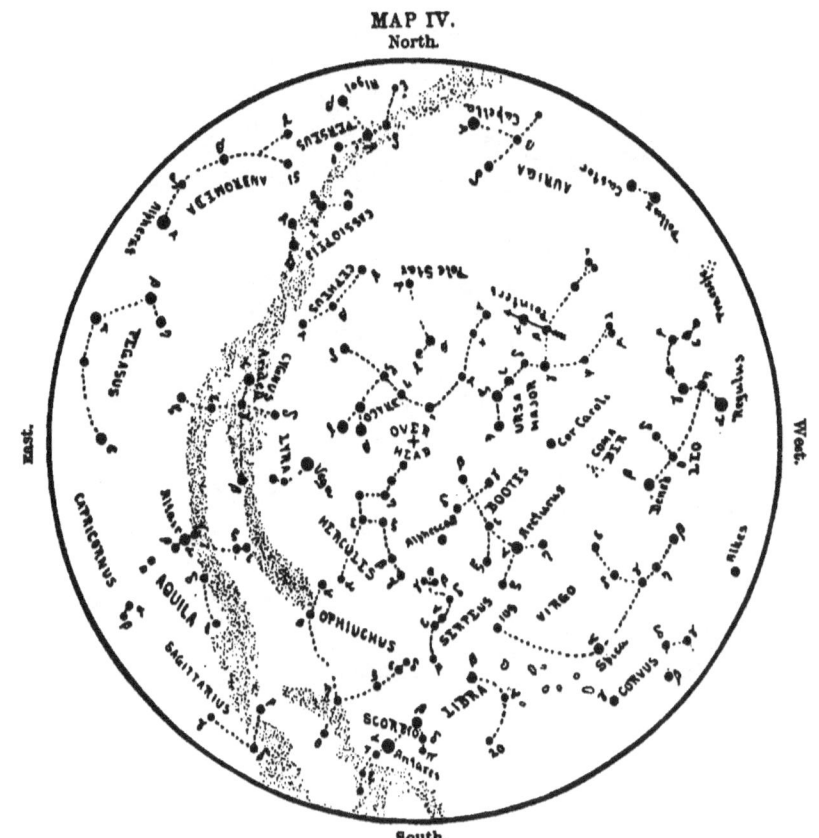

MAP IV.
North.

South.

FIG. 217.

The sky on May 21, at 12 o'clock P.M.
June 5, at 11 o'clock P.M.
June 21, at 10 o'clock P.M.
July 7, at 9 o'clock P.M.
July 22, at 8 o'clock P.M.

MAP V.

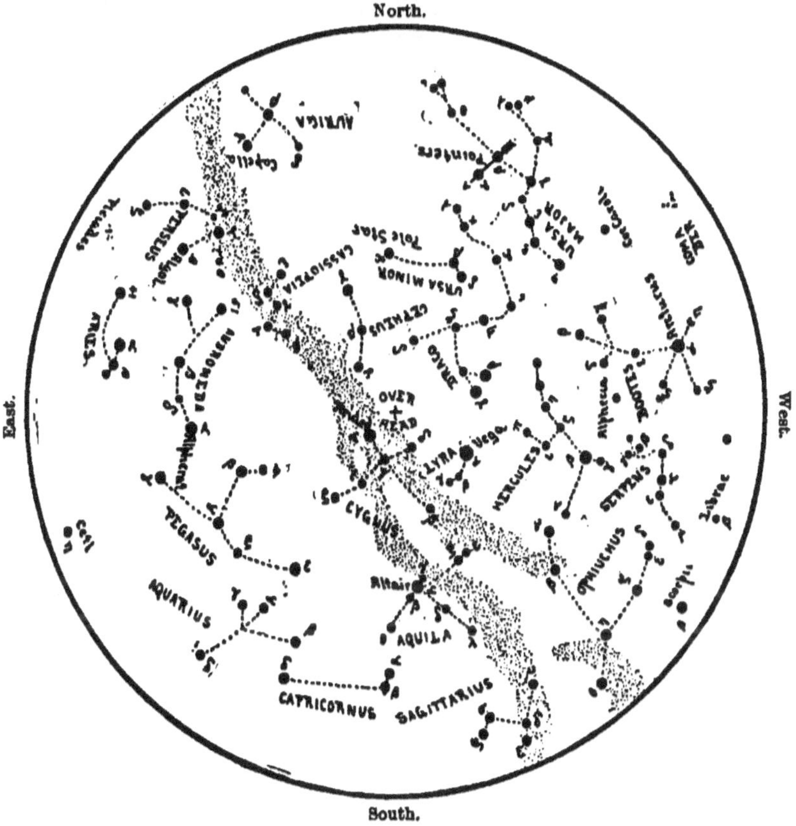

North.

South.

FIG. 218.

The sky on July   22, at 12 o'clock P.M.
          August   7, at 11 o'clock P M.
          August 23, at 10 o'clock P.M.
        September 8, at 9 o'clock P.M.
        September 23, at 8 o'clock P.M.

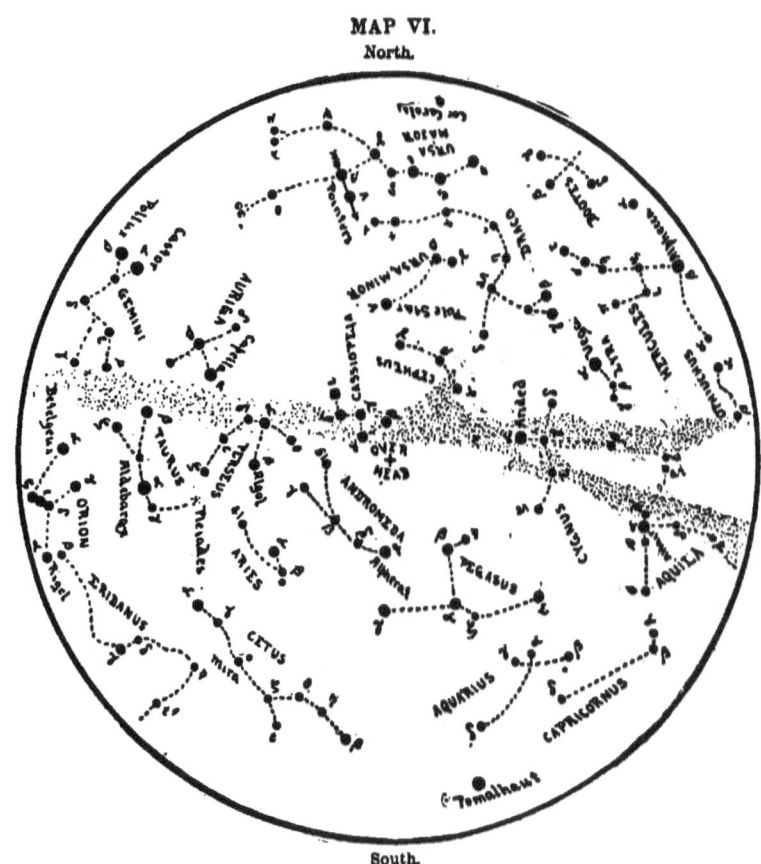

MAP VI.
North.

South.

Fig. 219.

The sky on September 23, at 12 o'clock P.M.
October　　8, at 11 o'clock P.M.
October　　23, at 10 o'clock P.M.
November　7, at　9 o'clock P.M.
November 22, at　8 o'clock P.M.

APPENDIX.

SPECTRUM ANALYSIS.

ALTHOUGH the subject of Spectrum Analysis belongs properly to physics, a brief account of its relations to astronomy may be useful here.

To understand the instruments and methods of Spectrum Analysis it will be necessary to recall the optical properties of a prism, which are demonstrated in all treatises on physics.

The Prism.—When parallel rays of homogeneous light, red for example, fall on a face of a prism they are bent out of their course, and when they emerge from the prism they are again bent, but they still remain parallel; thus the rays $r\,r$, $r''\,r''$, are bent into the final direction $r'\,r'$. This is true for parallel rays of every color. They remain parallel after deviation by the prism. This can be shown by experiment. If the *incident rays* $r\,r$, in Fig. 220, are *red*, they will come to the screen at $r'\,r'$. If they are *violet* rays, they will come to $v'\,v'$ on the screen, after having been bent more from their original course than the red rays. The violet rays, with the shortest wavelength, are the most refrangible. The red, with the longest wavelength, are the least refrangible.

The experiments of Sir ISAAC NEWTON (1704) proved that white light (as sunlight, moonlight, starlight) was not simple, but compound. That is, white light is made up of light of different wave-lengths. Difference of wave-length shows itself to the eye as difference of color. Seven colors were distinguished by NEWTON; viz., *violet, indigo, blue, green, yellow, orange, red.* (Memorize these in order. It is the order of the colors in the rainbow.) If parallel rays of white light, as sunlight, $r\,r$, fall on a prism, the red rays

433

of this beam will still fall at $r'r'$, and the violet rays will fall at $v'v'$. Between v' and r' the other rays will fall, in the order just given; that is, in the order of their refrangibility. The rainbow-colored streak on the screen is called the *spectrum;* it is a solar, a lunar, or a stellar spectrum according as the source of the rays is the Sun, Moon, or a

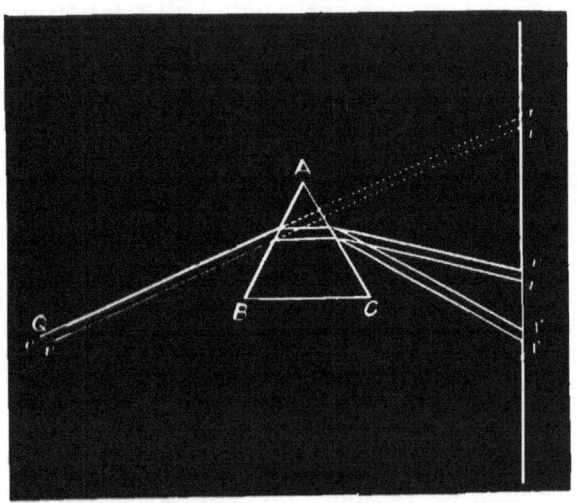

FIG. 220.—THE ACTION OF A PRISM ON A BEAM OF WHITE LIGHT.

star. The solar spectrum is very bright; the lunar spectrum is much fainter; and the spectrum of a star is far fainter than either.

If we let parallel rays, $r\,r$, of red light come through a circular hole at Q (Fig. 220), they will form a circular image of the hole at $r'\,r'$. If the hole is square or triangular, a square or a triangular image will be formed. If it is a narrow slit, a narrow streak of red light will be projected at $r'\,r'$.

When *white* light is passed through a circular hole at Q, circular images of the hole are formed all along the line $r'\,r'$ to $v'\,v'$: the red images at $r'\,r'$, the orange, yellow, green, blue images in succession, and the violet image at $v'\,v'$. If the hole is of any size these images will overlap, so that the colors are not pure. If white light falls through a narrow slit at Q, placed parallel to the edge A of the prism, the purest spectrum is obtained. The different spectra do not overlap.

FRAUNHOFER tried this experiment in 1804, and he found that the spectrum of the Sun was interrupted by certain *dark lines,* fixed in relative position. These are the Fraunhofer lines, so called. He made a map of the solar spectrum, and on the map he placed the various lines in their proper places. These lines appear in the same relative position no matter whether a slit or a very small cir-

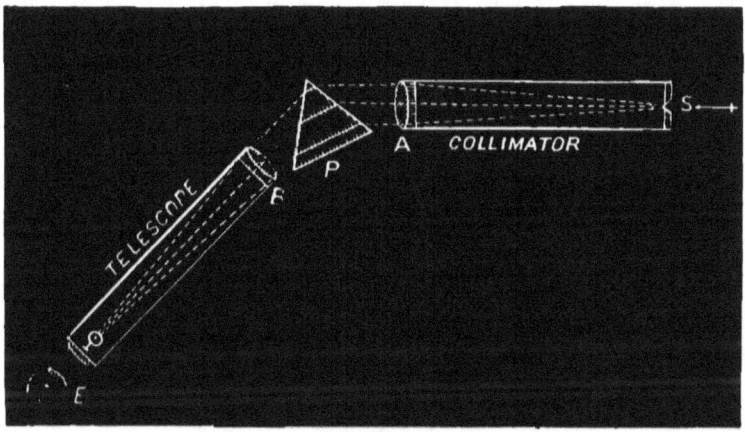

FIG. 221.—THE SPECTROSCOPE.

cular hole is used, and they belong to the incident light and are not produced by the apparatus. This simply renders them visible. They are not seen when the light comes through wide apertures, on account of the overlapping of the various images. (See Fig. 222.)

The Spectroscope.—A spectroscope consists essentially of one or more prisms (or any other device, as a diffraction grating) by means of which a spectrum is produced; of a means to make the spectrum pure (a slit and collimator), and of a means to see it well (a small telescope).

Fig. 221 shows the arrangement of a one-prism spectroscope. The light enters the slit *S*, which is exactly in the focus of the objective *A* of the collimator. The rays therefore emerge from *A* in parallel lines. They are deviated by the prism *P*, and enter the objective *B*, forming an image of the spectrum at *O*, which is viewed by the eye at *E*.

The Solar Spectrum.—Part of this image (of the solar spectrum) is shown in Fig. 222, except as to color. The

FIG. 222.—A PART OF THE SOLAR SPECTRUM.

various colors extend in succession from end to end of the spectrum.   In each color are certain dark lines which have a definite position.   The most conspicuous of these lines are called the Fraunhofer lines, and are lettered *A*, *B*, *C*, *D*, *E*, *F*, *G*, *H*.   *A* is below the easily visible red, *B* is at its lower edge, *C* is near the middle of the red, *D* is a double line in the orange, *E* is in the green, *F* is in the blue, *G* in the indigo, and *H* in the violet.   There are at least 500 lines besides which can be seen with spectroscopes of moderate power.   *Each and every one of these has a definite position.*

When the instrument drawn in Fig. 221 is pointed toward the Sun (so that the Sun's rays fall on *S*), the spectrum seen is that of the whole Sun. If we wish to examine the spectrum of a *part* of the Sun, as of a spot for example, we must attach the whole instrument to a telescope, so that *S* is in the principal focal plane of the telescope-objective. An *image* of the Sun will then be formed by the telescope-objective on the slit plate *S*, and the light from any part of that image can be examined at will. The spectroscope is also used in order to examine stars. We employ a telescope in this case so that its objective may collect more light and present it at the slit of the spectroscope.

Spectra of Solids and Gases.—A solid body, heated so intensely as to give off light, has a *continuous* spectrum. That is, there are no Fraunhofer lines in it, but prismatic colors only. A gaseous body, heated so intensely as to give off light, has a *discontinuous* spectrum.* That is, the colors red to violet are no longer seen, but on a dark background the spectrum shows one or more *bright* lines.

These lines have a definite relative position and are characteristic of the particular gas. The vapor of sodium, for example, gives two bright lines, whose relative position is always the same, as laboratory experiments show.

If the source of light is a solid body, intensely heated, the spectroscope will show a continuous spectrum without lines, as has been said. If between the solid body and the slit of the spectroscope we place a glass vessel containing the vapor of sodium, the spectrum will no longer be without lines. Two dark lines will appear in the orange. If we remove the vapor of sodium, the lines will go also. They are produced by the absorptive action of this vapor on the incident light.

If we register exactly the spot in the field of view of the spectroscope where each of these *dark* lines appears, and if we then remove the sodium vapor and replace the solid body (the source of light) by intensely heated sodium vapor, we shall find the new spectrum to be composed of two bright lines, as has been said ; and these two bright lines will occupy exactly the same places in the field of view that the two dark lines formerly occupied.

* Unless under great pressure, when the spectrum is continuous, as in the case of our Sun, and of stars of similar constitution to the Sun.

The two dark lines are a sign of the kind of light that is *absorbed* by sodium vapor ; the two bright lines are a sign of the kind of light that is *emitted* by sodium vapor. These two kinds are the same. What is true of sodium vapor is true or every gas. *Every gas absorbs light of the same kind* (wave length) *as that which it emits.*

If a spectroscopist had to determine what kind of gas was contained in a certain jar, he might do it in two ways. He might heat it intensely, and measure the positions of the *bright* lines of its spectrum; or he might place the gas between the slit of his spectroscope and a highly heated solid body, and measure the positions of the *dark* lines of its absorption-spectrum. The positions of the lines will be the same in both cases. By comparing the measures with previous measures for known gases, the name of the particular gas in question would become known to him. *New* chemical elements have been discovered by the spectroscope. The spectrum of the mixture that contained them showed previously unknown spectrum lines. They were first detected by the presence of these unknown lines and then separated from the known gases present in the mixture.

Comparison of the Spectra of Incandescent Gases with the Solar Spectrum.—Laboratory experiments on known gases show the positions of the spectral lines characteristic of each gas or vapor. The positions of the lines of magnesium or of hydrogen, for example, are accurately known. The positions of the dark lines in the solar spectrum are also known with accuracy. It is found that nearly every one of the thousands of dark lines of the solar spectrum has a position corresponding exactly to that of some one of the lines of some known gas or of the vapor of some known metal. For example, the vapor of iron has several hundred lines, whose positions are accurately known by laboratory experiments. In the solar spectrum there are several hundred whose positions precisely correspond to the lines of iron vapor. The same is true of many other substances, hydrogen, sodium, potassium, magnesium, nickel, copper, etc., etc.

From this it is inferred that the Sun's atmosphere contains the metal iron in an incandescent state, as well as the vapors of the other substances named.

Let us see the process of reasoning which led KIRCHHOFF and BUNSEN (1859) to this interpretation of the observation.

We have seen (Part II., Chap. XVI) that the Sun is composed of a luminous surface, the *photosphere*, surrounded by a gaseous envelope. The photosphere alone would give a continuous spectrum (with no dark lines). The gaseous envelope will absorb the kind of light that it would itself emit. The absorption is characteristic. If a solid incandescent body were placed in a laboratory and surrounded by the vapors of iron, hydrogen, sodium, etc., we should see the same spectrum that we do see when we examine the Sun.

The kind of evidence is easily understood from the foregoing. Only the spectroscopist can fully appreciate the force of it. The resulting inference that the Sun's atmosphere contains the vapors of the metals named is certain. These vapors exist *uncombined* in the Sun's atmosphere. The temperature and the pressure are too high to allow their chemical combination.

INDEX.

441